MARVEL
BLACK WIDOW
FOREVER RED

BY MARGARET STOHL

Los Angeles • New York

© 2016 MARVEL

All rights reserved. Published by Marvel Press, an imprint of Disney Book Group.
No part of this book may be reproduced or transmitted in any form or by
any means, electronic or mechanical, including photocopying, recording,
or by any information storage and retrieval system, without written permission
from the publisher. For information address Marvel Press, 1101 Flower Street,
Glendale, California 91201.

First Hardcover Edition, October 2015
First Paperback Edition, September 2016

10 9 8 7 6 5 4 3 2 1

FAC-020093-16204

Printed in the United States of America

Library of Congress Cataloging in Publication Control Number: 2016932824

ISBN 978-1-4847-7645-2

This book is set in Sabon
Designed by Tanya Ross-Hughes/Hotfoot Studio

Visit www.hyperionteens.com
www.marvel.com

THIS ONE IS FOR
KATE HAILEY PETERSON
KICKER OF BUTTS
BUILDER OF WORLDS
ROMANOFF IN SPIRIT

ACT ONE

"LOVE IS FOR CHILDREN."

— NATASHA ROMANOFF

EIGHT
YEARS AGO

SOMEWHERE
IN UKRAINE

ON THE OUTSKIRTS OF ODESSA, UKRAINE
NEAR THE BLACK SEA

atasha Romanoff hated pierogies—but more than that, she hated lies.

Lying she was fine with. Lying was a necessity, a tool of her tradecraft. It was being *lied to* that she hated, even if it was how she had been raised.

Everything Ivan used to say was a lie.

Ivan Somodorov, Ivan the Strange. She hadn't thought about him in a long time, not until tonight.

Years.

And right now, as Natasha clung to the side of a rusting Ukrainian warehouse on the edge of a waterlogged industrial dock, even the moon looked like just another one of Ivan's lies.

Welcome home, Natashka.

It was the dumpling moon that brought it all back now.

She climbed higher as she remembered the words, but even Natasha Romanoff, newly minted agent of S.H.I.E.L.D., former daughter of Mother Russia, couldn't escape Ivan Somodorov. Not any more than she could escape the snipers positioned on every neighboring rooftop or the barbed wire on the perimeter fence.

"See that moon?" Ivan had said when she was younger. "See that pale pierogi, hanging so low and heavy in the sky it wants to fall back into the boiling pot of salted water on your *baba*'s stove?" Natasha had nodded, though as an orphan of the war she remembered little about her baba—or for that matter, even her parents. "With a moon like that, your targets can see you as easily as you see them. Not a good night for hunting, or a clean kill. Not a good night for disappearing."

It was Ivan she remembered.

Ivan who had taught her how to shoot a Russian sniper rifle and to never use anything but a German pistol, preferably an HK or a Glock—no matter how you felt about the Germans. How to change out the barrel and action of an assault weapon in seconds and to modify her trigger so it broke like glass. How to cover her tracks, how to hide from the SVR and the FSB and the FSO—all the legitimate organizations that the KGB had become when it was the KGB no more. Those were her bosses' bosses, the groups they worked for but never with. The groups they vowed to follow, but who disavowed them. The groups with the names that could be mentioned in the headlines of the *Gazeta*, unlike her own.

4

Unlike the Red Room. Unlike Ivan's crew and, in particular, his favorites, *Devushki Ivana*. Ivan's girls.

Natasha took a breath and swung, springing through the moonlit night from side to side, making her way farther up the corrugated wall of the decaying warehouse. The rough metal siding bit into her palms. It was a miracle that she was still hanging on.

A miracle and years of training.

Natasha closed her eyes and tightened her grip. Truthfully, she didn't need her adhesive suit.

Even if I wanted to let go, I haven't been trained for that.

"I will teach you more than how to kill," Ivan had said. "I will make you into the weapon itself. You will become as automatic and unfeeling as a Kalashnikov, but twice as dangerous. Only then will I teach you how to take a life—how and when and where."

"And why?" Natasha had asked.

She had been young, then, or she would have known better. Child Natasha had been all eyes and shadows and angles. Alone and defenseless, half the time she felt like a thrashing rabbit caught in a winter trap.

He had laughed outright. "Not why, my Natashka. Never why. Why is for guitar players and Americans." Then he'd smiled. "We all have a time to die, and when it's mine, when they send you to sink a bullet into my head, just make sure not to do it on a pierogi moon." She'd nodded, but she couldn't tell if he was serious or not. "That's all I ask. A clean kill. A soldier's death. Do not shame me."

It was his favorite line. He'd said it maybe a thousand times.

And now, as Natasha stared up at the boiled-dumpling moon, she decided it was the one she'd repeat back to him tonight. When she finally killed him, just as he'd predicted she would.

He's not a martyr, she reminded herself. *We aren't saints. When we die, nobody mourns. That's the only way this ends, for all of us.*

Even if there were a hundred fat moons in the sky tonight, Natasha refused to feel any shame or any sorrow for Ivan Somodorov. She didn't want to feel anything at all, not for anyone, but least of all for him.

Because he felt nothing for you.

Natasha kicked her legs up, balancing on an air duct on the side of the warehouse. Now she had a full view of the building, which only made her shake her head. She had seen abandoned FSB doghouses in better conditions.

No. Outhouses.

She reached higher, grabbing another light fixture like a handle, hauling her body upward—until it came off in her hand, clattering to the rotting dock beneath her.

She froze.

Der'mo.

"*Vy slyshite-to?*" Beneath her, a fat dock guard moved toward the sound, his weapon still slung across his back. Two more guards followed.

Untrained. Not Ivan's guys. Unless he's really getting sloppy.

Natasha cursed to herself, flattening her hanging body against the side of the rusted wall beneath the shadowy eaves of the tin roof. Flashlight beams now swept across the warehouse, only centimeters beneath her. She held her breath.

You didn't hear anything, mudak. Just your old outhouse falling apart.

The guards moved on.

Natasha breathed, then flipped herself over the eaves, rolling toward a dirty skylight. The moves were instinct now, as automatic as breathing or blinking or the beat of her own heart. Slowly she eased her face above the cracked glass—taking in the view for the few seconds she could risk exposure. The world below was murky, and only two figures moved through the shadows in the central space between the shipping containers.

Two figures. One big, one small.

She could see a kid. A girl. Red haired. Dark eyed. From the looks of it, she was maybe eight or ten years old. They all looked the same to Natasha. Aside from her fellow strays in the Program, the only child she'd ever known had been herself—and she hadn't even really liked that one.

The girl turned her face away from Ivan, who stood between her and the window, and Natasha could now see she was crying. Holding on to a ballerina doll. *The kind with a ceramic head,* Natasha thought. *The kind they sell in the streets outside the Bolshoi Theatre.* She'd had one of her own, a few lifetimes ago.

Was that how I used to look at you, Ivan?

Because now, shoving the girl and the doll aside as he stepped into the moonlight, there was her old commander—and new target.

Ivan Somodorov.

The closest thing I had to a father.

Natasha hung farther over the skylight to get a better look. What was he doing? Putting something on the girl's head. Electrodes maybe? Definitely. On her temples. More wires on her arms, hands, even her chubby little legs. On the other end of the wires was a squat metal box the size of a phone booth, bolted to the concrete floor, patched and soldered on the surface, apparently kluged together from many lesser machines. It sprouted a mess of thickly bundled wire umbilical cords, curving and sparking in every direction. The wiring led to more boxes and then more wiring, as if it were a fundamental anatomical part of a much larger organism—one with no visible end.

An experiment. So the reports were true.

She's one of Ivan's little projects. Another Devushka Ivana.

Natasha stared. She didn't wince, and she didn't look away. The scene was all too familiar—though she'd been chained to a radiator, not strapped in a chair, and Ivan hadn't been into electrodes back then. All the same, it didn't matter. Enough was enough.

Natasha took in the scene in front of her, then rolled onto her back, raising her wrist to her mouth.

"Target is confirmed. Tell MI6 their tracking beacon worked. Intel is good."

"I'll send the Queen a fruit basket. God, you've got eyes on Ivan the Strange? London calls him Frankenstein." Coulson's voice crackled over the comm in her ear. "Human test subjects, that's really his thing now?"

She glanced at the skylight. "Looks that way."

"It's alive," Coulson said in his best mad scientist impression.

Natasha stared up at the dumpling moon. The view was even better here, from flat on her back on the top of the warehouse.

"Not for long. I'm going in."

ODESSA SHIPYARD WAREHOUSE, UKRAINE NEAR THE BLACK SEA

The moment Natasha Romanoff anchored her carabiner to the steel frame of the open skylight, her mind went into overdrive. Battle mode. The adrenaline kicked it up, and she rode the surge the way she did everything—fast and hard, with no apology and no regret. She hadn't felt it when she was unbolting the warehouse skylight's glass panels or when she was silently dislodging them from the metal frame that held them in place. She only felt it now that she was going in.

As she loosened her belay clip and rappelled silently down into the warehouse, her mind first ran through Ivan's obvious moves, then his logical moves, then his less logical ones; she knew them all. It was a one-woman game of speed battle chess—and when it was over, Natasha almost always won.

Like a Kalashnikov, she thought. *Like a Romanoff. This is who I am. This is what I do.*

Her eyes flickered across the interior of the warehouse as she read the room. *So you've got five thugs at the perimeter trying not to look like they're waiting for me. Where did you find these idiots, Ivan?*

Natasha dropped three feet farther, for a better look at her target.

I know you heard me rolling the last few feet of roof to the skylight. You taught me that move. What are you up to?

Natasha swung 180 degrees until she could see the little girl's face. *What about the kid? Looks genuinely scared. Kid. Vulnerability. Check.*

Natasha spun farther, counting heads as she turned. *Thick cabling coming through the walls, with a heavy smell of ozone and a scary amount of electricity. Check. Let's try not to blow the place up.*

It was time to do the real battle math.

Thug One is sticking close to Ivan at one o'clock, but just out of the light. Looks like he's the only grunt with a sidearm.

She raised an eyebrow.

Carrying Mexican style? Don't they ever worry about blowing their balls off? Which means they've been told to grab me, not shoot me. She rolled her eyes in spite of the darkness.

Good luck with that.

Thug One won't be the first to charge. He'll be hoping to get in a cheap shot from behind—if he needs to—while I take out Two and Three. They'll be coming from seven and nine o'clock as soon as I hit the floor.

Four looks like he'll be the fastest.

Her eyes picked out the last of the soldiers in the shadows.

Five looks lazy—he'll have a weapon—maybe a knife. Definitely a knife.

Once Thug One watches the other four go down, he'll realize it's over, panic, and go for his gun—look at him, he's already sweating—so I'll take him out somewhere in the middle. No need to get shot at if I don't have to.

She glanced back up at the ceiling above her. *The snipers are just insurance. They would have already engaged me. Ivan clearly wants to chat.*

Natasha loosened her grip on the cable and continued to rappel down toward the target. She was getting close now. She could see the bald sheen on the top of Ivan's head. He used to razor it every day to keep it shiny. She could see he still he still did. She wondered why he was sweating.

Because he knows I'm about to get the drop on him?

With that, Natasha Romanoff relaxed her hands and slid to the warehouse floor as quietly as a spider—but not quietly enough for Ivan Somodorov.

"Little Natashka," Ivan said, not looking up from the girl. "It's a dumpling moon. If you're going to be so obvious, next time just ring the doorbell." A tattoo of barbed wire circled its way around his neck, the sign of a stint in a Russian prison. He turned to look at her. "You shame me."

Natasha took in the rest of what she could see of him: a cheap leather jacket and chains, which, along with the dirty V-neck shirt, just made him look like a Russian mobster.

She sighed. "Knock-knock, Ivan. Who's there? S.H.I.E.L.D."

He looked at her blankly. "I don't get it."

Natasha punched him in the face as hard as she could. As he went flying back, she rubbed her fist. "Sorry. It's more punch than line."

The little girl began to scream—but Natasha couldn't hear a thing above her own heart pounding in her ears. She wasn't thinking now. This wasn't the time to think. This was pure movement and reflex. Action and reaction. Adrenaline. Muscle memory. And Natasha Romanoff's muscles had a nearly perfect memory.

Thugs Two through Five fell exactly as she had planned, except that Thug Five pulled out nunchakus—with a ninja flourish—instead of a knife.

"Are you kidding me?" She looked almost impressed. "But I appreciate the creativity." As she spoke, she dispatched her widow's cuff and sent the ninja flying with a bolt of electricity—and not in a very ninja way.

Thug One got off his shot, but not before Natasha shattered his arm with her left boot. The bullet went wide, and the shooter went down.

There was no one better at battle math than Natasha Romanoff.

Ivan Somodorov threw himself into the waiting chair next to the girl and attached the electrodes to his own head. The machine sparked between them. He grinned at his old protégée, his hand on the machine's lever. "Took you long enough. I've been waiting for weeks now. My Natashka."

Natasha stared at him, trying to figure out if he was lying, and what it meant if he wasn't. *The thugs were a distraction. The real game is just starting.*

Ivan snorted. "You come for me on a pierogi moon? And you don't bother to take out the security cameras first? Did I teach you nothing?"

"I wish." Natasha stepped in front of him, brushing an unruly curl of red hair out of her face.

"And how you've grown since the days when I schooled you in the Red Room." The look in his eye would make any girl shiver, but Natasha didn't flinch. "You looked like a lost little *ptenets* then, fallen right out of the nest."

Natasha ignored him. She couldn't take her eyes off the machine standing between him and the girl. It was marked "O.P.U.S.," in Russian military tagging. It was also why she was here, that tech—though S.H.I.E.L.D. hadn't filled her in on the details. She hadn't been with the American agency long, and they didn't tell her much. All she knew was that she was here to put three bullets into her old Yoda and bag the box.

"What is this thing? It looks like it belongs in a museum. And word on the street is Ivan the Strange's new gig is stranger than usual."

He waved one hand at the O.P.U.S. "Old Red Room tech. Something I've been playing with since our glorious union of the people collapsed. The Program has seen, you know, better days. But that doesn't mean we can't pick up a few of the pieces and make some money."

"Right. Last time I checked, you could barely hotwire a Yugo, Ivan."

"Who wants a Yugo? I drive a Prius now." He shrugged. "I've picked up a rogue physicist here and there. Red Room remnants." He grinned. "Dinosaurs like me, fighting extinction."

Natasha was unmoved, tilting her head toward the wide-eyed girl. "And the kid? Why is she here?"

He shrugged. "Does it matter? Another poor little unwanted *ptenets*." Now his smile was dark. "Sound familiar?"

Natasha Romanoff tightened her hand on her gun. "Was that what I was? Unwanted?"

"No. What you were was a pain in my *zadnitse*."

"Wrong answer." She smashed him with both wrists, once again unleashing the sting of her Widow's Bite cuffs. Ivan writhed under the surprise of the electric charge, his head snapping backward, smashing him into the chair.

Ivan lifted his head. His were the eyes of a madman now. "Forever red. That's what they call your kind. You may talk a big game, but you're no more American than I am."

"I'm nothing like you, Ivan." She leveled her gun at him. Her hand wavered.

Just do it. He deserves it.

You should have done it a long time ago.

Ivan's mouth curved into a twisted smile. "You're a ticking time bomb." His face was still pale from the shock. "Only a matter of time. You're not going to be able to cut this wire, *ptenets*. Not from me and not from Mother Russia." He spat blood from his mouth. "I just hope I'm there when you detonate."

But Natasha had stopped listening. This was all wrong. Something was off.

What's he waiting for? What's his game?

Natasha glanced at the soldiers blocking her exit, but as she did, Ivan reached out and grabbed the lever on the machine between the child and himself.

It's a signal. It's starting. Something's happening.

Natasha heard the first rounds fire the moment he pulled the lever. She catapulted forward, and the line of fire moved with her, driving her toward Ivan the Strange and his even stranger steel metal box. They were all caught in the firestorm—Natasha and the kid and Ivan.

Ivan shouted, but it was too late. A barrage of bullets riddled the machine. It exploded in a burst of fire and black smoke—and he went flying back from the impact.

Natasha dodged the stray rounds, diving away from Ivan and toward the girl. "I'm getting you out of here!" she shouted, reaching to take her from the chair. The child screamed with every gunshot, her arms and legs instinctively kicking, her dark eyes wide with fright.

Natasha yanked her free, and for a moment, the girl clung to her.

Only for a moment.

Before Natasha could set her down, a massive electrical pulse surged from the machine, flooding through the wiring to the electrodes, lifting the body of the girl almost into the air. Because she was still holding the girl, it lifted Natasha right along with her.

For a split second, Natasha Romanoff and the nameless red-haired child were frozen in the same white-blue light.

This is what he wanted. I walked right into it.

I failed the battle math. Endgame: zero.

Then it hurt too much to think about anything but the pain.

Nails, Natasha thought. *It feels like poison nails.*

Ripping through every part of my mind and body.

She had never been so exposed. A rush of images surged into her mind too quickly to process. Her brain burned hot, and the pain was overwhelming. She writhed beneath it.

But then the blue light was gone, if only because everything else was going up in flames around it. The entire warehouse was igniting.

A second explosion hit—this one much bigger than the first. Then another. And another.

Natasha realized now that the O.P.U.S. machine was no single piece of tech at all; rather, it was a collection of generators. By the ignition pattern, she figured almost every shipping container in the warehouse held one part or another, all wired together. Which meant the blast wave would be bigger than she was expecting.

Much, much bigger.

The kill zone will be too.

Ivan cried out, slumping to the floor, holding his head. Black smoke poured from the fried electrodes on his forehead.

Dead?

The little girl screamed. Natasha didn't hesitate.

She grabbed the kid and rolled beneath a weapons locker, the last of the electrodes snapping free. She held her hands over the child's ears as the locker and the warehouse and the world rolled around them.

RUINS OF SHIPYARD WAREHOUSE, UKRAINE
NEAR THE BLACK SEA

hen it was over, Natasha kicked off the locker. She rolled to her side, still holding the girl. Her own ears were ringing. Her vision cleared, and she took in the remains of the scene. Flames were spreading from shipping container to container. Soldiers were downed. Shrapnel had taken out the ones she hadn't.

Either way, it didn't matter now.

Natasha looked at the girl, who lay motionless on the concrete floor. Sirens blared from every direction as she lifted the child out of the rubble.

The girl's eyes fluttered open.

"You're okay," Natasha said, hoisting the girl into her arms and staggering toward the warehouse door. She shifted the child over her shoulder, ignoring the flames that now surrounded them. The flames and the ash and the bodies.

"Don't look." Once again, Natasha cursed Coulson for involving her in a mission with children.

The child's eyes reflected only loss and fear. She clutched her now blackened ballerina doll by the neck. "*Sestra*," she said. Sister. She reached to touch a lock of Black Widow's hair. Red, just like her own.

"Not exactly." Natasha almost dropped her. Because she felt something awkward, a certain kind of uncomfortable warmth, as it uncoiled inside her chest. *Sympathy. Familiarity. Some kind of connection.* It wasn't something she had experienced often, and it wasn't something she knew how to feel, or even understand. And Natasha Romanoff didn't like feelings she didn't understand. She didn't like feelings, period.

But she knew what it meant to be a child with those eyes.

Natasha lowered her voice, speaking Russian directly into the child's ear. "You'll be safe now. I don't know who your family is, but I promise I'll find you some nice people who will get you back to wherever you belong." Hesitating, she smoothed the little girl's hair as she carried her.

"*Mamotchka*," the girl said sadly.

"Your mother? Did he take you from her?" Natasha was grim. She didn't know if the child had any family or if there was even anything left for her to go home to. Knowing Ivan Somodorov as she did, the odds of either were slim to none.

But the little girl nodded, closing her eyes against Black Widow's shoulder. She let the doll drop to the floor as she collapsed, exhausted. Natasha could feel her other small hand still wrapped around her hair.

As Natasha carried her away from the burning warehouse, S.H.I.E.L.D. support patrols swarmed the place. Natasha knew the drill. Within minutes, Ivan, or what was left of him, would belong to S.H.I.E.L.D. Same for his tech, the O.P.U.S. whatever. The rest was just cleanup, not her problem. Even the agents had agents for this crap.

Thank God. She had had enough of Ivan Somodorov. She never wanted to see his face again. Natasha Romanoff had spent a lifetime putting a lifetime between the two of them. And with that, she dumped the kid into the waiting arms of a medical officer, who wrapped her in a blanket. Natasha was done.

The girl began to cry, reaching her arms out for her redheaded rescuer again. Natasha looked at her. The girl didn't stop. Natasha turned away. The girl kept crying. Natasha turned back, frustrated. She squatted in front of the child, speaking in Russian.

"*Kak tebya zovut, devochka?*" What's your name, kid?

"Ava," the girl said, sniffling. Her breath was ragged as she spoke.

Natasha nodded. "*Slushay, Ava. Perestan' plakat,' kak mladenets. Ty uzhe bol'shaya devochka.*" Roughly translated, it meant something like, *Listen, Ava. Don't be a crybaby. You're a big girl now.*

She tried not to feel bad for saying it. They had said the same thing to Natasha herself, hadn't they? On that day in Stalingrad so many years ago? When her own parents had died, and she had been taken by the KGB, and then to the Red Room.

And then to Ivan.

The girl stared at her, tears silently rolling down her face.

Natasha took another breath and tried again. *"Amerikantsy otvezu tebya domoy. Oni naydut tvoyumamu. Ya obeshchayu."* She had no idea if what she was saying was true, but she said it. *They'll take you home. They'll find your mother. I promise.* It was what the little girl needed to hear, she reasoned.

"Obeshaesh?" Promise?

"You can believe me, Ava. I'm just like you. See?" Natasha pulled on a curl of her own red hair. *"Ya kak i ty,"* she repeated. *I'm just like you.*

The girl tried to catch her breath, but she couldn't. The tears kept coming.

Natasha exhaled, standing up to grab a wallet off a passing soldier without him noticing. She pulled a five-euro note out of it as she let the rest fall to the ground. Then she yanked a pen off a senior officer passing by, who turned to look at her, confused.

Agent Coulson sighed. "Can I help you, Romanoff?"

She didn't look up as she ripped the euro in half and scribbled something on it. "No, Coulson, I can help you. I made sure to leave the security cameras running." She looked up at him. "You should have good tape, whatever that thing was."

Coulson held out his hand. "Great. But I want my pen back. That's a limited edition 1935 Montblanc tiger eye. . . ."

Natasha rolled her eyes and slapped the pen into his hand. "It's called a Sharpie. You might want to look into it."

"You do things your way; I'll do them mine." He took the pen. "Speaking of which, good job in there. Your file says you were Red Room too. This must have been personal for you. Emotionally complex."

"It wasn't," she said, trying to push past him.

Coulson smiled. "Well, that's probably for the best, seeing as most of a building just dropped on your friend Ivan."

"He's not my friend," Natasha said automatically. "I don't have friends."

"There's a shocker," said Coulson as he turned away. "And, for the record, not having friends? Very emotionally complex."

Natasha glared after him. "For the record, stay out of my file."

He didn't answer.

She moved past two S.H.I.E.L.D. medical officers, until she was once again kneeling in front of the little girl. She switched back to rapid Russian, pushing the ripped euro note into her hand.

"See this? If you need me, go to your embassy. Give them this. I'll keep the other half to remember you."

Ava nodded. Natasha whispered into her ear, still in Russian. "If you ask, I'll come, *sestrenka*. I promise, little sister." She pulled away. "But if I can do it, Ava, you can do it." She pointed to her red hair again. "Right? We're the same." *Tot zhe samoye.* The same.

With that, she was gone.

Ava looked down at the paper in her hand. On it there were two words and a crude drawing of an hourglass inside a circle.

BLACK WIDOW.

Her sign.

"I will remember, *moya starshaya sestra*," the little girl said, slowly. Big sister.

Then her eyes closed, and the fire and the chaos and the death and the noise disappeared.

Just like the red-haired woman.

EIGHT YEARS
AFTER ODESSA

SOMEWHERE
IN AMERICA

S.H.I.E.L.D. - CASE 121A415

REF: LINE-OF-DUTY DEATH [LODD] INVESTIGATION

FROM: AGENT PHILLIP COULSON

TO: S.H.I.E.L.D. DIRECTOR EX OFFICIO NICK FURY

SUBJ: SPECIAL INQUIRY

RE: AGENT NATASHA ROMANOFF A.K.A. BLACK WIDOW,
A.K.A. NATASHA ROMANOVA

AGENT IN COMMAND [AIC]: PHILLIP COULSON

S.H.I.E.L.D. CASE CODE NAMES: RED LEDGER, OPUS, SCHRODINGER,
ODESSA, RED WIDOW, WINTERSTORM

AUTHORIZATION: Inquiry follows Executive Order OVAL14AEE32
POTUS Eyes Only / Congressional Access Denied / Note: The following
summary includes excerpts from files, logs, correspondence, transcripts,
hearings, and findings resulting from NSA Special Inquiry S231X3P.

Autopsy results on remains of deceased [per S.H.I.E.L.D. Medical
Examiner] have been sealed. Designation for Presidential Medal of
Freedom [classified citation] is pending.

CHAPTER **4**: ALEX

DANTE CRUZ'S HOUSE
MONTCLAIR, NEW JERSEY

an-ta Claus! San-ta Claus!"
A group of middle school kids screamed for jolly old Saint
Nick as if he were a boy band. *The Jolly Old Saint Nicks,*
Alex Manor thought. *"I Beliebe in Christmas." "One
Direction to the North Pole."* His drugstore Santa hat
slipped down over one eye.

"What is this garbage? Can I get a Ru-dolph? Ru-dolph?
Nose so bright? Anyone?" Dante Cruz, Alex's best friend,
wheezed out the words from beneath his fake reindeer
antlers. "Jeez. Tough crowd."

Alex, a sweating, red-faced seventeen-year-old, looked
like he was about to pass out. Dante—equally sweaty and
equally seventeen—looked like he was enjoying it. The two
friends faced off over a swaying Ping-Pong table in what

appeared to be the arm-wrestling match of the century, or at least of the week, or at the very least of Dante's little sister's holiday party. The contest had started out as everything between them always did—first as a joke, then a dare, then a bet—and had quickly escalated into a fight to the death—the death of the ancient Ping-Pong table.

Alex Manor didn't have an off switch, not once his adrenaline was pumping. Dante Cruz was more in control, but equally competitive. Together they were the equivalent of a lit match and a stick of dynamite that had decided to become friends—or brothers.

"Had enough?" Alex looked at Dante over his fist.

"Why, can't take the pressure, Santa?" Dante smiled. His ruddy, brown-skinned face glowed with effort, and his laugh was contagious. Raised in a close-knit Puerto Rican family, Dante had adopted Alex the first day he'd shown up at their fencing club two years ago. Maybe because his dad was a cop, Dante knew a good partner when he saw one. And definitely because his dad was a police captain, there were never any parties at the Cruz house—not even the middle school variety—unless both parents were out of town.

"Pressure? What pressure?" Alex said, gritting his teeth. Alex was as good-looking as Dante, even if his long dark hair did hang halfway over his even darker eyes. A good two heads taller than his compact friend, the lanky Alex didn't look like a choirboy, but he wasn't a thug, either. And if there was something about him that seemed unsettled, a roughness or a restlessness that seemed to haunt from inside—something that left him with shadows under his eyes and the startle reflex of a trapped wolf cub—Alex himself would have been the last to know why it was or how to stop it. Alex Manor was just this side of the edge, at least for now.

This side of the edge, both in life and in this wrestling match.

Alex's arm bulged beneath his faded T-shirt, and the harder he shoved against Dante's arm, the more his tattoo slid beneath the edge of the material. It was red and black and circular. The pattern inside was shaped like an hourglass. There wasn't anyone in school who didn't know what that tattoo meant; it belonged to the Black Widow, who had become a hero to teens around the world, along with Iron Man, the Hulk, and Captain America. Plus, it was a cool tattoo. Everyone said it and Alex knew it, even if his mother didn't think so. That's how he played it off, anyway. But what Alex never told anyone was that he had no idea where he'd gotten it. He was so freaked out when he'd woken up with it that he'd had a full-blown panic attack and hadn't been able to sleep for a week. *Just another reason to stay sober and stay in school,* he thought. *But you would think I would remember something like that.*

Alex frowned and pushed harder.

"Dude, I'm Blitzened," Dante said.

"On energy drinks? At a middle school kickback?" Alex gritted his teeth, pressing down on Dante's arm. "That's your combat strategy? More caffeine?" He leaned in.

"Better than more Pringles," Dante said as his face turned even redder. Alex did have a bottomless appetite for junk food, and he couldn't help but laugh when Dante called him on it—which was apparently the opportunity Dante had been waiting for. He sprang forward, forcing Alex's arm almost down to the table.

The moment he did, Alex countered. He ran through the options in his head as he leveraged more and more of his weight against his target. *Dante's like a broken record. And now he's off balance. Which means it's almost time. Wait for it . . . not yet . . . let him get a little farther. Getting there. Almost. Three—two—one—*

Alex smashed Dante's arm down to the table, and it collapsed beneath them. Dante flopped onto his back into a tangle of net and painted plywood, and Alex went bounding up, arms over his head. "Victory goes to Santa! Christmas has been saved again! The crowd goes wild!" On his cue, the crew of wildly caffeinated, energy-drink-drunk, sugar-stoned eighth and ninth graders went even wilder.

Dante snorted in disgust.

Alex ignored him. "Thank you, Montclair Junior High, thank you very much." Alex waved at his adoring fans—some real, some imaginary—like a Tony Stark in the making. "You're all off my naughty list." They cheered. "Drinks are on me."

"They're actually on me," said Dante from the floor, strewn with red plastic cups, next to the food table. "Or maybe it just feels that way because I'm lying in a puddle."

"Technically speaking, *you're* on *them*." Alex smiled, searching the mostly empty pizza boxes for a spare slice. He found one—pepperoni—and dunked it into the sauce from the hot wings. As usual, the worse something was for him, the more he liked it, and at the moment this pizza was doing the trick just fine.

Dante groaned. "Seriously? You're disgusting."

Alex shrugged. "Whatever."

His mouth was still full when a sound in the distance caught his attention. He looked out into the darkness of the backyard, beyond the strands of colored lights hanging from the roof, and even beyond the flock of reindeer pulling the fake sled across the lawn. It sounded like a snapping branch or maybe an animal.

"Did you hear that?" For a second, it looked like something fluttered in the shadows of the far hedge. Alex narrowed his eyes. *Something's back there.*

"You got a dog now, D?"

"Yeah, my sister." Dante winked. He was still lying on the floor. "Why?"

Alex frowned. "Nothing. Just heard a stray, I guess."

"Nah, she's ours," Dante said with a smile.

Dante's sister Sofi—a pretty, younger girl in a vintage Planet Thor T-shirt—stepped up over her brother, jabbing at his ribs with her high-wedge sandal. "Did you just call me a dog? Really? Which one of us used to eat kibble for money, Dante Cruz?"

"You *did*?" Alex was already laughing.

Dante rolled over. "I was eight."

Sofi looked at the broken Ping-Pong table. "Dad's gonna freak. He's still mad from when you smashed up all his rakes for your stupid game." Sofi shook her head.

"Rakes? You mean our broadswords?" Dante was insulted. "And it's called LARPing, you pest. It's a sport." He grabbed her ankle from below. "Go back to bothering the middle school elves."

"Shut up, Rudolph." Sofi grabbed a bottle of soda from the wobbly card table and poured a new drink. "Why do you even hang out with my brother, Alex?"

Alex wiped his greasy hands on his jeans. "Charity. Pity. Because I'm nice."

Dante scoffed. "Tell that to the broken table."

"So I'm a little . . . competitive." Alex looked embarrassed. He was working on it, but he couldn't seem to stop himself, not when his instincts took over.

"A little? If I'm a dog, you're a pit bull, man." Dante pulled himself up on his elbows.

Sofi wagged her cup. "At least you have each other. I don't know why anyone else would hang out with you. Oh, wait—nobody does." She poured soda down on her brother's face.

Dante lunged for his sister's ankle as she stalked off.

Alex saw the porch light from the next house brighten for a second, as if something had only just moved out of its way.

Then he shook it off. *You're being paranoid. It's probably just Santa and his flying reindeer.*

But he found his eyes lingering on the dark back of the hedge. *What if something really is out there?*

Over at the far end of the yard, well beyond the shadows, a black-gloved hand pushed the hedge back into place.

Distant laughter drifted above the muted holiday music—all the sounds of someone else's party.

It was the sound of strangers having a good time, of the holidays proceeding as they should, at least for the average, everyday sort of people.

But not for everyone.

A face ducked back into the darkness, leaving the world of hedges and yards and red cups behind. Because Alex Manor was right; something was out there, even if it had more to do with destiny than flying reindeer.

LINE-OF-DUTY DEATH [LODD] INVESTIGATION
REF: S.H.I.E.L.D. CASE 121A415
AGENT IN COMMAND [AIC]: PHILLIP COULSON
RE: AGENT NATASHA ROMANOFF A.K.A. BLACK WIDOW,
A.K.A. NATASHA ROMANOVA
TRANSCRIPT: DEPARTMENT OF DEFENSE, LODD INQUIRY HEARINGS.

DOD: The boy. Let's start with the boy.
ROMANOFF: Yes, sir.

DOD: It seems, if we go back to this mountain of paperwork S.H.I.E.L.D. has so thoughtfully provided, that he had nothing to do with any of this.
ROMANOFF: It seems that way, yes.

DOD: Was that the case?
ROMANOFF: [pausing] That would be classified intel, sir.

DOD: And this would be a classified DOD/LODD hearing, Agent, would it not?
ROMANOFF: [sits back from mic]

DOD: Agent Romanoff? I want to remind you that you're under oath.
ROMANOFF: Look, let's cut the crap, sir. I know what I did, and I know why I'm responsible. If you want to know where things really went south, it all started with Ava and me. Is that what you wanted to hear?

DOD: What I want to hear, Agent, is why.
ROMANOFF: That's so—American.

DOD: I'm waiting.

FORT GREENE YWCA BASEMENT
BROOKLYN, NEW YORK

When Ava Orlova opened her eyes in the mornings, all she could hear was *Swan Lake*. Her mother had hummed Tchaikovsky as she had rocked Ava to sleep as a baby—then later, when she'd tucked her in at night as a little girl.

It was all Ava had left of her now. She didn't know what had happened to her mother, or even her father. She only knew that they were gone, and that by the time she left Odessa, all those years ago, she no longer had any reason to stay.

Ava could feel the hard floor beneath her thin, lumpy, and distinctly non-swanlike mattress. It radiated cold, and she pulled her sleeping bag (the one she'd stolen from the Auburn homeless shelter) up to her shoulders and shivered. Except for one scrawny kitten with an equally scrawny belly—Sasha Cat—Ava was alone in her nondescript room.

And possibly in the world.

A single lightbulb hung from her bedroom ceiling, if you could call the room a bedroom. The high, small windows were the first clue that her makeshift room was actually a basement. The second clue was the damp puddle on the concrete floor, the recycled newspapers stacked along the walls, and the bags of old cans and bottles.

It looked like a prison cell, but Ava wasn't a prisoner. Not technically, and not in anything resembling a jail. Not anymore. When S.H.I.E.L.D. had first brought her to this country, they'd taken her to three places: a baseball game (to experience America), a big-box store (to buy off-label American clothes), and 7B (a decommissioned American military bunker that still felt like a jail). The classified safe house had no name, so Ava thought of it as 7B—the numbers on her steel-reinforced bedroom door. For five years, her only companions were a dull rotation of tutors and security guards, an old television stuck on C-SPAN, and an endless supply of microwave macaroni and cheese.

Never again.

Ava had been on her own for three years now, and she'd never looked back. Not since her fourteenth birthday, when she'd ditched her handler and left 7B with only what she could steal and stuff into an old field bag. Ava didn't think of it as stealing so much as surviving. Aside from that, she'd been pilfering petty cash from the guards' jackets for years and found she had more than enough to get a one-way ticket to New York City, where she bounced from shelter to shelter until she found a place where she could come and go as she pleased. The benefit of living in the drafty basement of a YWCA was that nobody noticed when she left or cared when she came home. Freedom and independence were the perks of being a runaway.

Ava was seventeen years old now and nearly as scrawny as Sasha Cat, who had been in the basement when she'd discovered it. Ava's hair was still the same cinnamon color it had been when she was a child in Odessa, but now the freezing showers upstairs in the public locker rooms meant little time for things like conditioner. And combs. These days, her red curls were loose and twisting into wild knots. Ava would kill for a hot bath, not that she'd had that many since leaving S.H.I.E.L.D. custody. (Not that she'd had that many before, either; hot water wasn't much more reliable in Ukraine than it was at the Fort Greene Y.)

Sasha meowed, and Ava rolled over. She pulled a worn notebook from beneath her mattress and slipped her pencil from the spine. She began to sketch rapidly, without moving her eyes from the page; she had made a habit of drawing out her dreams the moment she woke up, if she could. If she had a bed and paper and a bit of charcoal or pencil. Which wasn't always.

Sasha bit the edge of the paper, and Ava pushed her off without looking up. She was already roughing out a picture of the boy she had seen when she'd closed her eyes. It was the same boy as always, the one with the dark eyes and the tattoo on his arm. *Tattoo Boy.* That was what Ava called him, at least to Sasha Cat, and sometimes to Oksana, when she talked about him. She'd never shown Oksana the sketches, though she was really the only friend Ava had made in this country. She didn't know how she could explain it—dreaming so often about a person she only felt like she knew—and anyway, Oksana had stayed on at the Auburn shelter when Ava left, so she didn't often see her sketching in the mornings.

Ava's hand curved across the page, and the graphite details took shape. The curve of his nose. The broad lines of his pronounced jaw, his cheekbones. His dark, wide-set eyes. The way his hair curled into unruly waves, almost hiding his face.

She drew him standing at the back of a crowded yard, staring straight at her.

My Alexei.

Alexei Manorovsky.

That was his name, at least in Russian, which was still the language of Ava's dreams. She heard someone call him Alex, which Ava found strange and short, like it was missing something. Tonight he was raising his arms in victory, playing some kind of game, she thought. It had looked like he was having fun just being with his friends, and it only made her lonelier to watch him.

You don't need friends, Ava. You need your brain. You need to stay strong like an ox and sharp like a razor. Promise me that much.

Her mother's last words to her whispered their way into Ava's mind as she stared at the page. As one of Eastern Europe's most important quantum physicists, Dr. Orlova had learned the hard way how to fight for everything she'd achieved.

Then another voice spoke up, though Ava tried to ignore it, just as she always did.

If I can do it, Ava, you can do it. . . . We're the same.

Tot zhe samoye. The same.

It was what the woman in black had said to her before she'd disappeared. But Ava wasn't the same as anyone—especially not her—and she knew that now. She was alone, and she always would be. She would stay strong and sharp.

Because my mother was right.

She sighed and added a final detail—the boy's Father Christmas hat. "Happy holidays, Sash." Sasha meowed back, nudging the paper gingerly with one paw.

Ava scratched beneath Sasha Cat's chin with one hand and flipped through her sketchbook with the other. The book was the only record of her crazy dreams, just as it had been for years. If she hadn't drawn it all herself, she wouldn't have believed it. There was an Alexei on almost every page. Fencing, kickboxing, riding on the back of a friend's motorcycle. Staring out a classroom window. Playing with a brown-eyed puppy. Ava rubbed the charcoal with her finger, blurring the smooth lines.

Who are you, Alexei Manorovsky?

Why do I only see you in my dreams?

And what do you have to do with me?

She turned the page without answering the question. There was home. Odessa and before that, Moscow, what she could remember of them.

Her mother's face above the collar of her lab coat.

Baked apples.

Her beloved old ballerina doll, the one with the ceramic head. Karolina. The doll had been a present from her parents, long lost now.

These were the scarce, salvaged moments of her childhood—so many scattered beads of a broken necklace come unstrung.

She wished she knew more.

She moved to a new drawing, to darker memories.

The Odessa warehouse where she'd lost everything, years ago.

The bald man with the barbed-wire pattern inked around his neck—the monster who had taken her whole world away. She always drew him with vacant black eyes, like a demon.

Which is what he was.

She couldn't remember much, but she remembered the black eyes taunting her. *No one will come for you, little ptenets. No one wants you. No one cares.*

Not even your precious mamotchka.

Ava turned more pages, forcing her mind to move on to other things.

Like the ghost words.

Beyond the sketches, she had scribbled strange words everywhere in the margins. Some appeared over and over, like the only pieces remaining from a missing puzzle. She no longer knew what they meant, aside from invoking her dreams, her memories, her past. Her head ached when she saw the familiar arrangement of letters, she'd stared at them so often.

KRASNAYA KOMNATA.

OPUS.

LUXPORT.

It was always the same. She remembered nothing more about the words, other than that they had something vaguely to do with the night S.H.I.E.L.D. had found her on the docks at Odessa. She remembered little else about them, nothing that made sense. And aside from those four words, she had only one other thing.

One meaningless scrap of paper.

Sasha Cat clawed at the edge of the page.

There it was, on the very last page, where she'd put it when she'd stopped carrying it in her pocket. It was the only thing that remained from her life in Ukraine—aside from a faded photo or two—an old euro, ripped in half, scribbled with two more words and an image, drawn in the shape of an hourglass.

BLACK WIDOW.

The sign that meant Natasha Romanoff. The woman in black who had haunted her dreams even before Tattoo Boy had.

The one who had rescued her from the madman who had murdered her mother—only to let her be tossed into custody, locked up, and forgotten about, one more unwanted refugee from an ocean away.

The Black Widow had given her this life. This privilege. To be homeless and motherless and alone. Always a stranger in a strange land.

Ava knew Natasha Romanoff was supposed to be a hero.

She and her powerful friends were supposed to take care of humanity. Natasha Romanoff was supposed to take care of *her*.

If you ask, I'll come, sestrenka. I promise, little sister.

Ava had asked. Ava had searched, clutching the faded euro with the hourglass symbol. But Natasha Romanoff had never come for her.

And Natasha Romanoff was an Avenger. They were better than the rest of us. That's what the world thought, anyway. Only Ava knew it wasn't the truth.

The Black Widow would never be a hero to Ava Orlova.

She would only be a disappointment.

Another one.

Sasha Cat leaped up from the sketchbook, settling into her customary perch on Ava's shoulders.

People disappointed you, even heroes. It was a lesson Ava never forgot. *Strong like an ox and sharp like a razor.* That was who she was now.

Her mother would have been proud.

S.H.I.E.L.D. EYES ONLY
CLEARANCE LEVEL X

LINE-OF-DUTY DEATH [LODD] INVESTIGATION
REF: S.H.I.E.L.D. CASE 121A415
AGENT IN COMMAND [AIC]: PHILLIP COULSON
RE: AGENT NATASHA ROMANOFF A.K.A. BLACK WIDOW, A.K.A. NATASHA ROMANOVA
TRANSCRIPT: DEPARTMENT OF DEFENSE, LODD INQUIRY HEARINGS.

DOD: So you knew there was a problem, even before you made contact with the asset?
ROMANOFF: No, sir. I did not.

DOD: But she was having the dreams. She was re-creating memories. She was clearly symptomatic.
ROMANOFF: I'm not a therapist, sir.

DOD: [laughs] Really?
ROMANOFF: Once the asset disappeared from the S.H.I.E.L.D. field office, we had no way of knowing how she was presenting, symptomatically. We didn't even know where she was.

DOD: What you're saying is, a facility run by *spies* couldn't hold this kid?
ROMANOFF: Your words, sir.

DOD: And the boy?
ROMANOFF: As I said—

DOD: I know, I know. It's classified. Humor me.
ROMANOFF: There's no humor in the situation, sir.

DOD: It's not a hearing, Agent, unless you give me something to hear.
ROMANOFF: You're not going to like it.

DOD: I rarely do.

ALEX MANOR'S HOUSE
MONTCLAIR, NEW JERSEY

The next morning, the pounding on the door began before the alarm went off. The ancient clock radio played an old song, "Nobody Loves the Hulk," by the Traits. It blared from the desk next to Alex's bed, but he didn't even flinch at the noise.

In fact, he snored at it.

Alex had stayed up late packing for his trip, which was why his room now rocked the tornado-swept look, with laundry everywhere (clean and dirty, as if those needed to be kept apart), stacks of comics and collectibles on all the shelves (but not in original packaging—Alex didn't want to be that guy), and an off-kilter poster of Iron Man hanging by one corner. (It didn't seem to matter to Alex that Taylor

Swift's head was pasted on Tony Stark's body. Taylor Stark was Dante's longest-running joke.)

At the far end of the room, a row of fencing medals dangled from a curtain rod, and they began to sway now, as the pounding on the door grew louder than the radio.

"Alex! Turn that off. You're already late for the bus." His mother's voice was worse than a thousand alarms. It was an instant dream killer.

Alex groaned. "Or I'm early for tomorrow's bus. Think about it." That only got him more pounding. He opened one eye and fumbled in his sheets.

There.

He pulled out a half-eaten apple and hurled it at the radio on his desk. The radio exploded into plastic parts—but at least the music stopped. His aim was better than his judgment.

Alex sat up. "Stop yelling. If you really want to know, I'm already totally dressed."

He got out of bed in his boxers, shivering as his feet hit the cold floor. The feel of it brought back his nightmare—that he had been lost in a forest in the winter, sinking deeper into the snow with every step, until he was up to his waist in the freezing white with only bare trees and white sky around him.

And then the snow covered my head, and I couldn't breathe at all. . . .

It didn't feel like a dream. It felt so real it was more like a memory. His feet were practically numb from frostbite.

"I don't hear moving," shouted the voice behind his door, interrupting him.

Alex moved.

His mother stopped him at the front door, yanking the earphones out of his ears. He took in her cat-hula-girl sweatshirt and mom jeans with a nod.

"New sweatshirt?" It wasn't, and he grinned as he said it.

Mrs. Manor rolled her eyes. She was a travel agent and had an exotic cat sweatshirt for every locale. This one said MEOW-NA KEA BEACH, HAWAII.

Of course it did.

Alex's mom firmly believed everyone needed to have a thing, and it seemed that cats and vacations—preferably cats *on* vacations—were hers. Stanley, her tabby, went everywhere with her.

"Forgetting something?" Mrs. Manor held up a bus ticket, looking smug.

"Never." Alex pocketed the printed ticket and grabbed his fencing bag from its spot by the closet, because he'd forgotten that, too. "Thanks, Ma."

"The bus leaves right after school. You're going straight to Penn Station. Stay with the team. Don't wander off from the coaches. If you get into trouble, I'll be at your grandparents' house." Mrs. Manor sounded stressed. By Alex's own calculations, this possibly had something to do with the last tournament, when the entire team had gotten busted while trying out the slots in Atlantic City.

Alex smirked. "What trouble? It's the North American Cup, Ma. Not a war zone."

She shook her head. "You're a *what trouble* magnet, Alexander Manor. It's in your blood. Everywhere you go is a war zone."

"Not—" Alex checked his ticket. "Philly." That was apparently where he was going. He made a mental note. *Cheesesteaks.*

He hugged her as well as he could, shouldering his backpack and dragging his fencing bag. "I'll behave. No trouble. No war. Not even a skirmish."

"No fighting, no biting," she said. "No black cards, this time. Please. Not even a red."

"Promise."

"Don't say that. I think we both know it will only lead to disappointment." She sighed. "Better to keep the bar low."

"How about, I won't get arrested? I could maybe promise you that." Alex kissed his mother's cheek. "Back on Sunday. Do *not* clean my room while I'm gone. I'll know if you throw one thing away."

She shrugged, unfazed. "And I already told you, I'm calling *Hoarders.* If they decide to pay us a visit, I'm not going to stand in their way."

"I told you, it's a collection. Not one thing. Not Taylor Stark. Not Jabba the Hut, not a single Avenger." He grinned, and his mother shrugged, still smiling. "Swear."

She answered by shoving his customary morning donut into his mouth.

As Alex bounded down the sidewalk, his mother's smile faded. For a moment, Mrs. Marilyn Manor looked as if she were made of steel. When Alex rounded the corner, she took out a cell phone and punched in a few numbers. Then she stepped farther out onto the porch, scanning the street as if she was looking for something. Her eyes darted from car to car, hedge to hedge, rooftop to rooftop. If there was anything there, she didn't seem to see it.

Mrs. Manor shivered despite her sweatshirt and pocketed her phone.

Behind a neighboring chimney, a black-gloved hand dropped a pair of binoculars. There was no doubt about it. Marilyn Manor was worried about the right problem; she was just looking in the wrong place.

There were eyes on the Manor family. That was the *what trouble* now. And whether or not trouble was in Alex Manor's blood, as his mother suspected, it made no difference. There was more to worry about, this time, than teenage boys let loose in Atlantic City.

S.H.I.E.L.D. EYES ONLY

CLEARANCE LEVEL X

LINE-OF-DUTY DEATH [LODD] INVESTIGATION
REF: S.H.I.E.L.D. CASE 121A415
AGENT IN COMMAND [AIC]: PHILLIP COULSON
RE: AGENT NATASHA ROMANOFF A.K.A. BLACK WIDOW,
A.K.A. NATASHA ROMANOVA
TRANSCRIPT: DEPARTMENT OF DEFENSE, LODD INQUIRY HEARINGS.

DOD: So we did have eyes on the boy?
COULSON: No, sir. Not to my knowledge.

DOD: Not S.H.I.E.L.D. eyes, Agent Coulson?
COULSON: Let me put it this way—whatever was going on with Alex Manor, or whatever you want to call him, it wasn't under my purview.

DOD: Then whose purview was it?
COULSON: Not mine. That's all I know.

DOD: And the girl? Ava Orlova? When did you first encounter her?
COULSON: That would be when Ivan Somodorov was trying to microwave her in Odessa, I guess. You know the rest. The hostage grab, when she was just a kid. And then Philly.

DOD: Ah. Which brings us to Philly.
COULSON: None of that was her fault.

DOD: Because she was your average teenage girl? I find that hard to believe.
COULSON: Ava Orlova was never your average teenage girl. But then, we wouldn't be having this conversation if she was, would we?

DOD: You tell me, Agent.

THE FORT GREENE YWCA
BROOKLYN, NEW YORK

"*P*rosypaysya, Ava!*" Wake up!

The slam of a fencing blade into her chest brought Ava back to reality. As she opened her eyes, the latest daydream faded.

Tattoo Boy saying good-bye to his mother, the one with the strangely hard eyes. But something else, too. Someone. Watching from across the street.

Someone with a gun.

The blade hit her again, and Ava found herself automatically kicking her foot beneath her attacker's outstretched leg—taking her down, slamming her to the floor beneath them. Her heart was pounding.

That's new.

Ava now stared awkwardly down at her friend Oksana, who was flat on her back on the wooden strip. "Sorry. I don't know why I just did that."

"Never mind why—where did you learn *how* to do that?" Oksana Davis was laughing—Ava could see her twinkling brown eyes and equally brown skin through the mesh of the mask. Still, she was surprised.

"Nowhere. It just sort of happened, I guess." Ava pulled off her mask. She knew it wasn't much of an explanation, but it was the truth; lately, all kinds of things had *just been happening* to Ava, and she couldn't explain any of them.

"Jeez. Your lessons are really starting to pay off." Oksana sat up.

The Y had started giving basic fencing classes two years ago, and Ava and Oksana never missed them if they could help it. They were allowed to use the equipment whenever they liked, so they found themselves hanging out at the Y most afternoons when toddler classes and retirees weren't occupying the room.

Both girls took to the sport. Neither girl fit anywhere particular in the world, and they'd gradually made a habit of not fitting in next to each other. When they'd met at the Auburn shelter in Fort Greene, Ava barely spoke—but Oksana spoke Russian. Her late mother had been a ballerina. Her father drove a cab. Every conversation Ava and Oksana had was a tiny glimpse of home for both of them. Even if Oksana had never been there herself, Russian had been her mother's tongue.

Which had brought them both to fencing, something Ava had begun back in Ukraine at her primary school when she was six years old. Oksana had let Ava drag her into their first épée class at the Y, but from then on, Oksana had been the one with the advantage, thanks to her endlessly long limbs. Though Ava was fast and strong and sometimes utterly fearless, she was a good two inches shorter than her willowy friend.

So why did I just win this bout today? Ava wondered. She didn't even remember practicing that attack. And she was still so disoriented from what she had seen in her daydream, she had been totally unprepared to defend herself.

"One lucky move." Oksana grinned. "Besides, you're thinking about your dream boyfriend again. Tattoo Boy inspires you." She pulled off her mask. Half her brown curls had escaped the boho scarf she wore wrapped around her head, as always.

"No I'm not." Ava could feel her face turning red. "I mean, he doesn't." She sat down against the wall and unzipped her borrowed fencing jacket, printed with the faded letters of somebody else's name.

"You know you're a terrible liar. It's one of your best qualities." Oksana sat herself down next to Ava. "So tell me. What is Tattoo Boy up to today?"

Ava hung her head. The dreams had almost become a joke between them, as if Tattoo Boy was their shared imaginary friend. "Something's wrong. And the dreams are changing." She looked at her friend. "They're turning into nightmares."

"Go on."

Ava looked away. "I don't know. It doesn't matter. It isn't real."

Oksana laughed. "This is America, Ava. Some people fly around in iron suits. Some climb buildings like spiders. Others pound cities into plaster with giant green fists or alien hammers. How do you know what's real anymore, *myshka*?"

Ava knew it was all too easy to fantasize about getting saved by a super hero, especially when you were stuck in the kind of life they had. She only shrugged. "Do you think those people are heroes, Sana?"

"Of course. Don't you?"

Ava didn't answer. She wanted to tell Oksana about Black Widow, just as she wanted to tell her everything about the dreams and show her the sketches. But there were some parts of yourself you just couldn't share, not even with your only friend. Because there were some parts of yourself that didn't make sense, not even to you.

Not even in a world where people flew around in iron suits.

Is Alexei real?

Maybe.

Possibly.

It was also possible that she'd invented him. But Ava knew she hadn't invented the Black Widow, and she—the woman in black, that was how she thought of her—was in her dreams too. Of course, they'd actually met, once, so maybe it was all some kind of psychological mumbo jumbo. Traumatic memories played out in the safety of dreamland or whatever.

But not Alexei.

He wasn't there in Odessa that night, was he?

As if on cue, the ghost words floated back into her head, the ones that had stayed with her for almost eight years now.

OPUS.

LUXPORT.

KRASNAYA KOMNATA.

When she was ten, she had snuck onto her tutor's laptop and looked up *OPUS*, but as far as she could tell, it was either some type of classical music composition or a cartoon character. *LUXPORT* was the name of a big Ukrainian export company, more boring than criminal-looking. *KRASNAYA KOMNATA*, that one she couldn't understand at all.

Krasnaya Komnata.

Red Room.

That was the literal translation. But so what? Which red room mattered to Ava, or even her mother? Red like the Russian flag? Red like her Russian blood?

Or maybe just red like the flames that had come after the warehouse exploded. Maybe her mind was just remembering that night, trying to make sense of it. Maybe the room was just her memory.

Red what?

Now Oksana was poking her with a blade. "Speaking of trips, we've got to leave really early tomorrow. Like six in the morning."

Ava tried to piece together what her friend had been talking about. "Six? That's the first bus? And how are we going to pay for a bus all the way to Philly?"

Oksana smiled. "Who said anything about a bus?" She unplugged her blade, letting it clatter to the floor. "I've called us a cab."

Ava looked surprised. "Your dad is going to drive us all the way to Philly?"

Oksana shrugged. "Once Nana said it was time we started competing, my dad said yes. He wasn't going to be the one to crush our dreams." She grinned. "Well, my dreams. We already know what your dreams are about."

Ava shoved her. "At least they're not about Nana." Nana was their volunteer coach, an Armenian firecracker who taught classes for free on Thursdays. Between the three of them, every other kid in the class now knew how to curse in Russian. "You know we have to register for tourneys." It was the best Ava could come up with. A fencing tournament was the farthest thing from her mind. She'd had an uneasy feeling all day, and now she felt sick to her stomach.

It's the gun in the dream. I can't stop thinking about it.

"What if I said same-day registration was still open? And that Nana told me she wanted us to go?" Oksana smiled.

"I guess I'd say we don't have equipment," Ava answered. She was still distracted.

Maybe it's an omen, she thought. *Maybe bad things are coming.*

Oksana looked around. "And then I'd say we could use this stuff."

"And then I'd say excellent. Because these gloves don't smell like someone died in them." Ava peeled hers off, dropping it on the floor.

Oksana smiled. "Oh my God, Ava. You're chicken? *Ty trushish?* Is that even possible?"

"I'm not chicken." Ava wiggled out of the jacket, which was three sizes too big.

"You? Ava Orlova, who fears nothing?" Oksana was amazed.

Ava shrugged. "I'm not scared of a little metal blade with rubber on the end, if that's what you're asking. I'm Russian."

I survived a madman in Odessa and an explosion and a Black Widow, too.

She had never talked about that night, not to Oksana. Not about the warehouse or Odessa. That didn't mean she didn't think about it, though.

The time when everything fell apart.

"Tournament blades don't have rubber tips, remember?" Oksana said, finally.

"Same difference."

"Okay," Sana gave up. "We don't have to go."

They sat side by side in silence. There was nothing more to say. Ava knew how much Oksana must have wanted to go to the tournament; Oksana barely spoke to her father unless she absolutely had to, as if he himself had something to do with her mother's death or the fact that she was now alone.

But she's not. We have each other.

Ava could feel Oksana's eyes on her.

"Okay," Ava said slowly. She shrugged off the feeling that had settled over her. There were no omens. The bad things had all already happened, and dream boys didn't die. As far as Ava knew, they didn't even live. "Okay, fine. You win. We'll go."

Oksana held up her fist with a smile and Ava bumped it. Then she leaned her head on Ava's sweaty shoulder and began to catalog the random collection of used fencing gear in the room.

Between the battered blades and smelly masks and oversized jackets and broken-zippered pants, Ava forgot all about the gun and the ghost words and the woman in black. She stopped wondering why or how her parents had disappeared—or who was responsible. She stopped thinking about boys who were not real and heroes who were not heroic.

By the time the girls hit the freezing-cold showers, everything was back to normal, if living in the basement of a Y like—and with—a stray cat could be considered normal. It was as normal as anything else Ava had known.

The icy blast of water was almost literally mind-numbing.

At least clarifying.

That's why Ava never minded the cold; she depended on it.

It pushed away her memories and made her head hurt less, which was important because the one thing Ava could not afford to do was feel.

She had felt too much already.

She already knew she was going to have to be her own hero.

LINE-OF-DUTY DEATH [LODD] INVESTIGATION
REF: S.H.I.E.L.D. CASE 121A415
AGENT IN COMMAND [AIC]: PHILLIP COULSON
RE: AGENT NATASHA ROMANOFF A.K.A. BLACK WIDOW,
A.K.A. NATASHA ROMANOVA
TRANSCRIPT: DEPARTMENT OF DEFENSE, LODD INQUIRY HEARINGS.

DOD: And you made zero contact with the asset prior to engaging?
ROMANOFF: No, sir. After further reflection, I had decided it would
be best to—to cut ties.

DOD: Why?
ROMANOFF: Sir?

DOD: Why cut ties? From what I've read, you pulled the asset from
burning wreckage. You spoke her language and identified with her
as an orphan of war, almost a sister.
ROMANOFF: I'm not sure I would say that.

DOD: Then I'd be curious to know what you would say. It strains
credulity, Agent Romanoff, that after you saved her life and brought
her to this country, you never spoke to the child again.
ROMANOFF: I'm not exactly the big-sister type, sir.

DOD: And yet you had no problem involving her in field ops? When
you knew yourself to be putting this minor asset's life at risk?
ROMANOFF: Yes, sir.

DOD: And? This didn't worry you?
ROMANOFF: Like I said, I'm not exactly the big-sister type.

DOD: I'm starting to pick up on that.

PHILADELPHIA CONVENTION CENTER— DOWNTOWN PHILLY THE CITY OF BROTHERLY LOVE

"**Y**ou're crazy." Dante shook his head. "And we're late."

But Alex wouldn't budge from the sidewalk in front of the convention center. "I'm serious. Someone's following us. A woman. It's creeping me out. I saw her at Penn Station, and I think I saw her just now." He looked from one end of the crowded downtown street to the other. As he did, he took a half cheesesteak out of his pocket and unwrapped the greasy paper. Alex always ate when he was stressed out—the junkier the better. He took a bite of congealed cheese-beef. "Maybe she's CIA."

"Is that the same cheesesteak from last night? Don't answer that. You have a problem." Dante looked slightly grossed out. "Either way, I'm not going to miss check-in, not even for a hot CIA agent."

"I didn't say she was hot." Alex scanned the street. He was sure she was out there.

Dante gave him a knowing look. "Then why do you care?"

Alex looked at him. "You're an idiot, you know that?"

Dante rolled his eyes. "Yeah, well, you can stand out here by yourself, Cheesesteak." He grabbed his bag and started moving. "And you think I'm the idiot." Alex followed his friend inside.

The boys' jackets said MONTCLAIR NJ FENCING ALLIANCE, but this wasn't New Jersey anymore. The convention center was crawling with similarly sweat-suited athletes from more than a hundred clubs like theirs. The rows of fencing strips looked like metal sidewalks, and there were so many that they filled the entire convention hall. The walls were littered with pennants and posters, flags and flyers, and the perimeter of the enormous room was lined with vendors. This was the North American Cup circuit, as it said on the flashing digital scoreboard. And a NAC tournament was no small deal.

It was almost as nerve-racking as being tailed by the CIA, Alex thought.

The boys made their way through the crowd to the place where a pile of guys and an even bigger pile of fencing bags slumped in a messy circle. Above them—plastered with duct tape—a slightly crooked MONTCLAIR ALLIANCE sign hung on the wall.

Alex frowned when he saw his teammates. "What is Jurek doing here? He wasn't on the train with us."

"I heard he missed the train by just two points." That was always the joke. Jeff Jurek, the Montclair Alliance team captain, never could just tell you his own results; he also knew yours and liked to tell you how close he had come to doing even better. According to him, he missed everything he deserved in life by *just two points.*

"Ah, man. If he makes us call him Cap again, he's going down," Alex scowled. Jurek idolized Captain America, which wasn't all that unusual; most high school kids worshipped one super hero or another—or at least identified with them. In this case, however, the irony was lost on no one that the fencing captain and the super-hero captain were nothing alike. "Where's a super villain when you need one?"

"Just stay away from that turd. Seriously, Mr. Black Card." Dante shook his head. "He's not worth it."

"I know," Alex said. "I just—"

"I know," Dante sighed.

They said nothing more and joined the others, who were all in various stages of getting ready to fence. It took a while to prep for any tournament, if only because of all the ballistic-nylon gear. You couldn't step on the strip at a NAC without wearing every last piece of protective equipment, according to USFA regulations. Not unless you wanted to end up like the Russian who had taken a blade through the brain at Worlds and died. Now there were white Kevlar underarm protectors and thicker white Kevlar jackets and even white Kevlar knickers that said USA, along with a stencil of the Stars and Stripes. Even before you fenced your first bout, you were sweating like a dog.

"Check it," Dante said, pointing across the room. He was always dressed first, which he said came from growing up with so many brothers and sisters. There were only so many clean socks; you had to move fast. "Manor and Cruz. Fame and glory. Just how we like it."

Alex looked up. On the digital scoreboard, Alex Manor was listed as first among the ranks of the Junior seeding. Dante Cruz was second. It was always that way, back and forth. Their main competition was with each other—which didn't make it any less fierce.

"Pound it," Alex said, holding out his fist.

"Except it really should say Cruz first, and then Manor," Dante pointed out, as they pounded fists.

"Sure it should," Alex said.

"After today, it will."

"In your dreams."

Alex picked up his mask, grabbing a handful of blades with his free hand. The back of his jacket said MANOR, but as tall and lanky as he was, he would have been unmistakable on the gym floor even without it.

"Yeah? I'm not dreaming now. *En garde*, loser." Dante held up a blade of his own. "Let's do this."

"All right, Cruz. But no crying this time." Alex turned to the nearest strip, the one that half of their team was already using for warm-up bouts.

The moment he turned, though, he felt a blade whack him on the back. He sprang back, instinctively, muscles tensed and heart pounding. He could feel his teeth grinding against each other.

Jeff Jurek laughed, wagging his weapon.

"Don't do that," Alex said automatically. He hated nothing more than getting hit with a blade, even as a joke. There was something about him that responded to every attack as if it were lethal. His body wasn't wired to tell the difference, though his brain should have been.

Try that again, turd. I dare you.

"Start running, *Miss Manners*. Then you can warm up." Jurek pointed at the strip with his blade. The guy was like every tristate cliché rolled into one, from his nonironic white tube socks to his thick gold chains. Jurek's difficult personality had also helped his despotic rise to captain; nobody wanted to be his cocaptain. Even now, the rest of the guys pretended not to see him.

Alex pushed the blade away, bristling at the nickname. "I'm good," he said. "I'll run later. Dante and I were just going to bout a little first."

"I'm good . . . ?" Jurek raised his voice inquiringly. He said the words like he was making a joke, but Alex knew he wasn't joking.

"I'm good, *Cap*." Alex rolled his eyes.

Jurek flicked his blade on Alex's leg. "Go on, warm up."

Alex flinched. "I told you not to do that." *Strike two.*

"He will. We are. Just give it a rest, Jurek." Dante tried to pull Alex away, as if he knew what was about to happen next. Which he did.

Jurek smiled. "Everyone runs. Even *Miss Manners*."

"*Super* original nickname. You come up with that yourself? Maybe you should use it *all the time*." Alex felt himself losing patience with the guy, though he was trying not to. He could already hear his mother scolding him in the back of his mind.

A short fuse blows up in your own face, Alex.

"And maybe you should get here on time." Now Jurek whacked Alex on the arm—and Alex grabbed the blade in his fist. That was it. He was done.

Strike three.

"Maybe you should make me." Alex couldn't keep the words from coming out. Worse, he couldn't stop himself from yanking the blade as hard as he could—sending both Jurek and his weapon stumbling.

Dante was already shaking his head, but it was too late.

Jurek swung back at Alex.

Now.

Alex let his mind go into overdrive—adrenaline did that to him. It happened during every bout, even if he was fencing Dante. Alex didn't really know how to describe it when he fell into the zone like this. It was almost like playing a video game, only Alex was somehow both the guy moving the controller and the character on the screen. All at the same time.

He'll start with his fists, but he's going to use his body. He's going to go for my head. The guy's like one giant head butt. That's all he knows how to do. Alex caught Jurek's fist in his hand, lightning fast.

Just as I thought. Alex smiled.

He already knew how it was all going to go down, based on the way Jurek was standing (low center of gravity), his height (six inch disadvantage), his weight (thirty pounds slower.) Also: how he thought (rage, instinct, general lack of strategy) and who he idolized (brute force over strategic advantage), as well as his insecurities (size, inferiority) and his behavioral tics (favoring the right side.)

Every battle was a new problem set, and every opponent required a new formula. Alex knew his work had to be disciplined and meticulous—even if these were the sort of calculations that left someone bruised and bloody.

And they were.

The moment Alex began to move, he became methodical, efficient. Like a trained soldier, ducking away, kicking out his legs and sideswiping Jurek with his feet.

It's almost too easy, Alex thought.

Almost.

As Alex and Jurek fell to the floor fighting, a horn sounded and the two boys were pulled off each other. Alex tried to catch his breath, but the wind was knocked out of him. One too many head butts.

Also as predicted.

Jurek's lip was as swollen as his eye was purple. It was only then that Alex realized how much trouble he was in.

Crap.

Trouble.

Again.

Alex tried to twist out of the hands of the two burly officials holding him back. A balding coach and a Senior fencer from the club had Jurek by both arms.

Here it comes.

Alex didn't understand why he did half the things he did. Sometimes he felt like he spent most of his life on autopilot. As if he was looking for some kind of never-ending fight. Whatever it was, Alex only knew he couldn't stop it or even regret it—not until it came down to this moment. Which it always did. One more black card Alex Manor didn't need. One more reason to be grounded and sidelined.

My mom is going to kill me.

Alex looked at the officials, beginning the familiar speech. "You don't understand. I wasn't doing anything. He started the whole thing." He'd been saying the same thing as long as he could remember.

He only wished he knew why.

S.H.I.E.L.D. EYES ONLY

CLEARANCE LEVEL X

LINE-OF-DUTY DEATH [LODD] INVESTIGATION
REF: S.H.I.E.L.D. CASE 121A415
AGENT IN COMMAND [AIC]: PHILLIP COULSON
RE: AGENT NATASHA ROMANOFF A.K.A. BLACK WIDOW, A.K.A. NATASHA ROMANOVA
TRANSCRIPT: DEPARTMENT OF DEFENSE, LODD INQUIRY HEARINGS.

DOD: So the boy had identified anger issues from the start.
ROMANOFF: I didn't say that. He wasn't an angel, but he wasn't a criminal, either. Not like—

DOD: Not like the rest of you?
ROMANOFF: Depends on who you ask, sir.

DOD: There is some thinking that you intended to bring the minor assets together. For the purposes of the mission.
ROMANOFF: No, sir.

DOD: And you didn't engineer the encounter?
ROMANOFF: It was a fencing tournament. I'm not the USFA.

DOD: You've been called many things, Agent Romanoff. That wouldn't surprise me at all.
ROMANOFF: It wasn't me.

DOD: Was that the first time you'd witnessed Alex Manor's combat abilities?
ROMANOFF: Yes. They were—surprising. I even contacted S.H.I.E.L.D. to see if he was one of ours.

DOD: And?
ROMANOFF: You know he was not.

DOD: Once again, I only know what I'm told, Agent.
ROMANOFF: And I'm telling you. Just a boy.

PHILADELPHIA CONVENTION CENTER—DOWNTOWN PHILLY
THE CITY OF BROTHERLY LOVE

"It's not a big deal. There's only like, what, three thousand people here? Four?" Oksana shrugged.

"I'd rather be in Grand Central during rush hour," Ava said, swallowing. "Maybe even Times Square."

The two girls stood side by side at the doors to the convention center, motionless in the crowd of identically white-suited athletes. Like everyone else, they were dressed head to toe in their own badly fitting, borrowed version of the regulation whites. That had been Oksana's idea, to show up already wearing their fencing clothes, so that they could blend in with the crowd more easily.

Less Y basement, more athlete.

But now it didn't matter, because neither Ava nor Oksana could bring herself to step inside the gym.

"This was a bad idea," Ava said. Last night she had dreamed nothing at all, which didn't happen very often. She didn't know what it meant, but it had made her nervous.

"Or a great idea," Oksana said. "We'll never know if we don't go in. Come on."

They didn't move.

Oksana took a deep breath. "Okay. You know how there's always someone you'd like to run through with a blade?"

"Just one?" Ava smiled, in spite of the sour feeling in her stomach.

"Pretend everyone you face today is that person." Oksana grabbed Ava's hand and squeezed, and that was it. No more stalling. "It's time to start fighting for what we want."

"Or at least time to walk into the building." Ava nodded.

But Oksana was right. It was time.

They let the crowd carry them through the doors—and into their first tournament. Ava had never seen anything like it. She was overwhelmed by the crush of uniforms and flags and faces and words. She saw club jackets referencing places she'd only heard about on the endless hum of C-SPAN back in 7B, when she thought she'd never be free to go anywhere at all. Some were still foreign. Windy City. Alamo. Chevy Chase. Bowling Green. But the famous American schools she knew, and those surfaced one colored warm-up at a time. Columbia. Harvard. Princeton. Stanford. Ava recognized the names from preppy sweatshirt-wearing Americans taking the Q train on their way to the trendy parts of Brooklyn to buy a scoop of ice cream for five dollars or homemade pickles in little jars.

Ava knew she would never set foot inside any school like that. She'd probably never go to school again at all. She tried not to care. School wasn't for everyone. She herself was the daughter of a quantum physicist and look how well that had turned out.

But as Ava watched a pair of girls in perfect braids walk by, she knew it wasn't just the schools. It was the bedrooms and the bathtubs and the swimming pools and the laundry rooms. The leashed dogs and the cut grass. She had no business being in a room with any of these people. They breathed a different kind of air than she did.

"Registration. And weapons check." Oksana's voice seemed to come from far away. "That's what Nana said to do next. But let's leave the gloves off until the last minute. They smell like cat pee."

Ava wasn't listening. She was too busy staring.

Aliens. They might as well be from another planet.

Then one of the braided girls looked back at her and laughed. She leaned in, whispering to her friend, who turned around to inspect Ava as well. They were both wearing shirts with enormous whale logos on them.

Why whales? Do rich people have a thing about whaling?

The longer the alien girls looked at her, the more Ava knew what they saw. The shabby, oversized jacket that only said her name on a piece of duct tape on the back. The sagging pants that she'd had to safety pin at the waist, with the one drooping suspender. The corkscrew curls she'd cut herself, using borrowed scissors. The holey sneakers that could barely pass for sneakers, let alone fencing shoes.

Ava touched a messy curl as she felt her face go red.

Der'mo.

And then—

Screw you.

She didn't have a choice about feeling like an outsider, but she didn't have to feel like a loser. She didn't have to let it get to her. She was tougher than that now.

Strong and sharp, Ava. Remember.

She followed the alien girls with her eyes as they moved around the perimeter of the gym, over to where a group of boys were warming up on a strip.

One in particular caught her eye.

He was taller than the others, and his brown hair curled into unruly waves that fell into his face as he laughed.

"Do not get near the gloves. I repeat. Not the gloves," Oksana laughed, but Ava almost couldn't hear what she was saying. Her own ears were ringing, and the blood was rushing to her head.

There's something so familiar—

Ava froze.

Oksana hit her on the arm. "*Privet?* Hello? *Ty slyshish'?* You listening? Earth to Ava?"

Ava couldn't answer. She was too busy staring at the boy on the far strip, across the crowded hall.

Now she could see his face—and she knew it. She recognized him.

It was impossible, but then everything about this boy had always been.

Because it was him. *Him.*

Alexei Manorovsky.

Tattoo Boy.

The boy from the dreams.

Ava was sure of it. It had to be him. He was right there, right there in front of her. Standing across the gym from her, talking to his friend.

"Oksana." Ava could barely get out the word. "There."

She couldn't look away.

He's here. Now. And I'm awake.

This is real. This is happening.

"What?" Oksana looked confused. "Are you okay?"

"That's him. Alexei," Ava breathed. The room was lurching and contracting around her. She thought for a moment that she was going to pass out.

Oksana relaxed. "Is this about Tattoo Boy?" She shook her head in mock dismay. She shook Ava by the arm. "Is he invisible? Can only you see him? Is he reaching out to you with his mind? Can you smell his blood, like in the vampire movies?"

"Oksana. I'm not joking. See for yourself." Ava fumbled in her backpack, pulling out her worn notebook from the fencing clothes and water bottles. Like most people she met in the shelters, she kept almost everything she owned with her—which wasn't much.

Now she turned the pages until she found a sketch of Alex, a decent likeness. One of the many.

"This." Ava held the smudged-charcoal portrait up in front of her friend. "Look. It's the same person."

"What?" Oksana looked at the page. "Hey. You're a really good artist. Why would you never show me your stuff?" She looked up. "Can I have this? Or maybe . . . could you do one for me of Thor?"

Ava rolled her eyes. "I'm not talking about the picture. Look at that one. Him. The one with the messy hair." She pointed, and Oksana looked across the gym to the farthest strip. Then Oksana frowned and glanced at the sketch again.

Ava watched as she compared the pictures. "I'm not crazy, right? Sana?"

Oksana didn't answer.

But it was him, and Ava knew there could be no doubting it. She believed, for the first time in her life, that she was looking at the real Alexei Manorovsky, or Alex Manor, or whatever you wanted to call him.

The tough-looking boy in front of her—the one with rowdy long hair and the rocker look—was unmistakable by now. He had the same wicked grin and dark eyes as always. Ava studied the familiar details with an artist's eye. He was tall and lean, with the body of a swimmer or a diver. His lanky arms only seemed that much longer with the blade in his hands, like now. Everything about his body, about his long arched back, about the loose-fitting white jacket that somehow covered and revealed just how powerful he was, all at once, seemed to belong to a warrior.

And then Tattoo Boy began to move.

He reached out and ripped a blade from the arm of an angry, red-faced boy, sending him flying.

The boy cursed and swung at him.

"Oh. My. God." After that, even Oksana, who was not speechless, who was never speechless, could not speak.

In one fluid movement, Alexei hurled himself down the strip, uncoiling like a spring had set him off and thrown him across the room. He had dropped his blade, and it wasn't so much that he was going for a touch, but that he was going for a kill.

That was what it looked like, predatory and beautiful, if such a thing was possible. As if such a thing was somehow meant to happen, and he himself was something meant to be—especially when he was in this kind of combat.

He's a fighter all right.

Ava grabbed Oksana by the hand. "I know I'm not crazy."

As she watched, it wasn't even a question anymore. Now Alexei was being held back from the skirmish by two burly men, both of whom looked like they wanted to toss him out of the tournament.

Oksana frowned as she looked from the picture to the boy in front of her. "It's incredible. Do you really think—?"

Ava nodded. She couldn't speak. They both stared back at him.

"Not imaginary." Ava couldn't believe it.

"Wow." Oksana's mouth hung open. "Definitely not imaginary."

"Right?" Ava looked at her friend. "You're absolutely sure you see him too, right? He's a hundred percent real?"

"Definitely real. Very, very real. And really, really—"

Just then, at that very moment, Alex turned their way. He was furious and embarrassed and upset—but both girls could see him, perfectly, for the very first time. And more embarrassing, Ava was almost certain that he could see them.

And that he was beautiful.

Oksana crossed herself as she grabbed Ava by the arm. "Really."

"This can't be a coincidence," Ava said, not moving her eyes.

"What else can it be?"

Ava didn't know how to answer, so she didn't try. Finally she looked away. "I'm going over there." She took a deep breath. "I have to, right?" Her heart was hammering in her chest like it was trying to get out.

"Don't look now, but I think you've been spotted." Oksana squeezed Ava's arm.

Ava let her eyes flicker back in his direction. He must have seen her staring at him. Now he was standing in the middle of the convention center, looking right back at her with his wildly dark eyes and his even wilder shag of hair. The men who had held him back were nowhere in sight.

The pink in Ava's cheeks turned to red, and she realized she was barely breathing. She let herself look at him—really look at him.

Alexei smiled at her, a bit awkwardly.

Let's do this. We're doing this. Here I am, doing this.

She forced herself to breathe.

She could feel him. She could feel his eyes exploring her, and she could feel the weight of their pull. She knew what he was doing. He was sizing her up the way Ava did when she waited for two fencers to finish a bout in class, knowing that she would fence the winner. Analyzing their strengths, their weaknesses, the patterns to their motion and their rhythm. As Nana liked to say, there was a kind of observation that was itself the overture to interaction. That was this, and Ava could feel it. What it meant or why he was doing it—that was a different story.

She had no idea.

Does he have them too? The dreams? Does he know me?

Ava felt so strange. Chemically, physiologically strange. Like there was some kind of crazy magnet pulling them together, which of course was what the dreams had always felt like, at least to Ava. Why else would she have imagined him into existence, right here in front of her?

She didn't know what was going on, not exactly, but she found that the longer she stood in the same room with this boy, the less she seemed to care.

Ava didn't realize her feet had actually begun to move until Oksana grabbed her by the arm.

"No, no. You can't."

"Why not?" The spell was broken, and Ava turned back to her friend.

"You'll look like an idiot. What are you going to do, hand him your drawing? Like, hello, beautiful boy, I'm really not just a serial killer or a stalker or something? You're going to scare him off." Oksana had a point.

Ava frowned. "I'm not going to throw myself at him. I just want to talk to him. I want to figure this whole thing out."

"This I-see-you-every-time-I-close-my-eyes thing? Yeah, that's not creepy." Oksana shook her head. "Look, I don't know what's going on here, but I know you have to play it cool. Normal rules still apply."

Ava knew she was right. "Well, what am I supposed to do?"

"You need a plan." Oksana looked at her. "And maybe a hairbrush."

Ava hesitated.

Maybe this is the plan.

Maybe it took me seventeen years to get here, but now that I have, maybe I'm here for a reason.

Maybe this is what destiny feels like.

A horn blew.

Oksana grabbed a handful of battered and bent épées out of the old bag. "Either way, it will have to wait. I didn't spend all those hours in a car with my father not to fence. He's up in the stands now. Registration is going to close in ten minutes. We have to get our weapons checked."

Ava knew it was true; even though this tournament was classified as open to the public, every fencer present still had to register—whether they came from Yale or the Y.

She looked across the room doubtfully. The boy who looked like Alexei was now deep in conversation with his friend, who also looked familiar. As she watched, she had to press her hand against her leg to stop it from shaking.

This is real. He's real.

It was all so confusing. She didn't know what was about to happen, but she also knew that some part of it had been happening for so long now that it would take more than any one person to stop it.

Strong as an ox. Be strong as an ox.

You have to think. You have to figure out what to do.

But it wasn't that easy. There were too many people everywhere she looked, making too much noise. Her heart was pounding, and she was beginning to panic. Where was the clarity of a freezing-cold shower when you needed it?

Maybe there's no shower, but at least—

Ava looked back to Oksana. "I'm going to find the locker room. I just need a minute. I'll meet you at the weapons check after that."

Oksana nodded, then grabbed Ava by both shoulders. "Breathe, myshka."

"Breathing," Ava said. "And I'm not a mouse." She smiled.

Myshka had been Oksana's pet name for her since they'd met in the rodent-ridden Dumpster alley behind the shelter.

Only a mouse would go hide in a locker room when the whole world had just opened in front of her.

And I'm not a mouse.

"We'll see," Oksana said as she disappeared into the crowd.

Ava slowly picked up her blades.

I'm not.

She turned in the direction of the boy and forced herself to start walking.

LINE-OF-DUTY [LODD] DEATH INVESTIGATION
REF: S.H.I.E.L.D. CASE 121A415
AGENT IN COMMAND [AIC]: PHILLIP COULSON
RE: AGENT NATASHA ROMANOFF A.K.A. BLACK WIDOW,
A.K.A. NATASHA ROMANOVA
TRANSCRIPT: DEPARTMENT OF DEFENSE, LODD INQUIRY HEARINGS.

DOD: And the friend?
ROMANOFF: Oksana Davis.

DOD: Russian national?
ROMANOFF: American citizen.

DOD: Tell me, did her Russian and American names give you pause?
Considering your history?
ROMANOFF: Every name gives me pause. Considering my history, sir.

DOD: Did you run a check on this friend?
ROMANOFF: I did not.

DOD: The father? The deceased mother? Stepsiblings? Living situation?
ROMANOFF: I wasn't planning for a LODD inquiry hearing at the
time, sir. And I didn't think she mattered.

DOD: Everyone matters, Agent Romanoff—
ROMANOFF: I'm touched, sir.

DOD: Especially once the bullets begin to fly.
ROMANOFF: And the blame?

DOD: Even more so.
ROMANOFF: And when the bullets stop?

DOD: Here we are.

PHILADELPHIA CONVENTION CENTER— DOWNTOWN PHILLY THE CITY OF BROTHERLY LOVE

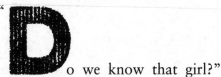

"**D**o we know that girl?" Alex couldn't help but notice the girl with hair the color of cinnamon who had been staring at him from across the gym. In a convention hall filled with thousands of people, she stood out.

"What girl? You mean, a girl who isn't from our school, Sofi's school, or the club?" Dante sighed, lacing up his last high-top Nike. "Probably not."

But it hadn't been Alex's imagination. There was a girl, and she was staring at him. Why? Alex looked down; he was holding the black card that meant he wasn't going to be doing any fencing today. In fact, he only had a few minutes to get his stuff together and get out of the gym.

That normally would have been all he could think about. But none of those things was as distracting as the striking girl on the far strip.

Alex couldn't bring himself to look away. He hadn't realized he was smiling, but he was.

Dante shoved him. "Dude. Stop staring. Be cool. For once." Alex snorted. "I'm not staring. She's staring. I'm being stared at."

"Who cares? She's . . . Wow. That is so *not* an eighth grader." Dante looked up, and then looked back down again. "I said be cool."

The horn sounded. The final warning.

"I gotta go." Dante punched Alex in the arm, a little lamely. "Sorry about the black card. Maybe next time you'll listen to me when I tell you to ignore Captain Underpants."

Alex wasn't listening. She was definitely looking at him, and when he met her eyes for the briefest of moments, they flashed with recognition. It was as if an electric current charged between them, and he felt his face going red. "Who is she?"

"A fencer, duh. Probably competing in Junior Women's, since it starts when our event does." Dante grinned. "I mean, when *my* event does."

"Don't tell my mom I got black-carded," Alex said automatically.

"Don't tell my dad, either. The noble Police Captain Guillermo Cruz already thinks you're going to drag me down. I can't give him the satisfaction of knowing how far you've fallen already."

"Me? Fallen?"

Dante laughed. "I gotta get to my strip." He pulled his mask halfway onto his head and picked up his water bottle, a spare electrical cord, and three blades. "Wish me luck."

As Alex looked back at the girl across the gym, he made up his mind. "Yeah, well. You wish *me* luck," he said.

Dante saw where he was looking and whistled. "You're going to need more than luck, compadre. What pretty girl would ever look at you?" he teased, holding up his fist, but Alex didn't pound it.

Not in front of her.

By the time he had made it across the hall, the cinnamon-haired girl was on the move with a handful of blades.

Not just on the move. In fact, she was moving right toward him.

Alex tried to compose himself.

Be cool.

She's just a girl.

He started to walk out to meet her, and that heady electric current—that magnetic charge between them—began to sizzle, sparking something inside him he'd never felt before.

Whoever she is, she isn't just a girl.

"Hey." Alex grinned, narrowly avoiding walking straight into a Gatorade-sponsored water cooler and knocking over the table that held it.

So much for cool.

"Hey." The girl smiled back, stopping in front of him, hesitantly. Her unruly curls flew around her face like red-gold fire, and her brown eyes were dark and wild.

There's something about her—but what?

She was beautiful, but it was more than just that.

It had to be.

There was a certain shadow to her face, something wistful and sad, that endeared her to Alex. Her smile may have been fragile, but there was a strength to her eyes as well. The way they sparked, he felt like there was something just barely kept in check, something that could explode at any moment—and he instantly understood. It was as familiar to him as looking in the mirror.

She was powerful, whether or not she or anyone else knew how powerful.

And probably a great fencer.

Alex didn't wonder at how he knew all this. He was too busy wondering how he could get to know her even more—and as soon as possible.

Why were you staring at me? Could I be that lucky?

"Hey," he repeated, not knowing what else to say, especially when what he really wanted to say couldn't be said.

Who are you? What do you want with me? Why are your eyes so sad?

Want to go away together?

"Hey," she echoed back. Now they were face-to-face in the center of the gym. All around them, blades were clanging as fencers thundered up and down metal strips—making the most of the last few minutes of warming up.

The silence was awkward, and Alex kicked himself for thinking this would be anything different from the way it usually went with girls his age. For all his confidence on the mat, he was shy. When it came to talking to most girls, he felt like he was trying to understand a whole different country, or even a different planet.

They stood there for another long minute.

Finally the girl spoke up. "So this will probably sound weird, but do I look familiar to you?"

He'd never seen her before in his life—he was certain of it. Still, she did seem almost familiar—if only in a way he couldn't articulate.

"Sure," Alex lied. "Totally."

"Right?" She tilted her head, staring into his eyes. "Do you know what I'm talking about?"

No idea.

Alex could feel the weight of her glance all the way down to his Nikes. He tried not to think about how much he was sweating—and he wasn't even wearing his fencing jacket. It was tied around his waist.

When she looked at him, the whole rest of the room blurred out, like some fish-eye-camera-filter effect.

Crazy.

The longer he stood there, the more it seemed like she was waiting for him to say something, so he did. "We met at Nationals, right? Did you go to Atlantic City?"

"Nope." The girl shook her head. "That's not it." He wasn't sure, but he thought she almost looked disappointed.

"You're from New Jersey?" He tried again.

"Brooklyn. Before that, Ukraine. And Moscow." She gave him an odd look. He was even more confused now.

"What's your club?" Alex rubbed his hand through his tangle of hair. This wasn't going as well as he had imagined. *Hoped.*

"No club," she said with a sigh.

"Ah, so you're independent. That's cool."

"So cool," she said with a laugh.

He smiled, relieved. "Yeah, I could tell. You know, you Brooklyn hipster types." He nodded at her triple piercings that dotted one ear.

"That's me." She laughed again. "And you're from Mountain Clear, right?"

"Montclair. Yeah. Close enough," Alex said. *Wait*— "But how did you know that?"

She looked startled, then pointed at the logo on his sweatpants. "Because I know how to read."

Alex forced himself to smile. "Duh." *Manor, you're an idiot.*

A buzzer sounded.

She shrugged, holding up her handful of blades. "I better go, or registration is going to close without me."

"You better."

She turned to go, but paused. "You really don't know who I am?"

God, but I wish I did.

And I want to.

He pretended to think. "Of course I do. I think it was driver's training. That's it. We were probably in driver's training together. With Mr. Marty? Big fat guy?"

"I don't drive. But keep trying," she said, pulling her blades to her chest. "I have to go."

"I will. Keep trying, that is. And good luck," Alex said.

"You too." She nodded.

"Yeah, it's a little late for that." Alex gestured at his faded T-shirt and the jacket wrapped around his waist. He wasn't suited up, which for a fencer only meant one of two things—that they'd been eliminated or that they weren't competing at all.

"You're not fencing?" A shadow flickered across her face. "Are you hurt—or something?"

"Only my pride. Black card," Alex said. "I'm Mr. Black Card. It's sort of a thing with me."

Her eyes widened. "Ah. I think I saw that happening. I've never had one."

"I've never not."

"Really?"

"No."

She laughed.

"So, yeah, see you around," he said.

"See you around, Alex." She smiled as she walked away.

Don't go. Come back.

Crap.

You suck at this, Manor.

Dante is never going to let you live this down.

Alex stood there, frozen in place for a moment. Then he turned and shouted after her, into the crowded convention hall. "Wait—what's *your* name?"

"Ava," she called, walking backward. "Ava Orlova. Let me know if it starts to ring any bells."

Then she was gone, and he felt like she had taken all the air in the room away with her.

Ava Orlova.

She thought he knew her, but he'd never seen her before in his life. He only wished he had.

Then he yanked his fencing jacket loose from his waist and stared at it. It was inside out, which meant she couldn't have read a single word on it.

And yet somehow she still knew his name.

S.H.I.E.L.D. EYES ONLY

CLEARANCE LEVEL X

LINE-OF-DUTY DEATH [LODD] INVESTIGATION
REF: S.H.I.E.L.D. CASE 121A415
AGENT IN COMMAND [AIC]: PHILLIP COULSON
RE: AGENT NATASHA ROMANOFF A.K.A. BLACK WIDOW,
A.K.A. NATASHA ROMANOVA
TRANSCRIPT: DEPARTMENT OF DEFENSE, LODD INQUIRY HEARINGS.

DOD: Dante Cruz is the child of a law enforcement officer in the state of New Jersey. Is that correct?
ROMANOFF: Yes, sir.

DOD: And the boy's friend. Closest friend.
ROMANOFF: [nodding]

DOD: And he's one of ours?
ROMANOFF: Sir?

DOD: This report states that Dante Cruz and/or Police Chief Captain Guillermo Cruz were cleared as possible candidates for surveillance assets placed in the field as eyes on the boy known as Alex Manor.
ROMANOFF: No, sir. I don't believe that.

DOD: That Dante Cruz was S.H.I.E.L.D.?
ROMANOFF: That Dante Cruz was anything that needed my attention, sir.

DOD: Why not?
ROMANOFF: I would have picked up on it. They were kids. They were into LARPing. And fencing. And . . . superheroes and comic books. And . . . superheroes.

DOD: Now, that's just ironic.

PHILLY CONVENTION CENTER LOBBY
THE CITY OF BROTHERLY LOVE

va stood in line at the registration desk, willing herself to calm down. Her stomach was roiling. Her head was pounding. It only got worse the longer she waited. She hoped she wasn't going to throw up.

This isn't like you, Ava Orlova.

Get your butt back out there, myshka.

Ava moved a few feet up in line.

So he doesn't know who you are. So he doesn't have the same dreams.

So what?

She stared at the head of the girl in front of her for a good long while. More perfect braids. Another alien. *Where do they all get these whale shirts?* This one was talking on a cell phone about a place called Squaw Valley. Ava wondered what a squaw was and why it had its own valley.

But nothing could distract her from her own racing pulse for long.

You know he's real now. You know he's here.

You both are.

Doesn't that have to mean something?

Isn't that the important thing?

Beyond that, why did it matter that she was still alone in her dreams? What had she expected—that his nights would be as magically full of her as hers were of him?

Who cared?

Maybe the dreams were just meant to bring us together.

Like fate. Or destiny.

Maybe I don't need them anymore.

Maybe this is what it was all always about.

Ava was almost at the registration desk now, but her mind was still a thousand miles away. And the pounding in her head felt like it could split her skull in two.

What would it be like to not have the dreams?

What would it be like to not feel a connection like that to anyone, except for maybe Oksana?

Could I be more alone than I am now?

She tried to summon her mother's face, but she could only remember her shadows. Her deep, dark eyes. The other edges, the hard ribs beneath her lab coat, when Ava hugged her.

Strong like an ox and sharp like a razor.

"Okay, Alexei Manorovsky," she said, if only to herself. "Let's do this."

"Do what?" a calm voice asked.

Ava was startled. She hadn't realized that she was at the very front of the line now, where an athletic-looking Asian woman in aviator sunglasses and a USFA cap was looking up at her from behind the desk.

Her name was Jasmine Yu. That's what her badge said, anyway.

Ava took a breath.

Jasmine spoke again. "Were you not talking to me?"

"No," Ava said, handing her a registration form. "Sorry, Ms. Yu."

"Same-day registration? Well, let's get you into the computer. You just made it on time." Jasmine typed a few words into her computer and frowned. "That's funny. There's some kind of problem."

Of course there is, Ava thought. "I don't understand."

"It says here that you don't have a birth certificate on file."

Of course I don't. She wondered if Oksana had one and realized she probably did. Ava tried to look unfazed. "That has to be a mistake." Then, in her best impression of an entitled teen: "My mom must have messed everything up. Again. She always does this."

Jasmine nodded at her sympathetically. "But I'm really not supposed to register you without one." She handed Ava back her registration form. "Do you have a parent here? Or one you can call?"

Of course not.

Ava pretended to think about it. "They're at work. But you could call my coach."

"Perfect. The forms are all in the office. Do you mind?" Jasmine motioned to her. "Come around the desk."

She put up a plastic sign. REGISTRATION CLOSED.

"Straight ahead now. This way. It'll just take a minute." Jasmine fumbled with a door, finally shoving it open.

As she did, Ava noticed there was no key in her hand.

It wasn't until Ava stepped through the door marked STAFF ONLY, however, that she really knew something was wrong.

They weren't in an office. They were in some kind of dim, industrial stairwell that appeared to run the full height of the convention center.

The door slammed shut behind them.

Ava panicked.

This isn't right. This isn't good—

Her instincts kicked in.

She turned to go, but Jasmine grabbed her jacketed arm. "That door is locked, kid. You're not going anywhere."

Ava stared at her in disbelief.

Even through the sleeve of her Kevlar jacket, her arm throbbed like it was on fire beneath the official's hand.

Every cell in Ava's body began to burn. She tried to wrench herself free, but it was no use. "Are you some kind of total psycho? Let go of me!"

"Not so fast, Ava. We just need to have a little chat."

Jasmine's grip on her Kevlar was as hard as her voice had become. Now Ava's arm was burning with searing pain.

"Yeah? The next person I chat with will be the cop who hauls your butt to jail," Ava said, forcing herself to calm down.

I have to think.

I have to get out of here.

Jasmine sighed. "Let's get some air, why don't we?" She yanked Ava up the convention center stairwell, pulling her by her side, a few steps at a time.

Her grasp on Ava's jacket was iron.

Ava's head now ached with such intensity she thought she might lose consciousness.

Up? That doesn't make sense. That's not the way out.

But Jasmine was surprisingly strong, and Ava knew she was in trouble. She screamed, but the sound echoed pointlessly through the abandoned stairwell.

At this close range, Ava could tell Jasmine Yu was no USFA official. Police? Or . . . worse? She wore all black—black jeans, a fitted black blouse, black boots. There were no other clues to her identity.

Jasmine—if that was her name—shoved her farther up the stairs.

Ava tried to get another look at her. A better look. Even her abductor's hair was jet black, from what she could see of it, with severe, geometric bangs and a chin-length crop poking out beneath her cap and her expensive-looking aviators. She looked like someone famous, like a star from a James Bond movie or something.

Probably not one of the good guys.

Now Jasmine was pushing her up through the stairwell so quickly, Ava almost felt like her feet weren't touching the ground.

They were within sight of a doorway. A sad-looking, rusted metal door, surrounded by a thin rectangle of light. They must have reached the roof.

Jasmine Yu kicked open the door with one leather-booted foot and shoved Ava into the light.

Ava stumbled out onto the roof. The woman stayed behind her, squarely between Ava and her only escape route.

Ava breathed as the pain in her arm faded away.

The sky was cloudless and blue, and all around them was cold winter sunshine and Philadelphia skyline. Ava edged toward the low wall at the perimeter of the building. She could see traffic moving, slow and oblivious, far below.

No way out.

Her head was no longer pounding but was still buzzing with static. She took a steadying breath and looked out toward the horizon—where the buildings met the shoreline—as she raised her voice. "Who are you?"

"You know who I am, *sestra.*"

The words hung in the air, low and grim.

It wasn't the answer Ava was looking for. It was, in almost every way, the opposite.

There was only one person who had ever called her that.

But that's impossible—

Ava was silent.

Everything came tumbling back to her now, slowly, randomly, like so many charred ashes falling through a burned-out Ukrainian warehouse.

The blast.

The woman in black knocking me to the floor.

The red hair.

The red flames.

The blood.

The burning face of the demon man himself.

"*Eto ty,*" Ava said, falling into Russian. It's you.

She turned to look at the woman who had taken her—slowly, finally.

The woman whose name had never really been Jasmine Yu.

"So it seems," the woman answered.

She hardly looked familiar, but Ava had learned not to trust her own eyes when it came to S.H.I.E.L.D.

Now the woman lowered her aviators and pushed back her cap, tapping once on the USFA tournament credentials hanging from her neck.

A tiny illuminated dot next to the printed name Jasmine Yu turned from green to red. Jasmine Yu's face—or what Ava had thought was her face—twisted into a digital glitch and flickered out.

You.

The badge hadn't been a badge at all, but some kind of remote holographic interface. S.H.I.E.L.D. tech. Ava had heard rumors about their capacity for holography, since her days at 7B.

Of course it's you. I should have known.

The face that looked back at her—the woman's real face—was unmistakable.

Behind the projection mask were the exquisitely cold eyes of Natasha Romanoff, agent of S.H.I.E.L.D., the infamous Black Widow herself.

Natasha Romanoff.

Avenger. Agent. Assassin.

Even though Ava hadn't seen her since she was a little girl, she could never forget that face. It had been burned into her memory by fire and death and disaster. Ava remembered it as a face that could bring the walls crashing down—because it had.

It was a terrible, beautiful face.

It was not a face to be dismissed or disregarded, especially not forgotten, not even by a little girl. There was nothing else like it, not anywhere in the world.

Natasha Romanoff's was a face of contradiction, with round curves and hard lines, features both rugged and soft. Her eyes were as cold and dark as her lips were full. However ironically, her face was heart shaped, with cheekbones so pronounced they seemed to cast their own shadows. *Not heart shaped*, Ava corrected herself. *Hard heart shaped.*

Natasha stood there in silence.

"What is that, your iFace?" Ava finally asked. She looked away.

"Something like that," Natasha said. She shrugged. "You know what they say. If it exists, S.H.I.E.L.D. has an app or crap for it, right?"

Nobody laughed.

Ava didn't want to give her abductor—*because that's what she was, wasn't she?*—the satisfaction of knowing how shocked she really was. So instead she steadied her words. "You never came back."

"No," Natasha said quietly. She slid the glasses back up and the cap back down, though there was no one else around to see her. She let her true face remain, but Ava didn't have to be a spy to realize that this was a person who preferred to stay in the shadows.

Ava sat down on the warm asphalt of the roof, her back to the parapet wall. It was a full minute before she spoke another word.

"You said you would come, but you never did. You handed me over to S.H.I.E.L.D. and left me to rot with the Americans."

"In some circles, that's known as *growing up*."

"I wrote to you. I went to the Ukrainian embassy and tried to cash in your stupid paper hourglass. They turned me away. They laughed."

"I know. Who do you think told them to do it?" Natasha didn't look remotely apologetic.

"But I knew no one. I was alone. No one cared. You might as well have left me to die."

"You didn't, did you?"

"Die? No, I didn't. No thanks to you. Now I know I can only depend on myself."

"Exactly." Natasha shrugged. "You're welcome."

Ava didn't respond.

Natasha sat down next to her. "Such Russian problems." She settled her back against the wall. "I know you're angry. Be as angry as you want. But no matter how you feel, we need to get out of here. Fair enough?"

"Why should I do anything you say?"

"Because you can trust me."

"Are you crazy? You're the one person I can't trust. You *taught* me not to trust you."

"No. I taught you not to trust *anyone*," Natasha said. "And that's something everyone has to learn. Especially every girl." She sounded as stubborn as Ava felt.

"So now I'm supposed to thank you for the lesson and move on?"

"Things have changed. Now you have to listen to me. Now you don't have a choice."

"This is America. Here I have a choice, *sestra*."

"No, you don't." Natasha frowned, and for a split second, an expression that looked entirely too human for the infamous Black Widow flickered across her face. "Not since six fifteen this morning, when customs officials flagged a passenger arriving on a flight from Manila, en route to Newark via Panama City."

"Panama what? Why?"

Natasha sighed. "Because Panama is the go-to airport for the modern cartel. And because the country does big business in cleaning up blood money."

Ava was confused. "And all of this has what to do with me?"

"Only that this passenger apparently had more than two

hundred Russian Belomorkanal cigarettes on him, which, as you probably don't know, is Panama's legal limit on imported brands." Natasha shook her head. "Disgusting."

"Cigarettes?" None of this was making sense to Ava.

"Not just any cigarettes. Belomorkanal is an old brand in Moscow, where it seems the passenger's flight originated." Natasha looked Ava in the eye. "Following a three-hour train ride from Odessa."

Ava froze.

"That customs inquiry triggered another, let's say, less official flag. Which caused one particular individual in a certain network of unlisted and unnamed friends to run a check on an unpublished number. Which in turn resulted in a single transmission via a secure broadcast." Natasha shrugged. "And here I am."

"What are you saying?" Ava couldn't breathe.

"Ivan Somodorov didn't die, Ava. He's not in hell where he belongs. He's in New Jersey."

The words fell between them with a dull weight. Ava felt like she'd been struck in the face. She thought she had forgotten the name, but she hadn't. Of course she hadn't. She only wished she could.

Ivan Somodorov.

She let her head drop into her hands.

Natasha's tone was more than serious as she got up from where she was sitting next to Ava. "He could have just disappeared off the face of the earth, but he didn't. He's still at it. Your name keeps coming up in chatter that all tracks back to Somodorov, now more than ever. He seems to have unfinished business with you, Ava. I believe he's been looking for you for eight years, and he's never going to stop."

Ava tried to think but found she could barely speak.

Because Ivan Somodorov is looking for me.

Ivan Somodorov is not finished with me.

Ivan Somodorov will be the end of me.

My demon.

"So?" Ava said finally. She felt the warm asphalt roof beneath her feet as she stood up. It was all she could manage.

"So the return of our friend Ivan changes everything." Natasha was pulling a bag out of a hidden corner in the roof.

Weapons, probably.

Ava forced herself to walk over to Natasha, despite the trembling in her legs. "Don't act like you care." Her head was already pounding, but she wasn't going to let Natasha know that.

"I didn't say I did." Natasha shrugged as she knelt beside the bag. She lowered her voice until the words were almost a whisper. "He's coming for us, and that's why I'm here. That's why we need to go. Your friend Oksana and your coach Nana and this boy, Alex—"

"Alexei," Ava corrected automatically. "Manorovsky."

Natasha Romanoff knows about Oksana? And Nana? And even the boy I dream about? She knows every detail of my entire life?

The thought was somehow thrilling and horrifying—though Ava hated herself for caring, either way.

Natasha smiled at Alex Manor's Russian name.

"*Alexei* and Oksana don't deserve to die. They don't deserve Ivan Somodorov. No clueless teenager deserves to get thrown into the middle of that."

"But I do?"

"Some of us don't get to choose, Ava." Natasha sounded sad, but that didn't change the truth of the words. "Children are disappearing from Ukrainian orphanages again. I don't think it's over. Not for Ivan and his mad Red Room science experiments. Not yet."

Ava flinched. When she tried to remember Odessa, she might as well be stepping on a jumbled pile of broken glass. Only the fragments remained.

Electrodes burning. Rope cutting at my wrists and ankles. Needles digging into my skin.

The black-eyed monster.

"Red Room?" Ava said sharply. "What's that?"

"*Krasnaya Komnata?*" Natasha shrugged as she stood up to face Ava, like it was nothing, but Ava recognized the words from her own dreams. They still made her shiver.

Natasha looked at her. "Those were the people Ivan worked for. The Red Room is also where Moscow's innocents are raised to be black-hearted spies like me. If you want to talk about not getting to choose."

Of course I don't, thought Ava.

And just like that, I'm alone in 7B once again.

Like always.

Natasha looked at her. "If I can get through this, you can too." She raised a single eyebrow, almost smiling. "We're the same, remember?"

Ava remembered.

She remembered those exact words, spoken in Russian, by her great rescuer. That was it. Something in her snapped. She couldn't take it, not another second.

She punched the Black Widow in the face as hard as she could.

For once, Natasha Romanoff didn't see it coming.

LINE-OF-DUTY DEATH [LODD] INVESTIGATION
REF: S.H.I.E.L.D. CASE 121A415
AGENT IN COMMAND [AIC]: PHILLIP COULSON
RE: AGENT NATASHA ROMANOFF A.K.A. BLACK WIDOW,
A.K.A. NATASHA ROMANOVA
TRANSCRIPT: DEPARTMENT OF DEFENSE, LODD INQUIRY HEARINGS.

DOD: Speaking of Russian orphans, you were born in Stalingrad?
ROMANOFF: That's right.

DOD: I'm surprised to learn even that much. There isn't a lot of
background in your background file, Agent. Even your birthdate is
redacted.
ROMANOFF: Yeah, I'm not a big birthday person.

DOD: And what's this reference note that says See Rogers, Steve
and Barnes, James?
ROMANOFF: [shrugs] They don't let me read my own file, sir. I guess
I don't have that level seven clearance.

DOD: I'll summarize. When your parents die, Moscow sends you
straight to spy school. The Red Room. The pride of the SVR. You and
every other lucky orphan of the state.
ROMANOFF: Oh, very lucky. You could say I won the orphan lottery,
sir.

DOD: Is that where you met Ivan Somodorov?
ROMANOFF: That's where he met me. Looking back, I didn't have a
whole lot of say in the matter.

DOD: As much say as he had in how you tried to blow him up?
Looking back?
ROMANOFF: I believe that's called karma, sir.

PHILLY CONVENTION CENTER ROOFTOP
THE CITY OF BROTHERLY LOVE

atasha Romanoff was still reeling from Ava's left hook when the door to the roof burst open. It swung wide, and the figure that came rolling through it landed on his feet.

Natasha's instincts erupted into movement, and she flung herself into attack position. Fists high, center of gravity low. Legs bent, like a predator ready to spring. Reflexively, she glanced over her shoulder to Ava, standing a few feet away.

Just have to keep the kid from getting hurt—

But to her surprise, the kid seemed plenty ready. In fact, Ava had assumed the same attack position as Natasha. She was the mirror image of the S.H.I.E.L.D. agent herself. Their instincts were identical. Fists high, gravity low. A *Systema* pose—all Red Room combatants were trained in the classic

Russian martial art. Which was strange, Natasha thought, considering only one of them had been trained there.

She frowned.

Seriously. It's not exactly Krav Maga. Even if the Secret Service uses it—would an orphaned Ukrainian immigrant girl?

It was like having a shadow—and Natasha Romanoff wasn't used to having a shadow. She was so startled she almost forgot she was under attack.

"Ava!" *A guy's voice.*

Natasha whipped her head back to their would-be attacker, who was now standing in front of them. Ava was nearly as fast.

But the assumed threat appeared now to be no threat at all.

"Look. It's a puppy. I think he's lost." Natasha sighed, relaxing to a standing position. She recognized him right away, and not just because he was the boy Ava had been flirting with at the tournament.

"Alex? What are you doing?" Ava sounded pretty shocked.

"Is this like, some kind of self-defense class?" Alex frowned, looking from one attacking Russian to the other.

"No," Ava said.

"Yes," Natasha said.

They looked at each other.

"I don't believe you," he said slowly. "So why don't we all go back downstairs and talk to the USFA about it?"

Natasha noticed that the boy—Alex—didn't drop his fists. Not even now.

Great. Not only a puppy. A junior Avenger puppy.
Just what I needed, on a day like this.

"Alex," Ava said, straightening back up. "Everything's okay. Really. I don't need you to rescue me."

"Aw," Natasha said. "That's so *cute*." The word was withering.

"I asked your friend where you went and she got super sketchy on me. Said you weren't even registered for the tournament."

"I—forgot. We got to talking. We were—catching up."

"You *forgot* to register for the NAC. Who does that?"

"She does," Natasha said with a scowl. *So the kid isn't an idiot. That isn't going to make anything any easier.*

"What conversation is worth missing the chance to compete at a national tournament?"

Ava glared. "A little hypocritical, don't you think? Mr. Black Card?"

He shook his head.

"Well, good on you, super sleuth," Natasha said, sounding annoyed. "You've checked it out, and she's fine. Now go away."

Ava looked at Natasha—then at Alex. "I am," she said. "Really. And again: I usually rescue myself."

Or I do, Natasha thought. Ava shot her a look, as if she knew what the agent was thinking.

But Alex still didn't drop his fists.

Now Natasha watched as he sized up the situation, taking in his options. *Junior Avenger. Not an idiot. Stubborn as hell. And worried about Ava.*

Interesting.

She shook her head. "Don't try it."

"Try what?" Alex asked, edging a few steps closer.

"Whatever you're thinking. I'm pretty good at taking the immobilizing shot. Right hamstring. It won't kill you, but you'll wish it did." She shrugged.

"I'm not too worried."

"I don't think you understand," Natasha said. "It's not a suggestion."

"Distance and speed. Momentum and angle of impact," Alex said, looking her right in the eye.

"What about it?"

"You just have to think it through. You know. Before."

"Before what?"

"This." He drew a breath, rolled into a crouch, and exploded toward Natasha. She wasn't expecting him to be able to move so quickly.

Still, being Natasha Romanoff, she moved *more* quickly and struck first—or was about to. But the moment before impact, she could feel the muscles in her jaw and shoulder tense, her center of gravity shift—and she watched in amazement as Alex read her perfectly. As perfectly as she was reading him. They matched each other, step for step, ducking blows, weaving between kicks, neither one landing a hit.

She was holding back—of course she was holding back. She wasn't going to destroy Ava's little friend.

But all the same, she hadn't been expecting this.

He seemed to sense exactly what she was going to do and to anticipate how she was going to do it, just as she did with him.

Finally he caught her fist in his hand. The two of them looked at each other, equally surprised.

Natasha shoved him off.

He's good. Very good. Very interesting.

Alex released her hand and spun, sweeping his leg. She avoided him effortlessly, anticipating the move.

"*Ty suma soshla*," Natasha muttered. You're crazy.

"Whatever that is, I don't speak it," Alex said. He didn't seem afraid of her, which she found intriguing.

Also annoying.

Natasha dropped her fists. "I don't have time for this game, little *Alexei*."

Ava interrupted. "Really? Because I don't have time for any of this." Now she was the one who sounded irritated.

"Leave Ava alone," Alex said to Natasha. "I know you're after me."

Natasha laughed. Ava did not.

"Seriously? You? Why would she be after you?" Ava was insulted.

"Why is the CIA ever after anyone?" Alex studied Natasha. "I saw you. This morning. You were following me."

"Don't flatter yourself. I was following her," Natasha said, motioning to Ava.

"I don't believe you," Alex repeated. "So I'm going to say it one more time. Just let her go."

"Oh please. I'm not CIA. Don't insult me." Natasha raised an eyebrow. "And besides, I don't negotiate with kids—so shove off, kid, before you hurt yourself."

"Rude," Ava said suddenly. "You don't get it, do you?"

"Me?" Alex looked surprised.

"Yes, tell him," Natasha said.

Ava glared. "I meant both of you, actually. I don't want to be rescued. I'm not some hopeless girl with a big fat target on her forehead. I can fend for myself."

You have no idea, Natasha thought, *how big that target is.*

"That's not what I meant," Alex insisted.

But—almost as if the universe wanted to drive home the point—a fraction of a second after Ava spoke, a shot rang out across the rooftop.

The bullet missed Ava's right temple by less than a centimeter.

The second bullet knocked her backpack off her shoulders.

The third whizzed past Alex Manor's head, clipping off a tangle of wavy brown hair. It drifted to the ground with an almost surreal slowness, like a falling leaf in a breeze.

Nothing else about the moment was slow.

Natasha Romanoff spun in the direction the shots came from her eyes narrowing as she calculated the trajectory of the rounds—

One o'clock.

Top floor.

Across the intersection.

Angle's off by maybe forty degrees.

—and she dove forward, yanking Ava down as hard as she could, until they were both lying flat against the asphalt roof.

Alex dropped right next to them, not a moment later.

"What the—"

Three more rounds answered him.

"Sniper," hissed Natasha, grabbing for the bag she had taken out of hiding just before the bullets began to fly. She could feel her brain speeding up. "Sounds like he took his silencer off for better range, which means he's at least a building or two away." She looked up, running the numbers in her head. "He's clearing what, four hundred meters? And hitting within maybe a half inch of target? Point five MOA? Or point three?" She shook her head.

"Is that bad?" Ava asked.

Natasha was grim. "Bad for us. It's a tough shot. So that's a highly trained military marksman. A pro, probably top dollar. Russian, I'd say—maybe an Orsis T-5000, from the sound of it."

"People are *shooting* at us?" Alex was in shock. "At a *fencing tournament?*"

"Not us," Ava said quietly. "Me."

Her eyes met Natasha's. "He's here, isn't he?" She sounded like she could hardly breathe.

Natasha shook her head. "I doubt it. Not in the flesh." Now she looked over her shoulder, taking in the skyline across from the roof. "But this is probably his guy. The profile fits."

Now do you believe me, kid? Is that real enough for you?
Ivan Somodorov hasn't forgotten either one of us.
Ivan doesn't forgive, and Ivan doesn't forget.

Natasha pulled off her sunglasses and tossed them into the sky above them. A series of shots ripped through the air in rapid succession, and the glasses shattered.

She sighed. "Correction. His *guys*, plural. Looks like he's got at least three on us."

"Whose guys? Who is *he*?" Alex's eyes narrowed in anger. Natasha ignored him, examining a bullet hole in the cracked surface of the cinderblock wall. "Look at that. Congratulations, Ava. They pulled out the big guns—those are .338 Lapua Magnums."

"Which means?" Ava asked.

"Moscow only likes a Lapua for high-value targets. You're a hot commodity. Those rounds don't come cheap—and Lapuas can eat through five layers of military body armor, so keep your hands in the car, kids."

"Can someone fill me in here? Snipers? High-value targets? What are you talking about?" Another shot rang out, and Alex ducked even lower, smacking his face against the asphalt.

"There isn't time to explain. Like I said, shove off, kid. You aren't part of this, and you don't want to be." Natasha studied a row of windows in a bank building down the block. She drew out two weapons from the bag—a compact-looking automatic assault weapon and a submachine gun—and crawled toward the low wall of the rooftop. "Stay down—"

Ava nodded, crouching low. Natasha snaked past her.

Good. The girl might be scared, but she's not showing it.

Out of the corner of her eye, Natasha saw Alex's hands instinctively curl into fists, though there was no one to use them on.

I hear you, buddy.

She knew how frustrated he felt, which is why she was rarely without a gun. Or three: her assault rife, preferably a

CZ 805, for real gunfights; her submachine gun, a PP-2000, for more discreet firepower; her HK P30 pistol, for always. Czech, Russian, German. The pistol was always German, even when she traded her HK out for her Glock. Just like Ivan taught her.

Which is why she'd use it on him, as soon as she found him.

She reached over her shoulder to yank the submachine gun from her back strap and rolled toward the ledge in one fluid motion.

Goodnight, Moon.

Without another word, Natasha Romanoff began to fire back at the sky.

S.H.I.E.L.D. EYES ONLY

CLEARANCE LEVEL X

LINE-OF-DUTY DEATH [LODD] INVESTIGATION
REF: S.H.I.E.L.D. CASE 121A415
AGENT IN COMMAND [AIC]: PHILLIP COULSON
RE: AGENT NATASHA ROMANOFF A.K.A. BLACK WIDOW, A.K.A. NATASHA ROMANOVA
TRANSCRIPT: DEPARTMENT OF DEFENSE, LODD INQUIRY HEARINGS.

DOD: According to this family tree, you're a descendant of the bloodline of the last czar of Russia.

ROMANOFF: Every Russian family line ends in a czar. That's the only way the genealogist gets paid, sir.

DOD: Does every Russian family have a lost fortune worth billions?

ROMANOFF: Enough of them. Consider it a Russian fairy tale.

DOD: So would that be a yes or a no, Agent?

ROMANOFF: Is this supposed to be some kind of joke, sir?

DOD: It goes to motivation, Agent. Some members of our task force believe Ivan Somodorov's interest in you was about more than the Red Room—and more than just physics.

ROMANOFF: He wanted me for my czarist gold? That's the best you can come up with?

DOD: Gold is gold, Agent.

ROMANOFF: Maybe to the capitalists, sir. Not so much to the physicists.

DOD: Tony Stark seems to have no problem with it.

ROMANOFF: If I had a piece of czarist gold for everything Tony Stark has no problem with—

DOD: We'd all be in Boca, Agent.

CHAPTER **13**: AVA

PHILADELPHIA STREETS—
DOWNTOWN PHILLY
THE CITY OF BROTHERLY LOVE

The bullets didn't stop coming.

They ripped across the roof, streaking past their targets by millimeters.

Ivan brought the big guns. Ivan wants me back, Ava thought, her palms cold and sweaty. Even his name made her want to retch.

No one will come for you, little ptenets. No one cares. Ava shook his voice out of her head.

"*Der'mo,*" muttered the Black Widow, shaking her head. "They're toying with us now. They've hit wide too many times in a row."

"I thought you said it's a tough shot?" Ava said, her voice low.

"Not for these guys. They're just keeping us busy now,

114

which means someone else is on their way to us. They don't want to kill us, they want to take us in. Looks like we're too valuable to kill." She nodded her head toward Ava. "At least some of us."

"How do you know?" Alex asked.

"Because we're not dead," Natasha said, matter-of-factly. "But we've got to get moving."

"Are you serious?" Alex asked.

"As the grave." Natasha shoved Ava in the direction of the door. "Now go—get inside."

Ava felt her heart hammering as she sprinted and dove behind the cinder-block walls housing the stairwell. Alex followed right behind her. He wasn't going anywhere, no matter how much Natasha wanted to get rid of him.

He will, Ava thought. *He'll leave. They all do. My mother and father and even Natasha Romanoff.*

It's the one certainty in my world.

That everyone leaves and there is nothing I can do to stop it.

But as Ava looked back over her shoulder, she saw that Natasha Romanoff wasn't behind them. Instead, she was discharging her weapons in the direction of the unseen snipers, only ducking behind the cinder-block walls when her magazines emptied.

She cursed and dropped both of her guns.

Natasha reached behind her back, pulled her pistol out of the waistband of her pants, and rose again from behind the cinder blocks, firing at the unseen enemy.

This isn't happening, Ava thought. *Also: How many guns can one person keep in their pants?*

Now Natasha was shouting back at them. "On my signal, do exactly as I say. I'll be right behind you. If they get the drop on me, you get your butt back to 7B and lay low. Got it?"

"What about him?" Ava asked, meaning Alex.

Natasha waved her pistol dismissively, and for a moment, Ava felt like she could almost hear what Natasha was thinking. *What about him? He's not my concern.*

Alex shrugged. "Got it."

"Okay." Natasha ducked another row of bullets. "I'm going to take that as a yes. Now—on my go—head down the stairs and into the convention hall."

"Wait—you want us to go back down to the tournament? While someone's trying to kill Ava? That's crazy." Alex looked confused.

Natasha rolled her eyes. "Would you rather she stayed out here?"

The wall exploded above them, raining plaster down on their heads.

"Good point." Alex nodded.

"Now!" Natasha Romanoff raced toward the stairwell and slammed open the door. They dove through it as she fired at the sky. The bullets followed.

Ava reached the bottom of the stairwell first, stumbling through the dim interior corridor and into the brightly lit lobby of the convention center. The easy-listening soundtrack piped through the public hall threw her off— until Alex came sprinting after her, and she remembered why they were running.

A moment later, Natasha appeared, stopping only to shove every firearm back into a strap, holster, or waistband that looked perfectly designed to camouflage its weapon. "Walk," she hissed. "Keep your head down and your back to the street entrance."

They slowed to what felt like an exaggerated stride. Now they pushed through the massive row of lobby doors that opened into Hall H, the crowded tournament space. The three of them threaded their way through, moving between strips where athletes were still fencing their first-round pools.

Ava winced as she heard the same lobby doors clang open again behind them. Natasha's voice followed a second later, low and deadly serious.

"You," she said to Alex. "You're not safe anymore, either. You have to keep moving or they'll take you to get to us."

"Got it, moving," he said.

Natasha didn't falter. "Our friends are inside. Dark Windbreakers. Black backpacks. Maybe twenty meters behind. Whatever you do, don't turn around. And whatever you see, keep going." She pulled her cap down over her face.

"Shouldn't we be running?" Ava asked, her eyes on the floor.

Natasha shook her head, almost imperceptibly. "No. You're dressed like everyone else in this room, right? These really *stylish* fencing uniforms?" She glanced sideways. "So split up and blend in. Don't draw attention. Cross through the convention hall to the far exit, the one closest to the river. I'll meet you on the street."

Alex nodded. Ava didn't say a word.

Natasha moved her hand to the concealed pistol at her waistband and cut away from them without another warning.

Ava felt the adrenaline course through her body. It all seemed so desperate and so dangerous. For all she knew this could be a trap, meant to make her think the Avenger was on her side, if only so she would let her guard down.

And even if we make it, then what?

Ava didn't want to think about it.

She had to trust Black Widow, at least for now.

She didn't have a choice, even if all she believed were the sounds of the guns pointed in her direction. There was no other way.

Ava was interrupted by a familiar shout, and she turned to catch a glimpse of Oksana hurtling toward an opponent on the strip.

Suddenly the idea of competing with rubber-tipped blades seemed a whole lot less intimidating than it ever had. The blades in this room were fake; the guns were very real.

And what if we don't make it? Ava imagined the shots ringing out, the people running. The chaos and the crowding as everyone tried to get to the exits.

Red blood spattered across white Kevlar, dripping off the American flags—

Ava shuddered. She glanced over her shoulder to the metal strip, almost involuntarily. Oksana's arms were raised in victory, and she ripped off her mask.

It all seemed so pointless now—

Still, it gave her an idea. The mask.

Keep your head down. Blend in. Wasn't that what Natasha said?

Ava ducked into the crowd of cheering bystanders next to Oksana's strip, swiping a mask from where it sat unused on the gym floor and ripping off the duct tape bearing her name from her back.

She slid it over her head without breaking stride. When she reached the next strip, she pulled a random blade from a fencing bag resting on a folding chair.

Across the gym, Alex took her cue and pulled his white jacket on over his T-shirt, swiping a USFA cap off the vendor tables as he passed by.

Along the perimeter, Natasha Romanoff casually joined a team of medics carrying an injured boy off the floor—grabbing his bandaged legs with her hand.

As the men in black fanned out through the hall, searching for them, fencers kept scoring and horns kept sounding and crowds kept cheering.

It was the longest walk of Ava's life, but she made it.

They made it.

Natasha was the last one out. "We're not in the clear yet. Keep walking." She motioned to Alex and Ava, and they fell into step with her. "We've got to get to the river; come on."

"The river? Why the river?" Alex looked sideways at her.

"That's where our ride is," Natasha said. "Good parking." She held up her wrist, where something vaguely resembling a black digital watch glowed. "If we can make it."

Fine. To the river, thought Ava.

They kept heading toward the Delaware River waterfront that glittered in the distance, maybe eight blocks away. Ava couldn't seem to make the pavement move quickly enough beneath her feet.

Seven—

Six—

Five—

A black SUV skidded around the corner.

A man in black protective gear fired a machine gun at them from the open window of the SUV, spinning to get back into position.

Natasha rolled behind a parked minivan.

Ava and Alex took cover one car behind her.

Natasha seemed fearless—calm, even—in spite of automatic weapons targeting the street around her. She shouted back at them. "I'm going to go have a little chat with our friend. I get the feeling he wants to tell me something. You guys keep going until you get down to the riverbank." Natasha took off, leaving Ava and Alex behind.

Alex glanced at Ava. "You know, your CIA friend is pretty hardcore. I almost feel bad for the shooter."

Ava didn't smile back. "She's really not CIA."

He raised an eyebrow. "Yeah, right. And those aren't really guns in her pants."

Ava took a breath.

This is wrong. He shouldn't be here, and he shouldn't be with me. Even if I want more than anything for him to stay.

Ava had to let him go. Push him away. She took a breath.

"But you're right. She can handle it from here." She tried to sound convincing. "And this isn't your problem. None of it is. If I were you, I'd go home, Alex."

"Right. Okay." Alex hesitated. "So why don't you, then?"

"Maybe I will," Ava said.

She didn't move, though. Neither did he.

In the distance, Ava could see Natasha was now engaging the SUV in some kind of firefight, baiting it into approaching her. Leading the car away from them.

Natasha looked back at them. "What are you waiting for?" she bellowed in their direction.

But Ava still didn't move. She couldn't. She found herself staring at the bumper in front of her.

Frozen.

We should just keep running. Go home. Both of us.

Only bad things happen when I'm around her, when anyone is.

Maybe that's why they call her the Black Widow.

The shooter must have seen them, because now he began to fire in their direction. Steam erupted from a bullet hole in the back of the car, just above Ava's head.

"Ava!" Alex grabbed her and pulled.

They crawled out from behind the car and started to walk, just as Natasha had shown them before. Heads down. Not looking back.

Alex kept his voice quiet, talking steadily as they moved down the street. "I have a weird feeling that I'm not supposed to leave you, Ava. Not like this."

"You get a lot of weird feelings?"

"Only when guns are involved." Alex didn't let go of her hand. "I'm not stupid. I know you're in trouble—and I know that cop isn't your friend."

"Yeah, well, she's not a cop, either," Ava said.

"Whatever she is and whatever this is, it's too much for one person. I mean, I can help." He looked at her. "If you want me."

Of course I want you. I spend every night with you, don't I?

But Ava said nothing.

The sound of gunfire ripping up the sidewalk behind them echoed in the distance as if to make his point, and they moved even faster.

Alex squeezed her hand. "You don't have to do this alone."

It's too late—I don't know any other way.

They were only a few blocks from the river now.

Ava didn't know what to say. What could she? That nobody could help, and nobody ever had? That she'd always known this day was coming? That Ivan would come back to her and finish what he'd started?

I can't trust anyone, Alexei Manorovsky. Not even you.

But she realized Alex was still holding her hand. He was still walking through the gunfire with her. He was still right there next to her. He hadn't taken off, and he hadn't let go. *Even though he barely knows me.*

Alex was somehow different. He was good, and he was innocent. He still had heroes, just like Oksana. Ava had watched him long enough every night to know that.

And for the first time since 7B, Ava wondered if she really was better off on her own. For a moment, she wondered if she ever really had been.

"Ava. I'm serious. Do you want me to stay?"

Ava glimpsed the same unbridled energy—the warrior Alex—that had gotten him the black card.

She could almost hear him thinking out loud.

Say the word, and I'll take on the world with you—

I'm ready to fight, so bring it—

Ava wanted to let him. But Alexei Manorovsky was never meant to be in this story. It wasn't his fault she had dreamed him into her life, however it had happened. It was still her dream, not his.

Dreams, she corrected herself. *Because there have been many. And because I've known you for a long time now, Alexei. Even if you don't know me.*

Ava had a sudden thought, for the second time that day.

Maybe this is what destiny feels like.

Maybe I can't stop this from happening.

I can't stop myself from dreaming, and I can't put aside my memories.

Maybe I can't even hide from Ivan Somodorov anymore.

The next time Alex asked, Ava let herself nod.

"Yes."

I can't do this alone, and I don't want to.

"Please. Stay." She squeezed his hand.

By the time the words were out of her mouth, Alex was off and running, pulling her toward the river as if he'd known what she was going to say all along.

Ava and Alex were only a half block or so away from the water when Ava looked behind her. Natasha was still in a firefight with the man in the black car. She could hear sirens in the distance, and she knew it would be over in a matter of minutes, one way or another.

What the—

Ava heard tires screech and looked up.

Alex was shouting.

A second black SUV spun around the corner, slamming into a parked car only a few feet away.

"Get out of there!" Natasha was yelling to her.

The parked car exploded into a ball of fire, and they took off, running as fast as they could.

Ava heard footsteps behind them.

Gunfire.

She only squeezed Alex's hand more tightly as they ran.

No—

Not now—

Not like this.

They sprinted across the last road between them and the river, slowing only at the edge of the bridge. The water loomed dangerously far below.

A round of bullets bit into the ground next to them. Rubble spewed into the air, and they dove to either side.

"The river. Now!" Alex didn't hesitate. "Come on!" He hurled himself over the railing and vanished over the edge of the bridge.

Ava hesitated—and then jumped over the barricade without a word.

I'm not going to die—

I'm not going to let Ivan Somodorov kill me—

I'm not finished yet.

Ava reached out with her arms and grabbed at the railing behind her as she fell. Instead of dropping into the freezing water, she anchored a hand to the rail and pushed off, in one smooth motion, twisting to break her fall by kicking, attack style, off the pilings below.

Ava flipped forward to land on two feet in the wet sand, splashing down into an inch of water before rising back to a standing position.

Alex, who was dangling by both hands from the bridge above her, kicked his legs over to the side.

He took a deep breath and bounced off the bridge a few times, scrabbling for a handhold as he dropped—finally managing to land in the water next to Ava.

One way or another.

They were safe.

Ava was still panting as she grinned and held out her fist. "That—was—awesome."

Alex bumped it with his own, nodding as he tried to catch his breath. "We're not dead—so yeah—more awesome than I thought."

"Not at all—dead," Ava agreed, taking one more deep breath.

He leaned his head back, gulping down oxygen. "Do you do this a lot?"

"Never in my life," Ava said, standing straight again.

In fact, she'd never done anything remotely like it before. As far as risky behaviors went, Ava had limited her own to hopping subway turnstiles and ripping off S.H.I.E.L.D.

So why now? What was changing?

"Me neither," Alex said. "Nothing like this, I mean." Then he smiled. "My mom would freak."

They looked back up to the bridge—just as Natasha Romanoff smashed the head of the second shooter into the metal railing.

His now unconscious body dropped to the ground, and Natasha straightened herself. She leaned forward over the railing and looked down to Ava and Alex.

"You stuck the landing," Natasha shouted, looking surprised. "Even a Russian judge would have to give that a ten."

Ava couldn't read the look on her face. It was only then that she scanned the entire height of the bridge.

By her calculation, they had jumped more than twenty-five feet.

I kicked Oksana's butt in a bout, I took sniper fire on the roof of a building, and I leaped off a bridge.

Ava watched as the Black Widow performed an almost identical move off the concrete girders and down to the sand below.

What is happening to me?

S.H.I.E.L.D. EYES ONLY

CLEARANCE LEVEL X

LINE-OF-DUTY DEATH [LODD] INVESTIGATION
REF: S.H.I.E.L.D. CASE 121A415
AGENT IN COMMAND [AIC]: PHILLIP COULSON
RE: AGENT NATASHA ROMANOFF A.K.A. BLACK WIDOW,
A.K.A. NATASHA ROMANOVA
TRANSCRIPT: DEPARTMENT OF DEFENSE, LODD INQUIRY HEARINGS.

DOD: Let's talk about Moscow's favorite finishing school for super
spies and sleeper agents.
ROMANOFF: The Red Room? It's all in my file, sir.

DOD: And the Black Widow program? Top Gun for Red Room girls,
as it were?
ROMANOFF: You already know all of this.

DOD: I know Black Widows were for deep cover. And, as such,
Moscow gave you false histories and manipulated your memories.
ROMANOFF: You mean brainwashing? You can just say it.

DOD: What about your handlers? They were trained to erase and
implant memories? To flip one switch in your head when they needed
a ballet dancer and to flip another one when they needed, what?
A ballet-dancer assassin?
ROMANOFF: I was whatever they told me to be.

DOD: You let them make that call.
ROMANOFF: I was serving my country, sir.

DOD: Like Ivan Somodorov.
ROMANOFF: Ivan Somodorov only serves Ivan Somodorov.

DOD: While you were what? A patriot?
ROMANOFF: A patriot and a ballet-dancer assassin.

THE DELAWARE RIVER
THE CITY OF BROTHERLY LOVE

irens wailed in the air, echoing off the pavement above them.

Down at the water's edge, safely hidden beneath the bridge overpass, the three convention-center escapees seemed to be safe.

At least for now.

The moment Natasha reached Ava and Alex, she could tell by their faces that the euphoria of escape was quickly fading into shock. She had been expecting it—from both of them, really. She was more surprised that they had kept it together this long.

People trying to kill you. It's unsettling. But you get used to it.

I did.

"First they're on the roof, then in the convention center; now they're on the streets." Alex shook his head. "Whoever hired these guys, he's really getting his money's worth."

"Yeah, well." Natasha wiped her forehead on her sleeve. "Russian mercenaries. There's a certain pride in workmanship there. Speaking of which, I had a nice chat with our shooter in the black SUV."

"Was he Ivan's?" Ava asked.

Natasha nodded. "Ivan Somodorov's personal military police force. And—spoiler alert—there's plenty more where he came from."

"This guy has his own police department?" Alex asked, incredulous.

"Devoted entirely to Ava, it seems." Natasha looked at her, clapping her arm awkwardly down on her shoulder. "Welcome home, *sestra*."

Ava pulled her arm away, but she didn't attempt a right hook, so Natasha considered it progress.

"Wait—*more* where he came from? How many more?" Alex asked.

"Does it matter?" Natasha shrugged. She knew it didn't. *It only takes one bullet to kill a person, ptenets.* Ivan had taught her that before the Russian alphabet.

"How long until they get here?" asked Ava quietly.

"According to my talkative friend, not long at all."

"Okay. Can someone finally explain what's going on around here? What does this Ivan person want with Ava? And what kind of cop are you, exactly?"

"Excuse me?" Natasha stared.

"In fact, how do we even know you're not working with them?"

"As what?" Natasha asked. "One of Ivan's hired guns?" For the first time today, she found herself laughing.

She felt sorry for the boy, more than he knew, but there was no turning back now. Natasha had tried to keep him out of it, and look where that had gotten them. She had two charges now, instead of one—and Ivan had three targets.

I'm going to have to improvise. I hate improvising.

"It's not funny." Alex seemed exasperated. "Seriously. There are bad cops. How do we know you're not working with the people who were trying to *kill* us five minutes ago."

Natasha laughed again.

"She's not," Ava said wearily.

"How do you know? She was definitely following me earlier. I know she was." He looked from Ava to Natasha. "What if she's lying?"

"Oh, she's always lying," Ava said. "Just not about this."

Natasha had stopped laughing. Now she contemplated decking the kid, he was so irritating. "If you hadn't noticed, I was shooting back at them. Which wouldn't exactly make me mercenary of the month, would it?" She reloaded one of her weapons as she spoke. "We need to get out of here, so the rest of your questions will have to wait. Hilarious though they may be."

She raised her wrist to her mouth and spoke into the tiny microphone woven into the black cuff beneath her sleeve. "Romanoff is standing by. I have the asses—I mean assets—ready for extract. Over."

Her wrist crackled back at her.

"Reading you five by five. Roger that, Agent." Coulson sounded relieved, even over the comm. "Extract on the way. Out."

"Why does that voice sound so familiar? Or am I just imagining it?" Ava looked panicked. "Do I know him?"

Natasha shrugged. "Everyone else seems to."

"Who was that?" Alex asked.

"Coulson," Natasha said, knowing full well that the name would mean nothing to either of them. "He'll want to debrief you." Alex looked at her blankly. "I mean, he'll probably have a few questions for you." *Either way,* she thought, *I'm not leaving you around to answer anyone else's.*

"What's happening in five? What did he mean?" Ava frowned.

Natasha waved her off, ignoring the question. The more she thought about it, though, the more she had a few of her own.

"Where did you learn how to jump off bridges like that?"

"I didn't learn. I just knew," Ava said, annoyed. "Where did you learn to shoot people like that?"

"School, obviously," Natasha said tonelessly. "Top of my class."

"Of course you were. Valedictorian of the shoot-'em-up." Ava sat herself down on the rocks, looking like she wanted the conversation to be over. She lay back.

Natasha shrugged. "That, and combined arms. Tactical. Close-quarters combat. Naval aviation. Navigation. Military engineering. Artillery—"

"We got it," Alex said, cutting her off. "You're amazing."

"After years of training. But somehow Ava expects me to believe she became an Olympic-level bridge-vaulting gymnast when I wasn't looking?"

"When were you ever looking?" Ava didn't bother to sit up.

Natasha eyed the girl, still. Something wasn't adding up. *A flip kick into a front flip with a full three sixty rotation? Nobody on the planet 'just knows' how to do that.*

She shook her head. Ava had executed a move that was textbook Red Room, and Natasha didn't like it.

Not at all.

Alex looked up from brushing powdery concrete dust off his limbs. "You can probably put those away now," he said, pointing to Natasha. "Unless you're going to, you know, shoot us."

Natasha hadn't realized she was still holding a weapon in each hand. She shoved one weapon into her waistband and slid the other down her back.

Careless. Ivan's getting to you. Even now, after all this time. Don't give him that.

"What's with the inquisition, anyway?" Ava said, looking up at the sky. "I thought we were getting out of here." She closed her eyes, rubbing her temple with one hand. "I hope we are. My head is starting to pound."

Natasha bristled. "It's not an inquisition."

"Then what is it? A pop quiz?" Alex frowned.

"I'm not a teacher, and I'm not a babysitter. If you want to take on Ivan Somodorov alone, go ahead. Don't act like this is a favor to me. I owed you the warning, and that's all."

"Agreed," Ava said, her eyes still closed. Now she had one hand on each temple. "Don't worry, you're not doing anyone any favors, and you're probably the world's worst babysitter. But hey, I do appreciate the warning."

Natasha moved toward her and held out her hand. "Get up."

Ava opened one eye.

"You're a sitting target." Natasha sighed. "You can't stay here. Not unless you were hoping to meet the rest of Ivan's goon squad for—"

Ava grabbed Natasha's hand and pulled herself up—or tried to. As soon as she was halfway standing, she doubled over on the rocks, moaning.

Something was wrong.

"Are you okay?" Alex looked worried.

Ava tried to stand up again but found that she couldn't. "I'm dizzy. I think . . . I'm going to throw up."

"Please don't," Natasha said, annoyed.

Ava stumbled up the bank, slamming the heel of her hand against her own forehead. "My brain is melting."

"I know," Alex said, pointing to his own. "My ears are still ringing from the gunshots. It's probably from that."

"Not melting—brain freeze." Ava managed to force the words out as she lurched forward. "Major brain freeze."

She stumbled into Natasha, knocking her off-kilter wig from her head. It tumbled loose, dropping into the craggy rocks at her feet—

—and Natasha Romanoff's infamous curls of red hair tumbled free.

Ava froze.

Natasha just stood there. She knew exactly what had happened.

Red hair.

Cap off.

Glasses shattered.

Digital mask down.

Der'mo—

In head-to-toe black, with her leather jacket and her triple firepower—her trademark red-gold hair blazing down to her shoulders—there was only one operative in the world who looked like that.

And that one operative hadn't exactly managed to keep a low profile.

Not since the Avengers Initiative.

Natasha Romanoff might have still considered herself a S.H.I.E.L.D. agent—but she wasn't just any S.H.I.E.L.D. agent.

In fact, the Black Widow was hardly unknown to anyone who had ever idolized Tony Stark or Captain America or a certain physicist with rage issues—not to mention an Asgardian king in the making. Last year, she had turned down more Hollywood premiers than Tony Stark. *(Which wasn't hard, since he never turns down any.)* Valentino had offered to dress her for the Met Gala. *(No grazie.)* She'd found her face on the cover of *Time* magazine's 100 Women Who Rule issue. *(Only a hundred?)* She'd even been asked around for bowling at the White House.

In her own way—whether or not she wanted it—Natasha Romanoff was a celebrity now. That had been the price of taking up the sacred responsibility of protecting the entire planet from dangers that no one else would or could. The cameras and the headlines and the coverage. There was nobody who wouldn't recognize the Black Widow now, no matter how much harder that made it for her to do her job.

"It's you."

Sure enough, Alex was staring at her as if he was seeing a ghost or a movie star or even the ghost of a movie star. He couldn't seem to believe what he was seeing. He was paralyzed. He couldn't look away, and he couldn't move.

"You're y-you," he stammered.

"She is," Ava said, putting a hand on his shoulder.

"So this—this is all real." Alex seemed to need to say it aloud.

"Afraid so." Natasha said.

"Those were *real* Russian mercenaries shooting at us." He was still staring.

"Bingo," Natasha said.

"And Ava's in *real* trouble. Because you're—you're the Black Widow."

Natasha sighed. She always hated this moment, no matter how inevitable it was—the revelation of her true identity. She had learned as a child to keep her secrets close; the less anyone knew about her, the safer she would be. Besides, being any of her covers was usually much less painful (and far less dangerous) than being Natasha Romanoff.

But blowing her disguise was infinitely worse now that the Avengers had become household names. Since then, everything had changed—from the way people spoke to her to the way they looked at her and most of all, to the things they expected from her.

Which was the way the boy was looking at her now.

"Alex. It's okay." Ava's face was even paler now, almost gray.

"Did you know your—she—was—her?" Alex was trying to make words come out, but he was still pretty incoherent.

Ava was swaying to stay on her feet as she looked at Natasha wearily. "Yes. You'll get used to it."

"They all do." Natasha shrugged. She glanced up at the sky. *Coulson. Where are you?* She looked at Ava more closely. The girl's knees were starting to buckle. "Are you all right?"

"I'm fine," Ava said, stumbling again. "Dizzy."

Natasha caught her by the hand—

—and Ava's legs gave out.

As she fell to her knees, her body began to convulse. She looked for a moment as if she had been struck by lightning.

"Ava?" Alex moved to her side.

Natasha grabbed Ava. The kid's eyes were closed now. "Her pulse is going crazy," Natasha said. "Help me get her down."

They lowered her all the way to the ground.

Ava lay motionless, curled on her side, as if her heart had suddenly stopped beating, or all the energy in her body had simply left her.

"Ava?" Alex kept one arm around her. "She's out cold. We need to get her to a hospital."

Natasha stood back up. "Not much longer now." She

looked down the river, to where a shadow moved across the water. "Thirty seconds."

Alex held Ava's head cradled in his arm. "Wake up, Ava, wake up. Come on."

Natasha scanned the sky.

Come on, Coulson. What's taking you so long?

As if to answer, at long last, with a great roar filling the air, a mighty S.H.I.E.L.D. ship dropped into the water behind them—and Natasha Romanoff exhaled for the first time all day.

S.H.I.E.L.D. EYES ONLY

CLEARANCE LEVEL X

LINE-OF-DUTY DEATH [LODD] INVESTIGATION
REF: S.H.I.E.L.D. CASE 121A415
AGENT IN COMMAND [AIC]: PHILLIP COULSON
RE: AGENT NATASHA ROMANOFF A.K.A. BLACK WIDOW,
A.K.A. NATASHA ROMANOVA
TRANSCRIPT: DEPARTMENT OF DEFENSE, LODD INQUIRY HEARINGS.

Incident: Odessa 2005 B2
Note in file: P_Coulson Personal — text logs

ROMANOFF: Looking for off-mission air support, Coulson.
Possible extract, around 1300 hours, Philadelphia metro area.
You in?
COULSON: Agent Romanoff, are you saying you need a favor?

ROMANOFF: I'm saying I'm looking for off-mission air support.
COULSON: I've been told I'm highly supportive.

ROMANOFF: It's a yes-or-no question.
COULSON: I read it in my horoscope once.

ROMANOFF: We're a go on my signal. Activating field tracker
now. Don't call me, I'll call you.
COULSON: That was also in my horoscope.

ROMANOFF: . . .
COULSON: Ready in 5. Consider this my RSVP.

<<offline>>

ON S.H.I.E.L.D. TRANSPORT PLANE SOMEWHERE OVER THE EASTERN SEABOARD

It had taken Alex only minutes to hoist Ava up, sling her over his shoulder, and carry her from the riverbank to the plane, but he had been so worried about her—and about dropping her—that it had felt more like hours.

When Ava awoke to find herself somewhere over Pennsylvania—securely belted into a jump seat on the plane's transport deck, with Romanoff on one side and Alex on the other—she took it better than Alex expected.

Better than I would have.

Waking up on some kind of S.H.I.E.L.D. military aircraft?

She had looked panicked for a moment but rolled with it as soon as she realized they were in the air. It meant Ava had already been through a lot, Alex figured, as he watched her from the next seat. He was barely able to process the events he had just fallen into.

If she expects things like this to happen to her.

To get shot at by Russian mercenaries or carried away on a military plane.

Why would she, though?

And what does it have to do with Natasha Romanoff?

He stole a glance at the infamous operative. She was deep in conversation with the other agent guy.

Natasha Romanoff. The Natasha Romanoff.

People called her the Black Widow. She knew Iron Man. She knew everyone, every hero he'd ever had.

Black freaking Widow. Alex wondered if anyone had ever called her that to her face. *What do you call someone like that? Natasha? Ms. Widow? Agent Romanoff?*

He tried to process this new reality he'd stumbled into, but there was no point. Alex couldn't figure Ava—or anything else—out.

He knew Ava was holding back, or just holding out on him. There was more to her story. That much he could tell by the way she resisted both friendly smiles and enemy gunfire. The way she took on the whole world as if she expected to do nothing less, and to do it alone.

He knew the feeling, and he was intrigued that she felt it too.

Alex wanted to be her ally, if he could.

Maybe more than that. If she'd let me.

She made him want to try.

Alex looked back to Ava, in the seat next to him. He felt better now that she was conscious again, though her face was still the wrong color, and her breathing was uneven. The plane pitched and rolled as it climbed above the cloud bank to a higher altitude, which probably wasn't helping.

Alex tightened the buckle that held him to his own seat.

"She should keep drinking that water." The agent strapped in across from them spoke up.

Ava looked irritated but took an obedient sip from the water bottle.

Alex couldn't remember the guy's name, only that he was the reason Ava was now awake. It hadn't taken much more than a whiff of some nasty-smelling capsule the agent had broken open beneath her nose until she'd come coughing right back into consciousness.

Alex had been grateful for that, but the way the S.H.I.E.L.D. guy (*Kelson, or maybe Cullen?*) stared at all three of them now, you would have thought they were about to jump out of the plane.

"She could be hurt. We need to get her to a doctor," Alex said. He touched her icy fingers. "People don't just pass out for no reason. And she's freezing." He frowned. "Is that shock? I thought cold hands meant shock." He let his fingers linger on hers. He didn't care if she noticed.

If he was honest with himself, maybe he even hoped she did.

"She'll be fine," Romanoff answered. "As long as we take care of Somodorov." She looked at the other agent. "Otherwise, she'll be dead."

"Hello? *She's* sitting right here," Ava said. She screwed the cap back on the bottle. "Maybe you should try asking *her* what *she* wants to do?"

Romanoff ignored her. "We need a coordinated response. Ivan brought the threat to American soil. The chatter is building. We can't stand by and watch while he shoots up whole cities. He's escalating."

"She's right." Ava held the water bottle against her head. "And I hate to break it to you, but if Ivan's back from the dead, he didn't manage that on his own. Where's he been all this time? Who's bankrolling him? Where's his base of operations?"

"Bankrolling? Did you just say bankrolling? Who talks like that?" Alex poked Ava in the side. She swatted his hand away, but he kept his eyes on her.

Romanoff looked at the other agent. "It's your call, Coulson. So make it."

Coulson. That's his name.

Agent Coulson shook his head. "It's not my call, actually. I'm your handler, Romanoff. I promised backup, maybe an extraction. Not a mission—and certainly not a war on an army of Russian mercenaries. My hands are tied."

"What are you talking about? No war on armies of mercenaries? That's practically our bread and butter, Coulson."

"Not this time."

"So you're saying if they don't make a trading card for it,

you're not interested? You only do the splashy stuff now? Aliens and Nazi throwbacks and bio-engineered super soldiers?" Romanoff snorted.

Alex looked at Agent Coulson with new interest. "Really? Aliens? Like, alien aliens? Or like, the guy with the big guns?"

"*Big guns* are two words that apply to most of the people I know," Coulson said. "And their planes. Sometimes even their flying cars."

"I was talking about the buff dude, you know, with the hammer."

"Why is he here, again?" Coulson looked back at Romanoff.

"Come on, *Phil.*" She sounded annoyed. "Your hands are tied? So untie them. You were there that night in Odessa. If Somodorov is alive, he's coming straight for Ava, to finish what he started."

Ava acted like she hadn't even heard the comment—but Alex knew otherwise, because her icy hand was suddenly clenching his.

So what did happen that night—and who is this Ivan guy really?

And why is everyone so afraid of him?

But Alex knew there was no point in asking. He wasn't certain what exactly S.H.I.E.L.D. did—aside from being some kind of shady intelligence agency—but whoever they were, they didn't seem much more forthcoming with information than the CIA, from what he could tell.

"Forget the Russian," Alex said. "We need a hospital. Ava might have something seriously wrong with her. If she had blacked out any earlier, when we were back on that street in Philly . . ." He didn't finish the sentence.

"She could have gotten killed," Romanoff said. "Or gotten us all killed." She had no problem finishing difficult sentences, because she was Natasha Romanoff. At least, that's what Alex figured. *Russians.*

"But *she* didn't," Ava said.

Coulson was shaking his head, and he looked more than a little unhappy. "You should have thought of all that before you brought a couple of kids into the mix, Agent Romanoff."

"Kids? We're kids now?" Ava protested.

"Oh please." Romanoff shrugged. "Keeping Ava from Ivan was my job—how was I supposed to know the boy would follow us?" She looked at Alex. "The boy's the real problem—he complicates everything. We've got to dump him. Then we'll figure out what to do with her."

"Dump me?" The plane swayed, and Alex grabbed the chest strap that held him to his seat with his free hand. "What did I do? I was only trying to help."

"You should have stayed out of it." Romanoff frowned. "You didn't need to open that door, and you absolutely didn't need to come nosing around on that roof."

"First a pretty girl is flirting with me and then I think I see her getting kidnapped, so I get involved. Is that so wrong?" Alex couldn't believe it. *You would think I was the one doing the attacking.*

"Flirting with you?" Ava's cheeks went pink. She pulled

her cold fingers away from him. "Was that the reason you came after me? Because you thought I was cute?"

"Of course not," Alex said, embarrassed. He could feel himself starting to redden. "I mean, you are cute."

Ava looked like she wanted to slap him. "Seriously? In a life or death situation, you were evaluating my attractiveness?"

"No," he said, uncertain of what to say or do. He didn't have a whole lot of experience with girls. "That was earlier."

She glared at him. Alex knew he was only making things worse.

Back it up, son. Get out. Get out while you can.

He tried to find the right defense, but he was on foreign territory now. "Just for the record, you weren't *not* flirting with me." He jiggled his foot up and down on the vibrating metal floor beneath him, a nervous habit.

Ava looked away. "If that was flirting what is this? A date?"

"Enough!" Romanoff barked. "Look around you. You're on a military transport. Nobody's flirting. S.H.I.E.L.D. does not run a *dating* service."

"Well," Coulson said, "technically it's frowned upon, but I'd be lying if—"

Romanoff glared at Coulson, and he fell silent. She looked back at Alex and Ava. "You two don't know each other, and you don't know what's going on here. So how about everyone shuts up already?"

They shut up.

"I don't think that's how you talk to children, Agent," Coulson ventured.

"They're not children. They're collateral damage."

"In the form of children," Coulson said carefully. "Collaterally damaged children—who you are probably collaterally damaging even more."

Ava growled.

Alex could feel the tension on the deck rising.

Instinctively he felt in his pocket, where a soggy lump of Snickers bar remained. He pulled it out. He was desperate.

Romanoff glanced at Coulson. "Children or not, those were Somodorov's thugs on our tail. I'm sure of it."

"You mean you think it," Coulson corrected.

"I mean I had a little powwow with one of Ivan's hired guns. Given the choice between talking and bleeding out, he went with talking."

"Smart guy." Coulson looked interested.

"Ivan hired at least ten of them. PMCs, private military, all of them. All Russian, of course. At least he's consistent."

"He really thought he was going to take you out with a few rent-a-shots?" Coulson smiled at the thought.

Romanoff shook her head. "That's the thing. According to our friend, the contract wasn't shoot to kill."

"Why else would you shoot someone?" Alex frowned.

"Shoot to wound," Romanoff said. "To control them. Or acquire them. Or reposition them. It could be as simple as that."

Coulson seemed surprised. "You think he was herding you like cattle?"

"That's one theory," Romanoff said. She sat back. "This

mission, to attack us? He said it had a name." Her eyes met Coulson's. "Forever Red."

"Yeah? Snappy. Does that ring any bells?" Coulson raised an eyebrow.

"Just one," she said slowly. "It was something Ivan said to me. That night in Odessa."

"Anything else?"

"This." Natasha held up a black cell phone with a badly cracked screen. "Our PMC had sent a text to Ivan, right before I took him down. Two words."

The others looked at her, waiting. She held up the phone. *Synchronization complete.* She tossed it to Coulson. "Looks like we were set up. Odds are, I played right into his hands. Again." Her expression was pained.

"So Ivan goes after Ava because he knows you'll come." Coulson studied the cell phone as he spoke.

"That's ironic," Ava snorted.

"Not that ironic. I'm here now, aren't I?" Natasha glared.

"Sure. Eight years late." Ava looked at Coulson. "There has to be more to it than that," she said. "What's the point? Why me, after all this time?"

"And what was being synchronized?" Alex was confused.

"And why did Ava sack out back there?" Natasha looked at the others. "I don't know, but considering Ivan the Strange and his history with human experiments, I'm thinking it all might be related." She shook her head. "Which is why I don't think taking her to a civilian hospital is going to help."

Ava looked down, suddenly interested in her water bottle.

"So that's what this is? Ivan and his unfinished business?" Coulson was somber.

"Who knows?" Natasha looked at Ava. "But I have a feeling things are only going to keep getting weirder until we figure it out."

Alex noticed the bottle was shaking in Ava's fingers, and he reached over to replace it with his own warm hand. Their eyes met.

I know. I'm worried too.

"We can't move on Ivan," Coulson said. "Not yet. The DOD hasn't even verified that he's stateside. Nobody's had eyes on him since Panama. As far as we know, he's still officially dead."

Romanoff sighed. "Red tape is your department, Coulson."

Coulson sat forward in his seat, a serious expression on his face. "We'll need to prove he's actually in the country. Bring in some hard evidence it's Somodorov on your tail. If we can show beyond a doubt that Ivan's back in play, we'll have the full resources of S.H.I.E.L.D. behind us." He sat back. "Then I can make the red tape disappear."

"Or, we do it my way." Romanoff shrugged.

He stared at her. "Do I even want to know what that is?"

"Do you ever?" She shot him a dark look. "It's time for some answers. Put us down where I can get them, or I'll land this thing myself."

"And where exactly is that, Agent?"

"S.H.I.E.L.D.'s high-security mainframe. I'm thinking the New York Triskeleon. I need to track down a piece of tech, and in a level ten classified world, this one goes to eleven." She glanced at Ava. "We can have a S.H.I.E.L.D. medic take a look at Ava while we're at the base."

"The Triskeleon? Now?" Ava was clearly spooked. Whatever it was that S.H.I.E.L.D. had to do with her, Alex could tell she wasn't a fan.

"Right now," Natasha said.

Coulson's eyes narrowed. "Let me guess. This piece of tech belongs to Ivan Somodorov?"

Romanoff nodded. "It did, until you and I stole it from him in Odessa."

Ava had gone ashen.

"They're not going to like it," Coulson said.

"They don't have to." Romanoff's voice was ice. "I don't like any of this myself."

"Like it? What about me? I hate it." Ava shook her head.

"You got a better idea? I'm waiting." Romanoff looked at her. "Yeah, didn't think so."

"Ava, come on. She's right. You probably should get checked out by a doctor," Alex began.

"Don't," Ava said. "Not you."

But even Alex knew Natasha Romanoff was right. There wasn't a better option—and there was nothing else to say.

A long minute later, Coulson sighed. "Then it's settled. We head to S.H.I.E.L.D. I'll get you as far as the East River docking bay."

"And then?" Natasha looked at him.

"And then, you're right. If you do have a way to walk two highly unclassified civilian kids into a highly classified facility, I'm pretty sure I don't want to know."

She nodded. "That's okay. I've got friends in low places."

S.H.I.E.L.D. EYES ONLY

CLEARANCE LEVEL X

LINE-OF-DUTY DEATH [LODD] INVESTIGATION

REF: S.H.I.E.L.D. CASE 121A415

AGENT IN COMMAND [AIC]: PHILLIP COULSON

RE: AGENT NATASHA ROMANOFF A.K.A. BLACK WIDOW,
A.K.A. NATASHA ROMANOVA

TRANSCRIPT: DEPARTMENT OF DEFENSE, LODD INQUIRY HEARINGS.

DOD: The New York Triskeleon?
ROMANOFF: You sound surprised, sir.

DOD: What is it you people do in there anyway? At any of the Triskeleon bases around the world?
ROMANOFF: Slumber parties. S'mores. Truth or dare. The usual
stuff.

DOD: And it never occurred to you that there might be an issue with
things like bringing unvetted civilian minors into high-
sensitivity situations requiring security clearances?
ROMANOFF: It occurred to me, sir.

DOD: Situations that may or may not involve matters of national security?
ROMANOFF: I weighed those issues.

DOD: And?
ROMANOFF: Ivan Somodorov had just come back from the dead. I
wasn't going to let a little red tape keep me from doing what I had
to do.

DOD: Which was?
ROMANOFF: Putting Ivan back into the grave. Then, you know. The
s'mores.

CHAPTER **16**: AVA

S.H.I.E.L.D. TRISKELEON BASE
THE GREAT CITY OF NEW YORK—
EAST RIVER

s the S.H.I.E.L.D. plane lost altitude, Manhattan came into sight. Ava had never seen it from this perspective. From way up here, none of it seemed real.

She traced her finger on the double-paned window of the aircraft, drawing an imaginary line from Central Park to the Empire State Building down to Battery Park, at the very bottom of the island. She drew another one out into the water, where S.H.I.E.L.D.'s massive Triskeleon base rose up round and tall with three protruding legs, becoming arguably the most dramatic New York landmark of them all.

The circle with three branches.

She couldn't remember what the Triskeleon symbol was supposed to mean, but she knew it meant something. She'd spent too many solitary hours stuck in a facility with only S.H.I.E.L.D. tutors not to know that. Even so, she made a point of never going near it, no matter what it meant.

She dropped her hand from the window.

Prison. That's all it means to me now.

Inmates didn't generally voluntarily walk back into prisons if they didn't have to—not the smart ones. But as Ava followed Natasha and Alex along the neon-yellow-painted walkway toward the heavily defended entrance to New York City's S.H.I.E.L.D. stronghold, she knew she was doing just that.

The plane had landed in a half-empty docking bay beneath the East River; it had opened in front of them as soon as they'd radioed in for permission to approach. All that was left of their journey now was the short hike through the glorified aircraft parking lot into the interior of the building—maybe a hundred yards through the airstrip.

Just keep walking.

"You okay?" Alex looked at her curiously.

"Fine." As soon as Ava said the word, the roof of the docking bay began to slide shut over her head, and she felt herself beginning to panic. They were shutting her in again.

What if they never let me go?

She watched as the sliver of New York City afternoon sky grew smaller and smaller—until all that was left was the steel-reinforced gloom of the docking bay itself.

It's not 7B. Keep walking.

Ava slowed down when she saw the glass doors to the S.H.I.E.L.D. base in the distance. She couldn't help but hang back; she honestly didn't know if she could talk her body into walking through the doorway.

But I'm not staying. Natasha promised.

The more Ava tried not to think about it, the harder it was to keep walking. Again, Alex was the one who noticed, and Alex was the one who waited for her to catch up. "Come on." He held out his hand, and she took it. She'd almost gotten used to taking it, and that surprised her. *I'm here, Ava.* That's what the touch of his fingers said. She tried to believe them, just as she tried to believe herself that nothing bad was going to happen.

Which was impossible.

But not when Ava held Alex's hand. Then she felt steady.

When even a single finger brushed against his, she felt like they were connected—even if she couldn't explain exactly why.

When, like now, their shoulders pushed against each other, letting their jacketed arms fall side by side, she felt like he knew her, liked her, even in some small way belonged to her.

He was the boy she touched now, today, and that meant something. It felt like something. Either something very new, or something very old.

He feels like home.

With her hand in his, Ava forced herself to keep moving one step at a time, until she found they had reached the base entrance. She took a deep breath.

A buzzer sounded—some kind of security door. A two-foot-thick, shatterproof, flame-resistant, steel-reinforced security door.

As it slid open, the first face that appeared caught everyone by surprise. As far as faces went, this one was a good one. It was undoubtedly handsome, incredibly animated, fairly well kept, and utterly charming. Also—somewhat narcissistic, slightly rakish, borderline wicked—and surprisingly battle worn.

Very, very battle worn.

"Is that—?" Alex stopped dead in his tracks.

Natasha shrugged. "I told you. Friends in low places."

"Agent Romanoff," Tony Stark called from the now open doorway. "What are you doing here? Or do you just happen to be stopping by to submit your proprietary plan for alternative energy subsidies too?" He grinned.

"Not so much," she said, pulling him in for a hug. "I was hoping you'd be here, actually."

"First Saturday of the month. Where else would I be?" He cocked his head. "I thought you were hunting bad guys in Bahrain?"

"Turns out the bad guys are hunting me," Natasha said. "Surprise."

"Wherever you go, guns follow, Agent Romanoff. Why would that surprise me now?"

"The guns I can handle," Natasha said. "It's the rest of it that's getting to me."

"You mean the rest of *them*?" Tony looked past her to where Ava and Alex were standing. Ava felt her face going red.

Natasha nodded. "Ava, Alex, this is Tony Stark."

"Look. It's a small human. Hello, small human." He waved, and Ava froze. She couldn't help it. Like everyone else, she'd heard the sound bites from Tony Stark of Iron Man fame—of Stark Industries fame—of tabloid and headlines and fast cars and fast everything fame. Even when the only channel she had was C-SPAN.

"Hi, Mr.—Iron—Stark." Ava smoothed her copper curls with one hand, suddenly appearing self-conscious.

Alex himself seemed unable to speak, until eventually he managed to choke out the words. "You're—you're him."

"Well, I'm not her." Tony smiled, looking at Alex.

"The kid says that a lot." Natasha shrugged.

"What's going on?" Tony gestured, and the two of them began to walk inside the S.H.I.E.L.D. facility. Alex and Ava hung back, following at a distance.

"You have no idea," Natasha said.

As the two spoke, only Ava noticed the sudden sound of the massive exterior doors locking together as they sealed off the docking bay behind them.

Tony stroked his chin. "Let's see. You show up at S.H.I.E.L.D. nerve central with two small humans in tow, and one of them seems to be a redheaded Russian girl. Why is that familiar? Why?"

"Are you finished?"

"Oh, I think I'm just getting started."

As soon as they set foot inside the base, the combined influence of Natasha Romanoff and Tony Stark—following up a few well-placed calls from Phil Coulson—was more than evident. Within minutes of their arrival, Alex and Ava were handed standard-issue S.H.I.E.L.D. regulation sweats—black fleece jackets and pants, all bearing the familiar steel-gray logo—as well as slightly less impressive foil-wrapped sandwiches.

"What, no S.H.I.E.L.D. toothbrush? Socks? Sleep mask?" Alex examined his sandwich pack.

Tony Stark looked at him. "Knock yourself out. They're in the gift shop."

"They have a gift shop?"

"No."

Then Natasha stepped in, and before she knew enough to complain, Ava was dispatched to the medical wing, where she was poked and prodded and examined within an inch of her life, while Alex refused to budge from her side. The moment Ava was pronounced healthy—remarkably so, given the day's events—she was out the door with the others.

Meanwhile, the full-court press that was Tony Stark and Natasha Romanoff ("Half the Avengers," Natasha had pointed out. "The cute half," Tony had added.) attacked the ranking brass, lobbying to get access to the Triskeleon's infamous proprietary mainframe. The double-teaming paid off; there was no resisting the power of a Stark-Romanoff alliance for long.

They were in.

Within an hour, Ava and Alex—now outfitted in black like every other regulation S.H.I.E.L.D. recruit—and Tony and Natasha were ensconced several floors beneath the East

River, in what Tony called the Brain Trust. The dark room appeared to be the size of a football field, though in reality it wasn't much more than fifty feet in any one direction. It was the information flowing through it that threw off the perspective.

The place was virtually larger than life.

As Ava and Alex stood side by side in the back of the chamber, they couldn't help but marvel at the free flow of data surrounding them.

"All right. This is cool." Alex nodded. He no longer seemed thrown off by the presence of Iron Man, or even the threat of Ivan's army.

Ava wished it were that easy for her. She was still wary. S.H.I.E.L.D. had taught her to be that way; even this room was protected by three separately patrolled corridors, an alarm sequence that reset on the hour, and a two-foot steel door. For a girl who couldn't help but calculate escape routes from every room that she entered, this was a nightmare. She couldn't trust anything in the building—not even if it was called the Brain Trust.

"Yeah, super cool," Ava said.

Still, there was no denying that what was happening in this room was nothing like anything she had ever seen in 7B—or anywhere else in the world. Back in the safe house, she'd snuck over-the-shoulder glimpses at elaborately encrypted files and equally elaborately encrypted routines that could steal them, just like she'd seen tech that could start any car or open any door. She'd thought nothing of it.

But that wasn't this.

Now thousands of S.H.I.E.L.D. files streamed over the walls, encircling them with illuminated images and numbers and charts and graphs, as Natasha and Tony searched different sectors of the mainframe. They were drowning in data, and it all had to do with Ivan Somodorov in one way or another.

Natasha was silent and focused, but Tony talked as he worked. "Walk me through it again. Your not-so-dead long-lost Red Roomie shows up in Panama City. You're afraid he'll try to tangle with Natasha Junior, here."

Ava coughed. "Excuse me?"

"So you circle the wagons, pick up Mini-Me, take out Ivan's welcome party, hop on Coulson's good ship *Lollipop*, and hitch a ride to S.H.I.E.L.D.'s doorstep."

"Mini-Me? No." Ava still looked wounded.

"Yeah. More or less," Natasha said, not looking up.

Tony frowned. "And what about the boy?"

"Caught in the cross fire," Natasha said dismissively.

"Tell me about it." Alex sighed.

"Ivan wants something, and I think it has to do with Ava and me. That's why we're here," Natasha said.

Tony nodded from his keyboard. "Because you need help babysitting?"

"Because I'm trained for ballistics and military strategy and counterintelligence and not for this."

"Top of her class," Alex muttered, nudging Ava's foot.

"So?" Tony laughed once. "I'm trained for highballs and the high life and—well, high everything—but people adapt. Things change."

"Not everyone," Natasha said, trying to focus on the screen in front of her. She sounded uncomfortable.

Ava watched her from behind. You had to appreciate the irony. *My curse was for her to abandon me, and her curse will be that she can never escape me.*

Ava looked away.

"Yeah, well, it looks like Ivan doesn't change much either. Here. I've got something." Tony tapped on a tablet, and what looked like a set of blueprints projected itself on the wall of screens. "This is a scan of what S.H.I.E.L.D. recovered the night of the Odessa raid."

Natasha glanced up at the projected image in front of her.

"That's what you were looking for, right? I think—there's more." Tony kept moving new files on and off the screen. Immediately numbers and images began to fly as he mined the Triskeleon's powerful—and powerfully secure—mainframe.

Natasha grabbed his arm. "Stop. The O.P.U.S. project. That one. That's it."

Tony pulled the image off the screen, and now the model projected itself into the center of the room. It was far from complete—if anything, the model appeared to be damaged and only partially materialized—but even in that state, it hung in the air above them in three translucent dimensions.

He tapped again, and the model spun over and over, revealing every side of itself, every angle, every flaw. What looked like some sort of patched, riveted metal box, as tall as a person, with coils of cabling that dangled beneath it like a kind of dead octopus.

A familiar dead octopus.

Ava felt herself holding her breath as Alex tightened his arm around her shoulders. She was transfixed. "I remember now. That—that thing. It was there. In the warehouse with Ivan."

"*That thing* is how we blew the place up," Natasha said, studying the glowing white lines and numbers that dissected the open space in front of her. "So this is what was left of it? After?"

"Apparently." Tony's hands were flying. Every inch of the room was full of images and numbers.

Finally he sat back. "Even what's left of it is pretty spooky."

"Spooky?" Ava said from behind him. "I know why *I* think it's spooky. Why do you?"

"Not me. Einstein." Tony tapped the tablet again, and Albert Einstein's face appeared on the screens behind the rotating model. "Spooky physics. That's what Einstein called quantum entanglement."

"Wait, what?" Alex asked.

"Quantum entanglement. The total manipulation of physics across space and time. The idea that two distinct pieces of matter can affect each other over a span of vast distances."

Ava frowned. "Two pieces of matter?"

"He means people," Natasha said. She kept her eyes on the walls. "Two people."

Tony nodded. "Ask twins who feel each other's pain—or a mother who suddenly wakes up when her kid has a nightmare—or a dog who waits by his master's grave." He looked up. "You could argue that those are natural entanglements. But what if you could control them? What if you could entangle matter for yourself?"

Natasha sat back in her chair, staring at the data in front of her.

"The O.P.U.S. project, if these records are right, was Moscow's push to weaponize quantum entanglement—and then build it. If they got it done, they've found what amounts to the legendary lost unicorn of every physics department in the world."

Natasha shook her head, frustrated. "You know who also said that? Howard Stark, only he was talking about Vita-Rays. Bruce could have said the same thing about gamma radiation. I'm getting pretty tired of unicorns. Could we try to get a regular horse around here for once?"

Tony tapped the interface again. "I think this particular unicorn is already out of the gate, Agent Romanoff. There are hundreds of pages of files here that corroborate mentions of your O.P.U.S. project, involving dozens of Russian labs."

She gave up. "Fine. So we know this thing, whatever it was, was a priority, and not just for Ivan. For Moscow." Natasha reached forward to the interface, rotating the model again.

Alex spoke up. "What do you mean, weaponize?"

"I mean, when people become just as dangerous as weapons." Tony sat back. "Unless I'm mistaken, that device right there was an attempt to entangle the psyches of two unsuspecting parties. Like an adaptor, but for brains."

"And by people you mean me," Ava said slowly. Her eyes were fixed on the wall of data streaming past her. "I'm the weapon."

"Conceivably. *A* weapon," Tony corrected.

"That has to be impossible," Natasha said. "Please tell me that's impossible."

"I'm not so sure," Tony said. "Imagine a modern-day version of the Vulcan mind meld, only Spock is completely in the driver's seat now, and poor Captain Kirk doesn't even know his mind is being melded."

Natasha looked annoyed. "Is that before or after they blow up the Death Star?"

"I'm going to pretend you didn't say that." Alex laughed. Tony didn't.

"Think about it. It's the perfect way to spy on heads of state, tycoons of industry, military generals, Supreme Court justices. If the psyche of one person can connect to the psyche of another person, anyone could be a double agent, anywhere."

"Not anyone," Natasha said, staring at the model in front of her. "How old were you, Ava? Back in Odessa?"

"Eight," Ava said, barely able to speak. "I was eight. By the time I left I was almost ten."

"Exactly." Natasha pulled a Ukrainian newspaper article up on the screens. "And now children are disappearing and not just from Ukraine. The kidnappings range from Moscow to Moldova. Just like last time Ivan was running his operation."

"Makes sense. Better brains," Tony added. "More adaptive. More growth of neuron pathways. Until you're twenty-six, and then it all gets shot to hell. Unless you're a—what's the word for it? A Tony Stark?"

Alex laughed.

Ava glared at him. *Suck up.*

Tony tapped a button, and the illuminated model disappeared. What looked like typewritten, sometimes handwritten, Russian lab reports appeared in front of them.

POLNAYA SINKHRONIZATSIYA.

"Synchronization complete," Natasha said, staring at the words. "That was the message we intercepted too. What if they were talking about Ava and me?"

"That *might* be *a little* not good." Tony shrugged. "Ish."

"Would the connection be stronger when both parties were in physical proximity?"

"You tell me. As far as we know, you and Ava appear to be Ivan's only Entangled working prototype."

Natasha spun her chair toward Ava. "I grabbed Ava by the hand, twice. The first time made her so sick she almost couldn't stand up. The second time, she lost consciousness."

Ava nodded. "It felt like my body was on fire. Like I was being electrocuted or something."

"And then she was gone. Completely sacked out," Alex added.

Tony looked delighted, and his brain appeared to be racing "Like two live wires. That's amazing. That's unbelievable. And some kind of dopaminergic pathway? Mesolimbic and mesocortical? That's—"

Natasha cut him off. "A level seven classified breach? An intelligence disaster? An unparalleled vulnerability, not just for S.H.I.E.L.D. but for the entire Avengers Initiative?"

"I see your point," Tony said.

"I hate to bring it up, but what if they're not the only Entangled prototype?" Alex asked.

"Then we're in a lot more trouble than anyone knows." Tony hesitated. "This party's just getting started. Even if it is only Ava and Natasha who are Entangled, it's likely that the stronger the connection gets, the greater access Ava will have to Natasha's cerebral cortex."

"Which means?" Alex looked at Tony.

"Which means I won't just be leaping from bridges and using her combat moves, will I?" Ava asked.

Tony shook his head. "No. Natasha—Agent Romanoff—will eventually just start . . . leaking . . . leaching . . . into your brain."

"Super," Natasha said.

"I know *I'm* thrilled," Ava answered.

Tony looked at Natasha. "Prepare for exposure. And I'm only saying this because I've never seen you as an over-sharer," he said. "Or, and I'm just being honest here, even an under-sharer. Or, you know. Sharer."

The silence that answered him was awkward.

"Yay sharing," Alex said.

Tony spun his chair toward Natasha. "You'll have no secrets, Romanoff. Not about what we do, and not about your past. You'll be an open book, and not just for Ava but to anyone who can get to her."

Ava found she couldn't look at Natasha. It was all too strangely intimate now. "Why now? What changed?"

"I don't think it is just now. I think the initial connection probably booted itself up when the two of you first encountered this thing," Tony said. "In Odessa. You and Ivan."

Natasha nodded. She remembered the moment, and she suspected Ava did too. The blue light. The explosion of electricity. The shooting pain.

"But something has to be triggering it. Now. After all this time," Ava said.

"Maybe that's why this Ivan guy showed up," Alex said. "So that Agent Romanoff would come for Ava. Maybe just getting them together again was the synchronization he was talking about."

"Exactly." Tony looked from one redheaded Russian to the other. "As you said. Physical proximity. It's possible."

Natasha's eyes were now as cold as the New York City winter night. "So use that big brain of yours to find a way to shut it down, Tony."

"If I can," Tony said. Then he smiled. "Who are we kidding? Of course I can." He checked his watch. "But I have to get to Bora Bora by dinner. It's Date Night."

Natasha put her hand awkwardly on his arm. "Thanks, Tony. I mean it."

Tony sighed. "Just so long as it doesn't involve chaos. I promised Pepper—we're on a break from chaos."

"So I heard." Natasha did not look amused.

"It was a book," he said defensively. "She made me read it. I'll send it to you. *Break from Chaos*. That's apparently a thing."

"You're Tony Stark. Since when do you have to get permission for a life of chaos?"

"Things change, Agent Romanoff."

LINE-OF-DUTY DEATH [LODD] INVESTIGATION
REF: S.H.I.E.L.D. CASE 121A415
AGENT IN COMMAND [AIC]: PHILLIP COULSON
RE: AGENT NATASHA ROMANOFF A.K.A. BLACK WIDOW,
A.K.A. NATASHA ROMANOVA
TRANSCRIPT: DEPARTMENT OF DEFENSE, LODD INQUIRY HEARINGS.

DOD: You expect me to believe you knew nothing more about the identities of the civilian minors placed in your care?
ROMANOFF: Sir?

DOD: I just find it odd that a solo operative suddenly involved herself with not one but two minor assets.
ROMANOFF: Is that a question, sir?

DOD: Did you believe that they were each in some way connected to the case?
ROMANOFF: Ava was always a target, as far as Ivan was concerned. Alex was just—wrong place, wrong time.

DOD: Would you say a protective instinct emerged? One that an agent of your record would have found disorienting, given your own childhood history with Ivan Somodorov?
ROMANOFF: I find everything about children disorienting, sir.

DOD: So no instincts?
ROMANOFF: My only instincts are to shoot and to run, sir.

DOD: And the children?
ROMANOFF: I wouldn't say I'd shoot them, but they should probably still run. Just to be on the safe side.

DOD: So no instincts.
ROMANOFF: None whatsoever.

S.H.I.E.L.D. TRISKELEON BASE
THE GREAT CITY OF NEW YORK—
EAST RIVER

"**Y**ou know what they say. The fifteenth time's the charm," Tony said cheerfully.

"They don't say that." Natasha glared. "Ever."

"Actually, I think the fifteenth time is when they say to give up," Alex offered.

"They don't say it to me," Tony said, waving him off.

Tony's fourteenth attempt to sever the mental connection between Ava and Natasha had nearly incinerated half her head, and she was still resentful. She looked doubtfully at Ava, who sat on a metal stool in the center of the room, just as she did.

Like two sitting ducks.

"Is he always like this?" Ava asked her.

"Always," Natasha said.

"Come on. Haven't you seen the documentary?" Alex piped up from where he stood behind them. "*Tony Stark—Iron Will?* He's the original American optimist."

"Yeah. What he said." Tony smiled, holding up a blowtorch.

"Actually, he's not the original," Natasha said. "That would be Rogers. By about fifty years."

"I'm just getting started," Tony said, lowering a welding mask over his face. "Reverse dog years. What are those, cat years?"

"Super-Soldier Steve Rogers?" Alex swallowed.

"I like this kid," Tony said as sparks flew. "The kid stays."

Just as he said it, the sparks exploded around all four of them.

Natasha's vision blacked out, and she flashed on a split second of imagery—a blurry figure of a dancing girl, maybe? It was too quick to see who it was. She only knew it wasn't her.

But she'd also heard something.

A song.

Is that—Tchaikovsky?

It was too quick to understand, though, and Natasha's vision returned to normal just as Tony dropped the mass of burning wires on the tiled floor. Two dutiful lab technicians sprayed the smoking heap with white foam.

"I saw something that time," Natasha said. "I might have."

"Let me guess, you saw stars?" Alex eyed the ruined remains of trial fifteen.

Natasha thought about it.

What did I see?

Were those Ava's memories? Was I seeing into her mind?

She could feel her own pulse beginning to race.

It had been one thing to logically understand quantum entanglement. But to see it for herself? For the first time, Natasha realized Ava could really see into her mind. Could actually access her memories.

The thought was more than terrifying.

The idea of anyone seeing her past made her almost physically sick.

"I don't care. I'm not putting these things anywhere near my head," Ava said, ripping off her own smoking electrodes. "I don't have a death wish."

Natasha looked at the other fourteen charred piles on the floor. Though the Triskeleon's lab facilities were state of the art—at least they had been, before today—Tony didn't seem to be making much progress. In fact, he seemed to be making everything but progress.

Come on, Tony. Get her out of my head.

I don't know how much more of this I can take.

It was slow going. Tony had started the evening off with his improvised Stark Quantum Detangler—quickly followed by a Stark Quantum Retangler—soon detouring into a little Stark Quantum Hypnotic Regulator, a Stark Quantum Rapid Eye Movement Stimulator, and a Stark Quantum Ultrasound Scanner. Basically, if Tony could put the words *Stark* or *Quantum* in front of it, he was game.

He was now holding two sparking electrical wires in front

of Ava and Natasha—along with a handful of electrodes. "Round sixteen. New idea. The Stark Hypothalamus Buffer." He attached a new electrode to each of Ava's temples. "Or, if you think it's catchier, the Stark Hypothalami Sandwich. Just put it on—"

Ava yanked the electrodes off. "And subject myself to more Stark Quantum Electrical Shock? Forget it. This isn't helping anything."

Alex nodded. "Yeah, no offense or anything, but you might as well just tell them to each stick a fork in an electrical socket."

"Well, actually . . ." Tony said, staring up at the ceiling. But then he shook his head. "No, never mind. That was basically what we did on number seven. Let's try this instead." He held out the sparking wires again.

Ava looked at him like he was crazy—which at this point was a pretty fair assessment, Natasha had to admit. "Pass. How about you call me *after* you build the Stark Quantum Burn Unit. Until then, I can't take any more of this crap."

"My tech," Tony said, "is never *crap*. Almost never."

Alex looked at the fourteen abandoned prototypes around them and raised an eyebrow.

Tony shrugged. "Well, it's rare. Let's leave it at that."

"Ava, if there were any other way, we wouldn't be here," Natasha said. "Trust me."

"Why? Why should I?" Ava slid off the stool and backed away, knocking over half a lab table full of circuit diagrams, wire coils, electrical switches, even soldering irons—as well as tools of all sizes. Ava didn't look like she was about to let any of it near her head again.

"Why? How about national security? Or even international peacekeeping?" Natasha stood up. She had no idea how to talk to the girl—to someone who was so like her in so many ways, yet so different.

At only seventeen.

Natasha watched her now, surveying her options. *Another scared rabbit in a winter trap*, she thought. It was a familiar sight.

How much I was like her, at that age.

And yet, how much she hates me now.

Ava kept backing up until she'd made it nearly all the way to the airtight laboratory doors, when two armed MPs stepped in front of her. She folded her arms. "Really? You're going to force me to stay? And here I thought the point of all those locks was to keep people *out*."

The room was silent, until a stray spark ignited a nearby trash can.

It exploded, toppling a rolling lab cart into two technicians.

"Don't touch that!" Tony shouted at the more terrified-looking of the two techs. "What do you think that is, a toaster?" He paused. "Well, okay. I see your point. You *could* use it toast bread. French bread. Or, say, the entirety of France. But don't touch that. Just get out of here. Now."

The techs fled to the door, and an MP pressed a security code into the keypad next to the steel panels, sliding the doors open.

"Oh, so they can go? Just not me? I thought America was supposed to be a free country." Ava glared at him.

"Maybe we should take break," Alex suggested. "Like, a big one."

Natasha looked at Tony, who just shrugged.

Thanks for the help, Stark.

She followed Ava to the door, reaching awkwardly to put her hand on the teen's shoulder.

"Ava . . ." Natasha began. "I know this is hard."

"Oh please." Ava whirled around to face her. "What?"

"Don't. Just don't. Don't act like you want to be my friend. You're nobody's *sestra*. I don't have a sister and I don't even know what became of my parents, thanks to Ivan Somodorov." Ava sounded annoyed. Alex looked at her sympathetically.

Natasha nodded. "I know how it feels to lose your parents," she said. "If you'd just let me—"

"No. I'm not falling for that again. I'm not afraid of you. Not anymore."

Natasha was struck by the defiant look on Ava's face. The faith and the innocence of her own anger.

But you should be afraid, little one. You should be afraid of so many things.

The world is a cruel place for Ivan's girls.

Natasha paused for a long moment, considering her options. Finally she tried again. "Look, Ava. It might not seem like it, but I'm here to help. I'm trying to keep you from getting fried by Ivan the Strange for the second time. I know what that's like. I was there, remember?"

And I was just like you, once.

"You were there?" Ava scoffed. "You were never there when it mattered. You don't get to pop back into my life when you feel like it, to play the hero again. I've been doing fine on my own, just the way you left me."

"Fine?" Natasha raised an eyebrow. "You're a runaway. You live in a basement and eat at shelters and soup kitchens. You're basically a homeless person."

Alex looked startled.

Ava's cheeks turned bright red. "At least I'm not skulking around fencing tournaments scaring people with my *fake face*."

Tony smiled. "See, *this* is communication. Now we're getting somewhere. Now we're sharing."

Natasha glared. *I give up.*

"Did someone say break? I agree. Great idea." Alex reached for Ava's hand, but she pulled it away. She wasn't done.

Now her eyes were blazing. "Glad to know you've been watching, *sestra*. Glad to know you care." She yanked an old, scratched iPod out of her pocket and hurled it across the room. Natasha winced, but Ava wasn't finished.

"You can keep your iPod. In fact, you can keep all your crappy birthday presents, with no card and no name. I never wanted them," Ava said. "What I wanted was a friend. One familiar face in an entire country of strangers. I guess that was too much to ask."

"Let's go, Ava." Alex put his hand gently on her shoulder.

Natasha tried again. "Just hear me out. I have an idea. And I won't let Ivan Somodorov near you. I give you my word."

Take it.

Let me help you.

We need each other, whether you can admit it or not.

"Your word?" Ava scoffed. "Where was your word for the last eight years? Where were any of you? All S.H.I.E.L.D. has ever done is lock me in a room for my own good, which I can tell you was no good at all. It was no good to spend eight years alone in 7B—and alone in an unmarked van—and alone with a tutor in a S.H.I.E.L.D. field office, memorizing the constitution of a country I began to hate."

Now it was Natasha who was livid. "Hate? Because they beat you? Brainwashed you? Chained you up? Forced you to steal and lie and kill?" Natasha spat the words out before she could stop herself. "No? I'm sorry you didn't have enough playtimes. I'm sorry you didn't get to go to the big dance. I'm sorry you had people feeding you and clothing you and trying to keep you alive."

She shook away the memories as they rose to the surface of her mind again and again. The beatings and the bruisings. The failures and the threats. The scars Ivan had cut into her skin, and into her psyche.

"Keep me alive? Maybe my life would have been better if you hadn't."

Natasha's eyes were fierce and dark. "Don't say that. You have no idea what you're talking about. It wouldn't have been better; it would have been shorter—"

"Playdates." Alex interrupted.

The room went silent. Nobody seemed to know what to say.

Alex sat up. "The word is *playdates*, not playtimes. That's what kids have. I mean, regular kids. Not like, you know, you guys."

Natasha shot him a withering look. Ava seemed disgusted.

Alex didn't seem to care. He just shrugged. "And the big dance is called the prom. I'm guessing that wasn't on your calendars."

"What's your point?" Natasha stared.

"Only that you guys might have more in common than you think."

Natasha took a breath and turned to face Ava. "Was it the radiator or the headboard?"

You know what I'm talking about.

Ava stared.

Natasha leaned in. "Where did the handcuffs go?"

When he beat you.

When he kept you captive, like an animal.

Ava's eyes were shining.

Natasha shrugged. "When you cried or said you were hungry or asked to go to the bathroom. Or if you didn't thank him enough for choosing you to be one of his girls."

Or all of the above, Natasha thought. *Like he did for me.*

Nobody said a word.

Natasha turned to Tony. "I was wrong to come here. Let's drop Alex off at home and send Ava back to protective custody."

Your decision, ptenets.

Natasha wanted to say the words out loud to Ava, but she couldn't. She'd said too much already.

I can't help you. Not like this.

Whatever happens, Ava, you'll have to live with it now. Just like I do.

Natasha wondered if Ava could hear what she was thinking. She suspected not, at least not yet. And anyways, you didn't need a mind reader to know how Ivan Somodorov ran his Red Room.

"Fine," Tony said. "I'll have a car sent over." He put down his screwdriver with a shrug. "Done."

"The sink," Ava said suddenly. "It was a pipe beneath the sink."

Of course it was, Natasha thought, closing her eyes.

Better acoustics.

He wanted the others to hear you scream.

The room was silent.

"I can't remember very much, but I remember that. I think I got used to what he did. We all did. What he said—I never got used to that." Ava's voice was quiet, but not weak. If anything, talking about it only seemed to make her stronger.

And angrier.

Natasha could see it in her face.

Good.

You should be.

It will make you stronger.

All eyes were on Ava now, but she just shrugged. If she had something more to say, she wasn't saying it. Not here.

"Let's go," Natasha said. She was resolute, even more so than before. Because Natasha now understood the truth; Ava was as vulnerable and broken as Natasha herself was. It was up to Natasha to keep her safe, to keep them all safe. Ava was a vulnerability, and Natasha had to make sure she wasn't exploited.

By Ivan, or by anyone.

"You've got to take cover," Natasha said, finally.

"What?" Ava looked as hurt as if she'd struck her.

"S.H.I.E.L.D. is the safest place for you. You'll be off the grid in an hour. Nobody will be able to get to you. That's why they call it a safe house." Natasha shrugged.

Not safe. Just as safe as I can keep you.

At least until Tony can figure out how to sever the link.

"So your secrets will be safe? Isn't that all you care about? Because if they can get to me, they can get to you? Because I know which drawer is your underwear drawer and which closets have all the skeletons?" Ava was bitter.

"Ava. Don't," Natasha said.

"Or do," Tony said. He was riveted. "About the drawers."

Ava went on. "Because I know about how broken your heart is? About how afraid you are—not of dying, but of living?"

"Stop it," Natasha said, her voice rising.

"Why? Because I know more about you than you do? I hate to break it to you, Agent Romanov, but that's not saying much."

"This is over." Natasha was seething. "You. Me. All of it."

Ava laughed. "*This?* This never started. Your *whole life* never started, because you don't have one. No real friends, no real family. Is that your big secret? That those aren't memories in your head—that's a case file? That your problem isn't being a superhero, it's being a human?"

"Yes," Natasha said, suddenly, startling Ava.

Ava took a step back. "What?"

Tony's eyes flickered from Ava to Natasha.

Even Alex was staring now.

"Nailed it. You got me. Happy? Great. Now get your bags. We're leaving."

Ava's eyes were still blazing. She shook her head. "I can't go back there. Not to 7B."

"Ivan Somodorov is coming for you and me both, Ava. I can't do anything about that. Not as long as he's out there," Natasha said. "But if you really can read my mind, then you already know that. So if your little monologue is over, let's go."

"Let him come. I'm not being locked up again."

Ava looked at Tony. He shrugged. "Sorry, kid."

Ava looked at Alex desperately.

He reached out his hand, looking at the others.

"Just give Ava tonight, okay? Just give her until tomorrow—enough time to get her head around it. "

"Excuse me?" Ava gave Alex a scathing look.

He didn't let that stop him.

"After that, she'll do whatever she has to do to stay safe. I'll go with her to the safe house myself. We all want the same thing. Right, Ava?" Alex nodded at her encouragingly.

She looked at him like he was crazy. "We do?"

He squeezed her hand tight.

She shook her head, giving him a strange look. Then she turned back to Natasha. "Fine," Ava said. "Tomorrow. Then I'll go back to 7B."

Natasha nodded at the MP, and he tapped the keypad, allowing the doors to slide open. "Tomorrow."

But you're still going, ptenets.

One way or another.

"All I ask is one thing." Ava took a last hard look at Natasha. "After tomorrow, you leave me alone. I'll never see your face again. Promise me."

Natasha's expression was even harder. "Believe me, *sestra*, I wouldn't have it any other way."

S.H.I.E.L.D. EYES ONLY

CLEARANCE LEVEL X

LINE-OF-DUTY DEATH [LODD] INVESTIGATION
REF: S.H.I.E.L.D. CASE 121A415
AGENT IN COMMAND [AIC]: PHILLIP COULSON
RE: AGENT NATASHA ROMANOFF A.K.A. BLACK WIDOW,
A.K.A. NATASHA ROMANOVA
TRANSCRIPT: DEPARTMENT OF DEFENSE, LODD INQUIRY HEARINGS.

DOD: Was that distressing? To discover that a stranger would have access to your mind and your memories?
ROMANOFF: It wasn't the first time. As you've noted.

DOD: Of course not. Did that make it harder or easier to accept, Agent?
ROMANOFF: There's nothing easy about having your brain on display, sir.

DOD: For some of us more than others, Agent.
ROMANOFF: If you're asking if I had a problem with Ava being entangled with me, of course I did. If you're asking if I intentionally put her in harm's way, you don't know me at all, sir.

DOD: I only know what you tell me, Agent. As I keep trying to explain.
ROMANOFF: Did it ever occur to you that there might be other people worried about my memories becoming public knowledge?

DOD: For example?
ROMANOFF: You tell me. I'm not interrogating myself here. Who asked you to investigate me?

DOD: That's classified.
ROMANOFF: It's not a hearing if you don't give me something to hear, sir.

ACT TWO

"...KEEP YOUR TRUE SELF BURIED UNDER SEVERAL LAYERS OF UNTRUE SELVES..."

—NATASHA ROMANOFF

CHAPTER **18**: ALEX

S.H.I.E.L.D. TRISKELEON BASE THE GREAT CITY OF NEW YORK— EAST RIVER

Some S.H.I.E.L.D. bunkrooms were their own method of torture, Alex guessed.

The one that had been given to visiting civilian asset Ava Orlova—right next door to visiting civilian asset Alex Manor, which was itself next to unassigned operative Natasha Romanoff—was small and stuffy and windowless, with barely room for a single compact iron bunk bed.

It was even a miserable place to be miserable.

Ava lay curled sideways on the lower mattress, staring at the wall in front of her. Alex lay next to her, his arm flung protectively around her back. She had been so exhausted she'd passed out as soon as she'd arrived at the room; Alex had watched her toss and turn until her nightmares had finally gotten the better of her fitful sleep. Within an hour, Ava had woken up screaming the name Ivan Somodorov.

Alex rubbed her shoulder now. Her t-shirt was thin and soft, and her skin was warm beneath it. Lying here with her now, he almost forgot they were at a S.H.I.E.L.D. base at all. "We'll find him, Ava. And we'll find out what happened to your mother and your father. I promise. We won't stop until we do."

The room was quiet.

Slowly Ava turned to stare at him with her tear-streaked face. "*What* did you just say?"

He looked at her. What had he said? "Won't we?"

Ava frowned. "*Ty ser'yezno?*" She was still staring. "Are you serious?" She sat up suddenly, almost hitting her head on the bunk above her.

"What?" Alex pushed himself up on one elbow.

"What you said." Ava said the words slowly. "*My naydem yevo, Ava. I my uznayem, chto shluchilos' s tvoimi mamoy y papoy. Ya obeshchayu. My ne ostanovimsya, poka my eto ne delayem.*"

Because those had been Alex's exact words. He only thought he had said them in English.

In fact, he hadn't.

What Alex had spoken was perfect Russian.

A language he didn't know he knew.

Der'mo, Alex thought.

Ava was incredulous. "You speak Russian? Why didn't you tell me?"

"Because I don't. I swear I don't. This is crazy!" *Tak s uma.* So crazy.

She laughed in spite of everything, and it echoed through the tiny space. "And yet you just answered another Russian question in Russian."

"*Der'mo,*" Alex said, aloud this time.

"That's so strange." She rolled toward him. "Do you think this is the O.P.U.S.? Maybe you're somehow picking up on Natasha Romanoff too?"

"You mean I'm catching whatever it is the two of you have? Quantum Russian? No." He shook his head. "The Black Widow? How could I have a connection to her? I couldn't. She's a—*mystery* isn't even the right word for it. She might as well be from outer space. I don't understand her at all." He thought about it. "Except the combat part. That I get. She has some great counterattacks."

Ava rolled onto her back, reaching to pick at the bottom of the institutional striped mattress above them. "I don't know. Since the river—since Natasha grabbed my hand—everything seems different in my head. Have you ever felt something like that?"

I've never felt anything like this.

Alex turned toward Ava, laying his head on the pillow next to hers.

Like you.

He knew he was staring but he couldn't help it.

Like me, lying by your side.

"Everything seems different since I met you," he said slowly, without realizing quite what he was saying. Then he turned red, because he did. "But even that doesn't explain my suddenly being able to speak Russian." They were face-to-face now—his lips almost grazed her cheek when he spoke.

She smiled at him. "I guess not."

Alex pulled on a strand of cinnamon curl, studying her profile. She was so beautiful it was almost shocking to see in this depressing gray cell of a room.

How did I get to be here?

He looked at her. "Why did you come over and talk to me like that, in the middle of the tournament? It doesn't seem like something you'd do, now that I know you."

"What, talk?"

"To a stranger? Ava Orlova? No way. You keep to yourself."

"You weren't a stranger. I told you, I thought I knew you." Her eyes looked fleetingly sad, but her smile was soft.

He pulled on another curl. "Yeah, well, I said I thought I knew you—but that didn't mean I did. That only meant I *wanted* to."

"Maybe it was different for me," she said. Then she looked at him. "Do you still? Want to—I mean? You don't think I'm crazy? After I lost it back there?"

"Is that even a question?" Alex asked in Russian, pulling her toward him. She curved into him, warm and soft and welcoming.

Come closer, he thought.

Then she pulled back, smiling. "Even after all this? Getting shot at?"

"Yes." He nudged her and smiled. "Of course."

"Taking a dive off the bridge?" She laced her fingers through his.

"Definitely." Alex was still smiling, and he brought the back of her hand to his lips. His heart was pounding, but he didn't know if it was from nerves or adrenaline.

Probably both.

Ava pretended to think. "Being dragged onto a S.H.I.E.L.D. plane?"

Alex laughed. "That doesn't count; I did the dragging on that one."

She leaned closer to him. "Getting stuck in this hole with me?"

"I think I can handle it." He raised himself toward her. "Life with you is never boring, Ava. You're not like anyone else I've ever known."

"Not like the other girls in Mountain Clear?" She teased.

"Not like anyone on planet Earth," he said, hovering over her.

"I'm going to choose to take that as a compliment."

"Believe me, it is."

She was so close to him now, he could feel her breath burning on his cheek. *God, I want to kiss her.* He drew her even closer. "And who knows? It could be our last night . . ."

He closed his eyes and dropped his lips to hers—

Bad move.

Ava frowned and pulled away, sitting up. *Not yet, Alex.* That was the message, and he understood. She didn't really know him. She didn't trust him. He didn't blame her. He wasn't sure he'd trust himself, either.

He fell back on the mattress. "I shouldn't have said that."

"Why not? It's the truth."

"You don't know that," Alex said.

Ava sighed. "You're just being an optimist. You and Tony Stark."

"I'm not. I'm a realist." He shrugged.

"I don't think you know what the word means."

He took her hand in his again, kissing the back of it once more. "I do. It means I'm *real*-ly happy I met you."

She groaned. "Oh, that was bad."

"How bad? Scale of one to Tony Stark?" He raised an eyebrow.

"It was half a Tony bad." Ava smiled.

"I'll take it."

"Alex?" Now her voice was quiet.

"Yeah?"

"I'm scared."

"I know," Alex said, tightening his arm around her. "We both are. That's okay." *And we're probably not the only ones.*

He didn't even want to think about how worried his mother must be by now. If Dante hadn't already gone to his dad, which was the same as going to the police.

Ava looked at him. "That thing Natasha said back there, about how I lived at the shelter? It's true. I have. But I don't want you to feel sorry for me."

"Nothing's changed, Ava. You're just you."

She leaned over and kissed his cheek in response.

He took a deep breath when she pulled away.

"Ava?"

"Yes?"

I'll wait for you, he thought, as she lay her head back against his shoulder, relaxing for the first time since she'd woken up next to him.

"If I'm catching something, Ava, it's not just Russian."

"I know," she said softly. "We both are. That's okay too."

He rested his cheek on top of her curls. *When you finally do let me kiss you, Ava, maybe I won't ever stop.*

Hours later, it was only when they heard footsteps in the hall outside that they knew their time was running out. Even without Romanoff and Tony Stark around, there were probably more security guards monitoring the hall outside their door than could have fit in the room itself.

Alex felt Ava tense up, next to him. "We have to get out of here before they come back," she said, sitting up.

Romanoff and Tony Stark were still back in the lab. Alex guessed it was late, but it was hard to keep track of time in the perpetually lit underground levels of the S.H.I.E.L.D. base.

"Still. We need a plan, seeing as we have to get past about, I don't know, maybe twenty-five guys? With guns as big as Romanoff's?" Alex rubbed his hand through his tangle of hair—his thinking gesture.

Cutting out of here isn't going to be easy.

"Twenty-two," Ava said automatically. "Guns. In the halls, I mean."

Alex looked at her.

She rolled over to face him. "Two per floor, and we're

eleven floors down. We can take the utility elevator, but even then, that's at least six more guys in the annex, another four if we cut through the west atrium. Thirty-two armed, trained operatives, not including the standard perimeter guards out front."

"So you spent a lot of time around here?" He frowned.

"Not really," she said. Ava closed her eyes. "It must be the—you know—*her*. I don't really understand it myself."

"Ah," Alex said. "Right."

"It's like I can see parts of a movie playing in my head sometimes. Only it's not my movie." She looked at him. "It's hers."

"Which is why she wants you locked up," he said.

She looked him in the eye. "I'm not going back into hiding. Not now, and not tomorrow."

"Back to prison?" Alex said. "I didn't think so."

"I would die. Really. It would kill me." Ava sounded like she meant it, and Alex didn't doubt her. He didn't imagine her life had been easy, and he'd heard enough already to know she had reason enough for everything she felt.

She didn't seem to want to tell him more than that, and he didn't push her. *There's time,* he thought. *She will when she's ready.*

Her voice was dark and low now. "You know what they'll do to me? If they decide I'm too dangerous? What I know, what I've seen?" Ava looked at him. "Have you ever seen an agent get wiped?"

"I've never even seen an agent," Alex said quietly. "Not before today. Why? Is that even a thing S.H.I.E.L.D. can do?"

Ava nodded, almost imperceptibly. She looked like she was going to be sick—and so, so sad. Alex sat up on the bed next to her, so close that he could feel her heart pounding next to his. He slid an arm beneath her, and she pulled closer to him.

"Tell me," he whispered.

She leaned into his chest, as if she couldn't look into his eyes. As if it was all too hard to think, let alone say.

"I spent years in 7B hearing all the gossip on deprogramming and hypnotic suggestion. They're like S.H.I.E.L.D. ghost stories. It isn't only Moscow that knows how to do that. One day you're you, and supposedly, the next day you're—"

She stopped.

"What?" Alex honestly had no idea.

Ava looked up at him now. Her eyes were dark. "Nothing."

"Nothing?" Alex didn't even want to imagine what that would be like, what he would be like, without his mind and his memories.

"Or worse—they tell you you're something that you're not, and you believe them. Their lies. And it doesn't matter, because you'll never know the difference. You might as well already be dead."

Alex stared at her. "Do you believe it? That someone would actually do that?" He shivered.

She just looked at him. "You've met these people. You tell me."

"How about we don't stick around to find out?" Even talking about it made Alex want to bolt.

"And go where?" Ava sighed.

He rested his chin on the top of her head. "My house.

My mom doesn't know her way out of a litter box, but we can ask Dante's dad what to do. My friend's dad is a cop. He's good with stuff like this."

"With Russian mercenaries and Avengers and S.H.I.E.L.D. super spies?"

"Yes. No. I mean—he will be." *I hope.*

Ava raised an eyebrow. "What's your mom going to do when Iron Man and Black Widow show up to nuke our brains? Politely ask them to go away?"

"Talk them to death? Let them hold the cat?" he said, standing up to pace. "Yeah. Okay. We need a plan."

"What if we're making this harder than it is? What if it's simple? What if we just need to solve the whole Ivan Somodorov problem before getting rid of us becomes the solution?"

"Simple? How is that simple?" Alex shook his head. "You're thinking we just solve quantum entanglement? We don't even really know what QE is."

"So there you go. There's our first move."

"What, google *quantum entanglement*? Look for the QE Reddit?"

"Maybe we just have to go back to the beginning."

Alex looked at her. "The beginning of what? And why do I have a bad feeling you're not just talking about the beginning of this weekend?"

Ava shook her head. "I'm talking about the warehouse in Odessa."

"Odessa, Ukraine?" Alex stared.

She nodded.

"And you're serious." Alex was still staring.

Ava shrugged. "Why not? We have nowhere to go, and it's the last place he'll look for us." She grabbed his arm to still him. "Just think about it."

Alex thought about it—but it was hard to sort out what he thought from what he felt. Only one of those two things was perfectly clear.

How do I feel?

I feel like I'd go with her anywhere, anytime.

Ava bit her lip, and he realized she was still waiting for him to say something.

He sat back down beside her and reached over to zip her black S.H.I.E.L.D.-issue jacket up, all the way to her chin.

"Listen," he began.

"Yeah? I'm listening." She smiled.

Be cool, Manor. Don't scare her away. Not yet.

Alex gave up. "I guess it couldn't be worse than Philly." *Except for what my mom will do to me, when I get home. That will be ten times worse.*

He tried not to think about it. It wasn't going to be pretty.

"Philly? You clearly haven't been to Odessa." Ava poked him in the ribs.

Alex let a hand drop on each of her jacketed shoulders. "So, what now?"

"First things first," she said, standing up next to the bed. "We need to take out two guns per floor for eleven floors."

She offered Alex a hand, pulling him up next to her. He sighed. "Great. Is that all?"

"No. After that, we need a cab."

"We have to take out twenty-two guys, and you're worried about getting a cab?"

"This is New York. Transportation can be a real issue."

She hoisted her backpack over her shoulder and put her hand on the doorknob. She looked at him, and he nodded, raising his fists to his chin.

"You go left; I'll go right," Alex said.

She shook her head. "I've got a better idea."

"Hey," Ava called. The S.H.I.E.L.D. agent patrolling each end of the hall snapped to attention. She raised her hands. "It's just me. Can I ask you a favor?"

The agents looked at each other. The one on the left nodded, and they began the short walk down the hall to her door.

Ava pointed to the battered iPod in her hand. "I can't get this thing to work. Can I borrow one of your ear-thingies? So I know if mine are broken?"

"With this?" The agent on her left pointed to his fitted black earpiece.

"Why not?" She examined the jack on her iPod. "It's a kind of speaker, isn't it?"

He shrugged. "I guess." He unclipped it and handed it to her. She jammed it into her ear and plugged the other end into her device.

"Oh, awesome." She nodded, turning up the music. "Thanks, guys." She stepped back inside the door.

"Hey—I need that." The agent leaned in, holding out his hand for his earpiece back.

"Oh yeah. Silly me," she said.

And she slammed the door on the agent's head. The reinforced steel echoed as it made contact with his skull.

CRACK!

The guy went staggering back.

"Sorry, sorry, sorry—" Ava winced.

"What the—" The second agent lunged at her from the corridor.

And this time, Alex slammed his head against the iron frame of the bunk.

SMASH!

"Hurry," she said. They dragged the unconscious bodies into the room.

Alex grunted as he dropped the last booted foot next to the bed. "Jeez. These guys must be eating more than the lousy sandwiches they gave us."

Ava went through the pockets of the first agent. Alex yanked an earpiece off the other agent, jamming it into his ear.

"Got it," she said, holding up a key card. She consulted it. "Thanks . . . Elliot."

"What about those?" Alex looked at the first agent's sidearm.

They both stared, not knowing what to do.

It was Ava who finally spoke. "Take it."

"Really?"

She nodded. "We're going to have to do some shooting, Alex."

He looked at her. "I'm not—"

"I meant the cameras."

He took the gun, and she slammed the door behind them. They were down the hall and at the elevator within twelve seconds. Alex was about to push the button, but Ava grabbed his hand, pointing to her ear.

They're on the way.

Alex nodded.

Ava pushed open the door to the stairs, directly across the hall. She paused. "*Now* you take left; I'll take right."

He grinned.

On the way up, Ava learned three things about herself.

One, she now knew how to disengage a Glock with a drop kick to the wrist. It was a handy skill for this specific circumstance.

Two, she now had a highly developed instinct for avoiding mounted surveillance cameras, even before she and Alex had a chance to shoot them out.

Three, she now knew how to drive a motorboat.

Which she did, all the way to a slip marina halfway to Manhattan.

Tony Stark was right. Being entangled with Natasha Romanoff was not going to be a small thing. That twenty-five-foot jump had only been the beginning.

S.H.I.E.L.D. EYES ONLY

CLEARANCE LEVEL X

LINE-OF-DUTY DEATH [LODD] INVESTIGATION
REF: S.H.I.E.L.D. CASE 121A415
AGENT IN COMMAND [AIC]: PHILLIP COULSON
RE: AGENT NATASHA ROMANOFF A.K.A. BLACK WIDOW,
A.K.A. NATASHA ROMANOVA
TRANSCRIPT: DEPARTMENT OF DEFENSE, LODD INQUIRY HEARINGS.

DOD: Hold up. To be perfectly clear, our two civilian minors have now escaped not only half of that storied global peacekeeping force known as the Avengers Initiative, but also the balance of base security at a S.H.I.E.L.D. Triskeleon?
ROMANOFF: Everyone has an off night, sir.

DOD: Off? Where were you in all this, Agent Romanoff? Off the planet?
ROMANOFF: Stark and I were still focused on trying to sever the Quantum connection, back in the lab.

DOD: So you put your own discomfort over the needs of national security?
ROMANOFF: That "discomfort" was itself a breach of every security protocol S.H.I.E.L.D. has ever put in place, sir.

DOD: Because this QE business gave that girl access to your classified brain?
ROMANOFF: Because this QE business gave her the tools to take out twenty-two highly trained operatives on eleven floors beneath the East River.

DOD: So she became the priority?
ROMANOFF: She always was, sir.

LONG ISLAND CITY CABSTAND QUEENS, NEW YORK

It was the early hours of the morning when the taxi rattled up to a deserted Long Island City cabstand. There wasn't enough gas or gumption to get them all the way to JFK by boat, so Alex and Ava waited on a nearby concrete curb, huddling together for warmth.

The front passenger window rolled down.

"You've lost your mind," Oksana said, staring out at them from the front seat of the battered yellow cab. "Why am I not surprised? I feel like I should be more surprised."

Ava yanked open the door and slid into the back. Alex followed on the other side. Ava leaned forward. "Did you bring it?"

"Under my seat," Oksana said. "And I got all the old fish sticks from the soup-kitchen Dumpster, just like you said. Your precious Sasha Cat should be fine now."

"*Sumasshedshaya*," Sana added, under her breath. Crazy.

Ava reached down and pulled out what looked like a battered old attaché case. She looked relieved. "Can you take us to Kennedy Airport, Mr. Davis?" Oksana's father only nodded, saying nothing as he kept his hands on the wheel and his dark eyes on the rearview mirror, an enameled ballet-shoe charm swaying beneath it. His late wife, Oksana's mother, had been a dancer with a visiting Russian troupe when she had met Oksana's father and defected. Oksana and her father hadn't gotten along since he had remarried, and Oksana had moved out soon after. Now, even when she stayed in the shelter, they still had dinner together every weekend—which was how Ava had known she would have access to the car now.

"And you expect me to believe any of this? That you're being hunted by Moscow?" Oksana rolled her eyes. "That you dropped out of the tournament for reasons of life and death—and not that you were too chicken to compete?"

"*Ty mozesh verit' mne ili ne verit'.*" Believe me or don't. Ava looked out the window.

"Okay, I don't," Oksana said.

"*Ya znayu, chto eto stranno, no ya dolzhen eto sdelat',*" Ava said. I know this is weird, but I have to do it.

"*Ona delayet,*" Alex answered with a sigh. She does.

Oksana glared at him. "Don't do that; it freaks me out. Speak English, Dream Boy."

"Fine. But drop the Dream Boy, thanks?"

"But you're just so *dreamy*," Oksana said, looking at Ava pointedly. Ava turned back to the window.

"Crap. Today's Sunday. I need to call my mom," Alex said suddenly. "Dante and I are supposed to come home. She'll think I've gotten myself into trouble."

Ava looked at him pointedly.

He turned red. "More trouble, I mean. Slot-machines-in-Atlantic-City trouble."

"Not Moscow-assassin trouble?" Oksana raised an eyebrow.

He shook his head. "You don't get my mother."

"I know," Ava said, watching cars streak by on the highway. "I'm sorry."

I remember mothers, she thought. *Bits and pieces of my own. Cinnamon apples. Ballerina dolls. A mug of tea late at night.*

She pushed harder, focusing on the familiar images.

Gray skies. Cold concrete floors. Ceiling tiles covered in tiny dots. The pen stain on my mother's lab coat pocket. Barbed wire looping in cursive circles outside as we walked her to work . . .

Ava tried to hold on to the pieces that she could, but it was getting harder and harder. "We'll get in touch with her as soon as we can," she said, squeezing Alex's hand.

They had made only one call before Ava had slipped the SIM card out of Alex's phone and destroyed it. That was S.H.I.E.L.D. 101, Ava knew.

No SIM card meant no way to track or hijack the cell signal. The one call they did make had gotten them this far, though.

Oksana had come, just as Ava had known she would, no matter how much she complained. Ava had also known that they'd come in Oksana's father's cab—with the trunk where Oksana and Ava kept their most valuable possessions, the things they didn't dare leave in any shelter or borrowed basement.

For Ava, that possession was a S.H.I.E.L.D.-issue attaché case that she'd carried with her since leaving 7B three years ago. And that one bag was the whole reason she had needed Oksana to come now.

As the cab sped toward the airport, Ava stuffed the contents of the old case into her backpack. She had never known when she might need it, but she couldn't take any chances. She had been preparing to disappear for years, and she had the feeling the time to go was finally now.

I'm ready. Even if it's today, I'm ready.

Finally Ava reached over the seat and squeezed her best-and-only friend's shoulder. "Thanks, Sana. We'll come back as soon as we can, I promise."

"*We* will?" Oksana looked annoyed. Ava couldn't blame her. Neither one of them had ever heard that word from Ava's mouth, except when it applied to Oksana herself.

I know, Sana. I'm sorry.

Ava couldn't say the words out loud, but she also couldn't keep from thinking them. Being hunted and shot at and tracked down was strange—but having someone new in her *we* now was even stranger.

She could feel the pressure of Alex's knee against hers, and the familiarity of it made her blush, even in the darkness of the backseat. It was embarrassing, to openly care about someone like this. It felt dangerous, and also painfully, pitifully new.

That it was happening in the middle of such chaos only made it a little easier to pretend to ignore.

Alex changed the subject, looking down at the thick navy booklet in his hands. "This is bananas. I don't even have a passport yet in real life." He couldn't get over the fake passports Ava had produced from inside the innermost pocket of the old attaché case, which had made her smile.

"This is real life, Alex." Ava had spent long enough in 7B to know that the holographic S.H.I.E.L.D.-issued passports she'd stolen from the supply room were only the tip of the iceberg when it came to what the organization could do. They were, in terms of operative tech, not just last year's news, but four years' past news. And S.H.I.E.L.D. years were like dog years in that respect; Ava wouldn't be surprised if they got to passport control only to discover that they set off every alarm in the place with their outmoded tech.

It was a risk they'd have to take.

"This isn't what my real life usually looks like," Alex said. "A big night for me is a night when it's someone else's turn to clean out Stanley's litter box."

Oksana groaned from the front seat.

Ava just smiled. "Well, this isn't anything all that new for me. Trust me." By the time Ava had run away from 7B, she'd known better than to trust anyone with her future, and these passports were part of her official plan. While she couldn't believe she'd had the optimism to steal two—not having ever had an American friend by that point, the second one was strictly wishful thinking—she'd always thought she could barter away the extra for something else she might need.

Thank God she had it now.

Ava steadied herself. "We can't mess this up. I only have two of these, and I don't have a plan B." She held the passport in front of him in the backseat of the cab. A split second later, his face appeared in the box where the photograph was supposed to be.

"Perfect," Ava said, handing it to Alex. "And you really do look like a Peter Peterson."

Alex stared at it. "Peter Peterson? Is that even a real name? Where does S.H.I.E.L.D. get these things?"

"From dead people. And phone directories. And yearbooks," Ava said. He shot her a look, and she shrugged. "What? It's true."

"What do you know about yearbooks?"

Less than I know about dead people, she thought.

But all she said was, "I've seen them on TV."

Alex pocketed the passport. "I still can't believe you just had these lying around."

"I told you. I've been collecting this stuff since I was nine." She didn't let on how deep her collection actually went. The cell-phone microtransmitters and receivers. The latex fingerprint covers and digital face-recognition tech scramblers. Anything she had thought might come in handy when a person wanted or needed to disappear—as she'd always figured she would.

And it wasn't just that Ava had scavenged the biggest

collection of abandoned spy gear in five boroughs—she'd also spent all those years in 7B learning how to steal it, to hack it, and to use it.

Maybe she'd been unknowingly preparing for this moment, all her life. Maybe some part of her had known Ivan the Strange would be back.

Bring it on. I'm ready.

Ava held up her own passport as she spoke, transferring her fingerprints to the sensor inside the cover. "I basically grew up at a S.H.I.E.L.D. field office. I've been ignored by spies since you were in elementary school." Ava flashed her own face onto the passport. "There. Now I'm an American." She held it up and made a peace sign with her other hand. "Taylor Swift! Captain America! Disneyland! Do I look like a Melissa Johnston or what?"

Alex raised an eyebrow. "You're so Johnston it's not even funny. You're practically Minnie Mouse."

Ava held up the last thing she'd stolen, not from S.H.I.E.L.D. but from Tony Stark. She'd found it inside a hollowed-out copy of *Break from Chaos* in his open briefcase, which was something closer to a tool kit, only made of fine Roman leather—a thick clip of hundred-dollar bills. She shook her head. "Billionaires and S.H.I.E.L.D. agents. They always come so prepared. Always ready to take off, I guess."

Alex eyed it. "Looks like someone isn't planning to take a break from chaos yet."

Oksana was wide-eyed, and Ava thrust a wad of bills up to the front seat before she could even ask. "Are those... real?"

"Yes," Ava nodded. "And believe me, they won't be missed."

"Are they yours?" Oksana swallowed.

"No. Now they're yours." Ava's eyes met her friend's. "Take it." More than that, they didn't even have to say out loud.

What have you done, Myshka?

Something I can't undo, Sana.

But then there was no more time to worry, because the lights of JFK Airport were blaring in her eyes, and the cab pulled over in front of a doorway marked INTERNATIONAL DEPARTURES, and suddenly she was standing at the curb with her only friend in the world.

As Oksana threw her arms around her, Ava pressed a small, black object into her hand. "It's a burner phone. Old, but international and untraceable. There's a number in it. Call us if anything weird happens. Then trash it."

"Weird? How weird? You mean, weirder than this delusion of yours?"

"Sana, I'm not kidding. Strange things have been going on all week. I don't want you to get dragged into my mess."

"I'm already in your mess. Your mess is my mess."

"Just lay low. Maybe stay at your dad's." Ava kissed Oksana on each cheek. "Just make sure to take care of Sasha Cat for me, will you?"

Oksana nodded.

Alex followed with an awkward one-cheek kiss. "Uh, bye." He looked her in the eye. "You're a good friend, Sana."

"Americans." Oksana rolled her eyes. Still, Ava noticed she was smiling as she got back into the car.

Ava shouldered her backpack and stared up at the Kennedy international terminal looming in front of them, Alex by her side.

She heard the cab door slam, and felt a surge of panic.

What if this is good-bye?

What if something happens, and I never see her again?

Ava turned back and shouted, "You never told me. How did you do, Oksana? At the tournament?"

A hand shot up out of the passenger window as the cab jerked back into the traffic—waving a gold medal in the air, before disappearing again.

Ava laughed. Even Alex smiled.

A gold medal for Sana.

Maybe, finally, a good omen for all of us.

Then, without another word, Alex and Ava took each other by the hand and disappeared into the crowd, leaving everything as familiar as an old yellow cab far, far behind them.

S.H.I.E.L.D. EYES ONLY

CLEARANCE LEVEL X

LINE-OF-DUTY DEATH [LODD] INVESTIGATION
REF: S.H.I.E.L.D. CASE 121A415
AGENT IN COMMAND [AIC]: PHILLIP COULSON
RE: AGENT NATASHA ROMANOFF A.K.A. BLACK WIDOW,
A.K.A. NATASHA ROMANOVA
TRANSCRIPT: DEPARTMENT OF DEFENSE, LODD INQUIRY HEARINGS.

DOD: When did you see they were gone? What was the tip-off?
ROMANOFF: You mean, beyond the pile of unconscious S.H.I.E.L.D.
operatives? The disabled security cameras? The four stolen assault
rifles dumped without magazines at the entrance to the Triskeleon?

DOD: A miscalculation by any standard, Agent.
ROMANOFF: It's hard to believe it, but I didn't know, sir. What she
was capable of, and how quickly she could make her move.

DOD: But why did you seek out Mr. Stark—why did you come to the
Triskeleon base at all, Agent Romanoff?
ROMANOFF: It was coincidence, sir. I needed a secure computer.

DOD: So this link between you, it was more than just some kind of
on-and-off switch into your brain?
ROMANOFF: I could never feel it, sir. Not from my side.

DOD: Let me get this straight. This stray little waif, this homeless
Russian orphan, could infiltrate an experienced, decorated
operative's entire mind without her even once glimpsing what
she was doing?
ROMANOFF: Something like that.

CHAPTER **20**: AVA

UKRAINE AERO TICKETING COUNTER KENNEDY INTERNATIONAL AIRPORT— QUEENS, NEW YORK

"Two tickets to Odessa. Leaving as soon as possible," Ava said to the woman behind the Ukraine Aero counter. Her eyes flickered to the security cameras at ten and two o'clock. She angled her face down by forty-five degrees. Alex did the same, right behind her, as if on cue. After the way they had left the Triskeleon, they weren't taking any chances."

We have to get out of these clothes.

Black Widow's probably got eyes on us already.

Ava closed her eyes and tried to feel some kind of connection to Natasha Romanoff. She couldn't. However the quantum link worked, she didn't yet know how to control it.

Or how to use it to keep her away from me.

Ava realized she was holding her breath, and she reached for Alex's hand beneath the counter. He grabbed it, and she felt her insides begin to unclench.

The attendant at the computer looked up. "You'll have to stop in Moscow. There's a flight departing in fifty-five minutes, but I only have business class."

"We'll take it," Alex said from behind Ava, in Russian.

"We will?" Ava sounded surprised. She had almost forgotten he could speak it.

"Of course. It's a family emergency. Our baba's on her deathbed. We need to sleep while we can." Alex shrugged, continuing on in rapid Russian.

Ava tried not to smile. His accent was aristocratic, almost too perfect. Every time he opened his mouth, she wanted to start laughing at the ridiculousness of it all.

"Besides, our baba always hated economy travel." Alex put his hand on her shoulder sympathetically. "Do it for her."

The airline representative looked at them quizzically.

Ava counted out half the fat roll of Tony Stark's hundred-dollar bills, shaking her head. "If you say so, brother. We don't want to disappoint Baba."

The flight attendant eyed the pile of cash. Alex didn't blame her—it was the most cash he'd ever seen in his life.

"Papers, please," she finally said, clicking her long nails against the keys of a computer that seemed older than the airport itself.

Ava handed over their passports, and the woman examined

them. Then shrugged. If there was something fishy going on here, she didn't want to know about it. She pushed two airline tickets across the counter. "I'm sorry for your loss."

"Don't be sorry yet," Alex said. "Our baba's a fighter. Now, do these tickets get us into the lounge?" He smiled innocently. "And are there showers?"

The attendant raised an eyebrow.

"Not the lounge," Ava hissed, pulling him away by his backpack. "Another ticket counter. We're not done yet."

"We're not?"

"You think we can just buy a ticket to Ukraine without raising a few S.H.I.E.L.D. flags? They're probably on their way now."

Alex hadn't considered it. "Good point, *moya malen'kaya* Romanoff. So we have more tickets to buy?"

"Little Romanoff? I'm not a little Romanoff. But yes." Ava pulled out the roll of stolen bills again. It was still pretty thick, even if it wouldn't be for long. "I hope this is enough."

"What, are you going to buy a ticket to every airport in Eastern Europe?" Alex asked, eyeing the money.

"Maybe. Or maybe one on every continent. Can't be too careful. I grew up with spies—get used to it."

"I'm starting to."

Thirty minutes and eight airline tickets later—not to mention two more unused fares on the connector shuttle between Kennedy and Newark Airport—Ava found herself trying on a baseball cap at the Hudson News nearest to their gate.

Black, nylon. I ♥ NY. Cheap and scratchy. It would have to do. Their flight would be boarding soon.

Ava looked in the mirror, adjusting the Harley-Davidson sweatshirt she'd bought across the terminal. The S.H.I.E.L.D. sweatpants could stay. She checked the crowd behind her for the fifth time in as many minutes.

One TSA agent. Two JFK Airport police.

One big Chinese tour group.

Nothing too obvious. No one doubling back.

No one appearing twice.

No familiar faces from the other side of the security line.

Alex appeared behind her in the mirror.

She jumped, startled. "Don't do that."

"Just wanted to show you my sweet new lid." He grinned. "Am I right?"

He had changed into a navy blue knit cap with a Captain America shield on it and had pulled a red New Jersey Devils jersey over his jacket.

"Really?" Ava just stared. "You thought those would help you blend in?"

"There's no Captain Ukraine," Alex pointed out. "Plus, this is a hockey jersey. The whole world loves hockey."

"Sure they do." Ava handed him a sweatshirt with the outline of a whale on it. "Now take it off."

"That? No. That's like what half my school in Montclair is probably wearing right now."

Ava smiled. "So? That's a good thing, right? You'll blend right in."

"No. No whales. I have my principles. How about the Islanders?" Alex sighed, pulling the jersey over his head. "As much as it kills me, at least that one's blue."

"Done."

Ava paused as the TSA agent walked past her, slapping a pack of gum on the counter. She grabbed the Islanders jersey from Alex, lowering her voice as she did. "Now your shoes," she said, looking down at his feet.

"What about them?" he whispered back.

"Get rid of them," she hissed.

His voice grew louder. "Are you kidding me?"

She shot him a look.

He lowered his voice again, whispering loudly, "Who buys *shoes* at the airport?"

The TSA agent left. She put her cap down on the counter and yanked Alex's off his head. "We'll take these."

She turned back to Alex, keeping her voice down as she spoke. "You don't think an agent like Romanoff noticed your shoes? The first thing she's going to do is alert the Feds to look for a kid in Nike fencing sneakers."

"You think?"

Ava shrugged. "She knows it's harder to get new shoes than a cap or a sweatshirt. I'm surprised we even made it through security without getting pulled. She must really be off her game." She pulled a hundred-dollar bill out of Tony's money clip. "Shoes. Off."

"Fine," he said.

Ava glanced at the cashier, a surly-looking bald man trying his best to ignore her. "Excuse me. Do you know where my boyfriend could get new shoes?"

"That's right. I'm her boyfriend." Alex grinned.

The cashier didn't look up from sorting a pile of receipts. "Mazel tov."

"He just stepped in something really gross," Ava improvised. "You know. I guess someone really doesn't like to fly."

"Just clean them off in the bathroom," the cashier said, still not looking up. "That's what I do."

Ugh, disgusting. Ava frowned. "We tried."

The cashier grunted and pointed to a boutique across the way. "Only shoes in the terminal." Then he looked at her. "Seriously. Who buys shoes at an airport?"

"See?" Alex said.

"Size twelve," Alex said to the saleswoman. "And we're in a hurry." Ava leaned against the open glass doorway, tallying the faces that passed by in the crowded terminal.

Restroom attendant. Another cop, different badge.

Gate agent. Mother with stroller. Teen taking selfies.

No familiar faces. We're good.

"Our sizes are French," a bored-looking saleswoman said. She had a scarf twisted around her neck in a complicated knot that made Ava tired looking at it.

"Yeah?" Alex just looked at her. "So are my fries."

She frowned.

Alex shrugged. "Just a joke. Sorry, that would have been funnier if we'd actually had time to go to Five Guys, like I wanted to."

"Alex," Ava warned. She averted her eyes as two police officers suddenly stopped in front of the boutique.

Come on, guys. Why would cops want to hang out here? You're just blocking my view.

She pretended to try on a scarf in a mirror until they moved on. Then she put the scarf down on the counter behind her, noticing the price. "Is that for real?" She looked incredulously at the saleswoman.

Now two Chinese-looking girls floated into the store, chattering away in Mandarin.

Mainlanders. Accent sounds like Chengdu.

"Cute boy." The first girl looked at Alex.

"Do you think that's his sister or his girlfriend?"

Ava pushed her hand against her head. Natasha Romanoff must have pretty decent Mandarin. *Because you shouldn't even know that was Mandarin, on your own.*

You have your hands full with English.

The saleswoman ignored Ava, looking at Alex. "The shoes. What style?"

He shrugged. "Style? Something with good, you know, grip. That I can run in. And that won't slip if I only have one foot on the ground."

The saleswoman raised an eyebrow. "Where would the other one be?"

"In someone's face," he said. "Or maybe a door."

The saleswoman looked at him blankly.

"Alex," Ava said from the doorway, her eyes still on the passing crowd—and him—and the Chinese girls—and every security camera within fifty yards.

Alex smiled. "Just a joke. See? I got you again."

"Look. He's looking at shoes," one of the girls said still in Mandarin.

"Who buys shoes at the airport?" The other laughed.

Ava shook her head, picking up a belt from the counter. She kept listening—if only because it was hard to turn it off.

"And why is a TSA agent shopping at Hermès? How well does the TSA pay in New York?"

"Americans are so crazy."

Ava froze.

TSA guy? He was back? Again?

She angled slightly to see a man in a TSA jacket looking at a display of ties lying across a glass counter behind her. She couldn't see his face.

Is he the same one from Hudson News? Is he our tail?

The saleswoman pulled out a bright orange box with neat brown trim and placed it in front of Alex.

"Perfect," Ava said. "We'll take them."

The woman looked surprised. "That's only the box. Don't you want to look at the shoes?"

"No, we have to go," Ava said.

Alex looked at her curiously.

Ava inclined her head toward the TSA agent in the back of the shop.

Alex's eyes flickered in his direction.

Ava slung her arm around Alex, flirtatiously. Whispered into his ear, in Russian. "Do you see a gun?"

He nuzzled her cheek, whispering—also in Russian. "No, but that doesn't mean it's not there."

"What should we do about it?" Ava whisper-kissed back. She watched TSA guy's reflection in the mirrored wall as he moved toward a row of large umbrellas, practically weapons themselves. *Great.*

"Get a room," said one of the Mandarin-speaking girls.

"Really," said the other.

The saleswoman opened the shoe box. Inside was a pair of white high-tops with orange-and-black trim and a silver buckle. "Calfskin. Eleven hundred fifty before tax. The Quantum. That's the name of the shoe."

"Quantum?" Alex asked. "Wait, that's the name? Really?"

"Dollars?" Ava asked. "Wait, that's the price? Really?"

Alex looked at Ava.

The two Chinese girls looked at each other and giggled, leaning in to get a better look at the shoes.

And then the first girl grabbed Ava's head with both hands, slamming her forehead against the glass counter in front of her—

While the second pushed off against the counter to drop-kick both boots into Alex's gut.

"Chush' sobach'ya!" Ava cursed, yanking her head back up as hard and as fast as she could, until she made contact with her attacker's skull.

THWACK!

Ava heard a loud cracking noise, and the girl dropped to the floor.

The TSA agent looked startled, falling halfway into a row of umbrellas, clutching at his pack of chewing gum.

"*Chyort voz'mi!*" Alex cursed back, grabbing the girl's booted feet while they were still lodged in his side, hurling her into a steel-framed hanging coatrack of expensive-looking cashmere coats.

CRASH!

The girl grabbed the rack with both hands, swinging her legs out to catch either side of Alex—but he twisted until she hit the edge of the rectangular steel rail—

THUD!

—and dropped motionless into a pile of coats.

The saleswoman hit the alarm, loud and piercingly shrill.

Alex straightened, picking up his backpack. "Really? Now?"

Ava dumped the sneakers out of the box and grabbed a random pair of shoes off the counter. "Change of plans. We'll take these. . . ."

"Loafers?" Alex made a face.

"They've seen the others." She pulled a handful of bills out of her pocket. "Let's get out of here."

"Are you all right? I'm so sorry." The saleswoman shook her head, shouting over the noise. "If you wait for a minute, we can file a police report."

"Sorry, plane to catch!" Alex shouted back, dropping the shoes and jamming his feet into them.

"She must have really wanted those Quantums. Eleven fifty is pretty steep for some people—maybe she thought she could try to shoplift them and run?"

The money was on the counter and the shoes were out the door before the woman could stop him.

Twenty minutes later they were somewhere in the air over the Atlantic.

S.H.I.E.L.D. EYES ONLY

CLEARANCE LEVEL X

LINE-OF-DUTY DEATH [LODD] INVESTIGATION
REF: S.H.I.E.L.D. CASE 121A415
AGENT IN COMMAND [AIC]: PHILLIP COULSON
RE: AGENT NATASHA ROMANOFF A.K.A. BLACK WIDOW,
A.K.A. NATASHA ROMANOVA
TRANSCRIPT: DEPARTMENT OF DEFENSE, LODD INQUIRY HEARINGS.

DOD: So tracking their airline tickets was a dead end?
ROMANOFF: Not a dead end. But we didn't have a read on the stolen passports until much later, so we didn't know what names they were traveling under. All we had was facial recognition software and a whole lot of real-time JFK security footage.

DOD: From a girl who knows how to avoid security cameras.
ROMANOFF: Exactly. If Ivan hadn't already had muscle in every New York airport, it would have been even harder. But he had eyes on the airports, and we had eyes on his eyes—

DOD: And you were all looking for Ava?
ROMANOFF: One way or another.

DOD: But Ivan's guys found her first?
ROMANOFF: He tried to have two Triad pick her up at Kennedy.

DOD: How did that pan out?
ROMANOFF: It didn't. But it gave us one critical detail. We knew we were now looking for a boy in a pair of Richie Rich high-tops.

DOD: Funny how it always comes down to the shoes, doesn't it?

S.H.I.E.L.D. TRISKELEON BASE
THE GREAT CITY OF NEW YORK—
EAST RIVER

rounded for life,"
Natasha said. She'd made her way out to the perimeter
of the base, but then retreated back to Tony's disaster
scene of a lab to scroll through security footage. Four
fully trained operatives had been hauled away by medics.
When they had come back to consciousness, they'd been
more embarrassed than anything else, but that didn't
change the situation: Natasha was furious. "Both of
them."

Grounded? What are you saying, Romanoff?

You've taken out men for less.

"Sure. You do that. But first you'll have to find them,"
Tony said, watching the footage.

Natasha rewound, stopping the tape at the moment where Ava borrowed the headset from the guard. "Look. She's faking him out—drawing him in—closing the distance. And—boom. He's down."

It was a good move, clever and fast, which only made her angrier.

That ridiculous little—

Natasha slammed her hand on the keyboard. "Sociopath. That's what she is."

"Really? Sociopath? The kid?" Tony snorted. "Who do you think invented that move?"

"Shut up."

Not now, Tony.

She didn't want to hear it. Even if she knew he was right.

"Come on. It's textbook Natasha Romanoff. You know it is." Tony laughed.

"It's not funny."

Infuriating. Embarrassing. Humiliating. Irritating. Rude, even.

Just not funny.

"It's a little funny. That Natasha Romanoff finally meets her match—and it's what basically amounts to *another* Natasha Romanoff?" Tony grinned. "I'm personally enjoying the irony."

Natasha dropped into a chair in front of a plasma screen. "Met my match? Please. I'll have them back here in twenty minutes—and then I'll make sure they're both locked up for twenty years."

At least.

Longer, if Tony can't fix the wonder-twin brain leak.

Tony shrugged. "We both know you won't do that, Romanoff. But they don't know you won't. That's probably why they took off."

Natasha frowned. "Why do you say that?"

"Because you're standing here talking to me, right? You're not calling in the cavalry. You're not even ringing up Coulson, and that's usually your first move."

He's right. Why aren't I? Because I don't know who to trust? Or so they don't get into even more trouble?

"I don't need Coulson or the cavalry," Natasha said finally. "Please, I'm my own cavalry."

Tony sighed, putting down his screwdriver for a moment. "What you need to understand, N-Ro, is who you're dealing with. A teenager. I might be able to help you with that. According to Pepper, I haven't matured much past one."

"I can't imagine why."

"You backed her into a corner and she ran. Sound familiar?"

Of course.

"You're one to talk." Natasha glared.

Tony shrugged. "I'm a runner. You're a runner. I'm not judging. I get it."

"They both ran. And I didn't back *him* into a corner."

"Ah, well, his motivations are a different story. The oldest story in the book, maybe, but a different story. Boy meets girl and finds her . . . motivating." Tony grinned. "I know that feeling." He leaned forward. "I, too, enjoy some occasional *motivation*."

"You are just so *classy*." Natasha rolled her eyes. "And you're not helping."

"Have it your way."

"Look. It's not rocket science. I'll just do what I would normally do. Start with a trace. Alex has a phone, right?" She sounded determined as she opened a connection to S.H.I.E.L.D.'s mainframe. "First stop, the New York Phone Company."

Natasha sat back in her chair. "No signal. Not detecting a SIM card."

Der'mo!

"Good for them. They trashed the phone."

She sat up. "Okay. Facial recognition." She hit the keys again. "We'll search every airport, every train station. They can't have avoided every security camera in the tristate area."

Tony looked amused. "Really? Because I've seen you do it. Why couldn't she?"

Natasha frowned at the screen. "She'll make a mistake. It's just—well, I'm not getting anything yet."

Der'mo der'mo—

"Right."

She sighed and returned to the keyboard. "Fine. I can just search passenger manifests. Airlines. Trains. Bus lines."

"Yeah?"

Her hands flew. "Got it. She's on her way to . . . Tokyo." Natasha smirked. "Easy. I can be at Narita before they land."

"Really?" Tony pointed back at the screen. "Because your little blinker-thingy is going off again."

Natasha looked back at the screen. "And Heathrow. And . . . Moscow. And São Paulo. And Panama. And Budapest. And Paris." Her face was growing redder by the moment.

Der'mo der'mo der'mo—

Tony grinned. "Come on. Aren't you the teensiest bit proud of them? And they say kids today lack initiative." He shook his head. "It's great to see the next generation learning from their elders."

"This is ridiculous." Natasha sat back in her chair. She didn't know where else to begin. "It's like she's using all my own tricks against me."

"Of course she is. She literally is. Those *are* your tricks. Because she has access into your brain, Romanoff."

But she can't do it forever.

Just like you can't hide from yourself forever, Natasha.

She shivered, pushing away the thought. She'd let Ava rattle her enough already. "Stop with the shrink talk, Stark. All of this only means she's progressed more than we thought." Natasha stood. "I've got to find them. Now."

Tony picked up a half-burned-out hard drive from the steel lab table in front of him. "I'll keep looking into the QE tech. You find Mini-me and Romeo. Just saying, it might take more than twenty minutes, though."

She grabbed her jacket.

Tony looked up. "Just don't do what you would normally do. That's what she knows."

Natasha paused at the door. "What else can I do?"

"Look at it as a chance to change things up. Be someone new." He shrugged again. "Who knows? You might find a whole new bag of tricks." The drive in front of him erupted into sparks. Tony frowned. "Or not."

"Great pep talk."

"Anytime."

S.H.I.E.L.D. EYES ONLY

CLEARANCE LEVEL X

LINE-OF-DUTY DEATH [LODD] INVESTIGATION
REF: S.H.I.E.L.D. CASE 121A415
AGENT IN COMMAND [AIC]: PHILLIP COULSON
RE: AGENT NATASHA ROMANOFF A.K.A. BLACK WIDOW,
A.K.A. NATASHA ROMANOVA
TRANSCRIPT: DEPARTMENT OF DEFENSE, LODD INQUIRY HEARINGS.

// REQUESTED APPENDICES

S.H.I.E.L.D. FIELD BULLETIN

OUT TO ALL OPERATIVES

<< MISSING MINOR ASSETS>>
<<AGENT ROMANOFF, NATASHA>>
<<EYES ON ORLOVA, AVA / MANOR, ALEX>>
<<ASSUME TRAVELING UNDER ALIAS / ALIAS UNKNOWN>>
<<SPOTTED ON FLIGHT MANIFESTS FOR: ROME FIUMICINO–
LONDON HEATHROW–AMSTERDAM SCHIPHOL–
MOSCOW SHEREMETYEVO–RIO DE JANEIRO GALEÃO–
PANAMA TOCUMEN –TOKYO NARITA–ISTANBUL ATATÜRK–
SINGAPORE CHANGI>>
<<TICKETS PURCHASED IN CASH>>
<<NO CC TRACKING>>
<<NO CELL/SAT TRACKING>>
<<DETAIN UPON SIGHT>>

CHAPTER **22**: ALEX

UKRAINE AERO FLIGHT 649— BUSINESS CLASS CABIN SOMEWHERE OVER THE ATLANTIC OCEAN

ive hours into the flight, Alex still wasn't sleeping. He was staring straight up at the ceiling, one arm tucked beneath his head. A pair of abandoned loafers beneath his reclined seat.

He watched Ava squirm in the seat next to him, trying to get comfortable. She had dutifully accepted every offering from every flight attendant, she had marveled at every warm nut or curl of cocktail shrimp, and her tray table was littered with empty cranberry juices. But there was nothing comfortable about where they were now or where they were headed—not even in business class.

Finally Ava gave up, righting herself in her seat. She looked exhausted and ragged, but even still she couldn't sleep. The stress was starting to wear her down, and Alex wished he could do something to help.

"Tell me something," she said, curling against the plastic console that lay between them. He wished it weren't there.

"Anything you want to know," Alex said. He meant it.

He wasn't too great at talking to girls, but he had been thinking about her ever since they'd boarded the plane. Even when he closed his eyes he found he could see her, as clearly as if he were looking at her still. It was all he could do to sit next to her without reaching out and taking her into his arms, pulling her close—

"How about—the dog?" Ava mumbled, closing her eyes again.

"The what?" He hadn't been expecting that.

A cat, maybe. A dog? Yeah, right.

"Your dog. You had a dog, didn't you?" She was half asleep now. "Brown, and kind of mangy. You snuck him food. . . ."

Alex sighed. "I wish. I never had a dog."

"You did."

"I always wanted one, but my mom's a cat person. And that's putting it mildly."

"Weird. I could have sworn you had a dog." Ava opened her eyes again. "Potatoes," she said suddenly. "He liked potatoes."

"Who did?"

"Your dog. You fed him off your plate."

Alex looked at her strangely. "Except he's a cat and his name is Stanley and he has his own plate. With Santa Paws on it."

She looked amused. "Really? Santa Paws?"

"And a different custom collar for every holiday. This one has—wait for it—jingle bells."

"So no dog?"

"No dog."

Ava sat up, her hair tousled. "Hmm. I don't know. Did you always live in Mountain Clear?"

"Montclair? No. My mom never talks about it anymore, but I grew up in Vermont. I still dream about the trees in our old backyard. The trees and the snow."

He didn't mention that the dreams were nightmares, or that he was being chased into banks of snow higher than his head, sometimes while people were shooting at him. Sometimes the snow was spattered with his own blood. He figured Ava had enough nightmares of her own without having to hear about his.

"And then?"

"Then, the most boring story on earth. My parents split up and New Jersey happened. My mom became a travel agent. And, of course, a cat person, but I think we've covered that."

"But you're not. How did that happen?"

"She says I was switched at birth. We have basically nothing in common."

"She's not the Black Card type?"

"Not at all. She's not exactly looking for a fight."

"And you are?"

He shrugged.

Ava looked at him.

"What happened to your dad?"

"I don't know. I guess he left, and she just gave up on everything."

"Even your dog?"

"No dog, crazy." Alex looked past Ava, out into the aisle of the plane. "But I'll ask her if we had one that I've forgotten from when I was little. As soon as I get home. Or, you know. Call." He looked at his watch. It was Sunday afternoon in New Jersey now.

My mom's freaking out. She's calling Dante's dad. Dante's probably covering for me. He won't believe any of this, but I still wish I could tell him.

Then Alex felt a warm hand slip inside his own. "*Brat,*" Ava said suddenly, looking at him.

"Who, me?" His eyes were twinkling. "I'm insulted."

She shook her head with a smile. "I remember now. That was your dog's name."

Alex looked at her strangely. This whole conversation was quickly getting very weird. "How would you happen to know that I even had a dog? Let alone his name?"

"Brat?"

"And what kind of name is Brat, anyway?"

"Not brat. *Brat.* In Russian," she said, looking at him. "Think about it. Try to remember."

Alex leaned back on his seat tiredly. "Brat."

What is there to remember?

What kind of dog is Brat?

Brown, he thought suddenly.

He thought of brown fur, brown eyes, a brown nose.

Brown everything.

And warm.

He felt a warm heart beating and a warm furry lump curling up in his bed.

A ceramic dish brimming with dried kibble and breakfast potatoes.

The warm spot on the carpet beneath the ottoman, for sleeping.

A knotted length of rope, chewed soft as cabbage—

"Brother," Alex said suddenly. He sat up. "*Brat* means brother. Because that dog was like my brother."

"Do you remember? Really?" Ava's eyes were wide. She smiled. "I knew I wasn't imagining it."

Alex felt at once more confused and more certain. In his mind, doors were opening in places he didn't even know to look for them.

"When I was alone, that dog was the only family I had," he said slowly.

It was unsettling, but still somehow real.

I really did have a dog.

He looked at Ava. "How could I forget that? And why don't I remember my mom being there? Or even my dad, if it was so long ago?" Alex ran his hand through a lock of dark hair.

"People forget things," she said. "Even dogs."

It was making his head ache. He didn't want to think about it, but he had the strangest feeling that he should— the feeling that even a long-lost dog was somehow very important.

And that Ava was somehow connected to all of it.

He studied her face now.

"You didn't." He watched the shadows fall back over her eyes. "How do you remember anything about me, Ava? We've never met. I'm pretty sure of that. So how do you know things about me that I don't even remember?"

"Alex," Ava said slowly. "Sometimes I remember much, much more than that."

Alex looked at her, and by the look on her face he could tell that this was about something other than just a dog.

"You mean like how you know things about Natasha Romanoff? Or like how I know Russian?"

She nodded. The words came slowly and with great difficulty. "My dreams aren't always just about her." She looked up at him. "And they didn't just start now."

"Who are your dreams about? Besides the dog?" The realization dawned on him. "Wait—you mean me?"

Ava nodded again.

"What are you saying?" Alex was trying to push the pieces together in his mind, but he couldn't. There were too many of them, and they were too broken. Nothing made anything close to sense.

"I dreamed you," she said. "About you. Before I even met you."

He tried to logically process what she was saying, even if it wasn't rational. "Like a premonition?"

Ava shrugged. "A little more than that." She paused, staring at his face as if she were searching for something.

He wished he knew what.

"I used to think of it as destiny," she finally said, so softly that he had to lean close even to hear.

"The dreams?"

"Not just the dreams." Ava blushed. "It's stupid; I know it is. A person can't be a destiny." Alex watched the flush of her cheeks as it deepened from pink to red.

He still didn't quite get what she was saying, but he could see how important it was to her. And how nervous she seemed, how badly she wanted him to understand.

Help me, Ava.

Help me put the pieces together.

I want to remember.

I want to know everything.

Especially you.

"Destiny, eh?" He tucked a stray copper curl behind her ear. "How do you know what a destiny looks like?"

Then she took a breath. "Here. It's probably better if I just show you. Just don't freak out, okay?" She reached down to the backpack at her feet and pulled out what looked like a tattered old notebook. "I've never shown anyone but Oksana."

She put it in his lap and waited for him to open it. He only had to see the first sketch to understand why she was so unnerved.

"That's me?" He studied it. "That is me. And there's Brat. And the forest behind—I think it was our old house. I think I remember the forest. I've dreamed about that too. This is incredible."

The trees and the snow.

The ones from my nightmares.

Alex shivered and looked more closely. "That *is* Brat. No wonder you remembered him. God, these are incredible. You're an amazing artist."

Ava didn't respond. She could barely look at him, and he realized how difficult this was for her. How private she was. *Ava can't stand people looking through her underwear drawer any more than Natasha Romanoff can.*

His head was still pounding as he took in the sketches. *Maybe neither can I.*

As he turned the pages, the immense scope of what he was looking at struck him over and over again—like some kind of ancient church bell, ringing for the first time in years.

"But I don't remember most of this," he said slowly. The realization was still coming. "Why can't I?"

"I don't know," Ava said. "Why can I?"

He looked up from the sketchbook. "How could you possibly know more about my life than I do?"

"It doesn't make much sense to me, either."

Alex flipped through the pages, seeing the sketches without really seeing them. It was all he could do to make sense of the words in his own head.

She remembers things I don't know myself.

Things that happened to me years ago.

He turned another page.

How?

He flipped the page again.

And how is this real, either? How am I on a plane to Ukraine? Sitting with a girl who sees my life in her dreams?

He felt her hand on his arm.

And why doesn't this seem weirder than it does?

"Are you okay, Alex?"

"I'll be fine." Alex took a steadying breath and turned back to both Ava and the book. "This is my house in Montclair. Where I live now."

"That's what I thought." She smiled. "Mountain Clear. I should fix the caption. But did I get the house right?"

"Perfectly." He studied the drawing more closely. "You've pulled off a weird perspective, though. You'd basically have to be standing on the roof of the house across the street to see it like that." He smiled at her. "Have you been climbing the Flanagans' roof again?"

"You caught me," she said, mustering a smile.

He moved to another image.

"This one, this just happened."

"That's right. A few days ago."

"Sofi's party. On Dante's back porch. This one looks like you drew it from all the way at the end of their yard, where the hedge is." He shook his head. "Which is only weird because I thought I heard someone out there that night."

"Busted again." She smiled. "I've been living in Dante's hedge for three years now. He's not too observant."

"Tell me about it."

Now Alex studied a sketch of himself on the fencing strip. "So first you dreamed me. Then you just, what? Found me? Bumped into me at the NAC?"

Ava nodded slowly. "I wasn't expecting to. I was as surprised as you were."

"Which is why you said I looked familiar?" He looked back down at the massive sketchbook. "Because I did. Of course I did." He reached out and took her hand, even as he kept turning the pages. "How is this possible?"

"How is anything that's been happening lately possible?"

Alex didn't answer. He was examining a sketch of the Odessa warehouse. Now the surrounding docks. Now a city in winter. Now crumbling gray buildings and twisting streets. "And these?"

"Just bits of things I remember. My old home, mostly."

"So that's where we're headed now? Home to Odessa. That's crazy. I've never even left the country before this."

Ava looked at him wistfully. "I don't know if Odessa is my home. I barely remember it, except in pieces. Even then it's mostly things I don't want to remember. Nightmares. The warehouse. Soldiers. Ivan Somodorov. I don't know if I want to think of that as my home. Maybe nowhere is, now."

Alex understood. "So it's just a place you once lived. Sometimes I feel that way about New Jersey." He tried to get her to smile.

"It's a place I know my mother worked with Ivan Somodorov. And also the last place I saw my father." Her eyes were dark.

He squeezed her hand. "Also the last place you saw any of them, right?"

Ava nodded.

"And your mother was a scientist?"

"Both of my parents were, for the government. Quantum physicists. My mother was even head of a lab. Before Ivan took me away." She reached over to flip a few pages. "That's her. My mother."

Ava pulled an old photo of her mother loose from the page. In the picture—once black-and-white, now yellowing with age—she was standing on the docks.

"She was beautiful," Alex said. "She looked a lot like you."

"Maybe she did. I hope so. I tell myself she did," Ava said, handing him the photograph.

He flipped the picture over in his hand. There was one word written on the reverse side of the photograph, in fading pencil.

Odessa.

There could be no turning back now.

But as Ava's head settled against his shoulder, Alex knew it didn't matter. Not for him. He wasn't going anywhere without her. Not if he could help it.

Because Ava was wrong. Sometimes a person could be a destiny.

Sometimes there was no difference at all.

Ava didn't move her head from Alex's shoulder, not even when she heard his breathing fade into sleep. Not even when it turned to something halfway between a snort and a snore.

She found she still couldn't move. She couldn't do anything but think, because she had realized something. Something important, she thought. Alex was the one who had made her see it.

The one similarity in all her sketches. The odd distance,

the removed perspective.

The barrier that could never be crossed.

She never drew herself into the picture. Most of the time, she wasn't even in the same plane as Alex but at a noticeably different height or distance or even angle.

She had come to think of it romantically, as the space between the two of them—between living and dreaming, the real and the imaginary, real life and Tattoo Boy.

Now she wasn't so sure.

You'd basically have to be standing on the roof of the house across the street . . .

Check. Possible.

I thought I heard someone out there that night.

Check. Also possible.

Think. The one with the black gloves.

Check. She didn't know why she hadn't recognized them earlier.

The one with the gun.

Check. The pistol. The one she carried at her waist.

I'm not spying on Alex. But I think I know who is.

Natasha Romanoff. It's always been Natasha Romanoff.

Ava had known she was dreaming of Alex almost every night—but even though Ava wasn't dreaming *of* Natasha Romanoff—she was starting to have the feeling she was dreaming *as* her.

It would make sense, wouldn't it?

That I'm seeing things as Natasha Romanoff? Seeing the world through her eyes, when I'm asleep? When I'm not seeing it through my own?

Especially given the quantum entanglement link. When I'm unconscious, our brains could easily be even more intertwined and I might not even know it.

And if that's true—

Natasha is the connection to Alex.

She's watching him, and I can see it. I see it through her eyes.

But why? Why would Natasha Romanoff be watching Alex Manor?

And why would she have been, not just now, but for two years?

It didn't make sense.

It had to mean something.

You may want me to think this is all about Ivan Somodorov, sestra, but there's more going on here than that, isn't there?

Odessa would bring answers. It had to.

Not just for her, but for Alex, too.

The next time Ava found herself facing Natasha Romanoff, she wouldn't be caught by surprise. She'd know what to do and how to play it. She would also know what any part of the mess had to do with Alex Manor—for both of their sakes.

Ivan Somodorov or not.

What is your game, Black Widow?

Sleep never came again for her, and Ava watched the window until the clouds blew away and the bleak, gray sky welcomed them to Moscow.

S.H.I.E.L.D. EYES ONLY

CLEARANCE LEVEL X

LINE-OF-DUTY DEATH [LODD] INVESTIGATION
REF: S.H.I.E.L.D. CASE 121A415
AGENT IN COMMAND [AIC]: PHILLIP COULSON
RE: AGENT NATASHA ROMANOFF A.K.A. BLACK WIDOW,
A.K.A. NATASHA ROMANOVA
TRANSCRIPT: DEPARTMENT OF DEFENSE, LODD INQUIRY HEARINGS.

S.H.I.E.L.D. FIELD BULLETIN

OUT TO ALL OPERATIVES

<<MISSING MINOR ASSETS>>
<<AGENT ROMANOFF, NATASHA>>
<<EYES ON ORLOVA, AVA / MANOR, ALEX>>
<<TRAVELING UNDER ALIAS JOHNSTON, MELISSA / PETERSON, PETER>>
<<INVOLVED IN ALTERCATION AT KENNEDY AIRPORT, INTERNATIONAL DEPARTURES>>
<<HIGH-END BOUTIQUE ROBBERY/ASSAULT RESULTING IN CAPTURE OF TWO WANTED TRIAD OPERATIVES>>
<<CASH TRANSACTION, NO CC TRACKING>>
<<NO CELL/SAT TRACKING>>
<<LAST KNOWN CLOTHES RECOVERED FROM TERMINAL DUMPSTER>>
<<DETAIN UPON SIGHT>>

BLACK WIDOW'S APARTMENT
LITTLE ODESSA, BROOKLYN

va Orlova is only seventeen years old. How far can she really get?

Natasha sat in the empty kitchen of her apartment in Little Odessa, staring at the tiny black thumb drive in her hand. On it was everything S.H.I.E.L.D. had on either Alex or Ava.

If the QE link holds, Ava Orlova is not just a seventeen-year-old.

If the link holds, she's an experienced operative trained on two continents who speaks five languages and knows at least three ways to kill someone with her bare hands.

It was too complicated to take in—especially for someone whose life had already been as complicated as Natasha Romanoff's. She had tried to keep her life in this country as simple as this apartment. She had exactly three rooms and four pieces of furniture to her name in this country. A couch, a bed, and a small kitchen table, and a chair. And somehow, a cat with no name that wandered in and out as it pleased and that seemed surprised to see her now.

Natasha wondered when she'd last sat at this same kitchen table.

Three months ago? Six?

The plain square of varnished wood tabletop was perfectly reflective, as if even a fingerprint had never smudged it. The entire kitchen was like that. The white paint was fresh and the cupboards were bare, as though Natasha had just moved in, when really she'd lived there for years.

If you could call it a life.

She picked up one of the traditional babushka dolls called *matryoshka,* that sat in the center of the kitchen table, with red painted scarves on their heads and pink circles on their cheeks. They wore flowered aprons for dresses and had hearts for mouths. They were one of her few personal possessions in the whole apartment—the kind of thing a grandmother would have given a granddaughter, Natasha guessed.

If I still had a grandmother.

These were from Pepper Potts, after a business trip to Moscow. They fit together so neatly, you found yourself looking at twelve concentric babushkas trapped inside each other, when you had thought you were only looking at one. It was only a doll; Natasha didn't know why she found it to be so disturbing. The hidden-identity trick. Pepper had thought it was funny. "Look," she'd said, "the original Russian secret agent. She reminded me of you."

Is that what I am? What Ava is? A matryoshka?

Twelve different people and different pasts that only pretend to be one?

She pulled the hollow wooden dolls open, one after the other, until their empty halves lay on the table in front of her.

Inside the last set, the smallest, was a piece of worn paper, folded into a neat square. She didn't have to open it to know what it was.

The remaining half of an old, torn five euro note.

Natasha drew her knees up to her chest, balancing on her chair with crisscrossed legs, as she had when she was a child.

She stared at the hollow wooden figures.

Could I really be that full and that empty all at once?

And, except for the other versions of myself, that alone?

Natasha drank from a take-out cup of black coffee—this wasn't the kind of apartment that had appliances—and stared into the screen of her laptop. She needed to stop thinking. She needed to focus only on Ava's dossier.

Hold it together, Romanoff.

She picked up a pen and wrote another word on the take-out napkin she was using as paper. Now there were four. Four places Ava Orlova could be. Four places that she might think of as home, given her history.

BROOKLYN

DC

ODESSA

MOSCOW

She had moved in a reverse chronology through Ava's file to come up with the four possibilities. Brooklyn was her home now, if you could call it that. Natasha had visited the Y, and she was impressed. The kid was tough.

And then before that, the S.H.I.E.L.D. safe house in DC. For what, five years?

That had been a grim place too. Natasha had only seen it once a year, when she went to drop off a birthday present for the kid.

Even if it was without a card.

She shook her head.

Before that, Ava had lived in Odessa, and as a baby, in Moscow.

So, Ukraine. Odessa and the warehouse.

Would Ava want to go back there, to where it all started?

Maybe.

But would she dare to head that deep into Ivan Somodorov's stronghold?

If she's thinking like a Romanoff?

Yes.

She circled the word ODESSA and returned to scroll through Ava's dossier. Half the scanned pages linked back to Natasha Romanoff's own files. And like Natasha's files, half of every page was redacted. There were more blacked-out lines than not.

She was frustrated—wasting time and getting nowhere.

Meanwhile, Ava and Alex could be halfway around the world.

Natasha pulled up another file.

Let's try the boy.

Alex Manor.

Again.

She stared at the folder on her screen for a long time before clicking on it.

When she did, she saw that even for a civilian, it was thin. Alex Manor was a decent student at Montclair High School. Fencing team, mixed martial arts club. Marilyn Manor worked at New Beginnings Travel Agency. Specialized in honeymoons and pet-friendly getaways. The house was paid off. The car was used. The termite problem had been solved.

Nothing out of the ordinary—but not enough to be ordinary. There were no school records for Alex before high school. Nothing before tenth grade. No driver's license. No birth certificate. No mention of a father—not even divorce papers.

There should be more here.

Natasha scrolled through his dossier.

More strangely—especially for a civilian, and a minor—just as it was in Ava's file, half of what was there was redacted. For all the black bars running through Alex's paperwork, he might as well have been a spy.

Then she noticed a few words scribbled in the margin of the very last page of his file. She zoomed in.

Three words.

She had never noticed them before, which was strange.

Because this wasn't the first time she'd opened Alex Manor's file.

The first time she'd opened it had been the day after she found herself on the street outside his house, watching him as he left for school, without even knowing who he was or why she was there. She'd sat there for hours, three houses down, only to return the next day.

He means something to you, doesn't he?

It had been her secret. Nobody at S.H.I.E.L.D. knew—not Coulson or Bruce or Cap. Not even Tony.

But you know.

You've known it all this time.

That the boy matters.

She stared at the screen, not even seeing the words.

That's why you've had eyes on him, without even knowing why. Why you've watched his house, his friends. His tournaments.

Now she tried to focus on the three odd words in front of her. The ones she'd never noticed, almost illegibly scribbled, as they were, at the bottom of the margin on the very last page.

ALIAS ALEX MANOR.

Her head pounded with a sudden searing pain.

Alias?

Alex Manor is an alias?

Alexei Manorovsky isn't Alexei Manorovsky, after all?

It made no sense.

She scrolled farther.

SEE PROJECT BLANK SLATE.

Blank Slate?

What's Blank Slate?

The words themselves seemed to push and claw against her brain, like it hurt to even think them.

Natasha had never heard of the program, whatever is was. Nonetheless, Alex appeared to be some kind of participant.

Under whose supervision?

Because that someone has a little talking to do.

Natasha ran through his files. She could only locate one more mention of Blank Slate, which didn't help until she found that it was cross-linked to another buried S.H.I.E.L.D. server folder—and *that* folder had an owner.

Someone had created it.

Someone who was presumably in charge of Project Blank Slate.

And that someone was—

She clicked on the folder.

NATASHA ROMANOFF.

She wouldn't have believed it, but an authorization code appeared beneath the name, and the digits were strangely close to her own.

"What the—?"

Natasha Romanoff stood up, grabbing her jacket.

The door banged shut behind her, and the cat with no name jumped up on the table, staring at the now disassembled wooden parts of a girl that had once been a hollow doll.

* * *

Natasha Romanoff's motorcycle skidded to a stop in front of the Triskeleon, at the edge of the East River. The monologue didn't stop running through her head the entire time.

You have two choices, Romanoff.

"You? Nobody wants to see you here, Agent Romanoff." Even the guy working the front desk knew what had gone down, she guessed. He didn't look like he was about to buzz her in.

File flight plans for Odessa and get your butt to Ukraine before something happens to Ava or Alex—assuming they're even there.

"Yeah, yeah. Save it. I need to talk to Coulson. Or Maria Hill."

Or find a way into the Triskeleon mainframe and figure out what this is really about. Who you can trust—if anyone.

"Pretty sure they're in meetings all day, Agent. At least they are now." The guy smirked.

She raised an eyebrow.

My first choice keeps everyone alive, but for how long?

She held up the drive she'd just finished with.

"I just have to give them this. It's some stupid Mac thing Coulson gave me, but I have a PC, and I can't even get it to work. Computers, right?"

The door buzzed.

Natasha smiled.

My second choice is riskier, but in the long run might keep everyone safer.

The guy's head hit his desk with a slam, and a second gate opened.

His boots dragged across the slick lobby floor—and into a maintenance closet. The door closed behind him.

So make the call, Natasha.

Natasha walked through the atrium, letting her motorcycle helmet drop to the floor. She nodded at the suited man standing in the elevator next to her, then shoved him out of the way, just as the doors closed.

What do you need?

No more people in your head?

No more people getting hurt because of you?

The elevator doors slid open, and she moved down a pitch-dark hallway, lit only by a thick strip of luminous blue safety lights in the floor.

No more doctors, no more generals, no more Ivans getting inside your brain?

What did he call you, all those years ago?

A time bomb?

Is Ava Orlova in your head going to be one the thing that finally pushes you over the edge?

She was in a basement now.

Dark. Secure. Featureless.

A place to withstand any kind of attack—even the kind that S.H.I.E.L.D. seemed to most frequently attract, from within.

What do you need, Natasha? How about twenty-four hours?

Twenty-four hours to figure this out.

She found the door she was looking for.

The one marked DANGER—RADIATION EXPOSURE.

She backed away from the door, raising her sidearm.

German. In honor of Ivan Somodorov.

Even Ava and Alex can keep themselves alive for twenty-four hours.

She fired three rounds into the door.

Now hurry up and find this slate and unblank it.

The room was mostly empty. The walls were empty, a single lightbulb dangling from the ceiling. Only a small table sat in the center—big enough for one person, like a school desk—next to a folding chair.

This was the real Brain Trust.

She slid into the chair, tapping twice on the desk.

A hidden screen rose up from the surface, angled like the cover of a notebook computer. Then a keyboard.

Natasha punched in her own authorization code.

Then she took a breath and slowly typed in the variant code, the one she had found written in the margins of Alex Manor's file. The one that was only three digits off from her own.

Blank Slate? Come on. What is that?

The screen powered up.

A three dimensional model of a woman's face materialized in front of her.

Her own face.

The face spoke. "This is the Stark Personal Virtual Data Backup for Natasha Romanoff."

"Of course it is," Natasha muttered.

"If you're within earshot of my voice, you can thank Tony Stark for uploading a personal photographic scan and cloning all existing digital data, to secure it for future use, Natasha."

"Remind me to send him a note."

"I'm sorry. That exceeds my intended function as your VDB, Natasha." The model smiled. It was unsettling.

Now she beckoned for Natasha to come closer. "Natasha, I'll need to ask you to stop for retinal scan now, please."

A guide appeared on the screen, and Natasha leaned toward it.

"Hold still, Natasha," the on-screen voice said.

A red light flashed, and the flesh-and-blood Natasha sat back, blinking. "Wow."

"Identity confirmed. How can I help you today, Natasha?"

"All right." The real Natasha looked at the virtual one. "If you're really so smart. What is Project Blank Slate . . . Natasha?"

The Romanoff on the screen angled her head, as if she was thinking. Then she turned back to face Natasha and smiled brightly.

"Blank Slate is the adaptation of proprietary Red Room alpha-wave reconfiguration technology for use by the S.H.I.E.L.D. agency, Natasha."

"I don't understand. Rephrase. What is Blank Slate?"

"Blank Slate is a colloquialism. Blank Slate is a program. Blank Slate is a protocol. Blank Slate is also a state of mind, Natasha."

"I know that, *Natasha*. What I don't know is what anything you're saying means." Real Natasha was frustrated.

Digital Natasha shrugged. "I'm sorry. I'll try to be more clear, Natasha."

Real Natasha glared at her. "Who instigated the Blank Slate program?"

The face angled—thought—smiled—and answered. "You did, Natasha."

"Me? Why would I do that?"

"It is an advanced security protocol, Natasha."

"Whose security?"

"The minor asset with the alias of Alex Manor, Natasha. You negotiated it as part of his conditional release to the United States under the auspices of S.H.I.E.L.D., Natasha."

"Are you sure?"

"I am an uncorrupted record of saved data, Natasha."

"When was this?"

"Twenty-two months ago, Natasha."

She sat back in her chair.

Alex Manor? She should have known. She should have seen it coming.

Admit it.

At least admit it to yourself.

You've had eyes on Alex Manor for almost two years now.

You haven't told anyone—not Coulson or Tony or Cap or Bruce. Not even Pepper. Not anyone.

Why?

What can you possibly find to be so interesting about a teenage boy from Montclair, New Jersey?

And why are you so terrified of him?

It was Natasha Romanoff's private business, something she was handling herself, and something that was no clearer now than it had been at the start.

What did the boy matter to anyone—but most especially, to her?

The whole thing was so off the radar that she'd actually defied S.H.I.E.L.D. protocol to clear out her own schedule, if only so she could stay in the country long enough to check in on a fairly regular basis.

And she still didn't even know why.

You don't know why he bothers you, but you can't let it go.

It probably has something to do with the whole Ivan thing, but you don't even know what.

You don't know anything.

Why don't you know?

Why you?

Why—

Natasha looked up.

"So this Blank Slate," she said slowly. "It's me, isn't it?"

Virtual Natasha nodded. "Yes, Natasha."

"I've been wiped?" Real Natasha asked incredulously.

"Yes, Natasha. That is the colloquial expression that articulates the process by which the neurotransmitters in your hippocampus, amygdala, and striatum have been electromagnetically reconfigured, and in which your overall neurogenesis has been altered."

"And Alex, too?"

"Yes, Natasha."

Actual Natasha was reeling.

I've been wiped.

Me.

I'm missing pieces of myself.

So is Alex.

Why?

The avatar looked at her expectantly. "Do you need further assistance, Natasha?"

"I don't know," Real Natasha said helplessly, switching off the screen. "I'll have to get back to you on that."

Because I don't know anything, anymore.

She sat alone in the darkness, wondering who did.

LINE-OF-DUTY DEATH [LODD] INVESTIGATION
REF: S.H.I.E.L.D. CASE 121A415
AGENT IN COMMAND [AIC]: PHILLIP COULSON
RE: AGENT NATASHA ROMANOFF A.K.A. BLACK WIDOW,
A.K.A. NATASHA ROMANOVA
TRANSCRIPT: DEPARTMENT OF DEFENSE, LODD INQUIRY HEARINGS.

DOD: That's a lot to take in, Agent Romanoff.
ROMANOFF: Tell me about it. At that point, all I knew was that there was more to the story than Ivan Somodorov. First Ava, now Alex, and of course, me. We were all somehow part of this, and I was personally involved with both of them.

DOD: And you simply believed that? That someone had microwaved your brain and basically lobotomized you? Just because, what, your clone told you? Tony Stark's knockoff Natasha Romanoff?
ROMANOFF: I could feel it in my gut, sir. The wipe. I should have picked up on it earlier. Especially after all that time in the Red Room.

DOD: So this had been done to you before? When? How?
ROMANOFF: Two times that I know of. I'm sure many more that I don't.

DOD: Unbelievable. Those are some tall tales, Agent.
ROMANOFF: Tall doesn't make them not true. If it did, I would be out of a job.

DOD: Ah yes. The unicorns.
ROMANOFF: Always the unicorns.

STREETS OF ODESSA
BLACK SEA INDUSTRIAL PORT

"*O*dessa Verfi. That's it." Ava held up the old photo of her mother. In the picture, her mother was standing in front of a rough section of corrugated-metal siding, with what looked like the top of a ship visible to one side. ODESSA VERFI was barely visible on a freshly painted sign in front of the ship. "This has to be the dock."

"You think the answers are here somehow? The answer to how we can sever the link?" Alex looked over her shoulder at the photo—as if he expected it to answer him.

"Maybe. It all started here, didn't it?" Ava stared at the picture, just as she had during the connecting flight from Moscow to Odessa, memorizing every line on her mother's face. But that photograph had been taken long ago, when the dock—and Ava's family—had seen better days.

Alex squeezed her jacketed arm with his gloved hand. "At least nobody here is trying to lock you up. Or wipe our brains. That's good enough for me."

"It's an improvement," Ava agreed, holding the picture higher.

Now, in the winter moonlight, she tried to compare the photo to the shipyard itself. The docks didn't look like they did in the picture, or in her memories. From where she and Alex hid, crouching behind a row of empty oil drums at the edge of the water, she could see just how badly the ODESSA VERFI sign and everything around it had fallen into disrepair.

The general decay wasn't limited to the sign itself; the whole place was in shambles, as if it had never really recovered from the last time she had been here. Scrawny wild cats roamed the rusting, splintering ruins, and what looked like vultures circled in the clouded moonlight overhead. Most of the ancient electric lights around the perimeter fence flickered on and off at will. Even the snow looked dirty, and the sky was as dark as the sooty shipyard beneath it, full of the promise of another storm.

This is not a place for the living.

It's for ghosts like me.

Ava tried to breathe. She could feel her pulse racing and her heart hammering in her chest. She made a conscious effort to steady her hand, so the photo would stop shaking.

But this is it, isn't it? The infamous warehouse from the photo?

This is where it all started, and here I am again.

Logically, Ava knew she had come of her own volition, but even seeing the place made her feel like she would never get away; it had some kind of hold on her and would always draw her back, no matter how hard she tried to escape.

No. This isn't my life. This isn't me.

It's just a place I lived once.

Ava tried not to think about it, turning instead to Alex. "This has to be it. See the sign? Odessa Shipyard."

Alex compared the photo to the burned-out shell of the warehouse in front of them, assessing the ruins in the cold moonlight. "I think you're right. It seems like you've drawn this same warehouse at least ten times in that notebook of yours."

Ava shivered. "I know."

"So this is where the raid went down?"

She nodded.

He scanned the dockyard full of cargo ships. "This is probably also where Ivan smuggled in all his equipment. Straight off the boat. Pretty efficient." He shook his head. "You have to wonder what else this dock has seen over the years."

"Plenty. Fifty million tons of Black Sea traffic each year, and a direct connection to a major rail network—" Ava caught herself on QE overload and shrugged. "Can't be good, I mean."

"Look what else." Alex pointed to the top of the warehouse building in the photograph. "Not as many cops back then."

It was true; there were armed officers around the perimeter of the shipyard now. *Militsiya*. Ava could count their wooly gray *ushanka* trooper hats—and she was jealous of the earflaps. She and Alex had waited for a good forty-five minutes before managing to sneak into the restricted cargo dock, alongside a slow-rumbling truck that had offered only minimal cover.

"Pretty strange for a supposedly abandoned warehouse on an old dock, wouldn't you say?" Alex counted the hired guns lingering around the dock's gates. "To have a whole team of security?"

"Or pretty standard, when you're Ivan Somodorov and you're trying to cover up your history," Ava said, lowering her voice as yet another guard walked past them.

"Well, we can't take on that many of them. Not without setting off enough alarms to bring the entire Ukrainian police force down on us." Alex sounded frustrated.

"Not to mention the rest of Ivan's private militsiya," Ava said, looking grim.

"What's the play?" Alex looked at her, and she tried not to think of how much he sounded like a S.H.I.E.L.D. agent. "Ava. We got this. You can think like a Romanoff." He grinned. "And I'm pretty good in a fight."

Ava closed her eyes, then opened them. "You're right," she said. "We got this." She smiled. "But this time I'll take left; you take right."

* * *

260

They found themselves pushing open the rusting warehouse not four minutes and one neatly unconscious security guard later.

An uppercut beneath the jawbone. Contact at the mandibular angle. Generate minimal lateral movement. Snap the head straight up.

Ava had gone left; Alex had gone right.

We're getting to be quite a team, she thought.

"If nobody finds our friend here," she said, glancing back to the worn combat boots still sticking out from behind the oil drums, "we should have plenty of time to check things out inside."

"You're going to have to teach me that uppercut," Alex said, giving the guard's boots one final shove. "It seems handy."

"Handy for what? Your future career at S.H.I.E.L.D.?" Ava surprised herself by how irritated she sounded as she flipped out her tactical microflashlight.

"Says the girl with all the spy gear." He grinned. "But sure, why not? We can be partners. Bonnie and Clyde. Only for good guys. Like, Bonnie and Clyde Coulson." He laughed.

"How do you know we're the good guys?" Ava asked distractedly. She moved her flashlight through the darkness, across the cavernous interior of the warehouse. Even inside, it was so cold she could see the puffy white curls of her own breath.

She shivered. *Hard to imagine that all these years later the whole place could still seem so terrifying.*

Ava forced herself to keep talking. "Bonnie and Clyde? So we can use our fencing skills to right the wrongs of the international spy circuit?" *It's not a bad idea,* she told herself, trying to think about anything other than where she was and why she had come back there.

And if I could figure out how to rig some kind of folding blade. . .

"Exactly. And we'll only fly business class. With our dog, whose name will be Brat Junior." Alex took her by the hand. "Plus, when you're a brat, I can call you that and you'll still think I'm talking to the dog."

"I see you've got it all worked out," Ava said.

She studied the shadows around her. *Was that where Ivan strapped me down? Was it there?* She tried to think, but she couldn't control what appeared in the present, and what remained obscured by the terror and chaos of the past.

A bald man with eyes made of black shadows—
A maze of tattoos rising above his jacket collar—
The smell of sour cigarettes and strong coffee—
A belt with a brass buckle that sometimes left scars—
The lies, the lies that always did—

Alex squeezed her hand, gently but insistently, interrupting her thoughts. "But the cat? What will we name our cat?"

He wasn't giving up.

She knew he was saying, *I'm here. You're not alone. Talk. Keep talking.*

"Sasha Cat already has a name," Ava said as she looked up at the now gaping hole in the roof. Snow was falling softly through it.

There.

That's where I remember the row of big guns, she thought. *Snipers.*

"Not Jerk?" Alex said, poking her in the ribs, bringing her back to him. "Because I decided that was the secret name for every cat on the day I was made to change my first feline diaper." He poked her again. "Look it up; it's a thing."

"You're terrible. Sasha and I hate you." Ava smiled.

Seeing how hard Alex was working to cheer her up was its own kind of warmth. Ava began to calm herself, despite everything. She didn't know how he did it, but he made everything seem like it was going to be safe again.

Like it's all going to be okay someday.

She exhaled.

Suck it up. We get in. We get out. Give it twelve hours. That's what she told herself, but even she didn't believe it.

Then what? What's the next play? You're going to take out Ivan Somodorov? You think you've got enough Black Widow in you now to do that?

Ava imagined she could do it if she had to, technically speaking. She had the capability. She even had three S.H.I.E.L.D. microdarts in her pack, each containing enough toxin to put down an elephant.

That wasn't the problem.

She was.

It's one thing to disable a guard. It's another thing to kill one.

Those memories Natasha has in her mind, the ones that make you wake up screaming in the night?

Do you really want those for yourself?

"So this is it," Alex said, looking around. "Just one big, trashed room. And yet the clues to everything in your past might be here somewhere."

Ava nodded. "It looked really different, though. Before, you know. Ivan." She pulled a fraying length of cable up from the floor. "And the whole explosion and fire and destruction thing."

"And before Agent Romanoff," Alex said, squatting to pull a chunk of concrete off what looked like an old metal locker. "She didn't exactly let him go down easy."

Ava shivered.

"He seems to have that effect on everything. Places and people." Alex shook his head. "But I don't get it. This place is a dump. It's nothing." He kicked a pile of charred rubble. "What's still here that nobody wanted us to see? Why the security? Why the secrecy?"

"Good question." Ava looked over the blackened ruins around her. "Maybe Ivan isn't done here. Maybe there's something he can't afford to get rid of just yet."

She moved her flashlight across the floor around them, which was cracked in a thousand places, unstable and uneven under their feet.

"Or maybe it's a trap." Alex stopped to pick up a shiny scrap of metal from the rubble beneath his feet. He had only noticed it as Ava's flashlight had zoomed past.

It was stuck. "What's this?" The thing was wedged halfway into a deep fissure in the concrete floor.

Ava held her light over it. "No idea."

Alex knelt on the floor, tugging at the metal scrap with his fingers. "It looks like someone dropped it there."

"Probably impacted during the explosion." Ava knelt next to him with the light in one hand. With the other, she pulled a compact switchblade from her pocket.

He looked at her. "What are you, James Bond?"

She shrugged. "Other kids collected plastic ponies. I have a collection of old S.H.I.E.L.D. junk."

Alex shook his head. He took the blade and dug out the object, which turned out to be a strangely formed piece of metal. He turned it over in his hands, blowing off the dust. "What do you think? Some piece of machinery? It might be stamped with something. A number? And I think words?" He rubbed the metal with his sleeve.

"It's a key," Ava said, picking it up from his palm. The metal surface was warm from friction, and she touched the stamped letters with her finger. "Those aren't just numbers. That's a name. Luxport—I recognize it. I used to see it painted on big trucks on the highways out of town."

"Luxport?" Alex frowned. "That's in your sketchbook, right?"

"And my dreams."

"So maybe that's some kind of clue. How many keys can there be that could have this same serial number?"

"I don't know. Let's keep going and check the other side," Ava said. Now she was curious. Her mind was spinning. Four words had haunted her since Odessa. Stumbling across one of them now, and here, seemed like some kind of sign from her past.

It seemed almost hopeful.

They moved through the darkness, toward the far side of the warehouse, until Alex smacked right into a wall, or what he thought was one. "Wait—what's that?" Alex rapped on the object in front of him. "The warehouse doesn't end here. And look—this wall doesn't match the roofline."

"That's because it's not a wall," Ava said. She shoved the flashlight between her teeth and rubbed at a spot in the dust with her hand. "I think it's some kind of box. A shipping container, maybe. There's a word on the side. The paint or ink or whatever is coming off now, but I think I can still make it out."

LUXPORT.

"There it is again," Alex said. "Just like the key." They both stared.

This time, the word was painted in military stenciling.

Ava pulled her sketchbook out of her backpack. She held her flashlight so that Alex could see for himself. "From my dreams," she said. "Just like Brat."

KRASNAYA KOMNATA.

OPUS.

LUXPORT.

"That can't be a coincidence." Alex's eyes narrowed.

Ava shook her head. "For a long time, those words were the only things I could remember about this place. And that night. I didn't know if they were memories or dreams."

"But why those four words?"

"I don't know. Natasha never even thought of Luxport when she remembered this warehouse." Ava sounded confused.

"I was starting to think maybe Luxport had something to do with Ivan, but not on the night that S.H.I.E.L.D. found me."

"Maybe." Alex took a step backward, looking up. "This really is a giant shipping container. You could stack up what, a dozen of my mom's minivans? And you'd still have room for a Prius or two."

"Your mom drives a minivan?" Ava gave him a thumbs-up. "Cool."

"Now's not the time."

"Wait. Does that mean *you* sometimes drive a minivan?"

"I don't have my license yet. And you don't get to make those jokes until you learn how to drive," Alex said.

Ava ignored him, still smiling as she felt her way around the corner of the container until she found herself shaking a padlocked door in front of her.

"Luxport. For the third time. It says that on the lock as well."

She held out the key.

Alex took it. "So it's not a key to a warehouse."

"Not a shipping warehouse. A shipping container. And it's probably been sitting right here for eight years."

He slid the key into the ancient padlock. Groaning with rust, the lock slowly began to open.

S.H.I.E.L.D. EYES ONLY

CLEARANCE LEVEL X

LINE-OF-DUTY DEATH [LODD] INVESTIGATION
REF: S.H.I.E.L.D. CASE 121A415
AGENT IN COMMAND [AIC]: PHILLIP COULSON
RE: AGENT NATASHA ROMANOFF A.K.A. BLACK WIDOW, A.K.A. NATASHA ROMANOVA
TRANSCRIPT: DEPARTMENT OF DEFENSE, LODD INQUIRY HEARINGS.

DOD: So you went rogue, eh? AWOL? Mommy and Daddy must have loved that. That their number one agent now had it out for them?
ROMANOFF: I had just been told my brain had been wiped, sir. That's not S.H.I.E.L.D. proprietary tech. That's an old Moscow move. Pure Ivan Somodorov.

DOD: So you weren't taking any chances?
ROMANOFF: Of course not. For all I knew, my name had been forged. My authorization code stolen. I needed to retrench. Dig in. Would you have done anything any differently in my position, sir? Would anyone?

DOD: That's a tough question. Frankly, I can't imagine ever being in your position, Agent Romanoff, and I hope I never am.
ROMANOFF: I didn't know who to trust.

DOD: It doesn't seem like you often do.
ROMANOFF: You get used to it, sir.

DOD: I imagine folks over there are a little sensitive about that.
ROMANOFF: You have no idea.

DOD: Your director reports to the same president I do, Agent Romanoff—so believe me when I say I do.

ODESSA SHIPYARD WAREHOUSE NEAR THE BLACK SEA, UKRAINE

ust turning the key wasn't enough. The shipping container didn't appear to have been opened in years, which meant it had no interest in allowing itself to be opened now.

Great.

Alex shoved his shoulder against the metal garagelike door. It wouldn't budge. Ava joined him, which he had to admit was humiliating for his high-school-boy ego, but still better than going at it alone. Together they slammed against the metal until it finally gave way beneath them, starting to slide.

Alex yanked as hard as he could, and the door slowly groaned upward, revealing a further rectangle of darkness.

"Time to find out why Ivan has all those guards on the payroll." Ava checked her watch. "I'm not sure when security will move on us again."

"Got it, Agent Orlova."

Ava smiled, flipping her compact flashlight to a wider setting. "Not Agent Orlova. Red Widow. *Krasnaya Vdova*. That was the name I came up with when I was little." She ran the flashlight over the shipping container's walls.

"Hold on. Red Widow? You had a superhero name picked out and everything?" Alex laughed, but he was impressed.

"Of course I did. I was a kid and I was stuck sitting around in 7B all day. What else was I going to do? But yes." She inspected the wall more closely, ignoring the laughter. "I decided that I would be the opposite of the Black Widow in every way. She wore black, so I would wear white."

"Like a fencer?" Alex smiled.

"Stop laughing," Ava punched his arm.

"Ow. I'm not laughing." He rubbed his arm. "Those Kevlar uniforms are bulletproof and blade proof—you could do a lot worse."

"Right? And the Black Widow had her guns, so I would have my blades."

"Ah. I see. A little bulky when you're jumping off bridges, maybe?"

"A little."

"You'd have to work on that one."

"Clearly."

"And you might want to rethink the whole no guns thing, too."

She shrugged. "The Red Widow can be flexible."

"Does the Red Widow also have forty-five pounds of stolen spy equipment in her duffel bag?" Alex raised an eyebrow.

"Maybe in her lair."

"Oh, she has a lair now?"

"Where else would she keep her cat?"

"Right, okay. Now I'm getting it." He laughed.

Ava smiled, looking a little embarrassed. "I even practiced my autograph signature. First I'd draw her big red hourglass, and then I'd cross it out by drawing my own right over it."

"Double hourglass? Isn't that a cross?"

She looked like she was going to hit him again. "No, it's not a cross. Think about it."

"I'm thinking about it. You're saying you'd be the Red Cross? Because that's already a thing." Alex shook his head.

"Not a cross." Ava made a face.

"You mean, like a flower, then?"

"Not a flower." She punched him in the other arm.

"Ow, okay, fine. Why not a spider?"

"Hello, Spider-Man?" She rolled her eyes.

"You put a lot of thought into this, didn't you?"

Ava shrugged. "I had a lot of spare time."

"Apparently."

She ignored him, turning back to study the space around them. But the walls of the container were perfectly smooth—as smooth as the room itself was empty, except for the dust that now spiraled up into the air.

"Nothing's here," she said, sounding disappointed.

"That's because it's there." Alex pointed to an outline of a trapdoor cut into the floor of the container—and he guessed the warehouse itself, beneath it.

"Is that—?" Ava crouched over the trapdoor, running her hand along its seams. "A door."

"So this isn't a container at all. It's some kind of secret entrance," he said.

"Hidden in plain sight." Now Ava was on her knees. "Looks like Ivan was getting smart in his old age."

"Not smart enough to stay away from a Romanoff, I guess." Alex rapped on the door. "It's definitely hollow. So there's some kind of space below us."

He wrenched the rusted panel upward, and a shower of dust gave way as it finally creaked open.

A wooden stepladder descended into the darkness beneath the floor of the container. Alex stuck his head over the edge, trying to get an idea of what lay below. "I think it's some kind of secret basement." He pulled his head back up. "Let's check it out."

Ava was already holding her flashlight in front of her, and she began to move down the ladder. Alex followed right behind.

Once they entered the darker room below, the beam from the flashlight cut across the shadows, flickering off the far walls. The space under the warehouse was immense. Sealed and protected by a layer of concrete, the lower level had been perfectly preserved in time.

"This place is practically a bomb shelter," Ava said. "I mean, it even sort of looks like one. And I should know, I grew up in 7B."

"But it still makes no sense." Alex shook his head. "A bomb shelter? For protecting who—and from what?" He picked up a mug from what seemed to be some kind of security station. It left a perfect ring in the dust. "And why the guards, if nobody uses the place anymore?"

"I have no idea."

"Are you sure? Think about it. You're the one who brought us back here," he said, hesitating. He almost didn't want to ask the question, but he had to know. "How did you know we'd find this?"

Ava didn't answer. Instead, she moved the light in front of her, focusing it on what looked like a hallway. "Look. I think this part is even bigger than upstairs." She edged toward the hall, pulling Alex after her.

"That's not exactly an answer to my question."

"I didn't know that we'd find anything, Alex. Not for certain. I just knew we had to come back to where Ivan had taken me. Where he'd—" She gave up. "Where I met Natasha."

She was done talking about it.

Alex got the message.

Instead, they explored. The first hallway branched into others, until it became clear the basement was a whole little world of its own. Dusty old maps of Russia lined the walls, dotted with the locations of former safe houses, munitions depots, secure recon posts. Boxes of electrical parts—coils of wire and old circuitry—sat abandoned on empty desks next to what resembled outdated phone books and discarded departmental handbooks. An old kitchen with yellowing linoleum sat next to a room with a sagging couch and a long-dead television.

Ava turned on a rusting faucet at the sink. Nothing came out.

"I think people might have lived here. At least spent a whole lot of time here," Alex said. From where they now stood, they could see past the shadows extending out in front of them to where a row of doorways methodically punctuated the hallway walls.

"There. That's the way," Ava said, motioning to the wall of doorways.

"To what?"

"I don't know. I just—it feels like the way." Ava stopped. "I think—I know this place." She pushed onward through the shadows, reaching out to touch the first three doors that she passed, finally opening the fourth. "This one. This is it."

She stepped inside, transfixed.

It looked to Alex like she was moving through a waking dream, almost like Ava was becoming her old self. *She's remembering.*

"My mother would stay here with me." Ava rounded the corner slowly into the next office. "There. Right there. That's her desk. I used to call it my cave. One safe space all my own. I think I used to play house under it."

Ava crawled beneath, dragging a valley through the dust. "Her mind was always somewhere else, but I didn't care, because I knew where she'd be. Sitting right at this desk. So even when she seemed like she was a million miles away, I never minded."

Alex watched her in the shadows, all curled up now, hiding beneath the desk like a child. He let her talk. He let her do whatever it was that she'd needed to do. Whatever reason she'd come for, whether or not she even knew.

"Look," her voice echoed. "Come see. My name is still here. The one I wrote with permanent marker on the underside of the wood."

Alex sat down on the concrete floor next to Ava, who was huddled against her knees. "I wanted to make it permanent. This was my place, with my mom, even when my dad was in Moscow. If we had to be here, I wanted to be right by her side, forever."

Alex ducked his head next to her. They both couldn't fit, so he lowered his head to rest in Ava's lap.

She shone the flashlight on the wood across from her. There, in painstaking lettering, was her name.

AVA ANATALYA.

But above the name there was something more, and Alex reached for it carefully. Gently. "Ava," he said, pulling a dusty black-and-white photograph free from where it had been tucked away, hidden up in the wooden slats supporting the desk drawer.

Her hands shook as she took it from him.

It was a picture of Ava as a young girl, holding her mother by the hand. Alex recognized Dr. Orlova from the picture of her on the dock he'd seen earlier.

Here, Dr. Orlova looked thin and drawn, wearing some kind of government-issue lab coat that was a few sizes too large. Her dark, haunting eyes seemed too big for her face, and the grip she had on her daughter's hand was iron, judging by the angle of Ava's chubby arm beneath it. Ava was gripping something tightly in her arms.

"Karolina. My doll," Ava said sadly. She traced the picture of the doll with her finger. "I loved her almost as much as my parents. She was the closest thing I had to a sister when I was little. See?" She moved the flashlight, and now Alex could see two more words, written next to two little arrows on the wood.

MAMOTCHKA was written near the top of the desk.

KAROLINA was written near the bottom.

Ava wiped her eyes with her sleeve, blinking rapidly. "It's all gone now, isn't it? They're all gone?"

"It looks like they are," Alex said, reaching around her until his arms completely encircled her, and their two bodies were just one warm, beating thing. "They're gone but I'm here."

"I know," she said, letting the tears come. "This was my home, Alexei."

"It was, Ava Anatalya," he said, reaching his warm hand up to her face, rubbing away her tears as they fell. "You've come home."

"I'm broken," she said, her face wet. "I know I am."

"You're not," he answered. "You're strong. Look. You're the one who's still here, when everything else is gone." She nodded.

He hoped she believed him.

"Have you seen enough?" Alex asked. She nodded again. He slid outward, pulling himself free from the desk, then her. He lifted her in his arms until she was back on her feet, her toes barely touching the floor.

"I think I want to kiss you now, Alexei Manorovsky." She whispered the words into his cheek, as if pulling her face completely away from his was something she could not even imagine.

"I think I do too," he whispered back, lowering his mouth down to hers, as gently as if she were made of the snow that was falling steadily and silently from the sky outside.

She raised her tear-streaked face to his. The moment their lips first touched, in the first kiss of many, he knew.

He knew it from how he could feel the kiss in his toes, from how her fingers seemed to burn against his jaw where she touched him.

He knew it from how a single kiss could make him want to burst into laughter and tears all at once.

The feeling was so intoxicating that he craved even more of it—and so terrifying that he dreaded feeling it ever again.

It was all he could do not to tell her right then. He told himself there would be plenty of time for that later. Time when they weren't being hunted by madmen from afar or threatened by operatives at home.

Time when they weren't hiding in the secret basement of a burned-out warehouse in a snowy foreign land. Love could wait, even when so many other things could not.

Couldn't it?

* * *

277

As Alex and Ava were leaving Dr. Orlova's office, Alex noticed a row of identical gray metal filing cabinets lining the far wall of the room.

"What do you think?" He looked at Ava, and she swung her flashlight across the faces of the cabinets. She took a deep breath, steadying herself.

"My mother kept meticulous records," she said.

"Do we have time?"

Ava checked her watch. "Four minutes."

Alex took a closer look. Ava was right; it was her mother's carefully inked labels that caught his eye. The neat row of hand lettering kept to all capitals, as if whatever was inside this row of cabinets was particularly important, at least to the person writing the labels. He moved instinctively to the center of the cabinets.

O.P.U.S.

Alex paused at the sight of the label. *I'm broken.* He could still hear Ava saying the words. He didn't want to do this to her. *Not now.* She had been through enough, hadn't she?

It was Ava who spoke up from behind him. "No, you have to. We have to. It's why we're here." She moved her fingers to the handle next to his. "Don't worry about me. Whatever's in there, I'll be okay."

She didn't wait for him to answer. Ava pulled on the cabinet as hard as she could. The file drawer still didn't move.

"Locked," she said, taking out her switchblade.

"You going to Red Widow it?" Alex raised an eyebrow.

She rolled her eyes, then handed him the flashlight. "I

knew I was going to regret telling you that. Just give me two minutes."

It only took one. Ava yanked the cabinet open and scanned the collection of hanging files inside. "This is it. I think we hit the jackpot."

"Looks that way," Alex said, shaking his head. "Holy Mother."

Each institutional green-paper file was stuffed with graphs and charts and marked with a Russian name, followed by a series of numbers. Alex opened the first file. "They're the names of the test subjects," he said. "That's what it says here, on the front file."

He pointed. There it was—*ORLOVA, AVA ANATOLYEVA.* "That's you, right?"

She nodded. "My father was Anatoly, so I was Anatolyeva. Anatalya for short."

"So you were part of this O.P.U.S. project, Ava."

Ava went pale. "Test subject? I was a test subject?"

"That's what the report says." Alex nodded. "In Dr. Orlova's program."

"She was testing me? Her own child? She knew I was part of the study?" Ava looked like she'd just been slapped in the face. Two bright pink spots appeared on her cheeks. "So I wasn't here because Ivan took me. I hadn't been abducted. I was here because she gave me up. She was using me."

She was fighting tears, he could see it.

He could see she was fighting back tears. He wanted to reassure her, but he couldn't think how. If Ava was right, her mother was a monster who failed to protect her own child from even greater monsters.

If she was wrong—how would they ever know?

Alex thought about it.

"Your name in this file only explains how Somodorov found you." He opened another file. "We don't know anything for certain. Let's take these files and get out of here. Actually, we should probably grab as many as we can."

Ava nodded, but she still looked stricken as she turned back to the cabinet. He reached for her trembling hand and squeezed it tightly.

"Hey," he said. "Don't do this to yourself."

She didn't look at him. Instead, she grabbed handfuls of files, again and again, as if clearing out the old cabinets would somehow clarify the muddle in her own brain.

Alex gave up and did the same.

As he began pulling files, he couldn't help but check for his own name. Not that he was expecting to find it, but still.

You never know.

You speak Russian, don't you? It's possible.

Nobody's ever really explained that away.

There were no Alex Manors—not even any Alexei Manorovskys—in the cabinets, though, and he breathed a sigh of relief.

By the time they'd stuffed two dusty cardboard boxes with everything they could fit, Alex had stopped worrying about it altogether.

It was Ava who found the photo.

"Wait. What's this?" Ava stood in front of the cabinet,

holding a second file in her hand, in addition to her own.

"What? I can't see. It's too dark in here."

She shone her flashlight on the folder for him. There was a photograph clipped to the file, and he found eyes as dark as his own staring out at him from the front of the green paper.

And a face. A childish, chubby-cheeked face under a head of sprouting curls. With a number stamped along one side of the folder, just like all the others.

"Look at this. He looks just like you."

"Isn't there a name?" He looked at the boy's face. He looked like Alex, but he was also a stranger.

"I don't see a name. Not in this part of the file." She looked at him.

"Does it say anything more about the program?" He was impatient.

"There's a whole stack of reports here." Ava split them in half and shoved a pile of paper into his arms. "Here. Look." Ava held another page beneath her flashlight. "This transcript calls it Ivan's spiritual companion to the Red Room program." She shivered.

"'But this time, he's not holding back'?" Alex looked up from the page he was reading. "That doesn't sound good."

"It's not." Ava frowned. "This says the children of O.P.U.S. are to be trained as master spies—listen to this—'until such a time as their placements with top foreign governments can be assured. Only the highest-level access, particularly with Western heads of state, will allow us to execute our glorious plan.'"

"That's crazy."

Ava looked like she was processing ten years at once. "But then the Black Widow showed up, and the warehouse got blown to oblivion, and after that I was nowhere to be found—"

Alex finished the thought. "And everyone thought Ivan was dead. End of program."

"Except now Ivan's back in town, and kids are disappearing again. . . ." Ava sifted through papers as she spoke.

Alex shook his head. "But if something's up and running, there's no way of knowing what targets have already been compromised, is there? Short of asking Ivan himself?"

Ava pulled a page out of the stack of files and froze. "Alex. That boy. There he is again, the one who looks like you."

"What about him?" Alex watched, now impatient. He wanted to get out of there. The dust was choking and the darkness was unsettling.

Ava pulled page after page out of his file, scanning each one rapidly. "He has a name, only I don't think it's Manor, or even Manorovsky."

She looked up at him with dark eyes—holding out the paper.

"It's Romanova."

Alex stared.

Ava repeated the word, this time in English. "You know. Romanoff."

He heard the words, but he couldn't understand what she was saying. He couldn't and he didn't want to hear it.

She pressed the open file into his motionless hands.

"And I think he's you."

S.H.I.E.L.D. EYES ONLY

CLEARANCE LEVEL X

LINE-OF-DUTY DEATH [LODD] INVESTIGATION
REF: S.H.I.E.L.D. CASE 121A415
AGENT IN COMMAND [AIC]: PHILLIP COULSON
RE: AGENT NATASHA ROMANOFF A.K.A. BLACK WIDOW,
A.K.A. NATASHA ROMANOVA
TRANSCRIPT: DEPARTMENT OF DEFENSE, LODD INQUIRY HEARINGS.

DOD: Did it ever occur to you that you were in too far? All three of you?
ROMANOFF: I'm always in too far, sir.

DOD: It just seems to me that, even for you, Agent Romanoff, this one was different.
ROMANOFF: That's what deep cover is all about. Your government isn't going to come bail you out from a black-ops mission that never officially happened. You have to know that going in. I did.

DOD: Maybe so. But they're also not going to force you into a permanent cover by taking your own brain from you, without even consulting you. That's not how we usually do things in this part of the world, Agent.
ROMANOFF: Really, sir?

DOD: Let's keep it to the inquiry, Agent.
ROMANOFF: Either way, I wasn't thinking about myself at that point. I was worried about Alex and Ava. I wasn't certain they could get themselves out of whatever they'd gotten themselves into since leaving the base.

DOD: Were you right?
ROMANOFF: I was close enough, sir.

LUXPORT BASEMENT ARCHIVE
ODESSA DOCKYARD, UKRAINE

lex Manor. Alex Roman.
Alexei Manorovsky. Alexi Romanovsky.

Alexei Romanoff.

A Romanoff.

Ava stared at him. The walls of the tiny room seemed to be closing in on them. Alex looked like he could not speak, he could not physically say the words.

Ava knew the feeling. Even when you only thought them in your own mind, some words still sounded like lies.

Is it true? Is it even possible?

She watched in sympathy as Alex slumped against the wall, letting himself sink to the floor.

Ava sat down beside him, gently touching his knee. "Do you think—could it have been—could that be you?"

"A Romanoff? As in Natasha Romanoff? And me?" Alex shook his head. "No. Not possible." He let his head fall into his hands.

"Anything is possible," Ava said gently. "You said that yourself. And it would explain the Russian."

He shook his head almost violently. "I have a mother. She's a travel agent. With a cat named Stanley."

"But you had a dog named Brat."

"We live in suburban New Jersey."

Ava thought about it. "You remember Vermont. And the woods. And the snow." She shrugged. "What if it's not Vermont you're remembering?"

He looked stunned. "My best friend is Dante. His dad is a cop."

"Maybe that's why. Maybe they've been watching you." Ava sighed. There was one more thing. She felt like she had no choice but to tell him now. "When I dream, Alex, I think I'm dreaming through her eyes. I think Natasha Romanoff has been watching you."

He didn't answer. He looked like he couldn't.

Finally he said the words. "Natasha and Alexei Romanoff? The Romanoff children? The Black Widow herself has a little brother? How is that possible?"

"I don't know, Alexei."

"What part of my life is real? Is any of it?"

She said nothing.

"If that file folder with my face on it is right, then everything else about my life is wrong."

Alexei Romanoff.

Ava thought about it.

The two words made his whole existence a lie, and yet somehow, if they were true, they would also explain everything. Everything he'd ever wanted to confide in her.

The feeling that he wasn't a perfect fit for his own life.

The fear that he had nothing in common with his mother.

The restlessness. The need to fight. The competitive drive.

Like a Romanoff.

Ava sighed, rolling herself to her side on the floor. "It could be worse. My mother is the physics mastermind behind O.P.U.S., according to half of those documents. That means I was my mother's guinea pig."

He pulled Ava's head up into his lap. She curled up against his leg.

"That also means I've been blaming Ivan Somodorov and Natasha Romanoff for everything that's ever happened to me, and all along it was my mother."

Jet lag was hitting, and her eyes were halfway closed already. She felt his hand curl against her cheek.

"Get some sleep. I'll keep an eye on the room. We can still get out of here before first light and avoid security."

She nodded, exhausted. She was too tired to answer.

She didn't imagine Alex would be sleeping, though. She knew he had too many questions—his mind wouldn't slow down enough to not think them.

She had enough of her own.

If my mother is behind the O.P.U.S. project, why would she agree to use her own daughter like that?

Can she really be that much of an animal?

Does Natasha know all of this?

Does she know about Alexei?

And, most of all—

Can Alexei really be a Romanoff?

"Alexei. Alexei, wake up." Ava slid her hand over his mouth to keep him from shouting out as he awoke. Her voice was low. "It's time. We have to go."

She pulled him to his feet. He woke up, all at once, grabbing his pack and stumbling after her.

She even heard a hoarse whisper as she fumbled her way to the stairs.

"Toropis." Hurry!

"You're speaking in Russian again," Ava whispered over her shoulder, pausing as she began to climb back up the wooden ladder and through the trapdoor—the way out. "We both are, *da?*"

"Da," he answered.

"Now we need to switch to English." She yanked her backpack through the trapdoor after her. Alex followed. "Mostly because if they catch us, you don't want to be able to understand a word anyone is saying. Got it?"

"Nemyye Amerikantsy," he agreed. Dumb Americans.

Ava latched the shipping container shut behind them and ran through the warehouse, Alex following closely behind.

By the time they made it to open the warehouse door, there were at least half a dozen guards assembling on the dock.

"I guess they found our friend from yesterday," Alex said.

"Der'mo," Ava cursed. "There's no other way out."

"What now?" Alex looked at her. "And by that I mean, you want to take left, or right?"

She pulled an ancient-looking gun out of her backpack. The one from her mother's desk drawer.

"Ava," he said.

She stared past him to the dock and the guards. She was already making the same quick calculations the Black Widow would have.

Grab their attention—

Focus them on you as the target—

Take One and Six out first—

Find cover while Two and Five get off a round—

Take position on the other side of the oil drums—

Alex hissed at her. "Ava, stop. You're not taking on all those guys. It's too risky, even with the QE link."

"I can do it." She looked at him. "I have to."

"You've never even fired one of those things before."

But she shouldered past him, aligning herself with the edge of the warehouse door. "Alex. I've got this."

She wedged her pistol into the open doorway, raising it until it was level with her eyes.

She hesitated. . . .

Closed her eyes.

Ready—

But before she could squeeze the trigger, an oil drum behind the guards exploded into a ball of fire.

A second oil drum exploded, and then a third.

The guards who were still standing went running.

"What?" Ava stood there, stunned. She pushed through the doors and out onto the burning dock.

Alex was right behind her. "Oh my God," he said.

It was her.

Natasha Romanoff rolled down off the roof.

Alex watched as Natasha landed on the ground in front of them on two steady feet, sliding away her weapon. "Sorry. Didn't mean to sneak up on you like that. I had the drop on them, so I took it."

Natasha looked from Ava to the gun she was holding, finally taking in the scene. "Oh God. What are you doing with that thing? Put it down. You could have blown your own head off."

Ava just stood there, in apparent shock. Alex, right behind her, found he couldn't speak, couldn't move. He could hardly register a thought, beyond the obvious.

Who am I?

Who is she to me?

Then Ava grabbed Natasha and hugged her with relief. "Thank God."

Natasha looked like she'd rather take a bullet, but she said nothing as she turned her eyes past Ava to Alex.

"Natasha Romanoff. Imagine that. What are you doing here?" Alex finally spoke.

He felt undone.

Hard and cracked and so hurt that it didn't matter what happened anymore.

The dock was on fire around them, but Alex didn't care if it burned. He didn't care if it didn't. He didn't know what to care about.

The world had changed since he'd last seen Natasha Romanoff.

The world and his world and everything in it.

It was an entirely different place now.

And I'm a different person.

"This fire is only going to get bigger. We need to go." Natasha looked over to Ava for help, but Ava said nothing.

"Alex?"

Alex raised an eyebrow, folding his arms in front of him. "Is that even my name?"

"Fine, *Alexei*. It doesn't matter what we call you, as long as we get you out of here before the police decide to show up," Natasha said in Russian.

"I'm not going anywhere with you," Alex said. In English.

Natasha took a step toward him, her hands out in front of her as if to say, *Take it easy*. "I'm just here to talk." Almost as if on cue, the flaming oil drums behind Alex exploded, sending smoke and fire to the docks around them.

He didn't flinch.

"That's funny. Because I'm sick of talking, *sestrenka*." He moved toward her as if he was back on the fencing strip and trying to pick his attack.

I'm sick of lies.

Of confusion.

Of nothing making any sense.

Natasha seemed to know exactly what he was doing. "What

are you going to do? *Fight me?* I'm a trained assassin, and you're barely more than a child." She backed away.

"Am I? Really? How would I know?" He closed the distance between them.

"Don't be stupid."

"But I am stupid. That's the point, isn't it? I'm so stupid I didn't even know my own name." Alex picked up a long piece of abandoned pipe from the dockyard debris and swung it. "I'm so stupid I don't even know how I got this way."

"Alexei," Natasha warned. She grabbed a splintering piece of two-by-four just in time for Alex's pipe to smash into it.

"My whole life has been wrong, even felt wrong. I have nothing in common with what I thought was my family. I get into fights for no reason, and when I do, I win every one of them. I'm restless. I can't sit still. I think everyone and everything is an attack. And now I'm supposed to just believe that this is why? That you're the answer to everything that has never made sense about my own life?" Alex swung again. "I don't think so."

Natasha ducked the pipe, extending her hands in peace. "Alexei. Don't test me."

"Why not? Here's the whole test. It's only one question. Are you or are you not my sister, Natasha Romanoff?"

"It's not that simple," Natasha said.

Alex swung the pipe again, lurching with the weight of the metal. "Oh, I think it is. I found my name on a list of O.P.U.S. test subjects. Only it was your name too."

"I can explain, if you'll just let me talk—"

"There's nothing to talk about. It's a yes-or-no question. Am I or am I not Alexei Romanoff? I have a right to know, don't I? Who I am and where I come from?" He staggered toward her, swinging recklessly. *"Da, Natalyska?"*

"Careful, Alexei—" Now even Ava was starting to get nervous. She kept her distance, though; she knew better than to interrupt what was about to happen.

Alexei wagged the pipe in the air. "Maybe we should start with this one. True or false—the woman who lives in my house and pretends to be my mother?"

"Alex," Natasha began.

He swung at her head wildly. "Ding-ding-ding! It's true! She's false!"

Natasha held out her hand. "Give me the pipe."

"Now for extra credit—and this is a tough one. What is my own mother's name?" He swung at her legs, but she leaped over the pipe.

"Who cares?" Natasha dropped the beam. Now she looked as angry as he did.

"Wrong answer!" Alex lunged at her, and she leaped away from him, grabbing his own pipe and smashing it down into him.

He smashed it back.

Natasha shook her head, pushing him off.

"Alex!" Ava shouted.

He heard, but he couldn't stop. It was too late.

"If it matters, Alexei, I only just found out myself." Natasha ducked Alexei's next attack.

"It doesn't." Alex parried with a broken length of siding now, flinging it at her.

"I was in the dark too. It took me this long to put the truth together. And even then, it took breaking into my own classified file to get it out."

"The truth? What do you know about the truth? You're so good at lying you don't even know when you're lying to yourself."

Alex was furious. He let go of his makeshift weapon and lunged at her—and she pinned him.

She tried again. "We both escaped from Ivan. As part of my deal with S.H.I.E.L.D.—and to keep you safe—our memories were wiped. They hid you in New Jersey for your own protection."

"But our bond couldn't be erased?" Alex scoffed.

"Something like that." Natasha pressed his face against the dock. "But I have to say, your attack really isn't so bad," she said, twisting his arm behind his back. "For a kid."

"For a Romanoff?" he said, laughing.

"For a little one," she said.

"Better than when you stalked my last tournament?" He forced the words out through his gritted teeth.

"Somewhat. Marginally." Natasha twisted harder. "Maybe in your footwork."

"How long?"

"What?"

"How long have you been stalking me?" Alex tried to flip her off him, but Natasha smashed him back down. "And is it just at fencing, or do you also like to hang with the moms at my judo class?"

"Two years now. Mostly fencing tournaments. And your house. And the occasional party." She shrugged. "I've been busy."

He stared up at her. "Why? Why did you do it?"

She looked almost embarrassed. "I didn't know why at first. I only knew that it was something I had to do. To be honest, I thought you might have been the son of one of my . . . targets." Alex kicked at her, and Natasha pushed him back. "Which could have been awkward," she added.

He sighed, holding up his hands for the moment. A sign of truce. "Listen. If I judo your ass will you finally tell me what's going on?"

Natasha stood up, releasing him.

Alex staggered to his feet in front of her, boxing stance.

"I'm Natasha Romanoff. Nobody judos my ass," she said. "Not even my little brother."

Natasha knocked her brother to the ground with her left hook.

He went down hard and fast.

Ava was there with him a moment later. She looked terrified, and Natasha didn't blame her.

Alex groaned, rolling to his side, holding his jaw.

"*Sestra.*"

Then his eyes rolled upward and he passed out.

The warehouse burst into flames around him, and without saying another word, Natasha Romanoff picked up her only brother and carried him into her life.

S.H.I.E.L.D. EYES ONLY

CLEARANCE LEVEL X

LINE-OF-DUTY DEATH [LODD] INVESTIGATION
REF: S.H.I.E.L.D. CASE 121A415
AGENT IN COMMAND [AIC]: PHILLIP COULSON
RE: AGENT NATASHA ROMANOFF A.K.A. BLACK WIDOW,
A.K.A. NATASHA ROMANOVA
TRANSCRIPT: DEPARTMENT OF DEFENSE, LODD INQUIRY HEARINGS.

DOD: So the Romanoff family is reunited at last. God, I love a happy ending, Agent.
ROMANOFF: And yet here we are.

DOD: Why didn't you disappear when you had the chance?
ROMANOFF: Because I wanted my brain back. Even if it had been wiped.

DOD: So a wiped brain is still better than an Entangled one?
ROMANOFF: It is if you're a government agent.

DOD: And because you were a government agent, you knew your work wasn't done?
ROMANOFF: Ivan was still out there.

DOD: And his Entangled test subjects?
ROMANOFF: At least a hundred more names, according to the files Alex and Ava stole from the warehouse.

DOD: A hundred potentially Entangled leaders of nations?
ROMANOFF: A hundred human land mines, buried for years across the globe, waiting to go off.

DOD: Forever Red, Agent?
ROMANOFF: No. Just forever Ivan the Strange.

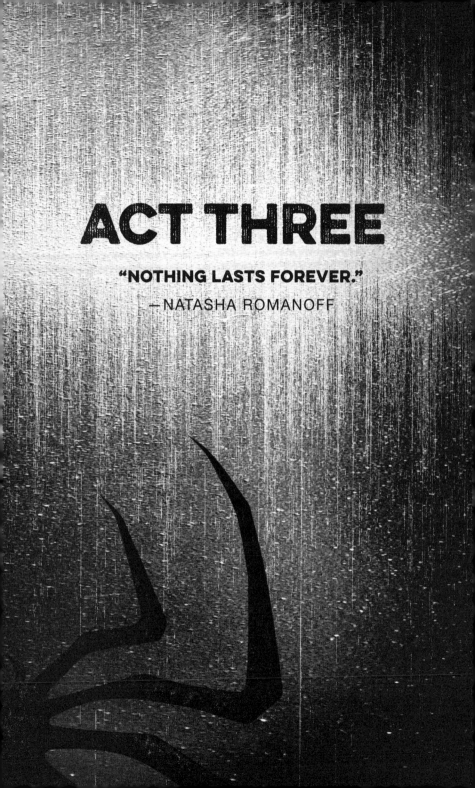

ACT THREE

"NOTHING LASTS FOREVER."

— NATASHA ROMANOFF

DACHA ODESSA HOTEL
ODESSA CITY CENTER, UKRAINE

"No more secrets," Alex said. "No more lies." Alex and Natasha had spent the better part of an hour comparing notes. Between the files Alex and Ava had found, and the digital archive Natasha had found, there could be no doubting it.

Alexei and Natasha were brother and sister—the last of the Romanoffs.

"No more secrets," Natasha agreed. *But when was that ever something I could promise anyone?*

A siren wailed in the distance. *Politsiya.* She paused to look out a dirty window, reinforced with chicken wire inside the glass. She could feel the cold seeping through the flimsy panes. They were sitting in a hotel room in the seediest corner of Odessa. The only amenity in the room was a trash can, and even that was chained to the floor.

Alex snorted from where he had flopped on the bare bed. "But you can't give up the lies?"

Natasha pressed a half-melted bag of ice harder against her head.

Now she heard cursing. Russian. Ava was still trying to use the tiny shower in the next room. Natasha knew better than to try.

Even the cold water is colder here.

The silence in the room hung there between them. Natasha looked away from Alex awkwardly. She wasn't used to this much . . . talking.

Her brother—*Because that's what he is, right?*—rolled over, staring up at the ceiling. "You know, the last time I saw you, I thought I was an only child from Jersey. Now it turns out I have a sister from Russia and a girlfriend from Ukraine—"

"Girlfriend?" Natasha asked. "You met her when? A few days ago?"

Great.

"And a headache the size of the Atlantic," he said, ignoring her. He rubbed his temple.

You're still just a kid.

She felt sorry for him. For both of them, really.

He looked so young, lying there on the cheap mattress, surrounded by dirty carpeting and peeling wallpaper and water-stained plaster.

And she suddenly felt so old.

"It hurts, right? When you try to remember?" Natasha moved to sit by him on the bed, handing him her bag of ice. "The first time the Red Room wiped me, I felt like my head was going to explode. I thought I had a brain tumor. I was almost relieved when Ivan told me the truth."

"Relieved?" He sat up, taking the ice.

"Well, those were my Red Room days. The bar was low." She looked at him. "Even now, the pain comes back when I try to think about certain things."

"Like me?" Alex draped the bag of ice across his forehead, tipping his head back against the mattress.

"Like you."

He pressed the ice against his eyes now. "I actually think someone dropped a grenade into my skull."

"Here. You want to hit the nerve, right . . . there." Natasha repositioned the ice for him. Her eyes flickered down to his. "Speaking of potential hazards, you and Ava seem pretty. . . close."

"Smooth." Alex tried to sit up, but Natasha shoved him back down.

"You need to rest."

He groaned. "Oh my God. You've been my sister for what, two minutes? And you're going to start lecturing me about *girls*?"

She looked more uncomfortable than he did. "Just—be careful. A relationship is dangerous for both of you, at least in our world. People will use your feelings against you. Look what happened to the two of us."

"I don't know what world you live in. My planet is Earth, and there, people are allowed to like each other." He shook his head. "What happened to you, Agent—" He paused suddenly. "What do I call you? What did I call you?"

She didn't say anything. She didn't know.

Alex tried again. "What happened to make you . . . like this, *Natasha*?"

Where do I begin?

"I got shot at. Blown up. Betrayed. Dropped out of planes. Attacked with knives. Hit by every kind of moving vehicle on the planet. Any other questions?"

"Yeah." Alex replaced the ice pack on his pounding head. "Who did this to us, and why would they do it?" He winced.

"Let me." Natasha reached out, tentatively, and took the ice pack from him, holding it in place. It was a caring gesture, one of the few she had. At least a Romanoff version of one. She was pretty good with a flesh wound and a bandage, too. She let her hand rest against his forehead now.

What did you used to call me, little brother?

Why don't I know? How is that fair?

It's our life.

It was.

It was our life, and they took it.

Finally Natasha looked up at him.

"Tasha." She looked at her brother over the ice bag. "That's what my friends used to call me, I think. From what I remember. I don't know if it's real."

Alex nodded. "Tasha, then."

She stood up, suddenly embarrassed.

"And it was Project Blank Slate. The people who did this to us. It appears to be some kind of radical security protocol, and it looks like S.H.I.E.L.D. had something to do with it. They must have somehow gotten us to agree to it. I found the name in our files, but I can't tell you much more than that. Not yet. Basically, all I know is that you're in hiding."

"And what does any of this have to do with Ivan the Strange?"

"It's possible that he's the thing you're hiding from. Maybe we all should be." Natasha pushed the ice against his head even harder. "But like I said, I don't have all the answers. I didn't even know the questions before Sunday."

Alex looked past her, to the dirty window. "So, no Vermont? Where do I come from, really?"

She looked shy. "Probably Stalingrad. That's where my family—our family—is from."

He nodded, trying to keep his face composed. "And New Jersey?"

She shrugged. "A cover. For your own protection."

Alex sighed. "Well, I guess that explains my love of New Jersey junk food. I've only had it for two years." His eyes flickered to her. "Which would make my mom an agent?"

Natasha hesitated. "Highly trained operative. One of the best. That's not a small job." She looked at his hand, as if she wanted to take it. "I'm sure she cares about you."

"Super," Alex said. "That makes everything better." He looked away. "At least now I know why I got this." He pulled up his sleeve to show Natasha the red hourglass inked on his bicep.

Her face lost all its color. "Where did you get that?"

"A tattoo parlor, probably."

She glared at him.

"What? I just woke up with it one morning." He tried to pull his arm away. "I think."

She shook her head. "That's no random tattoo. That's a message. For me."

"Message? What kind of message?"

"That they can get to you. That you're not safe. No one is."

"But I am safe. I'm right here. Nothing happened to me."

And what would I do if it did?

Slowly, awkwardly—for the first time in years, most likely—Natasha Romanoff reached out and touched her brother's hand.

"Alexei—"

She took his hand in hers.

Alex cried out suddenly, like all the air was being sucked out of the room.

The cheap mattress shook as he grabbed his sister with both arms and cried into her shoulder as hard as he could.

Ava clutched her towel to her chest as she pressed her hand against the bathroom door. The warping door was sticky with steam beneath her fingers, but she didn't even notice. The water was still running; she hadn't wanted them to know she was out.

Ava closed her eyes.

She was only a few meters from Natasha now—just on the other side of the door—and as far as their quantum entanglement was concerned, she might as well have been standing next to a bonfire.

Ava could feel it all.

Disbelief and confusion and relief and sadness and guilt and—

What is that?

That other feeling?

It fluttered in her chest, rippling all the way to her fingertips. There were other feelings too, but this one was new.

It ricocheted through her, even now, straight through her heart.

Love.

Natasha Romanoff loved her brother more than anything in the world.

It wasn't something she would ever admit—and it wasn't something Ava had ever felt from her before.

Could Natasha Romanoff be . . . happy?

I'm from a family of superheroes.

As the three of them rode the public bus into the center of Odessa, Alexei Romanoff was reeling.

He had a sister now, and a girlfriend, and he was sitting behind both of them.

What he didn't have was a mother, though it was impossible to imagine that the person he'd thought was his mother was not, and that she—whoever she was—was not actually going to ground him for the rest of his life when he got back to New Jersey.

Who was going to ground him now?

The Black Widow? Was she his guardian? She was certainly his closest living relative. That wasn't speculation. It was the truth. He knew it; he just didn't know how to process it, and he certainly didn't know how he felt about it.

He stared out the window as Odessa streaked by.

The bus dumped them out on the corner of Deribasovskaya and Havannaya, into a startling, piercing cold that seemed to entirely negate the late-morning sunshine. They'd plodded across the snowy street in silence—Alex kicking the snow out of his stupid loafers—until they reached the far sidewalk. Then they'd crawled gratefully out of the snow and into a warm corner table at the first lit café they could find, ordering platefuls of eggs and steaming milky cappuccinos and fruity hot *kompot*.

Alex smothered his confusion with sugar and pastry. As he managed his fourth plate of strudel, Natasha and Ava studied the stolen O.P.U.S. project files.

"I can't believe I missed it." Natasha was annoyed.

Ava nodded. "That his lab was right beneath the warehouse all along? All of S.H.I.E.L.D. seems to have missed it."

Natasha frowned. "And these names are test subjects? All of them? How can that be? There are more than a hundred names on this list." She looked up from the folder. "A hundred test subjects means there could be a hundred more Entangled Avas out there."

Ava picked up her coffee.

"You mean a hundred deep-cover operatives waiting to start psychically linking to a hundred heads of state or CEOs or dignitaries the minute Ivan Somodorov gives them the high sign." Alex put down his fork, shoving away his latest empty plate.

"Depending on what kind of access those children grew up with, Ivan could have positioned every single one of them to now be exactly where he wants them." Natasha turned a page. "As his spies or operatives. Or even an army of assassins."

"His own massive, worldwide Red Room." Ava shook her head. But something more seemed to be bothering her. "A hundred Entangled children? Like me? Where were they on the night of the raid?"

Natasha looked at her. "I didn't find any other test subjects but you. Ivan was dragging you around as if you were the only one."

"It's all a blur." Ava sighed.

"My name is on that list too, right? So where was I?" Alex asked.

"Maybe this mission was about Ava," Natasha said.

"But that probably was the whole point, right? That Ava was the only one you found?" Alex stared at his empty plate ruefully, as if he had eaten the answers he wanted.

"What are you getting at?" Natasha asked.

"What if Ivan wanted you to rescue Ava, because he wanted you to bring her back to the United States? What if he wanted an entry point to S.H.I.E.L.D.—and to you, Tash? What if it was all a setup?"

Natasha's eyes flickered over at her brother. *Tash?*

He shrugged good-naturedly.

"Even if it was, what do we do?" Ava was frustrated. "If he really does have a hundred Entangled zombies in place, taking out Ivan himself can't even stop it. We don't know who or where the targets are. What the threat is. We only have this list of names from what, eight years ago? They could be anywhere."

"So we'd better get started." Natasha looked at them. "We find Ivan and move before things get any more complicated."

Alex looked from Ava to Natasha. "So we take this to S.H.I.E.L.D.?"

Ava winced. "After how we left the Triskeleon? They're not going to be too happy with us."

"I'm not happy with them," Natasha said fiercely. "They're the last place we can take this. Someone at S.H.I.E.L.D. wiped our memories, and I don't know who we can trust."

Nobody said a word.

"So what now?" Ava tossed her napkin to the table, discouraged.

"Maybe there is a way," Natasha said slowly. She glanced at Ava. "I hate to even bring it up—"

"But you're about to," Alex said. "Eh, Tash?"

She ignored him, speaking only to Ava. "If the documents in these files are right, and O.P.U.S. was your mother's program—"

"It was." Ava cut her off. It clearly wasn't her favorite subject.

"That just might give us the advantage."

"How?" Alex leaned forward over the table.

Natasha looked at Ava. "She's your mother. You were there at her side the whole time. You probably know more about her than anyone—including her scientific brain. Which means you might even know more about the O.P.U.S. than you think you do."

"We can't be sure of that," Ava said uncertainly. "And I don't know anything about her. Why she let Ivan take me, what became of her. What she was doing working with Ivan in the first place. I don't know what good I could do."

"You did remember much more about the warehouse than you thought you would," Alex said, looking at her. "Maybe it was starting to come back?"

Ava didn't answer. A waitress came by, shoving their empty plates onto her tray. Nobody said anything until she was gone again.

Natasha lowered her voice. "So we try to amp up our QE connection, one more time. Just you and me, like it was back at the river. Or like with Tony's machines. I swear I saw a glimpse of something, before one of his machines exploded."

"Because that was so great?" Ava looked skeptical.

"Think about it. We make the most powerful connection we can. You let me in, and I'll see what I can find about O.P.U.S. in your own memories."

"It's too dangerous. Last time Ava couldn't even stay conscious." Alex sounded panicked.

"I know," Natasha said. "But there's no other way."

Alex reached for Ava's hand. "I still don't think it's a good idea."

Ava looked at him. "But she's right. Reestablishing our connection could be the key to figuring out how to break the entanglement."

"Or it's not," Alex said, "and you risk it all for nothing."

"Not for nothing. For every other person Ivan ever held in that warehouse."

The conversation was over. Ava's mind was made up.

LINE-OF-DUTY DEATH [LODD] INVESTIGATION
REF: S.H.I.E.L.D. CASE 121A415
AGENT IN COMMAND [AIC]: PHILLIP COULSON
RE: AGENT NATASHA ROMANOFF A.K.A. BLACK WIDOW,
A.K.A. NATASHA ROMANOVA
TRANSCRIPT: DEPARTMENT OF DEFENSE, LODD INQUIRY HEARINGS.

DOD: You mean to tell me, upon learning you yourself had been the recipient of some kind of compulsory cognitive reset—
ROMANOFF: Call it what it is. Just say it. Brain wipe.

DOD: You had zero qualms about conducting an unauthorized cognition experiment of your own, on a minor asset? In some fleabag hotel room in Ukraine? On Ivan Somodorov's own doorstep?
ROMANOFF: No, sir. That would not be a truthful statement.

DOD: Excuse me?
ROMANOFF: There were not zero qualms. There were qualms. There are always qualms, sir.

DOD: Yet you didn't stop for one minute to consider the validity of your own concerns? You didn't once ask yourself why you were doing any of this "Kumbaya" mumbo-jumbo brain garbage at all?
ROMANOFF: No, sir.

DOD: Why not?
ROMANOFF: Only guitar players and Americans do that, sir.

DACHA ODESSA HOTEL
ODESSA CITY CENTER, UKRAINE

Ava and Natasha sat cross-legged, facing each other on the sagging bed. Alex leaned uneasily against the only door to the room, waiting.

"Give me your hand," Natasha said.

Ava didn't want to, even if she didn't have a choice. And Natasha Romanoff didn't exactly want it either. But this was where they were. This was the moment they'd found each other at now. This impasse, or this opportunity—depending on the moment that came after.

For once in their lives, both *Devushki Ivana* knew they had to force themselves to drop their mental defenses.

Even the idea of it was torture to Ivan's girls.

Ivan had done terrible things to them—to both of them.

Not just in the Red Room for Natasha. Or in the labs of the

O.P.U.S. project for Ava. The cold reach of Ivan Somodorov went much deeper than that.

Ivan had condemned them to always live their lives in the solitary shadows, to always believe they were alone, that they could never be anything but alone. That was life beneath Ivan's dumpling moon. That was his curse.

Deep down, neither girl had ever thought it could be broken.

There was nothing more powerful in the universe than the cold truth of Ivan Somodorov, than their hatred of him and their fear.

Or so they had thought.

Until now. Until there were two of them—

Entangled into something bigger, something more.

An irrefutable truth of their own.

Together, they reached for each other's hands. Together, they looked into each other's eyes. And together, they did the last thing anyone expected them to be able to do.

They let it happen.

As Ava's fingers touched Natasha's, their minds rolled forward, intertwined, endlessly combining and recombining, Ava gave in to the pain that always came with linking to Natasha's psyche—but the moment she stopped trying to resist it, the sensation overwhelmed her, swallowing her whole, until she could no longer separate what hurt from what did not, the way a fish could no longer sense the water.

Whether the pain swallowed her or she swallowed the pain became impossible to say, and she felt nothing at all.

She felt nothing, but saw everything.

Soon it was almost impossible to tell one memory from another—or even to know whose mind they were in one moment to the next.

They were both. They were always.

They were at the end and the beginning, all at once.

The memories flowed.

A scared Tasha presses herself against elaborately painted wallpaper in Stalingrad, as heavy boots tramp down cobblestone streets and shots ring out beyond her playroom windows. Tasha reaches through the bars of the crib next to her. Don't cry, Alexei. I'm not going to let the bad men hurt you. *She looks down at the little brown puppy, whining by her feet.* Will we?

A young Ava refuses to let go of her father's hand, following him down the stairs to the street as she begs him not to leave their old Moscow apartment. I don't care if it's your job. Mama and I don't want to go to Odessa without you.

Tasha's hand clutches the railing as she stumbles, fast as she can, carrying her baby brother down the cellar steps. The puppy scampers after them. Her mother calls frantically for her father in the distance. Tasha covers her ears while shrapnel explodes through the old stone dacha.

Ava plays on the rug with her new china doll, Karolina, sent in the mail from her father, who works abroad. Her mother, surrounded by the endless stacks of her work papers, watches, with tired eyes.

Natasha holds her baby brother in her lap next to a flag-draped coffin lying in the snow at their parents' memorial service. The brown dog curls under their chair. Dark-eyed and solemn, she refuses to let anyone else hold her brother. You still have me, Alexei. You will always have me.

Ava practices her ballet positions, holding on to the back of her mother's chair in the windowless office of her Odessa lab.

An older Natasha sobs in secret in a Moscow Red Room dormitory, her face buried beneath the pillow of a low iron cot. Alexei. He needs me.

Ava practices a dance routine in an old Odessa ballet studio, twirling in circles across a mosaic floor. A number sixty-two is painted inside a yellow sun in the center of the tile. As Ava dances across the mosaic, she sings to her doll. Karolina, Karolina, Karolina—learn the steps, the steps are key, keep you safe and you keep me—one two three, one two three, one two three—

Natasha assembles and disassembles an assault rifle over and over again beneath Ivan's watchful eye. You shame me. Slow as a fat American. What are you going to do in the field? Stop and ask for more time? *Natasha's finger curls around the trigger.*

Ava pirouettes in the ballet studio, pointing her toes as she hits the tiled number six over and over and over again— but with only her left foot, and only on the downbeats of the rhythm.

Natasha faces Ivan, wearing only a tank top. He pulls a hunting knife from a sheath at his waist. Before she can say anything, the blade flashes and blood streaks across her upper arm. He laughs. I attack, ptenets. You defend. If you don't want your shirt cut to shreds, I suggest you move quickly. Otherwise, I clip your wings. *She takes a step back, but he's too quick, and he cuts her arm again, still laughing.*

Ava twirls, hitting the number two—and only with her right foot—far fewer times. Her mind is filled with left sixes and right twos. Her mother looks up from her papers nearby. Learn the dance, Ava—your recital is very soon, as soon as your father comes back.

From the city with the Blue Mosque, Mama?

The very one, Ava.

Natasha stands over the toilet, vomiting. Now she tries to wash the blood from her shaking hands, but it won't come off, and the whole sink turns red with her efforts. Ivan laughs behind her. Your first Red Room kill, ptenets, and there you stand, wild-eyed and weeping. For what, a deer? What will you do when Moscow sends you hunting for me? You really should be an American.

Ava walks with her mother into a military office but refuses to go inside. Her mother panics, slapping her. Ava is stunned. General Somodorov is a powerful man, Ava. You need to do what he says, for your father's sake.

Natasha practices her pliés at the barre, one slim black leotard in a company of fifty others, stretching her graceful arms toward the rafters of the theater while avoiding the concealed pistol strapped to her upper thigh, concealed by her ballet skirt.

Ava sits on the floor against the wall of an institutional-looking bathroom. The tiles are green. She picks at the grout as she tries not to pull the chain holding her to the pipe beneath the sink. It hurts her wrist.

Natasha tears apart an assault rifle in seconds. Her face is stone. Ivan watches as he smokes a Belomorkanal, saying nothing.

Ava sits on a chair in the Odessa lab, one of a dozen children lined in a row. She has wires wrapped around her wrists and forehead. Ivan's voice counts down—"Tri, dva, odin"—and Ava winces as a loud crackling noise echoes through the room. A Red Room experiment. She glances at her mother, behind a glass wall, only to see that she is crying.

* * *

Natasha stares into a rusting mirror over a Red Room bathroom sink. She examines the scar on her upper arm, wincing. It is an X, almost like an hourglass. But her whole body is bruised and battered. She splashes water on her face, looking back into the mirror. One day I will kill you with my own hands, Ivan Somodorov.

Ava lies in a cot, staring at Karolina, her doll. Her wrists are bandaged. Her eyes are red from crying. She hums the song from the ballet studio even now. Tchaikovsky. I will escape you, Ivan Somodorov. One day, I will get as far from here as my father did. You will not own me, the way you own my mother—

And with that, the memories gave way to darkness and then, finally, light.

"She's waking up," Alex said. At least Ava thought it was Alex. His voice was faraway.

Ava opened her eyes. She was lying on the bed now. Alex was sitting next to her, his hand on her back. "Thank God. You're back. You made it." He kissed her on the cheek.

Natasha was pacing in the room. "I could see it all, Ava. Everything. I've never experienced anything like that. It was—"

"Quantum?" Alex suggested.

"That song," Ava murmured. "That was my mother's song."

"From your dance? *Swan Lake*." Natasha nodded. "You know what *Swan Lake* was, of course?"

"A lake? With swans?" Alex asked, reaching for Ava's hand.

"She sang it to me every night," Ava said. The corners of her eyes began to tear up.

"A ballet. Very famous, and very Russian." Natasha's eyes were flashing. "Generally regarded as an *opus*. Pyotr Ilich Tchaikovsky's opus, in fact. At the Bolshoi."

"An opus?" Ava stared.

"What can that mean?" Alex asked.

Natasha sat down on the bed next to Ava.

"It means I don't think Ava's dance was just a dance at all."

"You don't?" Ava sat up.

"No matter what else your mother did, she made certain that you would know one thing, regardless of just how deeply it was buried inside your mind. Dr. Orlova's own swan song—the last thing she ever worked on."

"You mean the dance?" Ava put it together. "'Learn the steps, the steps are key.' That's what my mother told me. At least that's how I remember it."

"Exactly. Literally. A key. I'm thinking some kind of key code. Possibly even for the very project she was working on. The one Ivan was testing on her child." She looked at Ava meaningfully.

Ava grabbed Natasha's arm. "You think I've carried it inside me all this time? A message from my mother? Since Odessa?"

"What?" Alex stared. "You think some dance has something to do with the O.P.U.S.? How is that possible?"

"Basically, I think it's some kind of genetic code rewritten as a mathematical sequence. I'm guessing based on Ava's own DNA . . ." Natasha shook her head, looking at Ava. "And that probably wasn't a ballet studio you're remembering. There were no other dancers in your memories, right? It might have been some kind of lab."

"On the floor of the warehouse lab," Ava said slowly. "We were just there. I saw it. There was some kind of faded pattern all over it, beneath the dust."

Natasha slid her laptop out of her pack, opening it on the bed in front of them. "I think your mother painted that number on the floor, and I think she devised a numerical sequence that you could memorize. And yes. I think that sequence might even act as some kind of key code to set off the O.P.U.S."

"Which might mean we could use it to shut it off?" Alex asked. "That's insane.

"We could at least try to control it," Natasha said. She was punching numbers on the keyboard as fast as she could. "I don't want to forget the code." She smiled at Ava. "Your mother must have been brilliant."

"And my father," Ava said slowly. "He worked for Somodorov too. That's what my mother said. In the city with the Blue Mosque."

"Istanbul," Natasha said. "Ivan must have another lab." She looked up from the keyboard. "Which means . . ."

"There it is. That's the answer. That's where Ivan has to be staging his big comeback from," Alex said.

"Seeing as we know he's not in Odessa," Ava added.

Natasha nodded. "If I can program the code into some kind of delivery device—something that we can use to override the circuitry of the O.P.U.S.—"

"How are you going to do that? This isn't exactly the S.H.I.E.L.D. Brain Trust," Alex said. He looked around at the shady setting. "I'm not even sure what this place is, but I know it's not that."

"Maybe we don't need S.H.I.E.L.D. Or not more S.H.I.E.L.D. than we already have." Natasha pulled her black leather jacket off the chair and rummaged through the pockets. She pulled out a small black drive. "This ought to do it. A little gift from Coulson. A high-yield microdrive, straight from the Brain Trust itself."

"And you think we can use that thing to jam the O.P.U.S. with Dr. Orlova's code?" Alex took the device from his sister's hand.

"I think we should try," Natasha said. "Ava's mother worked pretty hard to get her daughter that message. Let's make sure it doesn't go to waste."

"My mother didn't give up. She was trying to help me get free of Ivan the only way she knew how. *Swan Lake.*" Ava looked at Natasha, overwhelmed. "I would never have known."

Natasha shrugged.

"Thank you, sestra." Ava reached for her suddenly, kissing first Natasha's left cheek, then her right. Russian style. "Strong like an ox and sharp like a razor, that's what my mother would say about you."

Natasha pulled away from the hug, looking embarrassed.

"Good job, Tash." Alex clapped his hand on his sister's shoulder.

Her mouth twisted into a smile at the name. "You're right, by the way. You did call me Tasha, once you were

319

old enough to talk. I remembered when Ava and I were linked."

"You did?" Alex looked surprised.

She nodded. "And Brat? The puppy was mine. I told you to keep an eye on him for me when I was sent to the Krasnaya Komnata." She looked at him sternly. "Thief."

"Wait. Really?" He stared at her. "You did?"

She leaned against the wall for support. "You were crying. You didn't want me to go away with the soldiers. You hated soldiers because of what had happened to our parents."

Alex sank down to the bed. "I have nightmares sometimes. Bombs are going off. In the snow. There's lots of snow." He glanced up at Natasha. "So much I get buried."

"We hid in the cellar, in the winter. When our house was shelled, the snow fell right into the nursery. We were the only ones to survive."

"And Brat," Alex said slowly.

"And Brat. Only his name was Boris until I turned twelve and was sent to the Red Room."

"Boris?" Alex didn't look at her. He couldn't.

Natasha leaned her head back against the wall, looking up at the stained ceiling. Composing herself. "The day the soldiers came for me, I told you that you had to stop crying or you'd scare Boris. Because Boris was your responsibility now, and your little brother. You had to take care of him the way I took care of you—"

"And love him the way that I loved you," Alex said softly. Ava reached to take his hand.

Natasha didn't answer.

Alex wiped his eyes on his sleeve. "So I called him Brat. I let him sleep in my bed. I fed him my potatoes, right off my plate." He spoke in Russian. Ava never let go of his hand.

"I remember that. Trying to not make noise. Trying not to cry, with the dog beneath my blankets."

Natasha looked back at him now. "You wrote letters about that dog for years. Until you stopped."

"Why did I stop?" He frowned, trying to think.

"Because you turned twelve and then the soldiers came for you," she said quietly. "And Ivan's Red Room was no place for even a dog."

"I don't remember."

"I remember." Ava squeezed Alex's hand. "To Ivan Somodorov, we were the animals."

Late that night, Ava and Alex curled together on the bed. Ava could hear Natasha out in the hall, on the phone with Tony Stark, who was checking and cross-checking every name on Ivan's list of Entangled test cases.

Aside from Ava Orlova and Alex Romanoff.

At least Natasha trusted him enough to talk to him. She didn't trust anyone else at S.H.I.E.L.D. and didn't want to risk another Quantum connection.

We can't gamble on losing Ivan now. Not when we're so close.

Ava focused on the conversation. Natasha seemed to be arguing with Tony about how to neutralize the now eighty-seven confirmed Entangled assets on Ivan's list and whether or not to alert the 115 global intelligence networks potentially compromised by them.

Ivan's Entangled army.

If S.H.I.E.L.D. discovers it, they'll discover us.

Alex and me.

We're in those files too.

In the eyes of S.H.I.E.L.D., we're as dangerous as any of Ivan's zombies, aren't we?

If they find out—if anything happens—I'll never escape 7B.

Or worse, I'll have electrodes strapped to my head for the rest of my life.

She couldn't stand to think about it, and she suspected Natasha was outside in the hall, instead of in the room with them, because she was concerned about the same thing.

What will happen to us?

Ava lay in silence, listening to Alex's heart pound. Alex hadn't shown any signs of being compromised, but they couldn't rule it out. He must be as anxious as she was.

"Alex?" Ava raised her head off his chest in the darkness. "Do you think Natasha's right about my mother? That she was trying to save me?"

He slid his arm around her shoulders. "Yeah, I guess I do."

Ava lay her cheek back on his chest. "I hope it's true."

I'm still worried that it's not.

That we can't get out of this trouble, not even with Natasha Romanoff on our side.

That we don't know what we're getting ourselves into.

Alex pulled his arm even more tightly around her. "Don't

worry. Tash will figure out how to shut down Ivan's whole brainwashing machine, and everything will go back to normal again," he said. "You'll see."

"Everything?" Ava lay her hand against his cheek. "What if I don't want everything to go back to normal?" she asked. "What if I like some things the way they are now?"

"What things?" She could hear the smile in his voice.

She pulled her face up next to his and kissed him along his jawline. "I can think of a few." He wrapped his arms around her and rolled over with her held close to him.

After that, there really wasn't much thinking.

S.H.I.E.L.D. EYES ONLY

CLEARANCE LEVEL X

LINE-OF-DUTY DEATH [LODD] INVESTIGATION
REF: S.H.I.E.L.D. CASE 121A415
AGENT IN COMMAND [AIC]: PHILLIP COULSON
RE: AGENT NATASHA ROMANOFF A.K.A. BLACK WIDOW,
A.K.A. NATASHA ROMANOVA
TRANSCRIPT: DEPARTMENT OF DEFENSE, LODD INQUIRY HEARINGS.

DOD: Are you saying the minor asset had a weaponized memory?
ROMANOFF: One memory in particular. Yes, sir.

DOD: And a biological trigger was hidden inside a child's mind in the
form of a ballet dance?
ROMANOFF: I believe so, sir.

DOD: Does this sound remotely plausible to you now, in the light
of day?
ROMANOFF: As plausible as unicorns, sir.

DOD: And you believed it was some sort of security code for
O.P.U.S.?
ROMANOFF: I believed that if Dr. Orlova was smart enough to build
the program, she was smart enough to take it down, sir. And I think
she believed that she had made her daughter strong enough to do it.

DOD: So you took your Red Room witch hunt to Istanbul, all because
of some ballerina ghost story about her dead mommy from when
she was a kid?
ROMANOFF: That, because if the QE bond was that strong for Ava
and me, I didn't want to think about what the other ninety-nine
Entangled test cases could be doing.

CHAPTER **29**: ALEX

he flight was a straight shot,
ninety minutes south over the Black Sea. Istanbul was on
the horizon, and Natasha was at the controls.

Seeing as there were no trains and no buses that could
connect Odessa to Istanbul in the current political climate,
they had resorted to Natasha's commandeered S.H.I.E.L.D.
jet. She had ditched it in the empty stockyard of an abandoned steel mill in a barren stretch of land east of Odessa;
it had been difficult to even get a city taxi to venture that
far out.

Alex could only wonder what their driver had thought on
his way back to the city when the plane had ripped through
the sky almost on top of the road.

"This isn't exactly the stealth approach I had in mind," Natasha said. "But on short order, it's the best we can do. I'll put her down at a base outside of the city. It'll work out." She frowned. She was all operative now. She had stopped using unnecessary language when she'd strapped on her second semi-automatic.

"This all has to work out," Ava said, from the copilot's seat. "There isn't a plan B."

"Actually, there is," Natasha said.

"What? It's not like we can call in S.H.I.E.L.D.," Alex said.

"And I'm not going back to 7B," Ava repeated fiercely.

"Nobody's going to make you go back, Ava. And I'm not feeling all that charitable toward S.H.I.E.L.D. at the moment myself," Natasha said. "Seeing as I don't exactly love the idea of someone wiping my brain."

"So what's plan B?" Alex asked.

"We do what we have to do," Natasha said, keeping her eyes fixed on her radar screen.

It took a moment for the words to sink in.

Ava frowned. "We're not going to let anyone *neutralize* eighty-seven people like me, or for all we know even Alex. Eighty-seven more people who never had a choice about what Ivan did to them."

"Besides, you just got through telling us how wired in all of Ivan's Quantums are. We can't fire on the White House, the Pentagon, the Kremlin, Parliament, MI6, Beijing, and half of the Arabian Peninsula without expecting blowback. Talk about World War Three." Alex shook his head.

"That's why it's not plan A," Natasha said, sounding

grim. "But we also can't sit around and wait for one of those Quantums to give launch codes for a nuke or kill the radar for every airplane headed into JFK or LAX."

"There has to be another way," Ava said.

"Tony's monitoring the NSA feeds and the Stark sats. If we get a surge anywhere, and it looks like Ivan's army is beginning to deploy—well, we'll deal with that when and if it happens." Natasha sounded as unhappy about it as they did. "Until then, let's stay focused on our own play."

Ava stared at the small black drive that lay flat in the palm of her hand. Natasha had reprogrammed it with Dr. Orlova's O.P.U.S. sequence in the final few hours before leaving the Dacha Odessa Hotel. "We don't have much to go on. Just the *Swan Lake* code and that Ivan's other lab was in Istanbul." She turned the drive over in her hand. "It has to be enough. We have to make it work."

"It will," Alex said from behind her.

Natasha touched a screen on her control panel, and a map lit up on the surface, the satellite image of a city. "We've got one other thing, actually." Pulsing lights illuminated a three-inch circle in the center of what looked like a grid of dense urban blocks. "We're picking up a massive heat signature with a very small radius in the center of Istanbul. There."

"Is that the lab?" Alex asked his sister.

Natasha nodded. "It looks like we're within kilometers of Ivan's Turkish operation. And from the corresponding radiation numbers, I think we can also say that we've found his next O.P.U.S. power source. He appears to be draining power from the city grid even as we speak."

"Where?" Ava asked.

"The old city of Sultanahmet, right in the center of Istanbul." Natasha looked over at her. "You want to go over the play again?"

Ava held up the drive. "We find the device, locate the port somewhere on it, connect the drive, take the O.P.U.S. network offline."

"And?"

"The transfer can only take ten seconds. There's a counter on the drive. It'll start timing from the second I connect it to Ivan's device," Alex recited.

"You mean I connect it," Ava said.

"No," Alex said. "We don't know that you have to do it. We just know you had the code. You can give me the drive. I volunteer as tribute. Let me go. I'll disable the O.P.U.S. and get out. No big deal." He reached for the drive.

Ava snorted, holding it away from him. "The whole code is based on my DNA, remember?"

"You're not thinking straight, Ava. The second we take out the O.P.U.S., you'll lose all your Entanglement skills. You won't be a tough little Agent Romanoff Mini-Me anymore. You won't know how to fire your Glock or your Bloch or whatever."

Natasha looked back at him. "Glock. And it's times like this that I can't believe we're related."

Ava glared. "Oh my God. *Thank you* for the vote of confidence, but I can do this. Stop worrying."

Natasha held up a black-gloved hand. "Ava's our best shot at jamming the device—it's her code. But we need to get her close enough to do it and cover her while she does. None of those things will be easy. They might not even be possible."

Neither Ava nor Alex said a word.

Natasha checked her control panel. "Fifteen minutes out. We're cleared for an airfield just outside of the city," she said.

"And by cleared you mean . . . ?" Alex raised an eyebrow.

"We cleared ourselves." Natasha shrugged. "And it might not be so much of an airfield as a field."

Alex reached up for Ava's hand and held it, lacing his fingers through hers. He decided, right then, that he never wanted to let it go.

S.H.I.E.L.D. EYES ONLY

CLEARANCE LEVEL X

LINE-OF-DUTY DEATH [LODD] INVESTIGATION
REF: S.H.I.E.L.D. CASE 121A415
AGENT IN COMMAND [AIC]: PHILLIP COULSON
RE: AGENT NATASHA ROMANOFF A.K.A. BLACK WIDOW,
A.K.A. NATASHA ROMANOVA
TRANSCRIPT: DEPARTMENT OF DEFENSE, LODD INQUIRY HEARINGS.

DOD: So you approved not one but two minor assets for a black-ops, off-the-books mission in a country where we are in no way authorized to execute fieldwork?
ROMANOFF: Something like that. Sir.

DOD: And you thought this would be okay because?
ROMANOFF: Because that's my job. Because Ivan Somodorov was my responsibility eight years ago. Because I was supposed to keep him from getting to Ava Orlova the same way he'd gotten to me, the same way he'd gotten to her mother, and I failed. Because there was nothing I could do to save anyone, when it came to Ivan Somodorov, but God help me that wasn't going to keep me from trying.

DOD: Did you ever stop to think that there were other ways to go about that job, agent?
ROMANOFF: No, sir.

DOD: Because?
ROMANOFF: I guess I'm a Romanoff, sir.

DOD: And that's something you have to live with now.
ROMANOFF: We have to live with a lot of things, sir. That's the other part of being a Romanoff.

STREETS OF SULTANAHMET
ISTANBUL, TURKEY

It hadn't been hard to find Ivan's lab. It had taken longer to find a way from the dead farmland where they'd hidden the plane to the center of Istanbul. Natasha tagged Ivan's location twenty minutes after they'd rolled out of the back of a dusty truck, thanks to Russian wireless. There may have been sixty-eight million subscribers to MegaFon wireless, but very few of them happened to be in the part of Istanbul's old city where Ivan's lab was located. The combined wireless signals of an underground crew of Ukrainians and Russians practically formed an electronic WE ARE HERE.

Now Natasha led the way into a crowded marketplace.

"We think Ivan's working in Sultanahmet, right?" Alex said. He pointed to a street sign. "We're here."

"Must be the Turkish word for the part of the city with the most tourists, the most mosques, and the most men." Ava scanned the crowd.

"It's the old town. Ivan's back to hiding in plain sight," Natasha said. "It's kind of brilliant, actually. Every foot of this place is sacred. No government in the world could touch any of these buildings, even if Ivan Somodorov and his entire army were inside. Not without causing international chaos." She was impressed.

"Great. So he's a genius. Fifty points for Ivanclaw." Alex was grim.

Natasha tried to put it out of her mind. What was about to happen. What she was going to have to do.

She knew, when it came down to it, that she was going to be the one who had to pull the trigger. She always was, wasn't she?

Stay focused, Romanoff. It's all about the mission.

Keep your mind on the mission.

Natasha hadn't told them how impossible it would be—to do what they needed to do. She also hadn't mentioned how bad the situation was, considering what Stark had told her. The Entangled were hidden throughout the families of the Pentagon, not to mention Langley. In New York, they were invisible among the interns and the neighbors and the dog walkers and the gardeners and the children of diplomats working at the United Nations. The North American targets would be the first to go.

Children of senior members of the Kremlin were Entangled too. Moscow's FSB had over 250,000 employees by Natasha's count. Who would notice the irregular behavior of one agent, with one compromised family?

Students in Islamabad had been flagged. Pakistan's ISI could be compromised for months before S.H.I.E.L.D. ever knew the difference.

And names they'd found operating just outside MI6? In the center of London? Could be disastrous.

Or the son of the deputy minister in charge of India's Research and Analysis Wing? He was close enough to trouble to be strategically useful to Ivan.

And of course, the student analysts they'd found in Berlin. The BND knew far too much about the former Soviet world for Ivan to leave it standing. S.H.I.E.L.D. was working overtime to build their case now, but they were coming from behind.

Natasha shook her head.

It was going to be a bloody mess—that much she knew.

If she couldn't get to the O.P.U.S. before Ivan activated them all, it wasn't going to be up to Natasha or Tony or the kids.

S.H.I.E.L.D. would take them all out before anyone could stop them.

Including Ava Orlova.

And including my own brother.

So focus.

She looked at the two of them now.

They're just kids.

She looked past them to the spires rising in the distance. The *Ayasofya*, on her left, was the color of the rose-petal jam the street vendors offered up from their blankets. A complex compilation of shapes, boxy and sharp and round. The Blue Mosque, on her right, competed in the sunlight for size and significance. Glittering gold reflected as it twisted itself atop the spires, and crowds rushed the paths and archways into its courtyard.

"See? That's the Blue Mosque. Holiest spot in all of Sultanahmet." Natasha nodded with her head.

Ava looked up at the familiar name. "Where? I don't see it." She frowned. "By where those birds are?"

What birds?

Natasha never pointed, and she only gave the barest indication of where she was looking now. Ivan's very first lesson—never move in the direction you seem to be moving— was harder to shake than she had ever let on.

"And across the street, that's the *Ayasofya*, which was basically the building that caused the Crusades," Natasha said, keeping her eyes on the sky.

There they are.

The birds.

A whole group of them—tiny as swallows, nothing more than gray splotches that hovered over the cobblestone street in front of them, weaving from storefront to storefront.

"So it's pretty much the Helen of Troy of houses of worship?" Alex looked at the ancient building, interested.

Natasha kept her eyes trained above the buildings.

It's a pattern. A repeating pattern.

Birds don't fly like that.

Ava took in the crowded street corner. "I'm guessing we're a little late for the Crusades, but it seems like those same two blocks are still where everyone here is headed. Should we walk that way?"

Those aren't birds.

"Don't walk. Run—"

Natasha shoved them roughly in front of her and took off through the intersection.

Those are Ivan's drones.

As they ducked through the streets, Natasha kept her head down, letting only her eyes scan the streets around her. Ava and Alex followed.

"This way."

They skidded around a corner, sending a crowd scattering. A group of women in raincoats buttoned from collar to toe. Natasha looked over her shoulder.

At least six small gray objects still followed, maybe a hundred feet above the street. If she listened, she could make out the faint hum of their motors, even from here. Even above their pounding footsteps.

They had to get off the open street.

"In here," Natasha hissed.

Ava and Alex followed her down the pavement, pushing through a crowd of vendors, past scattered places where the sidewalk became a café or a shop. The road was so clogged now, it was like an outdoor mall without walls.

Dust flew as they moved.

The vendors called after them, even as they ran.

"You like a book? Why not?"

"English? German? Italian?"

"I remember you."

Natasha dove behind a stall of textiles, and a rack of colorful embroidered bags went flying.

Alex jumped over a pile of woven slippers and scarves. Ava dodged an old man holding a tray of walnuts and stumbled into the shadows behind Alex.

They caught their breath as Natasha pulled a small lens out from her jacket.

"What are those things?" Alex asked.

Natasha held the lens to her eye. "Drones. Nasty buggers. Sting so bad they'll incapacitate you. When they're not moving too much, you can see the lasers lighting up on their bellies."

The hovering machines roamed the sky above them even now. All three of them stared.

"Ivan's drones?" Ava watched them rotate across the street.

"Microdrones, actually. And yes," Natasha said.

"So those things are weapons?" Alex stared.

"And cameras. They're meant to find us as much as deter us." Natasha pocketed the lens. "Looks like we've found Ivan's lab. The drones just mean we've hit the perimeter."

"How do we get past them?" Ava looked at her.

Good question.

She worked through the logic out loud.

"They followed us when we ran, which means either they spotted us, or they're somehow connected to the O.P.U.S., and they've pinned one or both of you as Quantums."

"Great," Alex said. "Now what?"

Natasha took in the street around them.

Cobblestones and an El Torito. Thousand-year-old buildings and a McDonald's in the distance. They were caught between the ancient mosque and the Starbucks, in a chaotic confusion of time.

Like me, she thought. *And Ivan and my brother and Ava. What are any of us doing here?*

Did I choose this? I can't remember anymore.

How it began. What I wanted. Who I was.

Before Ivan Somodorov and his scars.

She turned to look the other way, to where the street and the crowd widened and hardened into a broad city square, beautiful and old. Everywhere there were trees and benches and people sprawled sitting under and on them, even in the winter sun.

Focus on the mission. How do you take out Ivan's drone perimeter without sounding all his alarms?

In every direction the bright day bustled on without them. A man tried to sell his Turkish novel from a white canvas stand. A mobile ATM pulled up next to him. Two cats watched from a white iron fence. A police car sat in the street nearby.

Not much to work with there.

An old man wandered down the street selling walnuts by the half.

Just past him, a row of men at stands sold ragged chunks of cold watermelon, burned chestnuts, and corn on sticks.

So, what? We throw chestnuts at them?

At the end of the row, another man wrapped something that looked like a pretzel in wax paper and handed it to a policeman on a parked motorcycle.

Cops are out in full force for lunch.

The solution came to her before she could look away.

"Give me a three-minute head start. Then move it." She kept her head down, taking off down the sidewalk toward the food stalls.

She looked behind her. The drones were still hovering over the last block.

It's the O.P.U.S.

Those things aren't even picking up on me.

They're there for Alex and Ava.

Even before she neared the first stall, she had her sleeve up and her widow's cuff buzzing.

"You try," the man said, holding up a stick of corn—as her cuff sparked, and his entire cart exploded into flames.

She pushed through the crowd.

The policeman dropped his pretzel—and the chestnut grill went up next.

Then the pretzel stand. Then the books.

The crowd began to run. The sky was now filled with billowing black smoke, the air with police sirens.

It was impossible to see the drones now—and impossible to be seen.

Eight seconds later, Alex and Ava appeared at Natasha's side, and they slipped through the chaos of the street without another word.

* * *

The smell of burned chestnuts, like burning rubber, was still in the air as they turned off the busy street a few blocks later. Police sirens were still echoing in the distance.

"This is it," she said, letting her pistol slide into the palm of her hand.

"How do you know?" Alex looked at her.

"This isn't my first last stand," Natasha said. She didn't smile. She had meant to, but she found she couldn't.

A ramp in front of them lead to a wide, dark doorway.

Natasha hesitated, but Alex was the one who spoke first.

"If something happens—"

"Don't," Natasha said. "Don't ever."

"I just wanted you to know. I'm glad we met. I mean, again. Now. I'm glad you found me, Tash."

"Technically," Natasha said gruffly, "you found me."

"Technically," Ava said simply, "I found you both."

They were silent.

Natasha's thoughts were reeling, but she couldn't seem to pull them in. Now that it was time, she was too exhausted to say anything. If she was being honest with herself, she was too scared.

But I want you to know, she thought, stealing a glance at her brother. *Everything.*

Natasha looked quickly down at her own black boots, now as battered as any soldier's.

She tried to think about what she would tell him, if she could. If she were the kind of person who could say things like that.

That you are important.

That you always were.

That I never wanted to leave you.

That I'm proud of you, every bit as proud as if I'd had something to do with the person you became.

That I always cared—even when I lost you.

That some part of me would not stop until I found you—and that some part of you was waiting.

It's in your eyes, she thought.

All of it.

Our parents and our past.

The beginning and the end.

She took a breath, looking up at the door in front of them. She focused on the peeling curls of paint, the splintered wood frame.

I hope you love this girl and that she keeps you happy. I hope you let me go, right away, and I hope you know that I never will.

She looked up at her brother's face and found that his eyes were bright and blurry, and in that moment she knew that he loved her, too.

"You have Romanoff eyes," she said finally. It was all she could bring herself to say. Alex nodded. He reached for his sister as she pulled away.

Enough.

We're Romanoffs.

Like Kalashnikovs, only tougher.

But her brother just stood there, waiting for her, until she finally, reluctantly, pulled him in for the quickest hug in history, not longer than the time it took for two brisk pats on her brother's back.

"*Yal yublyu tebya, Sestrenka.*" Love you, Sis.

Natasha nodded, a pained expression on her face. "Can we just shoot someone already?"

So the three of them went inside without saying another word. It was only when Natasha rounded the corner that she caught a glimpse of her brother and Ava, quietly kissing each other good-bye.

S.H.I.E.L.D. EYES ONLY

CLEARANCE LEVEL X

LINE-OF-DUTY DEATH [LODD] INVESTIGATION
REF: S.H.I.E.L.D. CASE 121A415
AGENT IN COMMAND [AIC]: PHILLIP COULSON
RE: AGENT NATASHA ROMANOFF A.K.A. BLACK WIDOW,
A.K.A. NATASHA ROMANOVA

TRANSCRIPT: DEPARTMENT OF DEFENSE, LODD INQUIRY HEARINGS.

DOD: You know the Turkish government isn't very happy with us right now.

ROMANOFF: We had no choice. With Dr. Orlova gone, it wasn't like Ivan Somodorov could build another O.P.U.S. We knew this was our best chance for a fatal hit.

DOD: You wanted to take out quantum entanglement for good? There was no part of you that was curious to see how the QE tech could progress? On American soil, under the safe and watchful eye of the American government?

ROMANOFF: Because we have such a great track record in that department? Some progress isn't progress at all, sir. Some progress causes as much damage as good.

DOD: Your so-called unicorns? Vita-Rays and gamma radiation?

ROMANOFF: Exactly, sir.

DOD: You're not the least bit tempted, Agent Romanoff?

ROMANOFF: If you told me I could turn back the clock and have Odessa never happen, that might be tempting.

DOD: But you can't, can you?

ROMANOFF: Nobody gets a reset, sir. Not even me.

CHAPTER **31**: AVA

SOMODOROV FACILITY, YEREBATAN SARAY JUST OFF THE CISTERNS, ISTANBUL

 curving ramp took the three of them below the ground.

When Ava looked up, her eyes adjusted to the darkness of the space, and as they did, she couldn't believe what emerged. Where she was, at this particular moment, didn't look like anything she had seen on earth before. Lit rows of columns mapped out the vastness, all hidden beneath the bustle of the old city. Some were thicker than others and lit with a strange red light.

They were at a cistern. Not a random cistern, but Yerebatan Saray, which in Turkish meant "underwater palace," at least according to the placard on the wall. It was a monument, the engraved paragraph said. Constantinople's only source for freshwater, despite being surrounded by water, was a little river called Lycus. Because it was insufficient to meet the needs of the growing city, the Turks had to build an aqueduct that brought water to the city and distributed it to various outdoor tanks. These were the cisterns.

So said the wall.

But the words couldn't possibly do justice to what Ava saw before her now.

She stood at the mouth of a vast, shadowy underground cavern, the size of maybe a football field, illuminated with only the faintest light.

Just enough light to count the hired guns, she thought.

She counted as she surveyed the length of the space. The place was heavily armed, but not impossibly. It was the kind of muscle you'd expect at a monument, not a military base.

So there's more.

The cavern was divided into smaller areas by a series of wooden walkway bridges that traversed the space, suspended over the reservoir of water that filled the rock floor. A handful of tourists moved along the paths.

Tourists. Check. Going to have to remember that.

In between the bridges, rows of enormous columns reached up at evenly spaced intervals, appearing to hold up the carved ceiling. The shafts and capitals were uneven and seemed absurdly luxurious, as if they had belonged to a previous building from a more glorious time.

This was not such a time.

Ava was overwhelmed.

My father came here to work every day? Can this really

be where Ivan keeps his lab? Somewhere this beautiful and peaceful?

Natasha held out her wrist. A light on it was flashing, and she yanked her black leather sleeve down to cover it, leaning in toward Ava and Alex.

Her voice was a low whisper. "Look for the entrance to his private facility."

"How could there be a lab? Here?" Ava answered.

"The cisterns are probably just a way to get underground unnoticed. Think of them as a giant lobby. We probably won't see anything that looks like a lab until we get to the far perimeter, but it'll be here somewhere. Hiding in plain sight, right? Just find the door." Natasha motioned toward the shadows.

"What about Ivan?" Alex looked at his sister.

"Leave him to me."

"What *aren't* we leaving to you?" Alex raised an eyebrow.

"Morale? I pretty much suck at that." Natasha almost smiled. "And you can cover me. That's why you're armed. But that's the only reason. If it has a pulse, it's mine. Got it?" Then she grabbed Ava's arm. "Ava?"

"I understand."

"You don't. You aren't me. You might think you are, but you're not. You don't know what's going to happen in there, even if you think you do."

"I have your memories," Ava reminded her. "I know what's going to go down."

"But you don't have my stomach. Not for this," Natasha said.

Ava said nothing.

"I'm serious." Natasha squeezed her arm more tightly.

Ava pulled it away. "I got it."

"You're the pro, Tash," Alex said.

Natasha met his eyes. "That's right. I am. So no heroics. Not from anyone else."

"Get me in," Ava said. "I do the thing with the drive and we get out of here." Her eyes darted around the room, searching for some sign of light that meant another entrance. "As fast as we can. Being this far underground is reminding me of a grave."

Flip the stupid switch. That's why I'm here.

She tried not to think about what would happen after. If Natasha was right, it would basically scramble every hardwired neuron in her body. With any luck, it would also scramble a hundred other Entangled assets, wherever they were around the world. Including Alex, possibly. He hadn't shown any of the signs, but that didn't mean he wasn't part of the program.

Ava tried to focus back on the conversation around her.

Alex spoke in low tones. "I'm pretty sure we just walked right in the back door, the one they use for the public visitors, which probably gives them their cover. Maybe we work backward from there? Start at the far end?"

"Affirmative." Natasha wagged her head toward the back of the cave. "Follow my lead, kids." With that, Ava and Alex followed Natasha Romanoff out of the light and into the darkness of history.

Ivan Somodorov's history.

Ava shook her head.

Good pick, Ivan. It's like the place was made for a fire-fight. And even better, it's hidden beneath a massive urban population—with a massive urban power grid. No wonder you set up camp here.

She took in her environment with her Entangled brain firing rapidly.

Perfect for snipers. You could get off a shot from any of the hidden nooks and crannies. Good coverage, but easy penetration. The water in the cistern, though. Need to get a read on how deep and how wide—

"Ava," Natasha hissed.

Ava looked up, startled.

"Bridge." Natasha motioned.

It was time to move.

They took the nearest bridge, keeping to the side where the shadows were the thickest. One after the other, they moved like rats through the darkness, darting from column to column, threading and winding their way through the wooden maze.

One bridge connected to another above the illuminated, rippling water of the cistern. The reflected light on the surface was beautiful and hypnotic and distracting—so Ava avoided it. Instead, she trained her eyes on the walls in the distance.

Look for the entrance to his private facility.

The cisterns are probably just a way to get underground unnoticed.

Think of them as a giant lobby.

That's what Natasha had said.

Now she hopped from one bridge to another, ducking behind a column just as a group of guards headed their way, deep in conversation.

Alex motioned to Ava and she froze behind him.

Der'mo.

Ava checked over her shoulder, but now there were two guards at her rear.

They're switching shifts.

She looked ahead. She could just make out the barrels of their guns, glinting in the reflected light.

A bridge didn't leave many options when it came to traffic patterns. Especially not when the traffic was armed with automatic weapons. And wearing more Kevlar than a fencer.

Those aren't guards.

They're soldiers.

Ivan's Russian mercenaries.

Natasha gestured—and slipped into the freezing, dark water without a splash. Alex slid in after her. Then Ava.

The cold bit through Ava's clothes. She kicked her way behind a bridge piling, pushing beneath the surface to another, then another—until she was well out of range of the guns.

Slowly, quietly, she broke the surface, next to the cave wall. Only her eyes emerged above the red-lit water, and only long enough to get her bearings.

Natasha's and Alex's heads were bobbing above the water next to her.

All clear.

As far as Ava could tell, they could use the unbroken shadow in this part of the cave for cover.

She followed the others up over the splintered edge of the bridge. Ava clamped her teeth tight to keep them from chattering. Her eyes were stinging.

Now they were in the darkest part of the cavern, farthest from the entrance. Ava tried to calculate the distance she had come; there were twenty-eight rows of twelve columns each in the cisterns. She had already made her way past twenty-two of them.

She did the strategic math.

If Ivan's lab correlates roughly to this space, the entrance will have to be close by now. A service entrance, maybe, or a closed-off security checkpoint. Nothing out of the ordinary, but inaccessible.

There.

There it was, not twenty meters away.

The telltale construction tape, zoning off a single wooden bridge in front of a lone, rusting steel door.

The door to the labs. That has to be it.

Ava suspected that the posted sign on the door meant "off limits."

The wood beneath her feet began to vibrate, and she didn't have to look to know there were soldiers coming up the walkway behind her.

Natasha slid past her, toward the door. She already had her blade out of her belt.

She slid it into the aging lock before she had time to reconsider; it sprang open on the fourth try.

Too easy.

Ivan had all but left the door open for them.

As usual, he would be waiting.

The three former Russians glanced at each other, one last silent communication. Ava knew they were all thinking the same thing.

Have it your way, Ivan.

Let's do this.

As Natasha pushed open the steel door, she saw that she wasn't the only thing that had changed since Odessa.

Ivan had gone high tech. This wasn't the old warehouse on the dying Ukrainian docks. This was a massive state-of-the-art scientific facility the size of an airplane hangar, which was exactly what it looked like. A underground military research base, devoted to one thing and one thing only—and that thing stood carefully elevated on a steel platform in the center of the room.

The O.P.U.S. itself.

Snipers surrounded the base of the platform, which, while only a few meters tall, spanned maybe ten meters across in either direction.

Mercenaries.

Again.

Now that there was enough light to really see them, she noticed they wore the short-sleeved black polo shirts, black bulletproof vests, and black military pants tucked into black combat boots of Istanbul's police force.

Their faces were hooded in black.

They're dressed as riot police.

Explains away the bigger guns and the body shields.

Natasha counted the guns as the three of them took cover behind a stack of crates leaning against a curving corner of the rock. There were too many to count.

Her eyes narrowed.

From this vantage point she could see more than just Ivan's hired guns. She could see everything—and one thing in particular.

Ivan Somodorov.

She watched as he stepped out from behind the O.P.U.S., high on the raised scaffolding that held the device in the center of the chamber.

The ghost from her past was a ghost no longer.

The old Russian grinned from above. "Natashka? I know you're out there. I said you would come, and you didn't disappoint. You never do, do you, *ptenets?*"

His hairless head shone beneath the fluorescent bulbs that hung from the cavern ceiling; it was the only part of him not hidden by his baggy, black nylon track suit. She looked away from his face, but couldn't move her eyes from the thick scrolling of tattoos that bisected his neck. She didn't have to see the pattern to know what it said.

"No Man No Problem."

It had been Stalin's infamous reason for making all of his political enemies disappear—and to the same ends, Ivan's.

Her stomach twisted into a slippery knot of muscle and bile.

Ivan looked down at his watch, shaking his head. "I'm afraid we're going to have to speed things up, however. We have a tight schedule. Twelve minutes, in fact. We can't keep the children waiting."

Natasha said nothing.

Alex and Ava looked at her.

"Come out and see your old friend, my baby bird," Ivan shouted again. His thickly-accented voice echoed in the room around her.

But Natasha Romanoff was done playing games with Ivan the Strange.

She'd been playing them her entire life. It had to end, and not with a bullet in her baby brother's back. It wasn't worth risking his life and Ava's.

Natasha knew that if it came down to it, she would sacrifice her life for them. She had always known; that had never been a question.

The only remaining question would have been why.

At first, it would have been because of duty. A sense of responsibility or loyalty. The nature of the job she'd loved so much and done so well. The greater good, for the most people.

It was an old Russian lesson, and she'd learned it well.

But now, everything had changed.

Now she was learning something else, something she was only just starting to understand. Something unlike anything else she'd felt in a very, very long time.

Love.

Natasha wasn't afraid.

She was determined.

She just had to distract Ivan long enough so that Ava could do what they'd come here to do.

Alex looked at her. "Tash? What are you—"

She took a step forward.

Ava reached for her arm. "Don't."

But Natasha pushed past both of them and took her place in the center of the room.

LINE-OF-DUTY DEATH [LODD] INVESTIGATION
REF: S.H.I.E.L.D. CASE 121A415
AGENT IN COMMAND [AIC]: PHILLIP COULSON
RE: AGENT NATASHA ROMANOFF A.K.A. BLACK WIDOW, A.K.A. NATASHA ROMANOVA
TRANSCRIPT: DEPARTMENT OF DEFENSE, LODD INQUIRY HEARINGS.

DOD: What did he really want from you? Ivan Somodorov. Because I can think of easier ways to eliminate a target than dragging her down into an ancient Turkish cistern.
ROMANOFF: There's an old saying from the gulag. If you mean to punish a man with three brothers, you make the first kill the second while the third watches.

DOD: And this is what you were now? The three gulag brothers?
ROMANOFF: It's just an old saying, sir.

DOD: I heard another old saying about the gulag.
ROMANOFF: What's that?

DOD: Don't go to the gulag.
ROMANOFF: I didn't have a choice. None of us did.

DOD: I think you're wrong. I think this was something you wanted. I think you sought Ivan Somodorov out, you went to him, all three of you. You took the fight to Odessa, and then Istanbul.
ROMANOFF: Just as he brought it to the United States before that. Just as he stole a child from her mother.

DOD: So the real question is, what did you want from him?
ROMANOFF: I don't think that's a question at all, sir.

SOMODOROV FACILITY,
YEREBATAN SARAY
JUST OFF THE CISTERNS, ISTANBUL

"**I**van," Natasha said, her voice a low warning. "We don't need to involve any of them. They're just children." She kept her hand moving, slowly, until her weapon was trained on Ivan's head. "This is between you and me."

The hooded soldiers aimed their guns at her, and she could feel the snipers moving into place around the perimeter of the room.

Outnumbered, at least ten to one.

Been there before.

Ivan shrugged. "Don't spoil it, Natashka. I have been waiting for this day for a long time. So have my young friends around the world." He grinned. "They may not know it now, but they will, very soon."

"You mean your underage army? The Quantums?"

"Catchy. I think I'll use that." Ivan nodded.

"Yeah, that whole quantum entanglement thing? That's not going to happen. I'm going to make sure of that," Natasha said. "We know what you're doing. You won't get away with it."

Ivan smiled.

"I don't think you understand. I already have. Look around. We're all here together. Who do you think I have fighting by my side, even now?"

They're here. The Entangled. These hooded soldiers.

Ivan has more than a hundred.

More than we know.

They're his hired guns.

His army.

And they're no older than my brother.

Natasha sounded as disgusted as she felt. "You're sick. They're barely old enough to fight."

Ivan shrugged. "I seem to remember you knew how to handle a Glock at that age." He smiled. "I am the father of this army, Natashka. Just as I was to you."

"You were nobody's father, Ivan."

"Of course I was. And my most successful quantum pair, both my girls. My long-lost ptenets and my key to the future. Think of it as our own little family reunion—only one that will change the world."

"No thanks," Ava said. "I think I'll pass."

The lights flickered on and off across the cavern ceiling. A power surge.

It's already happening, Natasha thought.

"Here we go." Ivan looked up. "We had to hijack most of the city's power grid. Keep your fingers crossed we don't end up with another Chernobyl. I told Moscow we weren't ready that time. But I also didn't have your help, my Devushki."

"Our help? We will never help you. Not ever," Ava said.

Natasha looked over her shoulder at Ava and then Alex. "Just like you kids practiced. You take left. You take right."

Then she looked back at Ivan. "Sorry. We're going to have to pass."

"Life is a series of crushing disappointments," Ivan said with a shrug.

Natasha shrugged back—and then attacked.

Alex broke left. Ava broke right.

Ava rammed herself into the soldier closest to her—he went down still firing—and rolled out of the way.

Alex grabbed a gun off the soldier next to him and slammed it into his head, dropping him like a rock.

Natasha launched herself at the remaining soldiers between her and the O.P.U.S. platform. She landed boots first—with one in the gut of each of two soldiers. While multiple rounds discharged past her head on either side, she kicked her legs up and free, landing on her feet just in time to kick a boot into the knees of the two thugs at the base of the ladder that led up to the platform.

I'm the distraction. Ava and Alex will be fine. They'll use me to get clear and get to cover. That's the play. That's what we practiced.

She drew as much fire as she could, moving closer and closer to the gleaming steel device encased on the platform.

Now she could see it was wired into a massive network of power cores, just as it had been back in the warehouse, eight years ago. It still had the vague look of some kind of horrible sea monster, a giant octopus with a tentacle in every ship.

Only this O.P.U.S. device was ten times larger than the one in Odessa—and this time it looked like it was connected to ten times more firepower. This blast radius just might take out half the city above.

No pressure, Romanoff.

Now she was so close she could see the timer on the surface of the device. They didn't have much time.

Ten minutes to shut this party down.

But there was nothing Natasha could do to end it without Ava and the drive.

A round of sniper fire bit the air around her, and Natasha ducked, crouching along the floor.

She rose above the steel surface of the O.P.U.S.

Ivan Somodorov looked back at her. It was only the two of them now. Just as it had been at the very beginning.

Natasha Romanoff and Ivan Somodorov.

She realized the snipers had stopped.

He's not letting them target me. Why not?

He wants to do the honors himself?

She shrugged.

"I've come to kill you, Ivan. It's time."

"I know you think that," he said. "And I have been waiting, my Natashka."

"I don't know why it had to be like this," Natasha said. "But it did."

"That's a bit philosophical," Ivan said. "But I'm afraid it doesn't matter now. I'm glad you're here to see it. Soon many pieces will fall into place, and a movement will be born. We will bring about the great rebirth of all that we have lost. The Red Room in all its glory. The empire of the people and the greatest federation the world has ever seen."

"Let it go, Ivan. You're starting to sound like kind of a loser. Let's just get this over with."

He smiled, which only made him look like some kind of feral animal. "Now? Is it a dumpling moon, tonight?"

"I didn't care enough to look."

"Of course you do. You always have. That's your greatest weakness, and your most terrible secret."

"Shut up, Ivan."

"Why do you think you were such a ripe target for the O.P.U.S.? All those lovely little connections, reaching out every which way, desperate to connect with someone, anyone." He chuckled, pulling out a cigarette.

A Belomorkanal.

Your last, she thought.

He lit it, taking a drag. "You must fit in so well, in America, ptenets."

"This gooey ball of mush?" she said. "I really do."

She raised her weapon.

Do it.

She heard the sound of the next squad of snipers at the door, moving into ready positions at the perimeter of the room.

Ivan's backup plan.

She counted the footsteps.

There were many—more than she would have liked.

He's been preparing for this. For us.

She listened.

At ten o'clock. At three. At five.

She didn't even have to look. The math didn't work.

Even so, she couldn't bring herself to lower her gun.

Ivan held up his hand.

"No need," he called over his shoulder. "She won't do it. She can't." He looked back at Natasha. "She never could."

"You seem pretty confident," Natasha said. "For a guy sitting at the center of my crosshairs."

"Of course. I should know." He pointed at her left arm, smiling his crooked-toothed smile. "I'm the one who clipped your wings."

She lined up the shot.

"It's not our moon, my Natashka. We still have much to accomplish together. I knew you'd come back to me. Why else would I have done any of this, if not for you?"

"Because you're a clinical psychopath, *comrade?*"

He moved closer. "Because it's your mission, ptenets. To be here, now. You just can't remember. You just don't know it. This lab contains the last remaining functional O.P.U.S. prototype."

"Or dysfunctional." Natasha shrugged. "Potato, potahto."

"You've done exactly as you were asked. You proved it could work." Ivan smiled. "All according to the plan of one Yulia Orlova, the only Soviet scientist ever to solve the puzzle of quantum entanglement." He gestured to the device in the center of the room. "I give you her O.P.U.S., named for her team."

"Spare me the details," Natasha said, but Ivan was transfixed.

Ivan pointed to the stark lettering on the side of the steel casing, one at a time. His finger barely touched the silver O. "See? Orlova. That's her. Before I turned her into something less than human."

Ivan moved his finger to the letter *P*. "This was Yulia's husband, of course. Anatoly Pavlov. He was the one who came up with the initial brain-computer interface. I killed him myself."

Ava's father, Natasha remembered.

Ivan pointed to the *U*. "Pyotr Usov. He was just a Red Room functionary, but he kept our lab open long after the others were closed. Until he, too, met an unfortunate end. They found him floating in a water tower, after asking for one too many promotions."

Ivan shrugged, moving his finger one last time. "Which brings us, humbly, to yours truly." Ivan smiled. "Ivan Somodorov, old army dog. Defender of the People. Patriot of the Red Room. Old friend of the Romanoffs, living and dead."

"Who stole everything from everyone and called it science," Natasha said matter-of-factly.

"Not science. Progress. You can't stop a new day from coming. This is bigger than you and me, Natashka."

"Orlova, Pavlov, Usov, Somodorov? What is that, a poem?" She gestured with the barrel of her gun to Ivan's face. "Written to the rhythm of Ava's DNA?"

"A rebellious act, in a misguided parenting moment." Ivan sighed. "No matter. You've done your job, and I commend you. You've come back to me and made an old man proud."

"Don't be." Her voice was flat.

He took a step, laying his hand on the barrel of her weapon. "You don't fool me. You'll always be Devushki Ivana." He pushed the barrel gently out of the way. "It's been a long time coming, but you've been waiting, and I'm touched."

"I'm not quite done," Natasha said. "There's one more thing I have to do. Also for my Devuskhi Ivana." He raised an eyebrow. She didn't look away from his cold Russian eyes. "You could say it's also been a long time coming, for all of Ivan's girls."

"*Da?*"

"*Da.*"

Before he could answer, she pulled the trigger.

It broke like glass.

The bullet flew through the hand that had chained her to the radiator on so many winter nights.

It pierced Ivan's jaw, shattering it into bone as fine as dust.

It shot through the base of his skull.

His eyes went blank.

His legs buckled beneath him.

She looked away before the body hit the ground.

S.H.I.E.L.D. EYES ONLY

CLEARANCE LEVEL X

LINE-OF-DUTY DEATH [LODD] INVESTIGATION
REF: S.H.I.E.L.D. CASE 121A415
AGENT IN COMMAND [AIC]: PHILLIP COULSON
RE: AGENT NATASHA ROMANOFF A.K.A. BLACK WIDOW,
A.K.A. NATASHA ROMANOVA
TRANSCRIPT: DEPARTMENT OF DEFENSE, LODD INQUIRY HEARINGS.

DOD: So you eliminated the target. Ivan Somodorov. There's one for your bucket list. Must have felt good.
ROMANOFF: [pausing] Have you ever killed someone, sir?

DOD: Afghanistan. From thirty-five thousand feet.
ROMANOFF: No offense, sir. It's not the same. And it never feels good.

DOD: How does it feel, Agent?
ROMANOFF: A gun might as well shoot both ways at once, sir. You want to take out the person in the crosshairs? You have to get okay with taking out the person at the trigger. You don't get to choose.

DOD: You seem to say that a lot.
ROMANOFF: I'm Russian.

DOD: You were.
ROMANOFF: I was, sir.

DOD: Either way. You crossed off Ivan Somodorov.
ROMANOFF: I think I've got to get a better bucket list.

DOD: What about the O.P.U.S.?
ROMANOFF: Next on the list.

CHAPTER **33**: AVA

SOMODOROV FACILITY, YEREBATAN SARAY JUST OFF THE CISTERNS, ISTANBUL

The burst of sniper fire that followed was deafening, even on the far side of the lab.

Ava ducked behind an overturned table. Alex slammed a hooded soldier into a supply rack behind him and crouched next to her.

"Natasha," Alex said, breathless. "Sounds like she's in trouble."

Ava looked back up at the platform where the O.P.U.S. was. A row of snipers remained between them and it.

It didn't matter.

"This is taking too long," Ava said. "We have to find a way to get up there."

He nodded. "How?"

I have to shut down the O.P.U.S.
Jam the drive into the device and take out the army.
My mother started it. Now it's up to me to end it.
She didn't say anything.
She just felt herself starting to move.
"Wait!" shouted Alex. He picked up a weapon from an unconscious soldier and handed it to her. She noticed, for the first time, that he was already carrying one himself.
"I'll draw them off you. You won't make it five feet if I don't."
"No way. It's too risky. Just cover me from back here."
He held up his weapon. "Just a few seconds. I'll keep moving. I'll meet you on the platform."
The firefight on the other side of the lab picked up.
Ava couldn't count the rounds.
Alex was already moving, and she knew she couldn't stop him. He pulled his other gun from his waistband and released the safety.
She looked at him. "You aren't trained for this."
"I'll be fine. I'm a Romanoff." He touched her cheek with his hand. "Just wait until they come after me. Then make your move."
Gunfire blew past him. They had been spotted.
"Get down!" Ava screamed, pulling him down as hard as she could.
"Hold on," he shouted back. "Cover me—"
With all the strength he had, he flung himself at the platform, diving headfirst into the line of fire. Hurling himself into the smoke and chaos.

Moments later he was shouting to her.

"Now!"

She bolted toward the platform.

She could just make out Natasha at the end of the room, her back pushed up against the far side of the raised steel scaffolding. She was outnumbered, but that had never stopped her before, Ava knew.

Half the room was on fire.

A few meters away, the central O.P.U.S. device was sparking and smoking. Only so much could survive the barrage of ammo this room had seen.

They would have to work quickly.

Alex dodged behind steel shelving, firing from both weapons. Ava followed as he cleared the path for her. She was paces behind him now, and every bit Natasha Romanoff's Quantum double.

Stay low—move quickly—head down—don't make eye contact—

Stealth is speed and motion—

Ava saw Natasha freeze from across the room. She heard the screaming in Russian.

"Get out of here, Brother!"

"Do it," he said under his breath. "Do it now, Ava."

He fired shot after shot.

Ava couldn't speak. She stumbled forward, kneeling in front of the O.P.U.S. She pulled at a side panel with both hands, searching for a port as bullets scattered past her head.

"I can't—I can't find it."

"Keep looking," Alex shouted.

He kept firing.

Ava spotted a sparking, burned side panel and rocked it back and forth, harder and harder until she found a generator cell loose enough to rip from the side of the nucleus device.

She yanked it free.

A bolt of electricity shot through her, and she saw the cabling dragging loose behind it. She dropped it to the ground. It burned as if it had been on fire.

"It's too damaged. I can't even see where I would put the drive."

Think.

You're not just Ava Orlova.

You have your mother's code and Natasha's memories.

Alexei's heart.

They're fighting with you and for you.

Find a way to make this work.

She stared at the mass of wiring in the body of the O.P.U.S. device.

It's a circuit.

Complex, but essentially a circuit, connecting to a CPU.

You should be able to hack it.

Natasha should.

She pulled a thick red wire from the mass. Then a blue one. Bit off the ends of each with her mouth and twisted bits of wire from each end together.

Then she reached deep into the center of the machine and pulled out its brain—a motherboard the size of a shoebox.

There.

I should be able to connect the drive, if I can just rewire that one section. . . .

It sparked in her hands, and a web of blue electricity spread across the entire device. It was all she could do not to drop it.

She looked up.

"The whole thing is live, Alex! This whole place could blow at any minute!"

Alex had seen it too.

"You have to keep going!" he shouted.

Just then, his arm jerked as a bullet grazed him, and he dropped his gun. Ava screamed. She heard another gunshot and picked up her gun and fired in the direction of the shooter. A sniper in the distance still targeted Alex—Ava could see the red light trained on his chest.

"Alexei!" she screamed. "Alex, don't—"

The shot rang out and found its target, but it wasn't Alexei Romanoff's chest. It was the sparking power cell, the one she'd ripped from the side of the device itself. His hands were black and burned from even touching it, but that didn't stop him.

"Who needs a blade?" Alex shouted. "If you want me, try to take me."

Ava knew what he was saying from the way he swung his weapon, cocking his neck and batting at bullets the way a giant bear might a lazy bee—

Until he crumbled next to her, right at her side.

Ava screamed. "Alex, no—"

Alex rolled to his back, opening his eyes. He forced the words out. *"Sdelaty eto—"* Do it.

Bullets riddled the device around her, and she ducked to the ground. Blood was seeping from Alex's wounds to the stone floor beneath him.

Natasha appeared next to her.

She didn't hesitate, grabbing the sparking power cell from Alex's hands.

She looked at Ava. "Kabul, remember?"

Ava nodded. It wasn't just the name of a city in Afghanistan; it was an operation. An infamous one.

She knew exactly what Natasha was thinking. Then she looked from Alex back to the O.P.U.S.

"Hurry."

Natasha sprinted through the doorway of the lab, dodging bullets, dragging the live cables after her.

When she reached the edge of the raised wooden walkway, she stopped. The sight was grim. Hundreds of Ivan's troops, dressed as Istanbul's police force, were streaming into the cavern and across the walkways in front of her.

Armed to the teeth.

She raised the surging mass of wiring and steel high over her head, kicking off the sniper who now tried to crawl up from the water beneath her.

Natasha cracked the power cell over the hired gun's head, and the guy sank back into the water—but not before she shoved the burning generator cell in after him.

A blue-white shock wave smashed through the cistern, leaping up off the surface of the water as if the liquid itself was burning.

That's the smell.

Burning.

The cistern is burning.

Even the water is on fire.

The screams of the gunmen still trapped in the water were furious. They wouldn't be dead, but they wouldn't necessarily be conscious, either.

Natasha Romanoff had shut down half of Somodorov's army.

In five seconds.

She backed away from the burning tsunami that enveloped the larger lake of the cistern, and then began to run as if her life depended on it.

Which it did.

S.H.I.E.L.D. EYES ONLY

CLEARANCE LEVEL X

LINE-OF-DUTY DEATH [LODD] INVESTIGATION
REF: S.H.I.E.L.D. CASE 121A415
AGENT IN COMMAND [AIC]: PHILLIP COULSON
RE: AGENT NATASHA ROMANOFF A.K.A. BLACK WIDOW,
A.K.A. NATASHA ROMANOVA
TRANSCRIPT: DEPARTMENT OF DEFENSE, LODD INQUIRY HEARINGS.

DOD: What then?
ROMANOFF: Turn off the tape.

DOD: I never turn off the tape.
ROMANOFF: Sir.

DOD: Keep talking.
ROMANOFF: This isn't about you, and this isn't about the United
States. This is where your part of the story ends.

DOD: That's not how this works.
ROMANOFF: The rest is personal. It isn't about saving American
lives. It isn't about saving anyone's life.

DOD: What do you imagine is personal about your life at this point,
Agent Romanoff?
ROMANOFF: No. This isn't yours. It's mine. Some things have to
be mine.

DOD: Says who?
ROMANOFF: This isn't about the Avengers Initiative or Turkish public
safety or any kind of global peacekeeping mission. This is my life.

DOD: You're the last line of defense for citizens of the United States
of America, not to mention the world. Act like it.

SOMODOROV FACILITY,
YEREBATAN SARAY
JUST OFF THE CISTERNS, ISTANBUL

va gripped Alex's hand tightly in her own. His skin was pale and clammy, and she squeezed it again and again. "Stay with me, Alex. We're getting close now."

He nodded but didn't open his eyes.

She turned her attention back to the device in front of her. The O.P.U.S. was practically glowing. Bright bursts of energy seemed to pulse from inside the massive nest of wiring. "It's going. I think I've got it working again. I should be able to short it out now."

It was time.

She fumbled for the black drive in her pocket.

It was all she needed now—the last step to disable Ivan's nightmare project. At least it was supposed to be. As long as the code Natasha had written was working.

She looked over at Alex, who she'd rolled over to one side so as to stop the bleeding from his right arm and leg. She still had her own hand pressed against his left arm.

"It's time, isn't it?" Alex's eyes blinked open.

She nodded.

"It'll work," he said.

"What if it doesn't?"

"Then we'll just do this all over again." He tried to smile, but instead he winced. "Go on. Do it."

"Ten seconds," she said.

She studied the motherboard. She could wedge the drive directly in . . . there.

"Five."

"What are you, chicken?" His eyes were closed, his voice weak. She knew he needed to get home before he lost more blood.

"At least I'm not a brat," she said, staring at the machine in front of her.

Three.

Two.

One.

Now.

She slammed the drive into the loose motherboard and connected the last sparking wire to complete the circuit.

There.

She closed her eyes and ducked next to Alex. His lips formed into a smile. It was the last thing she could feel against her cheek.

"*Molodets.*" Good job, kid.

Then the world exploded around her.

Around them.

Into millions and millions of shrapnel-sized pieces of their past.

Ava's and Alex's and Natasha Romanoff's.

Yulia Orlova's and Anatoly Pavlov's and Pyotr Usov's and especially Ivan Somodorov's.

Clouds of thick, black smoke ballooned over her, enveloping her and everyone still alive. It raced through the cistern cavern, erupting up through the tunnels and exploding out every entrance.

A baptism, she thought.

Only with smoke and fire and death and destruction—

And without the church.

The biggest of big bangs—

Only the kind that comes at the end of the universe—

Not the beginning.

Ava could feel herself losing consciousness, the power draining from her.

The vivid ghosting of Natasha Romanoff's eyes, beyond her own, was fading away.

It was working.

She was forgetting.

Not all of it—but the part that didn't belong to her.

Everything else she remembered.

Maybe that was a last gift from my mother.
The remembering.

Ava shoved the bent, burned sheet of metal off her. The bottom of the panel had melted completely away.

"It's over," Ava said, sitting up into the world of white dust and gray ash. "I mean, I think it's really over. I feel it." She laid her hand against Alex's warm cheek. "Come on, Alex. Let's get out of here. We'll get you fixed right up."

"Bossy," he muttered.

A shower.

That's what I want.

Clean sheets pulled up over our heads for a thousand years.

Alexei Romanoff by my side for a thousand more.

She looked at Alex. His face was pale, but his eyes were moving behind his closed lids. "Can you walk?"

She reached for his hand and squeezed it.

"For you? Anything." His lips barely moved as the words slipped out. "Always."

His last word was a whisper as he squeezed her hand back slowly. Tiredly.

Once—and then twice.

"Hang on," she said. "Just a few minutes more."

He had lost a lot of blood.

He was also the reason that she was still alive—and that her mind was her own again.

If he hadn't drawn the fire of half of Somodorov's snipers, would she have even been able to shut down the O.P.U.S.?

And if her mother hadn't taken the Luxport job—if she hadn't run the project—if her father hadn't worked in the Istanbul lab—would Ivan have taken her for his test subject?

But if he hadn't taken her, would she ever have met Natasha Romanoff?

And if she hadn't met Natasha Romanoff, would she ever have found her way to Alex?

Ava didn't even want to think about it.

She heard Natasha calling in the distance, picking her way through the rubble. "We've got to get out of here. The police—the real police—are everywhere."

"Over here," Ava shouted back.

But as the smoke cleared and her eyes stung, she knew there was still one thing missing.

Only one thing she had left to do.

Something she had never done before.

She rolled over on her side, even though she was cut and bleeding, and the rubble beneath her was as rough as a bed of broken glass and stones.

"I love you, whatever your name is. Alex Manor or Alexei Romanoff. Do you hear me? I love you. I want to play with your dog in the park and meet your stupid cat. I want to fence with you and dance with you and go get ice cream with you."

She smiled.

"And I want to kiss you, really kiss you, until I can't find the place where you leave off and I begin." She nuzzled into the Alexei smell of his shirt. "How does that sound?"

She heard a scraping noise as Natasha shoved a busted lab table out of the way.

"Alex?"

Ava leaned curled against him, listening for the solid, stoic beating of his heart, as she had when they were falling asleep in the Dacha Odessa Hotel the night before.

She waited.

She didn't hear it.

She listened again.

"Alexei?"

She frowned, pulling herself up next to him.

She touched the side of his bloody face.

It was cold.

Then she knew Natasha was shouting—but something was wrong, because Ava couldn't hear anything at all.

The world went silent—as if the blood were coming from her own punctured eardrum instead of his.

Everything stopped. Nothing moved. She didn't know if the fire on the water was still burning, or if ash was still falling through the air.

It didn't matter.

Nothing did.

Nothing

As she rolled him onto his side

Breathed air into his purple-blue mouth

Kissed his cold lips

Held his quiet face

In the distance, his sister shoved her fists against his ribs

Up and down

In and out
Breathe damn it
breathe
He's marble now, she thought
Already
Like my parents
Like Ivan
Like the snow that covered Alexei's face
in his nightmares
People shouldn't be marble
People should be warm
And they should stay
And they should touch
And they should whisper
And they should laugh and love
and weep and wait
and wait
Wait
Alexei Romanoff
You have to wait
wait for me
Alexei
Don't

S.H.I.E.L.D. EYES ONLY

CLEARANCE LEVEL X

LINE-OF-DUTY DEATH [LODD] INVESTIGATION
REF: S.H.I.E.L.D. CASE 121A415
AGENT IN COMMAND [AIC]: PHILLIP COULSON
RE: AGENT NATASHA ROMANOFF A.K.A. BLACK WIDOW, A.K.A. NATASHA ROMANOVA
TRANSCRIPT: DEPARTMENT OF DEFENSE, LODD INQUIRY HEARINGS.

EVIDENCE LOG: As received from S.H.I.E.L.D. Turkish Bureau, Istanbul Field Office.

O.P.U.S. tech remains charred, recovered, crated.

To be dispatched to secure S.H.I.E.L.D. holding facility for further research & development.

Note: All active output/input from device has been disconnected. Device has been deactivated and rendered inert.

Test subjects previously affected by O.P.U.S. tech have been restored to previous mental conditioning.

Classified information has been determined "NOT AT RISK."

[Romanoff_N]

S.H.I.E.L.D. TRANSPORT SOMEWHERE OVER THE MEDITERRANEAN

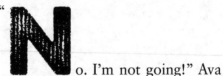"**N**o. I'm not going!" Ava was screaming in the cargo hold of the S.H.I.E.L.D. plane. Coulson's plane. Natasha couldn't think, let alone fly.

Ava pounded on the sealed metal door until her hand began to turn purple. "Let me off! We can't leave him here. We have to wait. Alex is going to come back."

The floor of the plane angled steeply up as Ava spoke. She stumbled, but Natasha kept her on her feet.

They were going, like it or not.

Natasha's S.H.I.E.L.D. brain was on autopilot. It was two hours and forty minutes to the Bulgarian border by car. On the plane, that meant only minutes until they were no longer in Turkish airspace.

Which meant they were gone.

She let her hand drop to the girl's shaking curls. "Ava,"

Natasha said gently. "Alexei's not going to come back. He's gone. Every part of him is gone. We both know that."

Ava sank to the floor of the cargo hold.

Natasha slid down onto her heels next to her.

Ava was shaking. She tried to talk, but her mouth was trembling so hard it was difficult to make out the words. "But he was here this morning. We were here, both of us. In the hotel."

It didn't seem possible.

It shouldn't be.

Natasha understood.

"I know. But he had to go." She slid her arm around Ava, who clung to her so tightly that she wondered if her gun was going to discharge.

Ava shuddered, still crying. "Why?"

Natasha focused her eyes on the window, willing them not to blur. "I don't know."

"Why does everyone leave? Why is it always only us?" The words were almost unintelligible.

Natasha found she couldn't look at Ava. She couldn't look anywhere but the far wall. She didn't know what would happen if she let herself look away. She tried to push everything she was feeling onto the solid blankness of the wall. "I don't know that, either."

"It's not fair," Ava said. Her voice was hoarse.

Natasha took a deep breath. "It's not."

"Don't let go," Ava said quietly.

"I won't," Natasha said. She looked up at the ceiling now. She was afraid the steel wall alone wasn't strong enough to hold everything she felt.

As she turned her eyes upward, she felt the burning weight begin to collect along her lashes.

No.

Not yet.

Not for me.

I don't get to cry now.

But it only took a few seconds for the ceiling to become as heavy as the walls, and even Natasha's eyes were beginning to burn from the pressure.

It was too much for anyone or anything to bear.

When will it be my turn?

When will I get to let go?

Who will be holding me?

Natasha Romanoff gave up.

She let the ceiling and the walls come crashing down. She let everything break into a thousand pieces around her. She let the world end.

My brother is gone.

My brother, the last of my family.

They've won and I've lost.

My brother and myself.

There is a part of me that will never come back now either.

They stole him from me for years, and now he's really gone.

Natasha closed her eyes and let the tears come.

They ran down her face, her neck, her hair.

They dripped down all the way to the top of Ava's head, cradled in her arms, but Ava was sobbing too hard to notice.

And if she did, she wouldn't have cared.

S.H.I.E.L.D. EYES ONLY

CLEARANCE LEVEL X

LINE-OF-DUTY DEATH [LODD] INVESTIGATION
REF: S.H.I.E.L.D. CASE 121A415
AGENT IN COMMAND [AIC]: PHILLIP COULSON
RE: AGENT NATASHA ROMANOFF A.K.A. BLACK WIDOW,
A.K.A. NATASHA ROMANOVA
TRANSCRIPT: DEPARTMENT OF DEFENSE, LODD INQUIRY HEARINGS.

Death Certificate: Teen Doe, Deceased Minor.

Name: xxxxxxxxxxxxxxxxxxxxxxxxxxxxxxxxx
Age: xxx
Gender: xxx
Citizenship: xxxxxxxxxxxxxxxxxxxxxxxxxxx
City of Birth: xxxxxxxxxxxxxxxxxxxxxxxxxxx

Date: xxxxxxxxxxx
Place: xxxxxxxxxxxxxx
Time: xxxxxx
Operation: xxxxxx
Cause of Death: xxxxxxxxxxxxxxxxx

[REDACTED]

MONTCLAIR ALL SAINTS CHURCH
SUBURBAN MONTCLAIR, NEW JERSEY

he Montclair High School orchestra played Tchaikovsky at the funeral.

Swan Lake.

Alex Manor's mother—or at least the veteran S.H.I.E.L.D. field agent playing the part of Alex Manor's mother—could not stop crying.

Her face was buried inside her handkerchief for the better part of an hour. She was not wearing a cat sweatshirt today. It was convincing, whoever she was. Ava had to give her that. Perhaps even an operative could become attached. Given that this was Alex, the tears were quite possibly real. He made people like him; that was one of his charms.

Just as his sister knows how to push them away.

Ava looked down the pews, willing herself not to cry.

Even behind her borrowed sunglasses, she still refused to do it. Not in front of these people.

These strangers.

The church was crammed with high school students, the same faces Ava had seen laughing in her dreams. It was strange to see them crying. It was only Alex's friend—Alex's best friend—Dante, who seemed strangely together.

He sat in front of the casket, along with five nameless, faceless boys Ava had only seen at the fencing tournament.

He never moved his arm from around his little sister's shaking shoulders.

That's Sofi.

Alex said her name was Sofi.

Ava sat in the back pew next to Natasha, who was incognito in a smooth blond wig and giant black glasses that made her look like some kind of jetlagged Parisian model. Coulson, on her other side, always just looked like Coulson.

He didn't seem to be able to help it.

Tony Stark had reluctantly stayed home, but then there would have been no way to explain the presence of Tony Stark at a random teen's funeral in suburban New Jersey.

Steve Rogers sent flowers in the shape of the American flag, out of respect for Natasha. So had Pepper Potts. Bruce Banner, the last of the Avengers, had sent only a note in a small, white envelope. Natasha still clutched it in her hand.

Ava stared at the paper program in her hands, the one with the picture of Alexei in his fencing jacket, holding a blade. He looked like himself, cocky and funny and full of attitude and life.

She touched the white streak in the photograph—his blade. His old fencing bag sat unused in Natasha's apartment, now. Natasha had given his gear to Ava; even she couldn't bear to throw it away. Ava herself didn't know how or when she would ever be able to open the bag again.

Maybe never.

Her breath caught in her throat.

Suddenly she found herself on her feet. She had to get out of there. She slid out to the aisle and disappeared into the parking lot of the church.

Where she found herself staring in horror at a waiting hearse.

Alexei's hearse.

The one that would take him to the cemetery, to his grave.

His real grave.

Where he would stay, forever.

No.

That's not real.

That can't be real.

Ava sank to the curb and let the tears finally begin to fall. She pulled off her sunglasses, finally letting her eyes adjust to the light. Behind her tears she could feel the now familiar burning sensation, just as she had ever since Istanbul.

She knew what she looked like: regular old Ava, except impossibly changed. Everything was different, and not just her broken heart. Her pupils sparked with a pulse of blue light that she couldn't explain, ever since the O.P.U.S. had detonated. And that wasn't the only change. . . .

You're gone, Alexei.

You left me, and now I'm alone with all this.

It's not fair.

va didn't know what any of it meant, and she didn't know how she was going to face it—whatever it was—without him.

She only knew she had to try, for both of them.

"You never think anyone you actually know will be riding in one of those things, do you?"

It was a friendly voice.

A stranger's.

Ava hurriedly wiped her eyes, startled.

She looked up to see Dante Cruz sitting on the curb next to her. His dress shirt was rolled up at the sleeves. His jacket was off. His eyes were red. He had been crying. When he saw her face, he looked as surprised as she did.

"It's you," Dante said. "What are you doing here?"

"What?" Ava was flustered.

She tried to compose herself, but her heart was pounding. She had nothing to say to Alex's friends, especially not this one.

Not in real life.

I never got to be in his real life.

"I'm Alex's friend Dante. Dante Cruz. And you're the girl from Philly. The one Alex was crushing on at the tournament," Dante said.

Of course.

That's all he knows.

She was relieved. She was heartbroken. "I'm Ava. Ava Orlova. And I don't know what you're talking about."

"No, you do. I recognize you. You were the one staring at Alex. The last time I ever saw my best friend."

Ava didn't know what to say. "I didn't—"

"I told the police about you when he disappeared. I tried to get them to look for you. I even described your face to a sketch artist at the precinct. Nobody turned up a clue."

"It wasn't me."

"Then why are you here?"

"Alexei and I were friends. I—I'll miss him too."

Dante looked skeptical.

"Alex. His name is Alex. You could at least get his name right." Dante sounded annoyed, and it caught Ava off guard.

He looked at her. When he did, he seemed every bit the son of a police captain. His eyes were dark, and the look on his face seemed to demand the truth.

"Fine. All right." Ava shivered. "I might have been there in Philly."

But he had already known, and he didn't need for her to tell him. Now he just shook his head. Ava shivered. "Just tell me one thing, Ava. If you hadn't come for him at the tournament, if you hadn't caught his eye—would my best friend still be alive?"

Ava couldn't answer him. She couldn't say it. She couldn't face it.

Not to Dante Cruz, of all people.

He was more a part of Alex's own family than even Natasha herself had ever been. The tears burned their way to the front of her eyes again.

You know it's my fault.

Of course it's my fault.

He would still be alive if he hadn't met me.

If I hadn't dreamed him.

If Natasha hadn't stalked him.

If I hadn't lived inside her head, every step of the way.

Everything that happened was because of one of us.

Natasha and me.

The two people who loved him more than anyone.

"I thought so," Dante said bitterly. He stood up, leaving her alone on the curb. "I have to get back in there. I have a coffin to carry and a best friend to bury." His eyes were dark. He slung his jacket over his shoulder.

"I'm sorry," Ava said miserably. "I miss him so much." Dante looked at her, but she couldn't stop the tears now.

She didn't try.

LINE-OF-DUTY DEATH [LODD] INVESTIGATION
REF: S.H.I.E.L.D. CASE 121A415
AGENT IN COMMAND [AIC]: PHILLIP COULSON
RE: AGENT NATASHA ROMANOFF A.K.A. BLACK WIDOW,
A.K.A. NATASHA ROMANOVA
TRANSCRIPT: DEPARTMENT OF DEFENSE, LODD INQUIRY HEARINGS.

DOD: What do you expect me to say?
ROMANOFF: My expectations are appallingly low, sir.

DOD: I can't decide if you should be suspended or incarcerated.
ROMANOFF: What I deserve is not the same question as what
should happen.

DOD: Because of you, a kid is dead.
ROMANOFF: You don't have to tell me that.

DOD: Duly noted. But you alone are responsible for your actions,
Agent. Start acting like it.
ROMANOFF: I always do.

DOD: Any last words?
ROMANOFF: It's not what I have to say that matters. It's what I have
to do.

DOD: Which is?
ROMANOFF: With all due respect, what happens now is none of your
business.

DOD: Are you finished?
ROMANOFF: No. Screw you. Sir. Now I'm finished.

DOD: That's the understatement of the century, Agent Romanoff—
and even that is probably an understatement—[rustling] Agent?
Where are you going? You can't just walk out on a federal—

ELEVEN
MONTHS
LATER

CHAPTER **37**: NATASHA

S.H.I.E.L.D. ACADEMY OF OPERATIONS
ADMINISTRATION BUILDING

atasha Romanoff strode through the main entrance to the Academy, brushing the snow from her black leather jacket.

She found herself stopping only in front of the Wall of Valor, the clandestine agency's carved-stone memorial to its own fallen.

She caught her breath when she saw his name. It was like seeing her own gravestone.

ALEXEI ROMANOFF.

She traced the letters with a black-gloved finger, leaning her head against the stone.

It's been what, almost a year now?

You're aren't gone.

You're laughing. You're learning how to ride your bike. Chasing a balloon at the frozen Moscow Zoo. Playing with a dog who jumps as high as your head.

Her eyes closed.

Did any of it happen like that? Our childhood? Was any of it real, outside of the Red Room? Will I ever know?

What have they left me of my own?

And what of theirs is still buried deep in my mind?

"Surprised?" Coulson spoke up from behind her.

Natasha opened her eyes, startled. She jerked her head away from the wall. "I wasn't expecting it. He wasn't an agent. Not yet."

"He would have been a great one. He certainly showed he had what it takes. And who knows how many lives he saved in Istanbul."

Natasha nodded, finally forcing herself to turn away. "And Ava?"

"Come on. I'll show you."

Natasha peered through the window of a nondescript door in a nondescript hallway. "Does she ever talk about it?"

"Not unless she has to."

"But it's not holding her back?"

"If anything, it's pushing her forward. She's the top of her class in every single subject, Agent Romanoff."

Natasha looked at Agent Coulson. "And her . . . condition?" She didn't know what else to call it—the mysterious blue electricity that had radiated from inside Ava, ever since the O.P.U.S. had exploded in Istanbul. She had gotten the worst of it, being closest to the blast radius.

If Alex had lived . . .

"Ava hasn't lost her spark, if that's what you're asking." Coulson nodded. "We still don't know much. We've let her experiment in the labs, though. She's rigged a couple of old fencing blades she had—now extendable and retractable. They seem to help her channel her power."

Alexei's blades. Natasha thought. The ones I gave her. So I'm not the only one who can't let him go.

She only nodded. "And?"

Coulson shrugged. "Let's just say, I'd hate to be the guy on the other end of that attack."

"And you've been monitoring her yourself?" Natasha asked.

"I drop in and out, as promised. But it's not just me, you know. She still talks to the cab driver's daughter. I think the girl takes care of Ava's cat."

"Oksana."

He nodded. "And Ava gets the occasional call from Tony Stark. Apparently he likes to tell her jokes."

Natasha rolled her eyes. *Who knows why Tony Stark does anything?*

"Anything else?" she asked.

"A letter now and then from a kid named Dante Cruz. He was—"

"My brother's friend. I know."

Natasha watched Ava make her way up the sheer face

of a climbing wall, her ponytail bobbing behind her. She looked weightless almost. Limitless. Nothing was holding her down now.

As if the wall in front of her was the only thing that mattered, the only thing she had to think about.

She doesn't seem almost a year older. She seems almost a year younger.

"Go on," Coulson said.

Natasha pushed her way inside.

A dozen Academy students—male and female—were suspended on cables, rappelling down from the soaring gymnasium ceiling.

Ava spun on her cable, sizing up the targets around her. She kicked up her boot and slid her sidearm into her fingers, taking out the surrounding targets without blinking an eye.

A perfect score.

It was only then that Natasha realized Ava hadn't fired a single bullet. The Glock she was holding was still crackling with the tell-tale blue light. From the looks of it, the weapon in Ava's hand had worked like an EMP device, discharging the girl's own energy. She might as well have been Zeus, firing lightning bolts from the sky.

Natasha raised an eyebrow.

"See what I mean?" Coulson smiled.

Natasha kept her eyes on Ava. "She's sparky all right."

A horn sounded, and the remaining cables dropped to the floor—dropping their recruits right along with them.

Ava raised her fist with a triumphant shout. "Yes!"

Natasha stared up at her. The girl with the cinnamon ponytail. It was hard to believe she was the same person. "She's ready?"

"She's something," Coulson said. "It's only been eleven months, but like I said, top of her class."

"And the nightmares?"

"A little better. Not gone, though. She needs a family, Agent Romanoff. A support team, something more than a friend. Maybe you could help?"

"I don't have any family," Natasha said automatically.

Ava didn't notice Natasha standing there until the other students began to whisper excitedly. Natasha Romanoff was the Black Widow, and at S.H.I.E.L.D.'s academies, the Avengers were more than celebrities.

They were heroes.

Ava looked over and caught her eye. Something close to a smile crept to her lips.

Then she kicked off from the cable, flipping forward— rotating three hundred and sixty degrees—just as she had off the bridge in Philly.

Only this time without Alex.

Natasha watched from the ground. The moment wasn't lost on her; neither was the message.

I'm here. I've got this. I know what I'm doing.

I'm not a child, anymore. That girl is gone.

As Ava dropped to the ground in front of the agents, her not-quite-regulation Academy jacket came into view. It was white Kevlar, long sleeved, high collared, and form fitting. From the looks of it, it was an old fencing jacket, taken apart and re-sewn to fit like a glove.

When Ava turned to pick up her water bottle, Natasha felt her heart stop. It wasn't just any jacket she was wearing. It was Alexei's. Faded regulation lettering still spelled out the name MANOR across Ava's back.

As the girl crossed the floor toward her, Natasha saw the familiar design hand-stitched and brightly emblazoned across her chest. Two red hourglass shapes that crossed, forming four bright red triangles that met together in the middle.

Natasha smiled, pointing at the red symbol.

"So, Red Widow, eh? How's the name sticking?"

Ava shrugged. "I'm giving it some time."

"Yeah? How much time do you need?" Natasha held up a set of keys. "See, I've got this plane, and S.H.I.E.L.D.'s got this base in Rio, and an old friend of mine's got this nasty little situation brewing in South America . . ."

"And?" Ava raised an eyebrow.

"And I owe him. And, of course, I could use the backup. Or at least, you know, the vacation."

Coulson looked surprised.

Natasha smiled. "What do you say? Want to help me get a little red out of my ledger—Red Widow?"

Ava shrugged. "If you want," she said finally. Playing it off.

Like looking into a mirror, Natasha thought. *She might as well be my shadow.* She smiled. "Go get your stuff. I'll meet you outside."

Ava looked hopefully at Coulson.

He nodded, and she disappeared out the doors before he could change his mind.

Smart girl.

By the time Coulson walked Natasha to the front doors of the Academy, she could see Ava standing outside in the evening snow, next to a gleaming red Harley and a duffel bag full of what Natasha suspected would be old spy gear.

Shivering.

Coulson nodded toward the motorcycle. "New hog?"

Natasha shook her head. "Tomorrow's Ava's birthday. That's her present."

"Ah." Coulson smiled. "Well, I hope this time you remembered a card."

Natasha pulled a card out of her pocket.

He felt in his pocket for a pen. "I happen to have a 1956 Montblanc fountain—"

"Already signed and everything." Natasha shrugged. "I used a Sharpie."

He laughed. "Go easy on her."

Natasha looked at him.

He sighed. "Fine. Go hard."

She reached for the door.

Coulson grabbed her arm. "She may not be your brother, Agent Romanoff, but she's still the closest thing you're ever going to find to a sister. Maybe even a friend."

Natasha pulled open the door. Then her mouth twisted

into something close to a smile. "You know, it's emotionally complex, Phil."

"Is it?" He smiled. "I'd say that's a start, Natasha."

"Well, it's not the end," she answered. And with that, she walked out into the snowy night.

LINE-OF-DUTY DEATH [LODD] INVESTIGATION
REF: S.H.I.E.L.D. CASE 121A415
AGENT IN COMMAND [AIC]: PHILLIP COULSON
RE: AGENT NATASHA ROMANOFF A.K.A. BLACK WIDOW,
A.K.A. NATASHA ROMANOVA
TRANSCRIPT: DEPARTMENT OF DEFENSE, LODD INQUIRY HEARINGS.
NOTE IN FILE: TEXT LOGS — SECURE TEXT.

Director's Note: What follows is the first existing file attributed to
case 121A415.

COULSON: Agent Romanoff, are you available for a mission? Director
Fury wants you to fly this one solo.
ROMANOFF: Kind of busy. New puppy.

COULSON: Wait—you got a puppy?
ROMANOFF: What do you think?

COULSON: Right. We need you in Odessa w/in 12. MI6 has new intel
on some old SVR we've been tracking.
ROMANOFF: Target?

COULSON: Think of it as a chance for you to reconnect with an old
friend. Ivan Somodorov.
ROMANOFF: I have as many friends as I have puppies. Be there in 6.

COULSON: It's never too late to make friends, Agent Romanoff.
ROMANOFF: It really is.

COULSON: You can call me Phil, for example.
ROMANOFF: Romanoff out.

PRIVATE ARCHIVES: BLANK SLATE
HIGHLY CLASSIFIED

FROM: Romanoff, Natasha
TO: Romanoff, Natasha
WITNESS: Coulson, Phillip

I, NATASHA ROMANOFF, DO SWEAR THAT ON THIS DATE <<SEE FILE>> I ASKED S.H.I.E.L.D. AGENT PHILLIP COULSON TO PERFORM A LEVEL SIX ALPHA WIPE ON MY OWN CEREBRAL CORTEX, AND ON THAT OF MY ONLY LIVING GENETIC BROTHER, ALEXEI ROMANOFF.

I, NATASHA ROMANOFF, DO ASSERT THAT BOTH MY BROTHER AND MYSELF AGREED TO THIS PROCEDURE IN HOPES OF HIDING THE SOLE SURVIVING MEMBERS OF OUR FAMILY FROM THE RED ROOM.

I, NATASHA ROMANOFF, DO PASS LEGAL GUARDIANSHIP OF ALEXEI ROMANOFF TO S.H.I.E.L.D. DIRECTOR PHILLIP COULSON FOLLOWING TODAY'S PROCEDURE. ALL FINANCIAL TRANSACTIONS WILL BE CLEARED THROUGH THE ROMANOFF FAMILY ESTATE, AS ADMINISTERED BY PEPPER POTTS.

I, NATASHA ROMANOFF, DO AFFIRM THAT I FACILITATED THE PROCEDURE VIA PRACTICES ADOPTED DURING MY RED ROOM TRAINING IN BLACK WIDOW OPS.

I, NATASHA ROMANOFF, DO ALSO AFFIRM THAT I SWORE DIRECTOR COULSON AND MS. POTTS TO SECRECY, EVEN FROM MYSELF.

I, NATASHA ROMANOFF, DO AFFIRM THAT THIS IS MY WILL AND TESTAMENT.

SO HELP ME GOD.

ACKNOWLEDGMENTS

As I've said before, being asked to write this book was probably the greatest honor of my life. I'll never forget the moment I got the call from my agent, Sarah Burnes, who had just herself gotten the call from my future editor, Emily Meehan. I was in Italy, in bare feet, standing on the balcony and holding a tomato. I mostly remember saying, "Tell them I'd do it for free," though to Sarah's credit, she ignored me.

Long before that moment—and this one—so many people have had a hand in bringing Natasha Romanoff to the world. Stan Lee (along with Don Rico and Don Heck) first introduced the Black Widow in 1964, but she's had many, many writers and artists since then, and they've all been a huge influence on this project. I'm a particular fan of Marjorie Liu and Daniel Acuna, as well as Nathan Edmondson and Phil Noto, edited by Ellie Pyle. Amazing work has also been done by Natasha's creative teams at Marvel Studios under Kevin Feige, along with Joss Whedon, Jon Favreau, Anthony Russo, Joe Russo, Zak Penn, Christopher Markus, Stephen McFeely, Ed Brubaker, and Justin Theroux, who have given the Black Widow a wider audience and a brighter spotlight.

And of course, it's now Scarlett Johansson whom the world sees as Natasha Romanoff, and rightly so. I myself can't help but see her when I write. Scarlett's Natasha manages to somehow remain both a flawed human and a force to be reckoned with. Someone who might be more comfortable saving the world than saving herself but who won't stop trying to do either. And if you make the mistake of under-estimating or belittling or stereotyping her? She's going to use it against you to take what she needs—and then slam both your head and your expectations against a wall. And oh yeah, she's a girl.

Word.

But the inaugural chapter in Black Widow's YA adventure has been shaped most of all by two particularly creative women—both personal (super) heroes of mine. I'm forever indebted to Editorial Director Emily Meehan at Disney Hyperion, who did a brilliant job editing this book—along with Elizabeth Schaefer—and who prompted the first fateful call that day in Italy. She is herself a huge talent, and a real friend. I'm also beholden to Marvel's director of content and character development, the singular visionary Sana Amanat, who oversaw our manuscript on the Marvel side, and who is impossible not to openly fangirl. Sana and Emily are each that rare combination of creative and champion; they get it, they get Natasha, and they get me. The preceding pages would have been radically different without them (and not in a good way!), as would the Red Widow teaser comic.

Beyond the simpatico synergy of Emily and Sana, I have to thank Andrew Sugerman at Disney Consumer Products, and Jeanne Mosure and Rich Thomas at Disney Publishing, for (Avengers) assembling a true dream team for Black Widow's YA debut. Publicity Director Seale Ballenger and Publicity Manager Mary Ann Zissimos do the impossible on a daily basis. Tim Retzlaff, Elke Villa, and Marina Shults in Marketing put together the best swag. Art Director Tyler Nevins oversaw our unbelievably perfect *Forever Red* cover, and illustrator Alessandro Taini and title font designer Russ Gray outdid themselves, as has the rest of my Disney team and family. On the Marvel side, every conversation and collaboration has been a pleasure, from Sana and Charles and Adri and Judy to Axel Alonso himself.

For my own team, thanks goes as always and as ever to my indefatigable agent Sarah Burnes (assisted by Logan Garrison) at the Gernert Company, for being not just smart but stalwart, and my friend. Thanks as well to Melissa de la Cruz, Michael Fletcher, and Julie Scheina for being my Black Widow critique oracles and my not-so-secret weapons. (And Mike, may your triggers always break like glass!) To my patient Russian translators Abbey Gardner, Dr. Kevin Platt, and Maria Grytsenko, who was also my Ukrainian expert. To Tori Hill and Shane Pangburn, my masters of social media, and to Joseph Moretti for the amazing author photo. To writer friends Marie Lu, Cassie Clare, Brendan Sanderson, and Rainbow Rowell, for agreeing to read (or even just pretending to) during deadlines. To Damon Conn, for sharing his Spider-Man comics with me, so long ago. To 7 Studios, for the trippy Fantastic Four days, which I now find myself thinking of often. To Kami Garcia, for being my personal Punisher and first partner in YA crime. To Veronica Roth, for talking me out of my trees (so many trees!). To my brother from another mother, Rafi Simon (along with Philip, Natalia, and India), and to my brother from the same mother, Dave Stohl (along with Ashly, Sara, Jake, and Charlie). *Thanks* is probably not even the right word anymore. To my whole tribe, a huge and heartfelt hug—you know who you are! It took me a long time to circle the wagons around all of you, but I'm so happy to have you in my life.

A special shout-out goes to the Women of Marvel, who rock in the extreme, both in the spotlight and behind the scenes. You guys really are changing the world; what an honor it is to join you. To the other half of those Women of Marvel panels, those hundreds of faces in the crowd: don't think we don't hear you. Talk about change—you're the reason this book exists at all.

And of course, the biggest, slobberiest smooch of all goes to my own heroic #nerdfamily, Lewis, Emma, May, and Kate Peterson, who are (along with Kiki and Jiji) the reason I get up in the morning. I know exactly how good I have it, because I have you (*and I'm not kitten you meow!*). What a lucky, lucky girl I am.

M. Stohl
May 2015

TURN THE PAGE FOR A SNEAK PEEK OF

MARVEL

BLACK WIDOW
RED
VENGEANCE

BY MARGARET STOHL

Los Angeles · New York

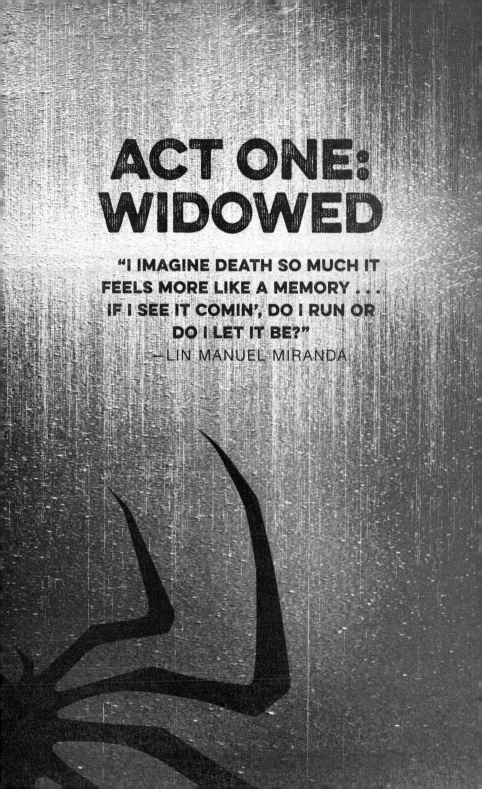

ACT ONE: WIDOWED

"I IMAGINE DEATH SO MUCH IT
FEELS MORE LIKE A MEMORY . . .
IF I SEE IT COMIN', DO I RUN OR
DO I LET IT BE?"
—LIN MANUEL MIRANDA

HIGH-DENSITY TARGET AREA, MIDTOWN MANHATTAN RADIATION ZONE ZERO, ZERO HOUR

Nothing like the Christmas tree at Rockefeller Center, thought Natasha Romanoff—*for terrorists, crackpots, and basic criminal scumbags.* As always, there were no visions of sugarplums dancing in the Black Widow's cold red head. The S.H.I.E.L.D. agent glanced up at the green-needled monolith—dusted with snowflakes and twinkling with lights and Swarovski crystals, the centerpiece of Manhattan's annual holiday party—and thought two words.

Merry Christmas? Try: target package.

Natasha knew that the famed Rockefeller Center tree was larger-than-life in a score of dangerously useful ways. Symbolic significance? *Check.* Media coverage? *Check,*

check. Mass casualties? *Check, check, check.* She sighed and touched her earpiece. "Black to base. No sign of their alpha."

"Copy that, but don't park your sleigh just yet, Black." Coulson's voice crackled into her ear as she moved through the crowd. "And check in with Red. We've lost her signal."

"Copy that, base. Black out." She kept moving.

A sea of raised arms, all holding cellphone cameras, now saluted the hundred-foot Norway spruce from every side, as if the yuletide monstrosity had crash-landed on some worshipful alien planet and assumed the role of supreme leader. *Yeah, a planet of sardines, more than a million a day, all packed squirming into one snowy city block,* Natasha thought.

And for what? To see a freaking plant.

It was a stormy Saturday afternoon in December, a bad time both for crowds and weather, which meant these were die-hard tree people—Natasha just hoped not literally.

Tourists plus terrorists? That always ends well.

The potential for disaster was staggering. Eyes up, defenses down—not one dazed worshipper was looking anywhere but the supersize tree—even though there was an entire holiday parade moving down Fifth Avenue at the far edge of the block.

Ever since the yuletide crowd had begun to surge and climb over the sludge-banked metal barricades at the edges of Rockefeller Center plaza—the corner of Forty-Ninth and Fifth—the NYPD had given up. Now they just cursed the cold afternoon, waiting out the end of their shifts on the safe side of the roadblocks, their breath curling upward in raggedy white puffs. *And they're strictly doughnut patrol, not top command.* That had probably also been a factor in the strategic acquisition of this target, she thought. *Human gridlock with only Paul Blart on your tail—*

Natasha touched her ear again. "Red, what's going on? Ava? You lost?"

All she got back was static.

That's not a good sound—

"Hey, happy holidays," said a harried-looking mom in a cheery red fleece, pushing a stroller zippered in plastic up the curb next to Natasha. "Great snowsuit—"

Natasha nodded, eyeing the kid as the patch of red disappeared into the snowflaked crowd. *Don't get distracted, Romanoff. Do your job and maybe this time nobody gets hurt.* She hitched her pack higher, pushing on toward Fifth Avenue.

Yeah, right.

The odds were good that this op was going to end in casualties—and the red in the snow wasn't going to be fleece. Natasha's hooded "snowsuit" was a C.B.R.N. (Chemical Biological Radiological Nuclear) state-of-the-art mop suit that only resembled snow gear; really, it was lined with filtering charcoal and striped with M-9 detection paper, so she could gauge what was being thrown at her in any given hot zone. And the goggles around her neck weren't for skiing but surviving—a mouth guard flipped down from inside, like a collapsible gas mask. (Dire biological functions aside, the whole getup also lowered the odds that one of the Black Widow's many superfans would recognize her infamous red hair.)

But it was the contents of her rucksack that really set her apart. Her requisition S.H.I.E.L.D. ruck held a M183 demolition charge assembly with enough C-4 (sixteen charges in all) to flatten a city block, if that's what it came to.

Unlike the rest of Manhattan, Natasha Romanoff hadn't come for the tree. She was there to take out the unknown number of hostiles who were plotting to use Rockefeller Center as holiday bait for civilian casualties. Her alpha priority was their leader, who had threatened to detonate the largest and most sophisticated chemical-weapons attack in the nation's history.

When it hit, the Northeast Megalopolis, the Boston–Washington corridor that was home to more than fifty million people, would be flooded with aerosolized chemical particulates. The invisible, odorless microbes would seize control of human neurons and eventually destroy them—unless Natasha could destroy the as-yet-unidentified dispersal device before the alpha triggered it, somewhere on this street, sometime on this day, at some point during this parade.

But no pressure.

This wasn't the first time she had carried a satchel charge through the streets of a populated area; off the top of her head, there had been Pristina and Grozny and Sana'a and Djibouti and even Bogotá before now. She had infiltrated Serbian revolutionaries and Chechen guerrillas and Yemeni pirates and Somali Armed Forces and Columbian mercenaries—but then, they had already known they were at war. It didn't make the ops any less devastating, only less of a surprise; those buildings had long been riddled by bullets, roads ravaged from IEDs, walls chiseled with rat holes for hostiles at every turn. Those cities had become operational theaters way before she'd gotten the call; everyone who could go had already gone.

At least, that was how Natasha had rationalized it to herself.

This, on the other hand, was Midtown Manhattan. This was a holiday attack perpetrated on American soil in the clear light of day during prime traffic for the highest-density urban population in the country. It was the sort of bad business only attempted by a depraved coalition of psychopaths grasping for global attention—because it worked. Every lethal move the opposition made brought them closer to achieving the desired result, to producing the headlines—*The worst! The deadliest! The bloodiest!*—that could shape or rule an era and force a country to its knees.

Not if someone stops them first.

She checked her watch.

Come on, Ava. Where are you?

They didn't have this kind of time to waste. For the next two hours, the parade would still be going, and Rockefeller Center would still be jammed with civilians. The timing wasn't an accident. *Pearl Harbor was hit at 7:53 a.m.; the first of the Twin Towers was 8:45.* If the attack succeeded, today would be worse by an order of magnitude.

From where Natasha stood, she knew she could shake up a Coke and spray fifty people without so much as tossing it. If she had to use it, the effect of a single stick of C-4 in a place like this, on a day like this, at a time like this, would be unimaginable. If she didn't use it, the number of people affected by the chemical attack would probably be worse. There was no easy answer, and there never had been.

Twenty-eight years of peace. That's all that this planet has known, since the beginning of recorded history. How can one person change that?

Even if that one person happened to be the Black Widow—

But it's not just you; there are two of you now.

I don't know why you keep forgetting that. Red and Black, remember?

You don't always have to be so alone, Natashkaya—

"Natashkaya!" She heard Ava's voice while her back was still turned. "I found the alpha. Right around the corner. There's just one thing—"

Natasha heard it in Ava's voice before she saw it. The flinty hardness, the push of adrenaline that inflected every syllable. Her hand went immediately to the back of her waistband.

It's not there—

"Touch one hair on that alpha's head and I'll shoot," Ava said. "I mean it."

"I know," Natasha said, raising her hands in surrender. And as she slowly turned to face all that remained of her family, she also found herself staring down the barrel of her own Glock revolver.

REWIND:
WEEKS EARLIER
IN SOUTH
AMERICA

S.H.I.E.L.D. EYES ONLY

CLEARANCE LEVEL X

CONFIDENTIAL: PHILLIP COULSON

CLASSIFIED / FOR OFFICIAL USE ONLY (FOUO) / CRITICAL PROGRAM INFORMATION (CPI) / LAW ENFORCEMENT SENSITIVE (LES) / TOP SECRET / SUITE AB ENCRYPTION / SIPRNET DISTRIBUTION ONLY (SIPDIS) / JCOS / S.H.I.E.L.D.

Phil, buddy:

Just heard from the Oval. It's not good. Keeping a "controlled specimen" under wraps is off the table—what did you think she would say? [CODE: REDROCK] is still too hot with the press.

What I can do is declare [CLASSIFIED SUBJECT] a Restricted Handling Asset, and name you to run the After Action Assessment. AAA is an easy sell, you have the expertise. Wrap it up, control the narrative, it all goes away.

Otherwise I'm hearing that [CLASSIFIED SUBJECT] faces quarantine in 1 of 3 high-security research facilities:

Amundsen-Scott S.P. Station (INT)
Superkamiokande (JP)
C.E.R.N. (SUI)

BUT: lab protocols would require [CLASSIFIED SUBJECT] to undergo a cerebral wipe and to be declared legally D.O.A.—rough stuff, even for S.H.I.E.L.D.

We are, after all, talking about a child.

That's the fallout from the [CODE:REDROCK] crapstorm. The N.S.A. vultures are circling. Good luck. Stay low—head down—ARTIE

Office of the Joint Chiefs of Staff
9999 Joint Staff Pentagon
Washington DC

S.H.I.E.L.D. EYES ONLY

CLEARANCE LEVEL X

SPECIAL CIRCUMSTANCES & INDIVIDUALS (SCI) INVESTIGATION
AGENT IN COMMAND (AIC): PHILLIP COULSON
RE: AGENT NATASHA ROMANOFF A.K.A. BLACK WIDOW
A.K.A. NATASHA ROMANOVA
AAA HEARING TRANSCRIPT
CC: DEPARTMENT OF DEFENSE, SCI INQUIRY

ROMANOFF: What am I doing here, Phil? I don't have time for this.

COULSON: You know the protocol. There's always an After Action Assessment. You're an S.M.E. now—
ROMANOFF: Subject Matter Expert? No, let's leave that to the wonks on the tenth floor.

COULSON: The real battles don't end on the battlefield. Control the narrative, Romanoff. Start at the beginning.
ROMANOFF: Why?

COULSON: *A beginning is a delicate time.*
ROMANOFF: Is that a quote? Are you quoting at me?

COULSON: *Dune.* Frank Herbert. You know it?
ROMANOFF: Not unless you're talking about a Desert Storm field manual.

COULSON: The beginning, Agent. There are people asking questions, and this doesn't end until we answer them.
ROMANOFF: I filed a report. Classified. Top secret. Encrypted. You know, the kind they keep in the little drawers with the combination locks?

COULSON: So let's just talk. I've been your friend longer than I've been your A.I.C.

ROMANOFF: You going Hallmark on me, Phil? Now you're that guy?

COULSON: You know I was always that guy. Start with the truth. They say it's out there.

ROMANOFF: Phil—

COULSON: I'll get you started. It ended in a national disaster and a global emergency. It began in Recife. Just tell me the truth about Recife.

ROMANOFF: Some stories aren't just classified. They're also personal.

COULSON: I think we both know you're not just a person anymore.

ROMANOFF: Okay. You want the truth? Then forget Recife. It started in Rio.

RIO DE JANEIRO, BRAZIL
CHRIST THE REDEEMER MONUMENT,
MOUNT CORCOVADO

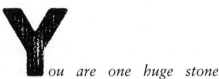

ou are one huge stone dude. You remind me of this big green friend of mine—

Natasha bit into a wild guava as she stood at the base of the massive stone Cristo overlooking Rio de Janeiro. She contemplated the statue, sucking on the ripe pinkish fruit, dribbling juice off her chin. The polished, graying soapstone arms were outstretched, as if the forty-meter giant of a messiah looming from the mountaintop above her truly believed he could gather up the entire city for a group hug. *Aw, bring it in you guys—*

"Tell me why we're here again?" Ava Orlova, the S.H.I.E.L.D. Academy rookie currently under Natasha's immediate supervision, glanced at the guava in Natasha's hand. "Huh. Wow. You don't seem like a fruit person."

"I'm a fruit person. Of course I'm a fruit person." Natasha swallowed. "What does that even mean?"

"Let's see." Ava began moving through the swarm of tourists crowding on to the observation deck with them, high above the city of Rio. "Thick rind. Sweet and mushy in places, I guess," she said, straight-faced. "Slightly seedy at the core, rotten in parts—"

"Funny," Natasha scowled. "What did you think I ate? Rocks?"

Ava moved along the railing, looked over her shoulder as she slipped away. "I don't know, rounds? Washed down with jet fuel?"

Natasha tried not to smile as she turned back toward the view. Their relationship had softened into an easy familiarity since they'd left New York. It made Natasha nervous. *Don't get to know me enough for opinions, kid. The only prize for winning that game is a bullet.*

The Widow eyed the pale sprawl of the city that unfolded below her, the broad blue sweep of ocean beyond that—and hurled the guava skin into the sky. It arched and fell, rolling down the mountainside. She wiped her sticky lips with the back of her sticky hand, still taking in the view. She always came up here, at least once every visit; she had for years. Despite the number of times the job had brought her here, she had never gotten used to the way Rio looked—especially not from the Cristo at Mount

Corcovado. It had always meant something to her, as silly as that was, and she'd wanted Ava to see it.

How can the world be so messed up and still look so magical?

It was true; the coastline seemed to be one of those surreal hand-drawn maps you might find in the front pages of old fantasy books. Everything she could see was too sharp or too steep or too brightly colored to be real.

Reality wasn't usually all that pretty.

Yet here it was. The vertical plateau of Sugarloaf Mountain rose up in front of her, sheer rock and cable cars and all; Ipanema (like the song) and Copacabana (like the other song) occupied the broad stripe of sand directly south of that—and then the curving seam of land and water broke into an abrupt handful of tiny jagged hills that poked up from the shallow surf, well beyond the row of grand beach hotels.

If she looked hard enough she could just make out the Copacabana Palace hotel, where back in the 1950s Howard Stark had fallen in love with the view of the sea (or, more likely, the women who swam in it) and purchased the sixth-floor penthouse Natasha and Ava had been using as a base of operations for weeks now.

Natasha had told Coulson she was taking Ava out of S.H.I.E.L.D. Academy so they could combine fieldwork with vacation, but the truth was clear: they had come to South America for one reason.

Vengeance.

FROM #1 *NEW YORK TIMES* BEST-SELLING AUT

MARGARET STOH

COMES THE HIGHLY ANTICIPATED SEQUE
TO **BLACK WIDOW: FOREVER RED**!

MARVEL

BLACK WIDOW
RED
VENGEANCE

#1 *NEW YORK TIMES* BEST-SELLING AUTHOR
MARGARET STOHL

WIDOW
FIRST STRIKE

THE GREAT CITY OF NEW YORK.

THERE'S NOTHING LIKE IT.

FOUR-INCH HEELS AND THREE-HOUR DINNERS...

YEAH, NOT MY LIFE.

I SHOP AT GOODWILL AND SLEEP AT THE Y.

AND BROADWAY?

AVA ANATALYA ORLOVA SPENDS HER LIFE TRYING TO KEEP HER NAME OUT OF THE LIGHTS...

...AND OUT OF THE LINE-UPS.

THIS AMERICAN DREAM WASN'T SOMETHING I ASKED FOR.

I WAS BROUGHT HERE FROM UKRAINE EIGHT YEARS AGO AS AN ORPHAN OF THE RUSSIAN MAFIA.

AT LEAST THAT'S WHAT THEY TOLD ME.

I SPENT FIVE YEARS IN LOCKDOWN IN A S.H.I.E.L.D. SAFE HOUSE. I ATE MICROWAVE MAC & CHEESE AND SURPLUS ARMY RATIONS ALONE IN FRONT OF A BUSTED TV WATCHING C-SPAN.

I DIDN'T EVEN KNOW THERE WERE OTHER CHANNELS.

STILL, I PICKED UP ON A FEW THINGS LIVING WITH SPIES-- AND I'M NOT JUST TALKING ABOUT ALL THE S.H.I.E.L.D. GEAR I LIFTED...

FORT GREENE SOUP KITCHEN

...I LEARNED HOW TO DISAPPEAR.

SO, ON MY FOURTEENTH BIRTHDAY I BUSTED OUT OF S.H.I.E.L.D.-CATRAZ.

I GUESS YOU COULD SAY I HEARD THE SIREN SONG OF THE CITY...

...OR MAYBE JUST THE SIRENS.

...THE RED WIDOW.

AND THIS TIME, SESTRA, I'LL BE THE ONE DOING THE SAVING.

RED WIDOW FIRST STRIKE

Writer: Margaret Stohl Artist: Nico Leon Colorist: Andres Mossa
Letterer: VC's Travis Lanham Editor: Charles Beacham Supervising Editor: Sana Amanat